BITTER FALL

BRUCE ROBERT COFFIN

Copyright © 2026 by Bruce Robert Coffin.

All rights reserved.

No part of this book may be reproduced in any form or by any electronic or mechanical means, including information storage and retrieval systems, without written permission from the author, except for the use of brief quotations in a book review.

Severn River Publishing
SevernRiverBooks.com

This is a work of fiction. Names, characters, businesses, places, events and incidents are either the products of the author's imagination or used in a fictitious manner. Any resemblance to actual persons, living or dead, or actual events is purely coincidental.

ISBN: 978-1-64875-730-3 (Paperback)

ALSO BY THE AUTHOR

The Detective Justice Series

Crimson Thaw

Bitter Fall

Dark Harbor

The Turner and Mosley Files

The General's Gold

The Cardinal's Curse

The Pirate's Secret

The Pharaoh's Tomb

The Emperor's Palace

Never miss a new release!

To find out more about Bruce Robert Coffin and his books, visit

severnriverbooks.com

For Joe Wambaugh, who blazed the trail. Semper cop.

"Life is neither amusing nor fair, but it's often ironic."
—Albert Justice

1

Tuesday, October 7, Greenville, Maine

Summer Randall sprinted along the gravel trail through the darkening forest, heart racing as she pumped her arms and legs as fast as she could. The all too real terror driving her forward was the stuff of nightmares and horror movies.

An avid runner, she was accustomed to pushing herself hard, testing the limits of her endurance, especially when preparing for the 10K road races she loved so much. The frequent cardio training left her muscles taut and well toned and her breathing exceptionally strong and efficient. The single thing sapping her strength now had nothing to do with conditioning. It was pure, unadulterated terror, for which she knew of no training regimen. Terror of her pursuer overtaking her, because the person chasing her clearly had homicidal intent.

She resisted the urge to look back for fear of breaking her stride or losing her balance. There was no need to check on her assailant's progress; she knew they were right behind her. This would only end in one of two ways. Either she reached the paved road and managed to flag a passing motorist for help, or she would meet her demise at the hands of a crazed attacker and die in the forest.

The glow of twilight had all but disappeared as darkness quickly descended beneath the thick canopy of trees. Even the well-worn and familiar cross-country jogging trail was difficult to navigate in the gloom. Summer concentrated on the one thing she knew she could do automatically: plant one foot in front of the other. Running as if her life depended upon it, because it did.

The pain emanating from the lower left side of her abdomen was growing more intense, affecting both her breathing and speed. What had initially felt like nothing more than a runner's stitch had turned into a bad cramp that was becoming more pronounced with each stride. She knew there would be no walking it off or willing it away. She startled to the sound of a tree branch snapping somewhere close behind. Her eyes widened in fear as she tried to calculate how close her pursuer was. Were they closing the distance? Was her pace slowing? She didn't think so. Curiosity got the better of Summer as she rounded a curve in the path and craned her neck ever so slightly to one side, hoping to catch a glimpse of her attacker. As she did so, her right foot landed awkwardly atop a tree root running perpendicularly to the path. She fought against the momentum pulling her off-balance by quickly planting her left foot on the path and pinwheeling her arms, but it was no use. Summer crashed headlong into a deadfall of fallen tree trunks and broken limbs at the boundary of the trail. A jumble of sharp sticks and branches stabbed through the thin material of her clothing, poking painfully into her arms and legs. As quickly as she could, Summer rolled onto her stomach and pushed herself up onto all fours. Bittersweet thorns tugged at her hair and clawed at her exposed face and hands as she backed onto the path.

Fighting off a wave of nausea and dizziness, she scrambled to her feet, testing her right ankle to see if it would support her and allow her to continue running. The joint was sore, but it held. Sore or not, there were no other options. If she couldn't outrun her pursuer, she would die out here in the woods. Punctuating the thought was the sound of another branch breaking, and this one, accompanied by the thump of rapidly approaching footfalls, was considerably closer than the last.

She resumed running.

Only a quarter of a mile left before she would reach the paved two-lane blacktop of Lily Bay Road and the help it might bring her.

Left, right, left, right, breathe in through the nose and out through the mouth. The voice in her head belonged to her track coach. *Long strides, arms pumping. Focus, Summer. Ignore the pain. You can do this. You must.*

Through a thin gap in the trees, she caught the flicker of light from a passing vehicle in the distance. Only a glimpse, but it meant she was drawing nearer to the road. The trailing footfalls and crunch of gravel were louder now. Clearer. Her pursuer was nearly on top of her. She redoubled her efforts, forcing herself to stretch out her strides, pushing through the searing pain in her abdomen as she navigated the last fifty yards.

A moment later, she burst through the tree line without slowing. Her energy nearly drained, it was only momentum that carried her up the side of the ravine and onto the pavement. She bent forward, hands on her hips to try and catch her breath. Large spots swam across her field of vision. The pain in her side felt like a soldering iron pressed into her skin. She staggered around to look back at the darkened forest from where she'd come but couldn't see a thing. Frantically she scanned the area for a rock or anything she might use as a weapon to defend herself but saw nothing.

The world began to spin as she turned to the sound of an approaching vehicle.

Bright lights blinded her as she attempted to lift her arms, intending to flag the driver down, but her arms wouldn't move. Something was wrong. The sport utility vehicle swerved from side to side. The driver wasn't slowing. Didn't see her. Summer recognized the danger a split second too late. She couldn't go back, not without running into her pursuer. Her only option was to continue to the far side of the road.

The SUV bathed her in the glare of its high beams. Summer staggered toward the safety of the far shoulder on legs she could no longer feel as blackness overtook her sight. A racing engine and the thump of metal on bone were the last sounds Summer heard.

2

Wednesday, October 8, 12:30 a.m

Maine State Police Detective Brock Justice stood just outside the yellow crime scene tape that hung across the desolate stretch of roadway. One end of the tape had been tied off to the diamond plate bumper of a fire engine and the other to the trunk of a nearby birch tree. Much like everything in law enforcement, the flimsy plastic barrier to the crime scene served as more of a psychological deterrent than anything, but still it illustrated the seriousness of what lay beyond.

The night was chilly and damp, coating everything in a thin sheen of dew. Diesel fumes from the idling truck choked the air while the flashing blue and red strobes of a half dozen emergency vehicles assaulted the darkness, reflecting off every surface and creating the illusion of movement where there was none.

Having arrived ahead of his partner, Chloe Wright, Brock used the time to his advantage, jotting notes into a clean investigator's notebook while formulating a mental image of exactly how the scene appeared upon arrival. Organized chaos.

Standing nearby was an adolescent-looking uniformed police officer holding a metal clipboard. He was dressed in black BDUs and a GPD baseball cap, chatting quietly with what appeared to be several members of the Greenville Fire Department. Each of the first responders stood transfixed by the carnage, oblivious to the arrival of a state police detective.

"Excuse me," Brock said as he approached the officer. "I need to sign in with you."

"And you are?" the officer said as he gave Brock the once-over.

Brock pulled back his windbreaker, revealing the badge clipped to the front of his belt. "Detective Justice, state police."

"Can I see your ID?"

Brock glanced at the man's name tag while the officer recorded his name, agency, and time of arrival in the crime scene log. Berce. It wasn't a surname Brock had ever seen, and he wondered about its origin.

"All set," Berce said as he returned Brock's credentials and lifted the tape for him.

"Thanks," Brock said. "But I'm gonna wait here for my partner."

"Suit yourself," the officer said as he strolled back to the firefighters.

An oversized EZ Up shelter had been erected near the center of the roadway, illuminated by several battery-powered high-intensity light stands that had been placed strategically to minimize any shadows. Beneath the shelter lay a single body crumpled and broken on the damp pavement. Two Tyvek-clad figures knelt at the far side of the body, one holding a large digital camera and flash attachment. Not far from the body, a charcoal-colored SUV rested on its caved-in roof. Its front end crumpled against the trunk of a massive pine. The driver's door of the vehicle had been sheared away near the hinges along with part of the windshield pillar. Both items lay on the pavement near the SUV. Brock could tell emergency responders had used the Jaws of Life to extricate at least one occupant from the vehicle.

At first glance, the scene appeared to be nothing more than a horrible vehicle-versus-pedestrian accident. But Brock knew there was more to whatever this was than met the eye. He and Chloe were homicide detectives from the Major Crimes Unit North working out of the Troop E barracks in Bangor. They weren't called to investigate fatal motor vehicle accidents.

Aside from two short telephone calls, one to Chloe and one to their boss, Lieutenant Penelope Cumberland, Brock hadn't spoken to a soul during the ninety-minute drive from Bangor to Greenville. He had spent the time clearing his head of any distractions and preparing mentally for the task awaiting them. Brock knew Chloe was doing the same thing. As if summoned by his very thought, approaching headlights illuminated the roadway behind him. He turned to see Chloe climbing out of her unmarked Ford Interceptor.

"Sorry I'm late," Chloe said breathlessly as she half jogged over to him before shrugging into her own windbreaker. "Have you spoken to anyone yet?"

"Just him," Brock said as he cocked a thumb in Officer Berce's direction. "I wanted to get the lay of the land first."

"You must be the partner," Berce said before repeating the sign-in dance with Chloe.

Brock's attention shifted to the foreground where a pair of white running shoes sat on the pavement. One shoe stood upright, its toe pointing toward the gravel shoulder as if its owner had been knocked out of it while crossing the road, and the other lay on its side approximately fifteen feet from the first. He glanced back to the body and confirmed that the one foot he could see was clad only in a sock.

"Jesus," Chloe said. "If I didn't know better, I'd think this was simply a fatal accident."

Brock didn't respond. He didn't need to. They both knew what it had to be, despite initial appearances.

Brock felt the all too familiar pang of guilt that came at the start of every homicide case he investigated. The guilt was a result of his conflicting emotions. Sadness for the victim juxtaposed with his own excitement at being tasked with chasing down the person responsible for the death. The hunter versus the hunted. It was the one thing every good homicide detective clung to. The chase propelled them forward.

A tall, uniformed deputy approached Brock and Chloe.

"Been expecting you guys," the deputy said. His name tag read: G. Easter.

"Hey, George," Chloe said. "Shitty night?"

"You could say that."

"George Easter, this is my partner, Brock Justice."

"Good to meet you," Easter said, with zero sincerity in either his tone or the limp handshake he offered.

Easter wasn't the first cop to take issue with Brock. Testifying in court against a fellow badge was always a sure-fire way to garner enemies within the field of law enforcement. Whether Easter would become an enemy or not had yet to be established.

"George and I went through the academy together," Chloe said, as if Brock might have been wondering about their familiarity. He wasn't.

"What do you have here?" Brock said.

"Yeah," Chloe said. "I hope you didn't drag us all the way up here for a car accident."

"Follow me."

3

Wednesday, October 8, 12:40 a.m

Brock and Chloe followed Easter toward the body, skirting several bright yellow markers placed along the pavement. Each tent-shaped marker displayed a letter to correspond with evidence located by the evidence response team, or ERT. Although this far north, resources were slim, giving the word *team* a more singular connotation. The marker system used by the ERT allowed for quick identification of each piece of evidence when photographing or recording it on the inventory log, or when explaining something later on to a jury.

As they neared the body, Brock recognized the dark-haired male state police ERT investigator, though he was unable to recall either his name or the nickname he went by. The other person, a diminutive female wearing glasses and kneeling over the body, Brock was entirely unfamiliar with.

"Chloe, Brock, this is Ginny Waite from the medical examiner's office," Easter said. "Ginny, Detectives Wright and Justice."

Waite looked up from her examination and greeted them with a curt nod.

"Heck of a night to get dragged all the way up here from Bangor," the ERT investigator said.

Brock couldn't agree more.

"And I assume you both know Clayton Veilleux, state police evidence aficionado," Easter said.

"Evening, Detectives," Veilleux said.

"Clay," Brock said, finally remembering the moniker.

"So, what makes you think this isn't simply a fatal?" Chloe said. "From where I'm standing, it sure looks like an accident."

"Step around behind me and I'll show you," Waite said, speaking for the first time.

"Mind the evidence markers," Veilleux said as he took a step back to make room for them.

Brock and Chloe did as they were instructed, stopping right behind Waite.

The victim, a young adult female with lifeless eyes, was dressed in black nylon running pants, a white undershirt, and an aqua-colored sweatshirt. She lay on her back with her left leg bent at an impossible angle. Brock saw the pale jagged end of a fractured bone protruding from the leggings on the right calf. The pants appeared to be soaked through with liquid, the origin of which Brock couldn't place. Her auburn hair had been pulled into a ponytail, though many strands had torn loose from the elastic and were now plastered to the bloody scrapes and scratches on the pale skin of her face and forehead. In addition to the bloodstains and smudges of dirt on her clothing, pine needles and leaves littered her hair as if she'd been dragged through the woods.

Waite slowly moved the beam of a small penlight around the body, pausing to highlight the various injuries. "As you can see, the victim suffered massive injuries to her torso, legs, and head. Fairly consistent with having been struck by a large vehicle. Point of impact appears to be right where her footwear is lying in the road."

Brock looked back at the sneakers, estimating them to be about forty feet from where the body lay. Their location also suggested that the driver of the SUV had been traveling on the wrong side of the roadway when the victim was struck.

"Excessive speed?" Chloe said.

Waite shook her head. "Based solely on the distance the victim traveled from the impact, I'd say no."

Easter weighed in. "The posted limit here is thirty-five miles per hour. There're still several other factors to take into consideration before drawing any kind of conclusion, but I'd say thirty-nine feet would be right in the ballpark."

"And the occupants of the SUV?" Brock said, gesturing toward the wreck.

"Just one," Easter said. "And he's alive. The local EMS guys cut him out of the vehicle using the Jaws of Life and transported him to Northern Light Hospital."

"Have we IDed everyone involved?" Brock said.

"Only the driver of the Tahoe," Easter said, handing Brock a Maine driver's license. "Jonathan Watters."

Brock copied the name and date of birth into his notebook. A quick calculation put the driver's age at forty-five.

"Resides in the next town over," Easter said. "Two prior OUI convictions."

"ETOH?" Chloe said, inquiring whether Watters was intoxicated.

"The guy certainly smelled like a brewery. We'll get preliminary BAC results from the hospital as soon as we can."

"What about HIPAA?" Chloe said, referring to the Health Insurance Portability and Accountability Act requiring the patient's permission to share medical information.

"Yeah, right," Easter said with a grin. "Like I said, we'll know soon enough."

Brock passed the license to Chloe, then readdressed Waite and Easter. "Nothing on her person that might help us ID her?"

"Just these," Easter said as he held up a set of keys attached to a leather fob. One of the keys clearly went to a vehicle equipped with keyless entry.

"No luck locating her vehicle?" Chloe said.

"Been a little busy," Easter said. "And you're assuming she had one."

"So, we're thinking what?" Brock said. "That this was intentional? Maybe the victim and driver knew each other?"

"Not sure about them knowing each other," Easter said. "And that isn't why we dragged you both out of bed."

"Then why?" Chloe said.

"This," Waite said as she lifted the victim's sweatshirt from her waist, revealing a bloodied white T-shirt underneath.

Brock noticed what appeared to be a thin vertical slice in the material. After pointing out the hole, Waite pulled the undershirt away from the bare skin beneath, displaying a small puncture wound in the left side of the victim's abdomen that corresponded with the slice in the T-shirt. The wound was no wider than the blade of a common kitchen or hunting knife. Brock found it curious that there was no corresponding cut to the sweatshirt.

"An injury sustained during impact with the SUV?" Chloe said.

Waite shook her head again. "This injury appears to be a single stab wound likely caused by a small, single-edged blade. And it occurred sometime prior to the accident."

"How can you tell?" Chloe said.

"Because the victim was already bleeding heavily before impact. Look, her running pants are saturated with blood."

The blood-soaked black material was hard to make out even under the high-intensity lamps.

"How long could she have continued before succumbing to that injury?" Brock asked.

"Hard to say without opening her up to see what the internal damage looks like," Waite said. "A lot of organs under here. Kidneys, small intestines. You'll have a more definitive answer after the autopsy."

"You're thinking that she was stabbed, then ran onto the road trying to get help?" Chloe said.

"Maybe," Brock said absently as he looked toward the woods in the opposite direction from where the victim's sneakers were pointing.

"Or maybe she was stabbed by the driver of the SUV during a fight, and she jumped out, only to have him return and try to finish the job with the vehicle," Easter opined.

"Good theory," Chloe offered. "Might explain why she's out here in the middle of nowhere without transportation."

"Let's press the pause button on theories for a moment," Brock said. He knew from experience that the worst thing any detective could do early on in an investigation was speculate. Developing a running theory without sufficient facts to back it up was a recipe for disaster. What they needed was something that pointed them in the right direction.

"What was the driver of the SUV wearing?" Brock said.

"Why?" Easter said.

"Humor me," Brock said.

"Um, jeans, dark tee, and a brown leather jacket. Smelled like he might have come from a local watering hole."

Brock looked back and forth from the victim to the sneakers. "Yet our victim is wearing spandex pants, a sweatshirt over a tee, and running shoes. Not exactly bar-hopping attire. Looks to me like she may have been out jogging when she was attacked and subsequently run down."

"I don't know, Brock," Chloe said. "Unlit road, desolate location, shitty shoulder, not really the best running route for an evening jog. And I'm a runner."

Brock addressed Easter again. "Are there any jogging paths around here? Maybe cross-country trails."

"All kinds of 'em," said the voice of a new arrival.

They all looked to see two more uniformed officers approaching, silhouetted by the bright lights.

"Chief," Easter said by way of a greeting.

"You must be the state detectives we've been waiting for," the older officer said. "Name's Rich Leavitt. I'm the chief of Greenville PD."

"Good to meet you, Chief," Chloe said, extending a hand in greeting. "Chloe Wright."

Brock gave a half-hearted handshake, but his attention was focused solely on the other recent arrival.

"And I believe you already know Deputy Evan Mathers from the Piscataquis County Sheriff's Department," Leavitt said.

"Hey, brother," Mathers said.

Brock felt his jaw tighten.

4

Wednesday, October 8, 12:50 a.m

Standing beside Leavitt, wearing a crooked smile, was former Maine State Trooper Evan Mathers. The trooper Brock had once worked alongside in Southern Maine before testifying against him in open court over a bad shooting. Brock's testimony in Mathers's manslaughter trial was the sole reason he had gotten transferred to MCU North in Bangor. It was a move that upended his entire life and derailed his career.

"Is this a surprise or what?" Mathers said to Brock as he gripped Chloe's outstretched hand.

"What the hell are you doing here?" Brock said, spitting out the words as he stared in disbelief at the badge gracing the breast of Mathers's uniform.

"I work here," Mathers said. "Three months now."

Brock said nothing.

"And is that any way to greet an old friend?" Mathers continued.

"We aren't friends," Brock growled.

"Do we have a problem here?" Leavitt said as he moved between the two men.

"No," Chloe said. "No problem at all, Chief. Is there, Brock?"

Brock held Mathers's gaze for a long moment before responding to Leavitt. "Nope. No problem, Chief."

"Glad to hear it," Leavitt said. "Especially since everyone here is expecting nothing less than a thorough and professional investigation into this woman's death."

Brock's attention shifted to the other investigators and first responders who had all stopped to watch the show. After a moment, they returned to whatever they'd been doing before his raised voice caught their attention. Brock addressed Chief Leavitt again. "Where exactly are these trails you mentioned?"

"The entrance to one of them is right over there," Leavitt said as he turned and trained the beam of his flashlight through a partially hidden opening in the trees. "That path leads to a network of trails that crisscross all through these woods."

"They get much use?" Chloe said.

"More popular with the summer folks than the locals," Leavitt said. "Not many of those left this time of year. The locals who are into working out tend to avail themselves of the air-conditioned comfort of the neighborhood gym."

"But where do the trails lead?" Brock said, not bothering to hide his growing annoyance. "There must be an exit point on the other side of the forest."

Mathers fixed Brock with a grin. "There are about seven different parking areas that this path will lead you to. And the lots are scattered all over."

"Thanks," Chloe said when Brock didn't respond.

"Don't mention it," Mathers said. "Happy to help."

"Don't suppose you've been able to ID the victim yet?" Leavitt said.

"No," Veilleux said. "Nothing on her person but keys."

Leavitt gave a slight nod but said nothing.

The grim look on the chief's face and his reaction to the answer gave Brock pause. It was only a gut feeling, but he wondered if the victim was familiar to the chief. In such a small town, assuming the woman was local, how could Leavitt not know her?

"What is it?" Brock said.

"It's probably nothing," Leavitt said. "Just that the sweatshirt looks familiar."

"Someone you know?" Chloe said.

"I'd rather not speculate until you get a solid ID."

"I get it," Chloe said.

Easter spoke up, "Chief, I was just telling them that we haven't been able to spare anyone to try and locate the victim's vehicle yet."

"We are stretched a little thin, Detectives," Leavitt said. "Matter of fact, I've got one of my officers tied up at the hospital with the driver and another taking a statement from the witness who happened upon the accident."

Brock turned to Chloe. "You want to take the witness? I'll stay here and see what else I can find out."

"I'm on it," Chloe said before turning to Leavitt and Mathers. "Don't suppose one of you could direct me to the station?"

"I was just about to head over to the hospital," Leavitt said. "But I'd be happy to—"

"I'll take that, Chief," Mathers said before addressing Chloe. "You have your own vehicle, or did the two of you ride up here together?"

"I have my own," Chloe said, after exchanging a wary glance with Brock.

"Good," Mathers said. "You can follow me."

"Thanks."

"I'll check in with you folks later," Leavitt said.

Brock shook his head as he watched Chloe, Mathers, and Leavitt duck under the crime scene tape and head back toward their respective vehicles.

"Bet you didn't expect to see Evan here," Easter said.

Brock ignored the comment and instead addressed Waite. "How soon can you post?"

"Won't be tonight. There aren't any local facilities to even do a proper viewing."

"Nothing at the hospital?"

"Detective Justice, this is a town of about fourteen hundred people. You won't find what you're undoubtedly used to in the southern part of Maine.

I've already contacted the local funeral home to transport the body down to Augusta. Dr. Isleborn will be performing the postmortem."

"When?"

"As soon as her schedule allows. I'd recommend contacting the office tomorrow after nine a.m."

"Thanks," Brock said sarcastically, biting his tongue to keep from saying something he would later regret. He wondered if one of the latest requirements to work for the medical examiner's office was giving up one's personality. Waite and Isleborn were like two humorless peas in a pod. As Brock turned away, his cell rang. He removed the phone from his pocket and checked the screen. The caller ID displayed one word: *Cumberland*.

Lieutenant Penelope Cumberland, the commander of Troop E out of Bangor, was the head of Major Crimes Unit North and Brock's immediate supervisor. And Brock knew she was already seeking an update.

"The boss?" Easter said.

"Yup," Brock said as he thumbed the ignore button.

"You've got brass ones, Justice," Easter said with a chuckle. "I'll give you that. I don't think I'd dare cross Penny Dreadful."

"Yet you don't seem to have any problem tossing around that ill-advised nickname," Brock said as he pocketed the phone.

"She isn't *my* boss," Easter countered.

"Doesn't mean she doesn't know yours."

"Whatever," Easter said. "It's not like I'm worried about it getting back to her."

"You should be," Veilleux said.

Easter scoffed. "All I'm saying is I can't wait until I have enough seniority with the sheriff's department to blow off my boss like that."

Careful what you wish for, Brock thought.

5

Wednesday, October 8, 1:15 a.m

Brock descended the steep gravel banking of the shoulder into the darkness of the drainage ditch that separated the road from the tree line where Chief Leavitt had indicated a trail. Brock was struggling to keep focused on the task before him and not on Piscataquis County's newly minted road deputy.

After climbing the far side of the ditch, Brock paused and trained the beam of his Mini Mag flashlight on the ground where the path first entered the forest. A small yellow-and-brown placard depicting the universal symbol of a hiker was affixed to a weathered post. Brock passed the sign, moving slowly and methodically, sweeping his light from side to side. The trail itself was nothing more than a five-foot-wide packed gravel track partially concealed under a layer of fallen leaves and evergreen needles. Carefully he studied each leaf, figuring if their mystery victim had truly been bleeding from a stab wound, as Waite had described, she would no doubt have left a blood trail behind her as she ran. It was a hunting lesson Brock's father, Albert, had tried to instill in both of his boys when tracking wounded prey.

Brock was about fifteen feet into the woods when his light hit upon something out of place. He knelt to examine a dark-colored blotch covering nearly half of a striped maple leaf. The dark crimson stain still glistened on the bright yellow leaf, leaving little doubt that it was blood, and it was fresh.

"What are you hoping to find out here?" Easter said as he came up behind Brock.

"This," Brock said without looking up.

"That what I think it is?"

"Looks like blood," Brock said.

"Then you were right," Easter said. "Our vic probably was attacked out here in the woods."

After snapping a close-up of the leaf with his phone's camera, Brock stood and turned to Easter. "I want this area sealed off too. Let's get Clay to document this with a real camera."

"You got it."

"Also, how soon can we get a K9 out here?"

Easter raised a brow. "That might take some doing. Probably won't happen until after daybreak, but I can make some calls."

Brock had hoped for something sooner. He knew the longer it took to start a track or an article search, the less likely it would be that they might locate the scene of the attack or recover any evidence left behind.

"Best you can do, then," Brock said as he headed back toward the roadway.

"Anything else?" Easter said. His tone dripping in sarcasm.

Brock stopped and turned toward Easter. "Yeah, where can I get a map of these running trails?"

Chloe followed Mathers's cruiser until it turned into the lot of the Greenville Public Safety Building. She continued past him, parking the unmarked Interceptor in a vacant space not far from the side entrance. She felt conflicted about Brock's reaction to seeing Evan Mathers in a law enforcement capacity again. Though Mathers had been found not guilty of manslaughter by a jury of his peers, it was clear that he and Brock still possessed some animosity toward one another. Chloe had never worked with or even met the former trooper, but she believed in forming her own opinion of others. She wondered whether Brock might be blowing things out of proportion and whether it would be a distraction from this investigation. She grabbed her briefcase off the passenger seat, then followed Mathers inside the building.

The pleasing aroma of freshly brewed coffee hit Chloe as soon as she entered the lobby. She followed Mathers down a short hallway to the administrative offices.

"You can use the chief's office if you want," Mathers said.

"Thanks."

Chloe wasn't sure what she had expected the chief's abode to look like after seeing the grandiose décor of some of the other department heads in her part of the state, but Leavitt's was a welcome change. There was little displayed on the walls aside from a group photo of the entire Greenville Police Department, civilians included, a clock featuring an enlarged version of the department's shoulder patch as a background, and a thirty-year retirement plaque from the Cumberland County Sheriff's Department. Atop his desk sat large stacks of paperwork and folders. It looked more like the desk of a detective than that of the department's top cop.

"Working chief," Mathers said, having caught her gaze.

Chloe nodded. "Small department."

"That and I don't think he sees himself as an administrator yet. Rich still likes to handle most problems personally."

"I totally get it," Chloe said, noting his familiar use of the chief's given name.

"You can hang your coat there if you want," Mathers offered, gesturing to an empty wall hook.

"Thanks," Chloe said as she shrugged off the windbreaker and slung it over the wooden peg. "You seem to know your way around the Greenville police station."

"We spend a lot of time here," Mathers said. "GPD is kind of like a substation for the county deputies. I assume you'd like to get started with the witness before they get too cranky about being kept here so long."

"That'd be great," Chloe said.

"Follow me."

Mathers led her along another short hallway past a small booking station equipped with an intoxilyzer and a closed door marked "Records." The last room on the right, also closed, was marked "Interview."

Mathers rapped once, then opened the door. Chloe saw an officer dressed in a Greenville PD uniform seated across from a slim, gray-haired man. His name tag read *L. Hastings*. The young flat-topped officer looked past Mathers. As he locked eyes with Chloe, a dark cloud drifted across his face, altering his expression. Even prior to the introductions, Chloe knew the officer was pissed about having the witness taken from him. As a detective in one of only three departments authorized to investigate homicides in the entire state, Chloe was quickly growing accustomed to that look.

"Sorry to interrupt, Leo," Mathers said. "Need to see you out here for a minute."

"Sure thing," the officer said before addressing the witness. "Be right back, Mr. Stanley."

Brock left the scene in the capable hands of Deputy Easter and Trooper Veilleux as he climbed inside his Ford armed with the victim's keys and a rudimentary hand-drawn map of the trail parking areas and their corresponding roads. Brock had scribbled out the directions from a mobile screen after finding the local trail club website. With only a single bar of coverage, the likelihood of maintaining cellular service while he searched was slim. The hand-drawn map was a precaution. Brock knew he was grasping at straws concerning the way the attack occurred, based on only his flimsy hypothesis and some blood droplets discovered in the woods, but the sooner they located the victim's vehicle, the sooner they could move the investigation forward.

The search area Brock needed to cover encapsulated ten square miles. Located on the outskirts of Greenville alongside Moosehead Lake between Lily Bay and Kokadjo, flanked to the east by White Cap Mountain, the remote wooded area was some of the least populated in the entire state. According to the map Brock had drawn, the forest where the victim may have been running was bordered by Lily Bay Road, Scammon Road, and something called Mount View Trail. While the first two at least sounded like paved thoroughfares, anything referred to as a trail meant "off road," meaning all-wheel drive would be a requirement. He was glad he had the Interceptor.

Brock marked small Xs along the route to approximate the location of the trail parking areas. Alongside each X, he added numerical designations clockwise along the route to keep track of his progress. The first two lots were located along Lily Bay Road, and both were empty. Brock continued up Lily Bay Road until it intersected with Mount View Trail. As he had expected, the "trail" was nothing more than a hard-packed gravel logging road, a bumpy cut-through connecting Lily Bay to Scammon. With frequent dips and the occasional washout, Brock kept his speed well below fifteen miles per hour. The last thing he needed out here was a flat tire and no cellular service.

After traveling approximately one mile along the Mount View Trail, Brock reached over to the passenger seat to pick up the map and assess his location when a flash of white appeared directly in front of the SUV.

"Shit," Brock said as he mashed the brake pedal. The front end of the Ford dipped dramatically, and everything not secured inside the passenger compartment slid forward onto the floor. The flash he had seen through the windscreen was the back end of a large white-tailed deer bounding gazelle-like across the dirt track in front of him. As the SUV came to a sliding stop, Brock watched the deer continue across the clearing and into the woods. Immediately following were two spotted fawns, one of which shot into the woods after what Brock assumed was its mother, while the other deer stopped in the center of the road, transfixed by the headlights of his vehicle.

Gradually Brock's heart rate began to slow as he sat face-to-face with the wide-eyed deer. After several moments, the fawn turned its head and trotted silently after the other two, leaving Brock alone on the deserted road. He glanced down at the passenger side footwell where his gloves, thermos, and map had settled in a heap. He had forgotten to replace the thermos cap, and the remaining coffee had leaked out into a sizable aromatic puddle, soaking everything.

"Perfect," he groaned.

As his attention returned to the road in front of him, Brock noticed something gleaming through the trees to his left about a hundred and fifty feet away. He took one last look around for wildlife, then continued slowly up the trail. The gleam that had caught his attention turned out to be chrome affixed to a mint-colored Subaru Outback parked in an unmarked dirt turnout not listed on the map he had drawn. Brock pulled into the lot and parked directly behind the wagon.

The Subaru was unoccupied, and the passenger side window had been smashed out. A Maine registration plate along with several colorful bumper stickers adorned the rear hatch, each one connected in some way to running and the outdoors. Hanging from the rearview mirror was a pair of tiny pink running shoes. He reached into his pocket and removed the keys Veilleux had given him and pressed the unlock button on the fob. The Subaru's marker lights flashed twice as the doors unlocked, confirming that he had located the victim's vehicle.

Once again, Brock was overcome by conflicting emotions. He had located the victim's vehicle, which was good. The downside was that they were about to turn the lives of everyone connected to this woman upside down as he and Chloe investigated the circumstances that had led to her murder. After all, prying into the most intimate aspects of the victim's daily life and the lives of those close to her as they worked to identify and build a case against her killer was the job of a homicide investigator.

Brock donned a pair of blue nitrile gloves and opened the driver's door, intentionally avoiding the broken window. It was time to find out who the Subaru belonged to and just maybe the identity of the woman lying dead in the middle of Lily Bay Road.

The glove box was open, and its contents were strewn across the floor of the vehicle. He saw no sign of a purse or pocketbook. Brock snapped several photos of the interior before he went looking for the registration certificate and insurance cards.

While Brock knew he could just as easily radio in the registration request to the dispatcher, it wasn't the kind of information he wanted over the airwaves for a variety of reasons, not the least of which was the possibility of the woman's identity getting back to her loved ones before they could be notified properly, or worse, having the registered owner turn out not to be the victim. It was every cop's worst nightmare.

6

Wednesday, October 8, 1:30 a.m

Chloe entered the interview room carrying two mugs of coffee in one hand and her battered leather briefcase in the other. She handed one of the mugs to the elderly witness, then sat directly across from him in the chair previously occupied by Officer Leo Hastings. Replacing Hastings turned out to be every bit as unenjoyable as Chloe had imagined. The officer's face had turned beet red when Mathers broke the bad news to him out in the hallway. And he'd glared at Chloe before storming off in the direction of the lobby. Being big-footed off a case by a detective from another agency wasn't something any cop wanted to be subjected to. Had their roles been reversed, Chloe knew she would feel the same as Hastings did. However, as this was no longer a simple motor vehicle accident but a possible homicide, it meant the state police had jurisdiction over the entire investigation.

"Thanks for the coffee, Detective," the man said after Chloe introduced herself. "Name's Norman Stanley, but you can call me Norm. Will Officer Hastings be joining us?"

"No, Norm," Chloe said. "The state police have taken over the case."

"Guess that's pretty routine when the accident is a fatal, huh?"

Chloe ignored the comment rather than risk corrupting a witness by sharing unnecessary details. After all, she was there to find out what Stanley had witnessed, not what he may have learned since. She removed a fresh legal-sized notepad and pen from her briefcase and set them on the table in front of her. She recorded the date, time, location of the interview, Stanley's name, and her own. Her attention then returned to Stanley.

"Why don't we start from the beginning, Norm. I'd like you to recount for me everything that happened tonight."

"I already told Officer Hastings everything I saw, which, to be honest, really wasn't all that much. I mean, the accident had already happened by the time I arrived."

"I understand, and I appreciate that you must be tired and want to get home, but I really need you to tell me everything. Okay?"

"Well, if you think it will help."

"I do."

Despite the length of time that had passed since the discovery and the fact that Stanley had already been interviewed, the man still appeared visibly shaken as he described the incident for Chloe.

"I've never seen anything like it," Stanley said as Chloe read back through his written statement. "She was just lying there in the middle of the road. It didn't seem real."

"I'm sure it was a shock," Chloe said.

"You know, I didn't even notice the rollover at first, just the body in the roadway. I pulled right over and stopped, of course."

"Did you attempt any kind of lifesaving measures or touch the victim in any way?"

The man shook his head. "No. I think I was meaning to, but as I got closer I could tell she was already dead. Her face and leg were just—it was horrible."

"Did you recognize the woman?"

"No, I can't say as I did. There was too much blood."

"What did you do after you realized she was dead?"

"I ran over to the overturned SUV to see if I could assist the passengers."

"And what did you find when you got there?"

"There was only one person inside. The driver was hanging upside down from his seat belt and bleeding from the face and head, but he was alive."

"How could you tell?"

"Because he was making little blood bubbles through his nose, so I knew he was still breathing. I tried to open the door to pull him out, in case the thing caught fire, but it was wedged shut from the collision with the tree."

"Why were you worried about it catching fire? Were there flames?"

"No," Stanley said. "But there was smoke inside the passenger compartment. One of the firefighters told me that it was most likely from the airbags going off. But I didn't know. Guess I've watched too many movies where the cars are always catching fire and blowing up after an accident. Isn't that what happens on every TV show?"

Chloe agreed it certainly seemed that way.

"Anyway, after that, I ran back to my truck, grabbed my phone from the charger, and called for help."

"Did you recognize the driver of the SUV?"

"Not at first because of the blood running down his face, and because like I said, he was upside down, but I did recognize the SUV. I know the owner. His name's Jonathan Watters."

"Did you see anyone else in the area? Other witnesses or people who may have been involved?"

"No. Not until the fire department and cops showed up."

Chloe nodded and added another line to the statement.

"Is that okay to say?" Stanley asked. "Cops?"

"It's fine, Mr. Stanley."

"I know when some people say it, it sounds derogatory. But that's not how I meant it."

"I know it isn't."

"Know what I keep thinking about, Detective?"

"What's that?" Chloe said.

"The woman's sneakers. They were just lyin' there in the middle of the road. Like she got knocked clean out of them. Guess I never knew that really happens."

Not knowing what to say, Chloe said nothing.

Stanley's voice cracked as he spoke again. "I'm afraid I'll end up seeing those sneakers in my dreams."

Brock stood by watching as the wrecker driver slowly winched the Subaru up the ramp of the flatbed. Prior to seizing the car, he had taken several photographs with his cell phone to document where he had located it. According to the paperwork Brock located inside the glove box, the Outback was registered to a woman named Summer Randall from Augusta, Maine. Brock texted the information to Chloe.

The tow truck operator turned and fixed Brock with a smirk. "Slow night, huh?"

"I don't follow," Brock said.

"Didn't know you staties patrolled the hiking lots for cars parked overnight."

"You should think about keeping your day job."

"What is that supposed to mean?"

"Your idea of humor could use some work, friend. I'm towing this vehicle because the owner was killed tonight. This is going to the Greenville police impound."

The driver's face reddened. He opened his mouth to respond but then apparently thought better of it and turned his attention back to the Subaru. Brock's cell phone rang with another call from Lt. Cumberland. Brock knew he couldn't put her off any longer.

"Lieutenant."

"This must be my lucky night," Cumberland said.

Brock knew she was setting him up and that she was pissed that he hadn't already provided an update. "Because?"

"Well, I figured since you hadn't called to check in, the cellular service in Greenville must be horrible."

"It is," Brock said.

"Uh-huh," she said, not sounding the least bit convinced. "Run the case down for me, Detective."

Brock brought Cumberland up to speed on what they had while the wrecker driver secured the Subaru to the flatbed. When he was finished, the driver stood, arms crossed, staring at Brock as he awaited further instructions. The smirk on his face had long since vanished.

Brock signaled to the driver that he would follow him back to the impound.

"Sounds like you've got a good start on this," Cumberland said. "How's Chloe doing?"

"At the moment, she's taking a statement from the only witness we have so far."

"A witness to the stabbing or the crash?"

"Far as I know, it's neither. Apparently the witness came across the accident and called it in. I don't mean to cut you off, LT, but I'm about to follow the wrecker back to the impound, and I'll probably lose you."

"Okay, we'll talk later on today. One more thing before you go."

"What's that?"

"Don't forget Chloe's your partner, Brock, not your gopher. She's there to learn from you. Got it?"

"Got it."

As he ended the call and pocketed his phone, Brock wondered if he should have mentioned Piscataquis County's newest road deputy. He also wondered how long it would be before Cumberland showed her face in town.

7

Wednesday, October 8, 3:40 a.m

After securing the Subaru inside the wrecker company's impound yard, Brock drove directly to 7 Minden Street, Greenville Police Department headquarters. Typical of many small Maine towns, the police department was located inside the public safety building rather than in its own free-standing facility, sharing space with the fire department. Brock parked in the side lot next to Chloe's Ford, then headed inside.

He found Chloe and Chief Leavitt waiting somberly inside. Thankfully, Evan Mathers was nowhere to be found.

"What gives?" Brock said.

"The RO on that Subaru you texted me," Chloe said, referring to the registered owner. "The chief knows her personally."

"You know Summer Randall?"

"I did," Leavitt said. "She's—was—very popular here and sort of a local."

"Sort of?"

"Summer actually hails from Augusta," Leavitt said. "She was a breath of fresh air and a hard worker. Came here to work these past few summers between her sophomore and senior years at UMO."

Brock knew Leavitt was referring to the University of Maine at Orono, located just outside of Bangor.

"What brought her to Greenville?" Brock said.

"Her parents got divorced," Leavitt said. "Taylor, her father, lives here now. Runs a business in town. He's a friend of mine."

"And the mother?" Brock said.

"She's a US congresswoman," Chloe said.

"Not Rhonda Randall," Brock said.

"The very same," Leavitt said.

Great, Brock thought as he took a moment to let the bad news sink in. The case had just gone from highly unusual to highly charged in an instant. Representative Rhonda Randall chaired the commission on police reform. If there was one member of the US House of Representatives they didn't need sticking her nose into this case, it was Randall. She had been a constant thorn in the side of law enforcement and a dyed-in-the-wool media hound. It also meant that keeping a lid on the details had just gotten a whole lot harder.

"How sure are you that Summer is the victim?" Leavitt said.

"Not a hundred percent," Brock said. "But the victim matches the general description on Summer's license, and the key we found at the scene unlocked her Subaru. I was hoping to wait until we could match her fingerprints with something on file before we made the notification."

"We've got to give her father a heads-up at least," Leavitt said. "Taylor will die if he finds out some other way."

"He's right," Chloe said.

Brock nodded.

"Where did Summer work?" Brock said.

"Until very recently, she was employed part-time at Balance Gym in Greenville Junction," Chloe said.

"But her main job was at Northern Light Hospital as a paid intern," Leavitt said. "Part of her college requirements, as I understand it. She was a senior this year."

"Why wasn't she back at Orono for the fall semester?" Brock said.

"Good question," Leavitt said. "I suspect she got a taste for freedom and a little money in her pocket and found it hard to go back. Wouldn't be the first."

Brock nodded. He too remembered that feeling as he neared his own graduation. The siren call of freedom was highly intoxicating.

"The chief was just telling me that Summer was an avid runner," Chloe said. "Most likely training in the woods when whatever happened to her happened tonight."

"She ran the occasional 10K road race to stay in competitive shape," Leavitt said. "Even ran in our local 5K race this past summer. It was kind of a fundraiser for Operation Sunrise. One of our community projects to assist the elderly."

"Do you happen to know where Summer was living?" Brock said.

"I do. She was renting a small apartment in town from Lucy and Zachery Corbett. They're the owners of the Moose Mountain Inn. Nice folks. Gave her a hell of a deal. Speaking of which, you two will probably be needing a place of your own while you're in town investigating."

"Can you help with that?" Chloe said.

"I might be able to pull some strings," Leavitt said as he checked his watch. "You hungry?"

"I could eat," Chloe said.

"Anything open this time of night?" Brock said.

"The coffee shop on Lakeview doesn't open until seven, but if you'd like to join me for breakfast, I'll see if I can get Jean to let us in early."

"Jean?" Brock said.

"Jean Prescott. She and her husband own the Greenville Grinds. Best cinnamon buns in the state."

"Sounds great," Chloe said.

"Thanks," Brock said. "Now about that death notification."

8

Wednesday, October 8, 4:45 a.m

Brock and Chloe stood beside each other one step down from Chief Leavitt on the darkened steps leading up to the side door of the large lakeside log cabin. They allowed Leavitt to take the lead on their initial contact with Taylor Randall. Death notifications were always unpleasant, but given the brutal way Randall's daughter had met her demise, this one had the potential to go very badly. Brock hoped that the chief's familiarity with the man would help to soften the blow.

Leavitt was about to knock a third time when the porch light illuminated, momentarily blinding them. The door swung inward, revealing a tall, burly man with a ruddy complexion and tousled sandy-colored hair. He wore gray sweatpants and a khaki T-shirt that stretched across the muscular chest of a weightlifter. He stood there for a long moment, wearing a look of confusion on his face as he attempted to process what was happening while his gaze shifted from Leavitt to Brock to Chloe.

"Taylor," Leavitt said at last, drawing the man's attention back to him.

"Rich," Randall said warily. "What brings you out here so early?"

"'Fraid I have some bad news," Leavitt said softly.

And then it happened. Brock saw Randall's stoic expression slide as something broke inside of him.

"It's Summer, isn't it?" Randall said, his voice barely audible.

Leavitt nodded.

"Please don't do this to me," Randall implored as his eyes welled with tears.

"May we come inside?"

Randall hesitated for a moment, as if denying their entry might prevent his worst fears from being realized. Relenting, he stepped back from the door and allowed them passage.

Brock and Chloe followed Chief Leavitt's lead. They sat at the kitchen table in awkward silence while Randall prepared coffee.

Brock had seen this scenario play out too many times to count. An aggrieved parent busying themselves rather than face the music. A subconscious attempt to delay the inevitable life-altering news. In this case the death of the man's only child. Rather than asking how they took their coffee, Randall simply poured four mugs and brought them to the table along with a half-empty carton of milk, a small ceramic container of sugar, and four spoons. He pulled out a chair and plopped down heavily at the far end of the table, nearest to Leavitt. Nobody touched their mugs as all eyes were fixed on Taylor Randall. He looked briefly at each one of them, as if reading their inner thoughts, before addressing Leavitt.

"My daughter is dead, isn't she?"

Randall said it in a matter-of-fact way, but Brock knew the man was a tight bundle of emotion, fighting to keep it from bubbling to the surface.

"Yes," Leavitt said.

"We still need to confirm Summer's identity," Brock added. "But we are confident that it is your daughter."

"What happened?"

"That's what we need to find out," Leavitt said. "These are detectives from the state police."

Randall nodded his understanding. "Figured that much out for myself."

Leavitt turned to Brock and Chloe. "Taylor was one of my reserve officers for a time. My best."

Brock, seeing that Leavitt was slipping from the task at hand, allowing his own grief at Summer's passing to creep through his professional veneer, weighed in again. "Mr. Randall, my name is Brock Justice, and this is my partner, Chloe Wright. Let me start by telling you how very sorry we both are for your loss."

"Thank you for coming here in person," Randall said. "It means a lot. I know how hard death notifications are. It sounds like you are still trying to piece together what exactly happened."

"We are," Chloe said. "Can you tell us the last time you spoke with Summer, Mr. Randall?"

"Taylor, please. If we're going to discuss the death of my little girl, then I guess we can dispense with the formalities. I spoke with Summer yesterday morning. She called me just to say hello. She did that a lot. We both are... were pretty busy and our schedules don't always align, but Summer always made time to check in with me."

Brock heard the anguish in the man's voice as he fought through the pain.

"I know you are all doing your best to skirt around what happened," Randall said. "But please, I need to know."

"Summer was killed in a motor vehicle accident," Chloe said. "It appears that she may have been crossing Lily Bay Road on foot when she was struck by a passing vehicle."

Randall looked to Leavitt as if for confirmation as a cascade of tears rolled down his cheeks, and the chief nodded his silent agreement.

"We have reason to believe that alcohol played a part in the accident," Leavitt added.

"But my Summer didn't drink," Randall said, wearing a confused expression. "She never touched a drop."

"We believe the operator of the vehicle that struck her had been drinking," Brock clarified.

Randall turned to Leavitt again. "Who was it, Rich? Who killed my little girl?"

"We don't need to get into—"

"Who?" Randall said, slamming his fist down on the tabletop, making the spoons clatter.

"It was Jonathan Watters. He was transported to the hospital with non-life-threatening injuries. But I don't know any more than that at present."

Brock watched a lightbulb go off inside Randall's head as he turned back to fix his hollow eyes on him.

"The state police don't send detectives out to investigate fatal motor vehicle accidents," Randall said. "The county can handle those. There is more to this than you're telling me. What is it?"

"We have reason to believe that your daughter may have been attacked prior to the accident that killed her," Chloe said.

"Attacked? By who?"

"That is what we need to find out," Brock said.

Leavitt weighed in again. "Summer was struck near the forest trails across from Sandy Bay."

"We think she may have been jogging in the woods when the attack happened," Chloe said.

"Can you think of anyone who might have wanted to harm your daughter?" Brock said.

Brock saw Randall lock eyes with Chief Leavitt again. Something clearly passed between them. After a moment, Randall turned back to face Brock and Chloe.

"No, I can't think of anyone who might want to hurt my Summer," Randall said.

Brock knew Randall was lying. What he didn't know was why.

"We understand that you and Summer's mother are divorced," Chloe said.

Randall nodded. "Rhonda."

"We'll need to notify her as well."

"I'll take care of that," Randall said gruffly. "Where is Summer's body?"

"She's been transported to the medical examiner's office for the post," Brock said.

Randall's eyes welled with tears again. Brock knew the man was thinking about the nature of an autopsy and what cruelty still lie ahead for his daughter. After the atrocity that had already been inflicted on her, Brock could only imagine the anguish Randall was feeling as he envisioned the next steps. Both men knew that a postmortem examination was the only way to obtain the answers necessary to identify the exact cause and manner of her death, the next step in finding the person responsible for putting her in the path of a drunk driver, but it didn't make the image of the procedure any easier to swallow.

"Will you keep me in the loop going forward?" Randall said.

"We will do all we can, Mr.—Taylor," Chloe said.

"We'll be in town for as long as it takes," Brock said as he handed Randall a business card. "I've written my cell phone number on the back."

Chloe passed him her card as well. "If you think of anything that might be helpful to our investigation, please contact one of us."

"Thank you. I will."

9

Wednesday, October 8, 6:40 a.m

True to his word, Chief Leavitt got them into Greenville Grinds twenty minutes before it opened. Only a stone's throw from Moosehead Lake, the coffee shop couldn't have had a better location. After setting them up at a four-top across from the breakfast bar in the back, Jean Prescott, owner of the establishment, poured each of them an extra-large cup of piping-hot coffee.

"There," she said. "That should get you started."

"Thanks, Jean," Leavitt said.

Brock and Chloe echoed their appreciation as Prescott returned to the kitchen. The yeasty aroma of cinnamon buns baking in the oven overpowered the small café. Brock wondered how they would ever manage to wait until seven before sampling one.

"I could kill for one of those," Chloe said, as if reading his very thoughts.

Her comment needed no clarification. Everyone seated at the table knew to what she was referring.

"Well, that went a whole lot better than I imagined," Leavitt said before taking a careful sip of coffee.

"I've definitely seen worse," Chloe said.

Still wondering if they could trust Leavitt, Brock delivered his opening salvo without fanfare.

"Any idea why Taylor lied to us back there, Rich?"

Leavitt, who was hoisting his cup for another sip, paused halfway to his mouth. Chloe's mouth dropped open as if she couldn't believe Brock would make such a blunt accusation.

"What about?" Leavitt said, cocking his head slightly and tossing the ball back to Brock.

"When I asked if he knew anyone who might want to harm Summer, Taylor hesitated before saying no. And something unspoken passed between the two of you. What was it?"

The chief returned the cup to the table without taking another sip. He pursed his lips and held eye contact with Brock for a long moment before responding.

"We had some trouble around here a little over a year ago."

"What kind of trouble?" Chloe said.

"The abusive boyfriend kind," Leavitt said. "Summer's high school sweetheart, Ronnie Libby."

"What happened?" Brock said.

"What always happens? Ronnie found drugs and alcohol, and they turned him into a real asshole. Gave Summer a black eye and split her lip. I locked Ronnie up for assault before Taylor could get a hold of him. I was worried he might kill the kid."

"That have anything to do with Taylor not being a reserve cop anymore?" Chloe said.

Leavitt nodded. "Taylor made some threats against the boy. I couldn't blame him, really, but letting him go was part of a plea deal. Didn't have a choice."

"How's that?" Brock said.

"Ronnie's parents got involved, as did Congresswoman Randall. Neither side wanted the negative publicity that a long, drawn-out domestic violence case would've brought to our little hamlet. In the end, Libby's parents agreed not to file criminal threatening charges against Taylor if they were allowed to put Ronnie into rehab and have the entire case against him filed for a year."

"I take it the Libbys have some clout around here," Brock said.

Leavitt nodded. "As do the Randalls. Small town."

"And what about what Summer wanted?" Chloe said. "After all, she was the real victim."

"I suspect Summer simply went along with her mother's wishes," Leavitt said.

"Have there been any problems this year?" Chloe said.

Leavitt shook his head. "None. Summer and Ronnie both seemed to have moved on from the incident. And to my knowledge, Ronnie has been clean and sober ever since he was released from the rehab facility over in Bangor."

"What does Libby do for work?" Brock said.

"He's a boat builder by trade. Been working on the *Kate* restoration."

"Kate?" Brock said.

"*Katahdin*. She's a historic steamboat docked right here in East Bay. Named after Mount Katahdin, the locals all call her *Kate* for short. *Kate's* been cruising people around Moosehead Lake for over a hundred years. She's more like a floating museum than a ferry, I suppose."

"What does this have to do with Ronnie?" Brock said.

"Anyway, when he's straight, Ronnie is one hell of a craftsman, and he is part of a team working to restore *Kate*. Ronnie's parents got some big money donors to pony up two million dollars for the project."

"I'll bet some Congressional money made its way into the coffers too," Chloe said.

Leavitt nodded. "Good guess."

"Strange bedfellows," Brock said.

Leavitt cracked a smile for the first time since departing Taylor's house. "Sounds like you're both familiar with politics."

"All too," Brock said as he thought back to Evan Mathers and the events that had led to his transfer to Northern Maine.

"Well, you're right," Leavitt said. "The Libbys donated half a million dollars to the project, citing the historic importance of the *Katahdin*, bringing it right to the two-million-dollar goal."

"Must be a coincidence that this happened right after Ronnie Libby's assault charge was filed," Brock said.

"Must be," Leavitt said, attempting to hide behind his coffee cup.

"And you had no say in any of this?" Chloe said.

"I had plenty to say about it," Leavitt said defensively. "But if you've ever dealt with elected DAs, you know exactly how little my opinion mattered."

"Handmaidens of the law," Brock said absently.

"That's all we are," Leavitt said. "Anyway, I said my piece, got overruled, and the Greenville Police Department lost its best reserve officer."

"Too bad Evan isn't available to fill it," Brock said, earning a glare from Chloe.

"You mean Deputy Mathers?"

"That's exactly who I mean," Brock said.

Leavitt placed his cup on the table. He seemed to be formulating his response. "I gather that some bad blood still exists between you and Evan."

"You're very perceptive," Brock said.

"Be that as it may, Evan was found not guilty and resigned his position with the state police voluntarily and in good standing."

"That what he told you?"

"That's what his superiors told me. I'm not sure how easy it is to find a trained cop with Evan's level of experience and expertise in Southern Maine, but up here, it's a bear. And the few, small, underfunded departments around here all end up fighting for the same scraps. In addition to that, it still takes a year or two before a new officer is up to speed and seasoned enough to be of any use. And you know as well as I that most probationary officers these days end up leaving for a larger department just as soon as they're trained. That is, assuming they even remain on the job. Bottom line is I had no reason not to hire Evan except I didn't have it in the budget to take on a full-timer. So, I spoke to Armand Pelletier, the sheriff of Piscataquis County, and he agreed to run Evan through their process. He breezed right through the hiring process and saved them a fortune by not needing to send a brand-new recruit through the academy."

Brock remained quiet.

"Evan's been a big help to me since he got assigned to this area. Even though he works for Armand, Evan has taken on kind of a mentoring role to some of my part-timers."

"Sounds like a win-win," Chloe said, a bit too cheerfully for Brock's liking.

"I get that you and Evan still have unresolved issues," Leavitt continued. "But that isn't my problem. I expect the two of you to play nice until this is resolved. I may only be the chief of an insignificant police agency in your eyes, but don't be fooled, I've been in this game a long time. Thirty years in Cumberland County Sheriff's Department. I have many friends in this business. If whatever issues you still have with Evan begin to spill over into this case, I'll make sure that your superiors reassign this murder so fast your head will spin. Do we understand each other, Detective Justice?"

After a moment and against his better judgment, Brock nodded.

"You think Ronnie could have done this?" Chloe said, breaking the awkward silence. "Attacked Summer with a knife?"

Leavitt finally tore his eyes away from Brock. He appeared to ponder the question before answering. "No, but then I couldn't see him beating her up either. Not before it happened."

"And you're sure Ronnie's still clean?" Brock said.

"Like I said, so far as I know, but you should check with his boss, Charlie Fasulo," Leavitt said before his attention shifted toward the kitchen door.

Jean approached their table carrying a tray with three plates. Upon each plate was the largest cinnamon bun Brock had ever seen, each one dripping with cream-colored icing.

"Who's hungry?"

10

Wednesday, October 8, 8:40 a.m

Autumn had yet to reach its crescendo in Piscataquis County, but the striking red foliage of the swamp maples was already on full display. Accompanying this were glints of gold and rust from the oaks and birches soon to follow. At first glance, the tranquil lakeside town of Greenville looked like something from a bygone era, the kind of place where nothing bad ever happened, like Maine's own version of Mayberry. But as Brock knew all too well, first appearances are often deceiving.

Still fuming over Leavitt's dressing-down, Brock drove in silence along Lily Bay Road. He lowered the windows, taking full advantage of the quickly warming air. He kept the radio off as he scrolled through a mental checklist of the case priorities and what he hoped to accomplish by the end of the day. Chloe followed right behind him in her own unmarked. He knew he didn't need to convey to her that this was the last bit of calm before the storm descended upon them and the town of Greenville. The murdered daughter of a congresswoman would own the local news cycle and beyond.

Though the pending K9 track, and any additional evidence discovered, including the location of the attack, was paramount, there were already several leads to be followed and people to talk to before word leaked out and alibis could be manufactured. Brock slowed as he neared the scene of the previous night's accident. He pulled onto the gravel shoulder and stopped.

Activating the SUV's emergency flashers, Brock opened the door and stepped out to survey the area. Discarded remnants of garish yellow crime scene ribbon still clung to several trees on either side of the roadway, fluttering in the breeze like obscene reminders of the collision that had punctuated the end of what by all accounts had been a promising young life. The life of Summer Randall.

"What the hell was that?" Chloe said as she approached him on foot. "Are you trying to get us kicked off this case?"

"Of course not."

"Then why are you poking the chief? Leavitt's been nothing but helpful so far. And if this case blows up, and it has all the earmarks of doing just that, we're going to need an ally in this town."

"I got that message just fine, thank you. I don't need you to recap our situation. I get it, okay?"

"And Evan Mathers? What about him?"

"I'll play nice with Evan, but only because I have to."

"Good."

"Just remember he and I have a history, Chloe. There are things you don't know about him."

Brock crossed to the far side of the roadway directly across from the trailhead.

"Where are you going?" Chloe said. "I thought we were going to walk the trail."

"We are. But first I want to remove the leftover crime scene tape before Summer's family sees it." *Or some heartless prick from social media uses the image as clickbait*, he thought to himself.

"This area will probably be loaded with flowers or wreaths soon enough anyway, Brock. Her family won't be able to escape it."

"Maybe not, but there's a big difference between a tasteful memorial and a police crime scene. Which one would you want to have etched into your brain if Summer was your daughter?"

Chloe said nothing as she walked into the scrub and untied the unsightly tape from the nearest tree.

Brock removed the plastic he found on the far side of the road along with a discarded latex glove, likely belonging to one of the first responders. He was pleased to see that the Greenville firefighters had at least made the effort to rinse Summer's blood from the pavement. He could only imagine Taylor's reaction to seeing that. As he returned across the road, he noticed how much more visible the entrance to the forest trail was by day. The narrow opening had been difficult to spot in the dark. He wondered why there wasn't additional signage identifying the trail. Maybe there had been, and local hoodlums absconded with it. Also visible by the light of day was a small dirt turnout about a hundred feet up the road from the trailhead.

"Know what I keep wondering?" Chloe said.

"No," Brock said.

"I wonder if the attack on Summer was random or if the suspect knew her routine. Knew she'd be running this specific trail last evening."

Brock had wondered the very same thing.

"It would help if we knew where the suspect parked their vehicle," Brock said, nodding toward the turnout.

"You don't think they hoofed it out here?" Chloe said.

"Seems too far from town to me."

"Not impossible, though," Chloe said.

"No. Not impossible."

They both turned to the sound of an approaching vehicle. It was a black Piscataquis County Sheriff's Department SUV with a large gold K9 decal affixed to its side. The deputy greeted them with a wave as he parked behind Chloe's Interceptor.

"Good morning," the deputy greeted.

"Morning," Brock said.

"We were worried you weren't coming," Chloe said.

"Yeah, sorry about that. I had some personal stuff at home to deal with. Either one of you have a teenager?"

They both shook their heads.

"Do yourself a favor, don't. Or maybe adopt a twenty-something and skip right over that fresh hell altogether."

"I'll try and remember that," Chloe chuckled.

"Name's Sam Rancourt," the deputy said.

"Chloe Wright," she said, extending her hand in greeting.

"Brock Justice," Brock said as he followed suit.

"Good to meet you both."

Brock was pleased that Rancourt didn't feel the need to mention that he'd heard Brock's name. It was refreshing to be introduced to someone in the law enforcement community who didn't feel any compulsion to mention his infamous reputation.

Deputy Rancourt retrieved some of his gear from inside the passenger compartment while his enthusiastic K9 bounced around in the back of the vehicle, whining loudly.

"Who's your partner?" Chloe said.

"This excitable young lady is Nikko. You ready to go to work, girl?"

Nikko gave a high-pitched bark in response.

"She's beautiful," Chloe said. "German shepherd?"

"Mix, actually. Half shepherd, half Akita."

"That a good mix?" Brock asked, not really knowing anything about dog breeds.

"I'll say. Means she's got a nose for bad guys and the bite to back it up."

Brock and Chloe watched Rancourt slip a tracking harness over Nikko, preparing her to work.

"Tell me again exactly what you're hoping to find?" Rancourt said as he stood.

"We believe our victim may have been out running in the woods last evening," Chloe said. "We have reason to think she was attacked somewhere along the trail and was attempting to flee her pursuer when she exited the woods only to be struck by a vehicle right here on the road just after dusk."

"Talk about bad luck," Rancourt said. "Do you have any idea where the victim came from? Where she started her run?"

"We do," Brock said, explaining that he had located her vehicle in a lot off the Mount View Trail.

Rancourt nodded. "So, you're hoping to try and figure out where the attack occurred?"

"Exactly," Chloe said.

"And any evidence that may have been left behind," Brock said. "There may have been a struggle."

"Well, let's see if we can find you some clues," Rancourt said as he turned his attention to Nikko. "You ready, girl?"

Nikko audibly responded in the positive.

11

Wednesday, October 8, 9:00 a.m

Nikko and Deputy Rancourt led the way with Brock and Chloe following from a short distance to avoid distracting the K9 from her track. Nikko kept her nose firmly to the ground while pulling Rancourt along at a brisk pace. Brock knew from experience that both things were clear signs that she was on the hunt. They had walked less than a quarter of a mile into the woods when Brock's cell chimed with an incoming text message. He removed the phone from the pocket of his windbreaker and checked the display.

Call me.

Brock recognized it for what it was, and it wasn't a request.

"Penny?" Chloe said with a knowing smirk.

"Who else," Brock said as he silenced the text messages and returned the phone to its previous location. He couldn't help but wonder which one of the influential parents had already reached out to Cumberland.

Lieutenant Penelope Cumberland, known informally among the rank and file as Penny Dreadful, was a tough, no-nonsense commander you only crossed once. And, as Brock quickly learned, she was equally capable of being a staunch ally or your worst nightmare. Her moniker was well earned. As the most recent arrival to MCU North, Brock still wasn't sure which role the lieutenant would play in his professional life.

"You think she knows about the political connection yet?" Chloe said as they moved through the woods at double time.

"If she doesn't already, she will soon enough. My guess? Her phone's blowing up right about now."

"Think it's a good idea to blow her off at this point?"

Brock knew it wasn't, but he also knew that she was likely already en route to Greenville to get a lay of the land and try to maintain some control over what was sure to be a dumpster fire of the highest order.

"I'll call her as soon as we finish the track," Brock said.

"Your funeral," Chloe said.

Despite the amount of physical rehabilitation Brock had undergone after being shot, his wounded left leg had atrophied. Not only was it visibly smaller than the right when he compared them in the mirror, but the muscles of that leg also tired more quickly, giving him a visible limp. He was doing his best to keep up with Chloe while at the same time hiding the handicap. Brock had spent significant time on both the treadmill and the elliptical as part of his recovery training, but there was a big difference between working out on precision-machined gym equipment and hurrying across the uneven ground of the Maine woods.

Rancourt radioed through a blast of static from up ahead where he and Nikko had stopped. "Think I got something."

Brock and Chloe reached them a short time later.

"What is it?" Brock said.

Rancourt knelt and pointed to a small piece of torn material caught in a deadfall just off the trail.

"What did you say your vic was wearing?"

"Dark running pants, white tee, and an aqua-colored sweatshirt," Chloe said.

"Did you happen to notice if the sweatshirt was torn?"

"There was a lot of damage from the collision," Brock said. "Impossible to know without matching it to the actual material."

"The color matches," Chloe said as she snapped several pictures of the find with her phone before removing a pair of purple nitrile gloves from her pocket. "I'll take it."

While Chloe seized the possible evidence, Brock examined the nearby ground and surrounding area. After a moment, he spotted what looked like dark crimson-colored stains on several of the lighter branches contained within the deadfall.

"The branches here are coated in what looks like dried blood," Brock said.

"I'll take a sample of that as well," Chloe said.

Brock stood back to examine the overall setting. The deadfall, approximately the size of a small automobile, was located near a sharp bend in the trail. Meaning if Summer had been running toward Lily Bay Road, she would have been coming out of the curve as she approached the deadfall. Brock studied the curve. It was severe enough that Summer could have lost her way or her footing in the dark, causing her to leave the trail and crash headlong into the pile of branches. It might explain the detritus they had seen in her hair. Brock moved carefully about the path until he found what he was searching for. The leaves and pine needles carpeting the forest floor were disturbed exactly where the trail turned. A swath of mud had been turned up, and though the imprint was smudged, it closely resembled the tread of a running shoe. A running shoe like the ones Summer Randall had been knocked out of at the accident scene. The muddy smear likely made a positive comparison impossible, but combined with the torn aqua-colored cloth, it appeared to confirm his theory that she had been chased through the woods by her assailant.

Nikko and Rancourt approached, trying to see what had piqued Brock's attention.

"Whatcha got?" Rancourt said.

"If Summer was running from her pursuer, like we think she was, this mud may be the reason she slipped and left the trail."

"Makes sense," Rancourt said. "If she was running toward the road and slipped right here, she could easily have pinwheeled into that brush. Man, that girl had one fucked-up last few minutes in this world."

"Not to mention her coda of being run down by a drunk driver," Chloe said.

Brock heard his cell phone ringing. A quick check confirmed it was Cumberland calling. He thumbed the ignore button and returned the phone to his pocket.

"Did you seize the cloth?" Brock said.

"Yup. And a couple of blood scrapings too so we can confirm this is Summer's blood."

"Wouldn't it be great if it belonged to her attacker," Rancourt said.

"Get some shots of this mud too," Brock said.

After gathering the evidence and recording the finds with photos, Brock and Chloe continued after Nikko and Rancourt. They hurried through the woods for another twenty minutes or so. Brock guessed that they had traveled well over a mile and a half from their starting point on Lily Bay Road, but they had yet to find anything resembling an attack scene. Though what that might look like was anyone's guess.

Nikko had begun to cheat, lifting her head to scent the air. No longer strictly following the trail left by Summer Randall as she fled through the woods, the K9's pace had slowed considerably. Nikko appeared to be focused on something more intermittent along the trail.

"You find something?" Chloe called out.

"Maybe," Rancourt said, once again kneeling for a closer look at the ground.

"What is it?"

"Bloodstain," Rancourt said, while wrestling to keep Nikko from nosing through it. "And the ground is disturbed here. Looks like this might be where a struggle ensued."

Brock examined the area closely. Two paths converged on the spot. And low-growth hemlocks bordering both sides of each trail would have provided concealment for the attacker. It looked like the perfect place to set an ambush.

"I agree," Brock said. "Not only does it look like this may have been the scene of the initial attack, but it is also the perfect place to lie in wait."

"Speaking of ambush," Chloe said, causing both men to look up. "The boss is calling."

Before he could stop her, Chloe answered the call.

"Good morning, Lieutenant," Chloe said.

"Damn," Brock mumbled.

12

Wednesday, October 8, 10:00 a.m

"Is there some reason that you keep ignoring my phone calls and texts?" Lt. Cumberland demanded after Chloe handed her phone over to Brock.

The tone of her voice made her displeasure with him crystal clear.

"Don't even try to make excuses. You'll only end up saying something to piss me off even more."

"The cell coverage up here is really spotty, LT," Brock said.

"And yet Detective Wright's phone doesn't seem to be having any difficulty."

Chloe mouthed the word "sorry" to Brock.

"You may want to check your own cell phone again, Detective Justice. I just texted a photo to you that may be of interest."

Brock's heart sunk as he studied the image on his phone screen. It was a screenshot of an online article written by a small-town newspaper reporter in Greenville that had somehow been picked up by the *Bangor Daily News* and then the Associated Press. The headline read: *Congresswoman's Daughter Murdered in Maine*.

The accompanying images were stock photos of Moosehead Lake, likely taken from the local newspaper archives or AP files, and a photo of Representative Rhonda Randall. Brock noted that the article contained very little detail about the murder, which was a good thing. The problem was that it made clear that Summer had been murdered, removing any chance he and Chloe would have to try and slow-walk the details from leaking out. They were officially out for the world to see. A world that would quickly be descending on them.

"Any idea how this got out?" Cumberland said.

"I don't," Brock said. "Chloe and I haven't spoken to anyone from the press."

"Doesn't really matter now, does it?" Cumberland barked. "Someone opened their yap, and now this has become the biggest story in the Northeast and beyond."

Brock said nothing. No amount of contrition would change things.

"Tell me where we're at," Cumberland said. "If I'm going to do damage control, I have to know what the hell I'm talking about."

Brock quickly ran down everything they had while Cumberland listened. Brock could hear the sound of pen on paper as the lieutenant scribbled notes.

"What about this drunk driver?" Cumberland said. "What's his story?"

"Jonathan Watters," Brock said. "We haven't been able to speak with him yet. He's still being treated at the hospital. They had to extricate him from the wreck."

"And we think, what? He was just in the wrong place at the wrong time with a head full of booze?"

"At this point, we don't have enough to rule him in or out as far as the stabbing goes," Brock said.

"And we're one hundred percent sure this was a murder?"

"The victim definitely received one stab wound while in the woods," Brock said. "Long before she reached Lily Bay Road."

"And the post?" Cumberland said.

"I put a call in to Dr. Isleborn's office first thing this morning," Brock said. "Just waiting to hear back, then I'll head down."

"Why are *you* going all the way to Augusta?" Cumberland asked.

"I figured Chloe could interview some of the locals while I'm at the autopsy," Brock said as he held Chloe's gaze.

"I want you up there, Brock," Cumberland said. "This is your mess. Chloe can handle the autopsy, right?"

Brock glanced at Chloe to see how she would respond. Her expression confirmed that she'd heard Cumberland's side of the conversation. Chloe's previous postmortem, and coincidentally her only, hadn't gone particularly well. She'd gotten sick, nearly passing out in the process.

"Of course," Chloe said after a moment's hesitation.

"Good," Cumberland said. "Glad we got that settled. Now, you both better get back to it before all hell breaks loose."

"How can it get any worse?" Brock said absently.

"I'll tell you how it can get worse, Detective," Cumberland snapped. "Congresswoman Randall is flying directly into Bangor from DC. She's scheduled to arrive just after two o'clock."

Everyone's attention, even Nikko's, was drawn to the ringing of Brock's cell.

"Is that your phone ringing, Detective?"

"It is."

"Oh good," Cumberland said. "Looks like you've got service again. See you soon."

Brock raised his own phone to his ear and answered the call. "Justice."

"Good morning, Detective."

"Morning, Doc," Brock said, instantly recognizing Dr. Isleborn's distinctly arid tone.

"I see you've stirred up another hornet's nest. Are you still up in Greenville?"

"I am."

"How soon can you get here for the post?"

Brock checked the time, then looked at Chloe. "Detective Wright will be there by one o'clock."

Twenty minutes later, they arrived back at their respective vehicles parked on Lily Bay Road. Most of the return trek through the woods had consisted of Chloe and Rancourt discussing Nikko while Brock brooded inside his own head.

"I figured Cumberland would have been a lot more pissed at us for letting that information get out."

"Oh, she hasn't finished with us yet," Brock said.

"Well, it looks like you guys are set for now," Rancourt said as he opened the rear hatch of his vehicle and signaled for Nikko to hop in.

"Thanks again for the quick assist," Brock said.

"Don't mention it. I'll email my supplemental report to both of you before the end of shift."

"Thanks," Chloe said. "And thank you, Nikko."

Nikko responded with a bark and playful tail wag.

"Holler if you need anything else."

Brock stopped Chloe before she drove off. "I'll check in at the hospital and start on a timeline for Summer while you're gone. You sure you're okay attending the autopsy?"

Embarrassment blossomed across Chloe's face. "Of course. Why wouldn't I be?"

Brock could see she was trying to mask her apprehension.

"No reason. Just thought I'd ask. Let me know as soon as Isleborn gives you something we can use. We need a clear-cut cause of death here."

"You'll be the first call I make."

And with that, Chloe was gone. Brock was about to climb inside his own vehicle when he noticed a black SUV approaching. Behind the wheel sat none other than Chief Leavitt.

13

Wednesday, October 8, 10:30 a.m

"Chief," Brock said as he watched Leavitt exit his police vehicle and approach on foot.

"Hoping I might catch you out here," Leavitt said.

"I'm a little busy now. What's up?"

"Want to apologize for the media leak. It shouldn't have happened."

Brock paused for a moment, attempting to parse his next words. If Leavitt really was an ally, the last thing he wanted was to alienate him further than he already had.

"I know you and I kinda got off to a bit of a rocky start, what with Evan Mathers, but I would never leak something like this to the press."

"Any idea how it happened?" Brock said.

"I'm still trying to sort that out. Best I can figure, one of my people or one of the EMT folks spoke to Joyce Peterson at the *Greenville Times*."

"What's her story?" Brock said.

"She's our local Woodward and Bernstein wannabe. She works for the only newspaper in town and has her tentacles into the public safety sector. Only a small group of folks knew about the stabbing. Obviously, someone spoke out of turn last night."

Brock couldn't help wondering if that someone might just be Evan Mathers.

"Any idea why they would do that?" Brock said. "You said Summer was well liked."

"Why do they ever do it? Trying to be the big deal with inside information, I suppose. We don't get many murders in this town. Especially when the victim is the daughter of such a prominent political figure as Congresswoman Randall."

"Don't suppose it matters much now, does it?" Brock said, silently wondering if there might have been a political reason for the leak.

"Guess not. Just wanted you to know I'm sorry it happened, and I'm gonna try to get to the bottom of it so it doesn't happen again."

"Appreciate it," Brock said.

"By the way, Jonathan Watters is awake at the hospital. Figured you'd want to know."

"Is he in custody?"

"Not yet. We still need his blood analysis to be able to officially charge him with operating under the influence. And I guess your investigation will likely impact our ability to charge him with vehicular manslaughter, right?"

Brock couldn't argue that point.

"I figured you'd probably want us to hold off for now to give you time to speak with him."

"Thanks, Rich."

The Northern Light CA Dean Hospital was located on Pritham Avenue in Greenville. A brand new, albeit small, state-of-the-art medical center, constructed on the former campus of the Greenville Medical Center. As Brock turned into the visitors' lot, he was struck by the irony that Summer Randall, a former intern who may well have taken part in treating Jonathan Watters for the injuries sustained in last night's accident, now lay on a cold steel table in the morgue at the medical examiner's office in Augusta while Watters convalesced in her hospital. Brock could hear the sound of his father, Albert, waxing poetic with the words: "Life is neither amusing nor fair, but it's often ironic."

After changing back into his street shoes and checking his clothing for any muddy remnants of his romp through the woods, Brock locked the Ford and walked toward the hospital's main entrance.

Brock caught the attention of an attractive thirty-something brunette manning the admissions desk. "May I help you?" she asked.

Brock displayed his credentials to the woman. "Detective Justice, state police. I'm hoping you can direct me to Jonathan Watters's room."

He waited while the woman studied his ID. She looked up at him with pleading eyes.

"Is it true that he killed Summer Randall?"

Brock hesitated a moment before responding. He knew anything he said at this point, even the simplest acknowledgment, might come back to bite him later. Assuming Joyce Peterson, the local reporter Chief Leavitt had mentioned, hadn't already spoken to hospital staff, she would soon enough. As would the legion of major media outlets likely to follow. The court of public opinion was no place to try a case, but over the last few years, that very thing had become the new normal. The last thing Brock wanted was to add fuel to that raging inferno.

Brock settled on, "We're still investigating exactly what did happen." His comment seemed to placate the woman.

"We really thought the world of her around here. I can't believe Summer is dead."

Brock waited another moment to see if she might provide him with Watters's room number. When she didn't, he prodded her. "Watters's room number?"

"Oh, I'm sorry. He's in 208."

Brock decided to check in at the nurses' station rather than go directly to Watters's room. If he had learned anything about hospital hierarchy during his many years in policing, it was that the nurses ran the show.

"May I help you?" the duty nurse said.

Brock repeated the process of identifying himself.

"Patient Watters?" the gray-haired nurse grumbled, making no attempt to mask her disdain for the man. "Yeah, he's up for visitors. You plan to question him about what he did to Summer Randall?"

"I plan to talk with him," Brock said as he returned his credentials to his back pocket.

"Let me know if he gives you any trouble."

Brock fought back a grin as he imagined to what lengths this nurse might go to get Watters to talk.

Brock hadn't been sure what to expect from Watters when he first entered the room, but some contrition and a bit of remorse, two emotions he seemed incapable of expressing, might have made conversing with the banged-up man slightly more palatable.

Watters lay on his back, inclined slightly in the hospital bed. Jet-black hair was matted to his forehead, and there were cuts and bruises scattered about his face. Based solely on the amount of damage sustained by the overturned truck, and the need for extrication, Brock had envisioned Watters's injuries would be much more severe.

"State police, huh?" Watters said. "First time dealing with you guys. I must be too much for the locals."

Brock ignored the comment. He knew Watters was attempting to provoke him, and he wasn't about to give the man the smug satisfaction of rising to the bait.

"I want to ask you about the accident," Brock said.

"What about it?"

"Do you remember anything from before or after the crash?"

"Am I in custody?"

"Do you see any restraints?"

"Nope. But we both know that doesn't mean I'm not in custody."

"You are not in custody, Mr. Watters. But I am investigating the death of a young woman in connection with your accident. Anything you can remember might be helpful."

"Helpful to who? Or is it *whom*? I can never remember."

"To her family," Brock said.

"Ah, so you're hoping to play the sympathy card with me, right? Talk about this girl's mother and father, sister and brother, and I'm supposed to get all weepy and emotional, is that it?"

"How about showing a little human compassion, Mr. Watters? You may have walked away nearly unscathed, but a woman is dead after being struck by your vehicle."

"Really? See, that's interesting, because the way I hear it, the woman may have been attacked before she ran out in front of my truck."

"Where did you hear that?"

Watters nodded toward the wall-mounted television. "TV news. Sounds like I'm just a victim of circumstances, Officer Justice."

"Detective."

"I stand corrected, Detective Justice. By the way, is that your real name? Justice?"

"It is."

"That's too much."

"So, you remember her running out in front of your truck."

"Who said that?"

"You did. You said, 'The way I hear it, the woman may have been attacked before she ran out in front of my truck.'"

"Ah, well, it's all a little fuzzy at the moment. Must be these great painkillers they got me on."

"This conversation is over, Detective," a voice said from the doorway.

Brock turned to find a slight, bespectacled man standing in the doorway holding a leather briefcase.

"Well, if it isn't the attorney du jour," Watters said. "About time, Henry."

"And you are?" Henry said to Brock.

"Allow me," Watters said. "This is Detective Justice from the Maine State Police. Detective Justice, this is my attorney, Henry Gifford."

"I'm guessing you specialize in OUIs," Brock said.

"I'll thank you not to mock me," Gifford said as he entered the room. "I hope you haven't been questioning my client in violation of his Miranda rights."

"Your client isn't in custody," Brock said. "And up until you interrupted our conversation, I had no idea he was even represented."

"Well, now you know," Gifford said as he removed a business card from the inside pocket of his suit coat and extended it toward Brock. "Any further questioning of Mr. Watters will have to wait until he's been released from the hospital and in my presence. Are we clear?"

"Nice chatting with you, Officer—um, I mean Detective Justice," Watters said with a wink. "See you 'round."

If Brock had been biting his tongue at that moment, he might well have bitten it off. He wondered how the public would react if they were ever allowed a glimpse into the callous side of many criminals instead of the well-manicured and well-practiced version crafted by their attorneys for use at trial.

"I'll be in touch," Brock said before his attention turned to Watters one last time. "By the way, in case you're still curious, it's *whom*."

14

Wednesday, October 8, 1:15 p.m

Chloe stood alone in the medical examiner's viewing area, peering through the glass as Dr. Isleborn and her assistant slowly and methodically conducted the autopsy on the pale, battered remains of Summer Randall. The so-called examination room looked like a cross between a surgical theater and the lair of a demented serial killer. Rows of stainless-steel tables, sinks, and hanging digital scales each bathed in unforgiving fluorescent lighting that presented everything, and everyone, with a ghoulish pallor.

Chloe couldn't help thinking what a waste it was that the life of such a promising young woman could be snuffed out so easily. With a single thrust of a blade, the killer—or killers—had stolen Summer Randall's life along with all that promise. It was an act too cruel for words. Chloe was only mildly aware of the presence of ERT Investigator Clayton Veilleux as he circled the room while snapping photos to document the procedure and any discoveries the doctor made.

To this point in the postmortem examination, Chloe had managed to stave off the inevitable nausea that had accompanied her previous visit. She wasn't sure why she reacted the way she had during her prior visit with

Brock. It wasn't as though she hadn't field-dressed the occasional deer with her father and three older brothers during the annual family hunting trips. She had experienced firsthand the removal of organs up close and personal. And this was a completely clinical experience in a climate-controlled setting with all the necessary safety procedures in place. Hell, she wasn't even in the same room where the dissection was happening. But still, there was something altogether different about watching a human corpse disemboweled.

"Did you hear what I said, Detective Wright?" Dr. Isleborn said, ripping Chloe from her own thoughts.

"Sorry, Doc," Chloe said. "Would you repeat that?"

Isleborn exchanged a glance with her female assistant before readdressing Chloe.

"I said it appears that exsanguination was the cause of death."

"How can you tell with all of those injuries?"

"This single deep-penetrating stab wound to her abdomen resulted in a massive loss of blood. I'd say class-four blood loss."

"Class four?" Chloe said.

"Approximately forty percent of the victim's blood supply had already been lost, meaning she would have exhibited signs of shock as her organs were starved of oxygen. Loss of blood pressure and increased heart rate would have rapidly impaired her cognitive abilities and decision-making."

"We think she was fleeing from her attacker to get help."

"Intense physical activity would only have served to speed up the blood loss. If she hadn't been struck by the drunk driver, she would have collapsed and died within minutes."

Chloe paused to let Isleborn's words sink in. If the doctor's assessment was right, Summer Randall was dead even before reaching the road. She just hadn't known it yet.

Chloe scribbled in her notebook, then underlined Isleborn's words, "Would have died within minutes."

Isleborn and her assistant continued the examination while Chloe speculated about the identity of the individual capable of inflicting such a cruel injury. And what kind of a sadistic person rejoiced in chasing their prey until they dropped? The abusive ex-boyfriend, Ronnie Libby? Some random encounter in the woods? Or someone in Summer's life yet to be discovered? A slight shiver ran through Chloe as she pictured Summer running for her very life like a wounded deer.

"Detective," Isleborn said again. "Would you mind coming in here for a moment?"

The doctor's normally brusque tone had noticeably softened, giving Chloe pause. Whatever Isleborn had found was important enough to garner an invite into the normally restricted inner sanctum, yet sensitive enough to remove even the doctor's hard edges. She wondered if Isleborn had found evidence of sexual assault.

Chloe walked around the glass partition and entered the examination room. As she approached the table, the pungent odors intensified. Up close, Summer Randall's body looked more like a biology course experiment than it had from the viewing area. Chloe was glad that Summer's parents were spared the indignity of seeing their only child reduced to this. She knew the search for answers in a case like this trumped everything else. This was a hunt for evidence, period. The cause and manner of death along with any evidence that might help them identify the perpetrator.

"What did you find?" Chloe said, just managing to croak the words out.

"See for yourself," Isleborn said.

Chloe stepped closer to the table than she was comfortable with, doing her best to remain focused and take shallow breaths. Whatever it was that she had been summoned to observe was important, and she had to stay sharp. She stopped walking and steeled herself for what was to come. Veilleux and Isleborn's assistant stepped back to give Chloe room. Isleborn stood on the opposite side of the table holding open a flap of skin just above the victim's pubic mound. It was at that moment Chloe realized what she was about to witness, even before the doctor's words reached her ears.

Summer Randall was pregnant.

She stared wordlessly at the partially developed fetus. Though it was clearly early in the pregnancy, the fetus was immediately identifiable. Chloe was doing her best to try and comprehend Isleborn's words, but they were garbled and distorted, as if she were speaking in an unfamiliar tongue. Chloe's attention shifted away from the womb to Isleborn's face, which seemed to contort right before her eyes. Something was wrong with the doctor, Chloe thought. She caught a sudden flash of movement from her left where Veilleux had been standing only a split second before. The entire examination room began to tip on its axis as Chloe's world went black.

Brock returned to the duty nurse's station, where the same middle-aged woman was holding court with several younger members of the staff. As she caught his approach, she sent them scattering.

"Did he come clean, or do you need me to find some sodium pentothal?"

Again, Brock was taken aback by her comment. Although he knew she was only joking, her calm demeanor and deadpan delivery made him uncomfortable. Kidding or not, she wasn't someone a patient would want to cross.

"I wanted to ask you about Summer Randall, Miss—"

"Ms. Florence Nadeau. But everyone around here calls me Nurse Flo."

"Perhaps I could speak with Summer's immediate supervisor, Flo?"

"That would be me. Give me a second to find someone to cover the desk."

Brock followed her eyes as she scanned the hallway.

"Irene," she called out to a dark-haired nurse. "What are you doing at this very moment?"

"Um, I was just about to—"

"Now you're going to cover the desk for me."

"Yes, ma'am."

Flo's attention returned to Brock. "I'm free now, Detective."

Brock was halfway across the parking lot when he heard someone shouting for him to stop. He turned to find a young brunette dressed in a nurse's uniform hurrying in his direction.

"I'm sorry about chasing you down like this," the woman said. "You're with the state police, right?"

"Detective Justice. What can I do for you?"

"My name is Brittney LaRoux, and I need to talk to you about Summer Randall."

"Okay. Do you know something about her death?"

LaRoux's eyes welled up with tears. "I'm sorry. I made a deal with myself that I wouldn't do this."

"It's okay. Would you like to find someplace quiet inside the hospital to talk?"

LaRoux looked back at the hospital with apprehension written on her face.

"Or we could talk right here in my vehicle," Brock offered.

She nodded. "Right here is better."

Brock unlocked the doors to the SUV, and they both climbed inside. After scrounging around inside the console, he handed her a tissue.

"Thanks," she said as she wiped her eyes.

"I take it you and Summer were close," Brock said.

"She was my best friend. And I think she might be dead because of me."

"Because of you?"

"We were supposed to do a training run together late yesterday afternoon, but I had to cancel at the last minute. Maybe if I'd…" Her words trailed off once again in sobs of grief.

15

Wednesday, October 8, 1:30 p.m

Brock departed from the hospital and was turning onto Pritham Avenue when his cell phone rang with a call from Chloe. He answered on the very first ring. "How did it go at the post?"

"Fine."

Chloe's accentuation of the word gave Brock pause. Something was wrong. He wondered if she'd suffered a repeat performance. Not wanting to embarrass her if she had passed out again, he moved on.

"Tell me the cause of death is settled."

"It is," Chloe said. "Dr. Isleborn confirmed that the cause of death was exsanguination from a single stab wound to the abdomen. The blade, which she estimated to be approximately four inches, punctured Summer's small intestine and kidney."

"Any signs of sexual assault?"

"None."

"And the injuries sustained from the collision?" Brock said. "No chance that they contributed to her death?"

"Not according to Isleborn. Broken bones and contusions. Not pretty to look at, but nothing that would have proved fatal. Bottom line, Summer was stabbed and bled out. Isleborn ruled the death a homicide."

Brock paused a moment to run the legal scenario through his head. He knew Henry Gifford, Watters's attorney, would undoubtedly avail himself of Dr. Isleborn's official finding to minimize the charges against his client. The Piscataquis County District Attorney would never make a case for vehicular manslaughter against Watters, not if the medical examiner's office listed Randall's stab wound as the official cause of death. At best, the DA might be able to charge elevated aggravated operating under the influence, assuming that Watters's blood alcohol level came back well over the legal limit. And it would be theoretically impossible to charge both Summer's attacker and Watters with causing her death. Either way, the accident had created serious issues for both the state and county prosecutors. But Brock knew they couldn't waste time worrying about that now. Their job was simple. Identify Summer Randall's attacker and build a solid case against them. Period.

"Did you hear what I just said?" Chloe asked.

"Yeah, sorry. Just thinking this thing through. Anything else noteworthy come from the examination?"

"One other thing. Summer was pregnant."

There it is, Brock thought. The reason Chloe sounded upset. Brock considered this latest revelation. If they were searching for the attacker's motive, Summer being pregnant might potentially fit the bill, but they would need to find out who she had been sleeping with.

"How far along?" Brock said.

"Doc said about eight weeks."

"And we got a sample for DNA testing?" Brock said.

"Yes. Clayton Veilleux seized it."

"Who else knows about the pregnancy?" Brock said.

"Besides you and me, only those attending the post. Isleborn, her assistant, and Veilleux."

"We need to make sure that her pregnancy remains inside information. Even from her parents."

"Jesus, Brock. That's cold, even for you."

"The stabbing got out, and we still don't know how." Though Brock had some very clear ideas on who may have leaked the information to the reporter. "We can't risk the same thing happening with this. So, we tell no one."

"What about Cumberland?"

"Especially the lieutenant. Penny needs deniability. Trust me on this, Chloe. Letting that little detail out now could absolutely sink this case. Besides, questioning people close to Summer will reveal if anyone knew."

"You're the expert, Brock, but I don't like it."

"Your objection is duly noted, partner. How long until you're back in Greenville?"

"Um, I'm probably still forty-five minutes out. Why?"

"I need you to go through Summer's apartment. Her car was already broken into."

"Meaning?"

"Meaning, if Summer was killed because of something she possessed, they might try again by burglarizing her apartment."

"I hadn't thought of that," Chloe said.

"Besides, we need to get in there and have a look around before Congresswoman Randall arrives in town," Brock said.

"You don't think she'd actually disturb Summer's things before we got a look."

"This is her daughter we're talking about, Chloe. Randall's first order of business will be to hide anything damaging or embarrassing to the family's reputation. Not to mention her own reputation. She is up for reelection, after all."

"Yeah, but wouldn't she put the investigation first? I mean, wouldn't she want justice for Summer?"

"Randall's a politician. A pragmatist. Getting justice for her daughter is an intangible. I'm betting she puts her career first. Just like she did last year with the domestic."

"You're right," Chloe said. "What about keys? I'll need those to gain access."

"I'm headed to the public safety building. You can swing by and grab the keys from me."

Chloe let out a deep breath as she ended the call with Brock. She was embarrassed about passing out at the autopsy again, and the last thing she needed was for it to get back to Brock. She could only hope that Clayton Veilleux was a standup guy.

Regardless of how their last case together had turned out, this one was a new start. A new opportunity to show Brock that she had what it took to be a proficient, reliable homicide investigator, and partner. Passing out or losing her cookies every time she was asked to attend a post didn't exactly exude confidence. And while she trusted Dr. Isleborn, and to a lesser extent her assistant, to keep the secret, she wasn't as sure about Clay.

Chloe exited the highway at Newport and pulled into the first drive-through she saw. In dire need of a caffeine fix, she purchased an extra-large to-go coffee, black. While the attendant was making change from her five-dollar bill, Chloe took a mouth-searing sip. As she swallowed the hot liquid, she began to feel more like herself. More alive. More focused. Back among the living. Though the image of Summer Randall's naked body and the damage inflicted on it was still firmly etched upon her brain. As was the unborn life snuffed out inside her.

"Here's your change," the attendant said, jarring her from her reverie.

"Keep it," Chloe said.

She pulled out of the lot onto Route 11. With the circus about to arrive in town, there was no time to waste.

Even if Brock hadn't warned her about the impending media onslaught, she knew staying ahead of the reporters would be paramount if they were going to crack this case. Every witness the media got to before Brock and Chloe was a witness tampered with and far less likely to be forthcoming with the police.

Brock and Chloe needed to find out everything they could about Summer. Who she hung with, worked with, and confided in. During their early morning conversation, Taylor Randall hadn't mentioned a significant other in Summer's life, not unless Ronnie Libby counted, and based solely on the abusive history described by Chief Leavitt, he shouldn't. But Chloe knew when it came to relationships, even the bad ones weren't always easy to break free from. Taylor had told them that Summer had decided to take at least one semester off from college. Chloe's own experience had taught her that there were only so many reasons for leaving college, even temporarily. Given that finances didn't appear to be an issue, that left only two likely possibilities. Either Summer had fallen in love, or she knew she was pregnant. And there was only one way to find out which one had upended her young life. It was time to conduct a deep dive into Summer Randall's world.

16

Wednesday, October 8, 2:45 p.m

After retrieving the keys from Brock at the PSB, Chloe drove directly to Summer Randall's Pleasant Street apartment. Normally they would have taken the time to secure a search warrant, but with confirmation from both Summer's father and the landlord that Summer lived alone in the one-bedroom apartment, there was zero chance that anyone might later claim a right to privacy.

The small efficiency unit was located above a detached two-car garage. Chloe parked in the empty space she imagined had been designated for Summer near the steep flight of stairs that led up to a newly refurbished pressure-treated deck and the entrance to the apartment. As she mounted the stairs, she noted the outside light next to the door was still illuminated. Chloe imagined Summer had left it on, expecting to return after dark from her run.

She removed a pair of nitrile gloves from her jacket pocket and worked her hands into them. Chloe had no way of knowing whether something of importance might turn up inside the apartment or not, but she would treat the area with due diligence as if it were a crime scene. As with any potential scene, the goal was to recover evidence, not corrupt it. The key Brock had given her slid smoothly into the lock. Chloe turned the handle and let herself inside. She paused to examine the latch and doorjamb for damage, but everything appeared in order. If someone had beaten her to the apartment, they would have needed a key. She closed the door behind her and turned on the interior lights after locating a bank of wall switches to her left.

The quaint space had been designed as an open concept, featuring a vaulted ceiling with two skylights and laminate flooring. A small island sat parallel to a long kitchen counter, and the stove and refrigerator were tucked neatly against the wall, creating a galley type space. The air smelled of bacon grease and something fruity that Chloe couldn't identify. The sink was stacked with dirty dishes, and a greasy fry pan, likely used to fry the bacon, sat atop the stove. On the opposite side of the island stood two wooden barstools, both doubling as clothes racks as several items of Summer's clothing were draped over the backs of each. The space reminded her of her own apartment, the typical abode of a single working woman who spent more time at her various places of employment than caring for her apartment.

On the floor beside the exterior door sat a long black plastic tray upon which a literal jumble of shoes and sneakers were piled. Using her phone, Chloe snapped a quick photograph of the shoes, noting at least one pair of what looked like white nursing shoes. She made a mental note to look for hospital scrubs to accompany the shoes.

The living room furniture consisted of a large cream-colored area rug, a well-worn beige sofa and matching overstuffed chair, and a wooden coffee table. Flanking both ends of the sofa were mismatched end tables and department store lamps. On the wall opposite the sofa hung a flat-screen television. Atop the sofa was a wrinkled comforter and a stack of throw pillows. Chloe pictured herself stretched out watching late-night television and gorging on unhealthy snacks. Once again, she couldn't help feeling that this young woman could have been her. It was a disturbing thought. One that left her feeling voyeuristic. Like she was violating Summer's privacy, because that was in fact what she was doing. She shook off the image and moved toward the apartment's only bedroom.

The sleeping area was even less tidy than the living room and kitchen had been. An unmade double bed was strewn with various exercise tops and bottoms, as if Summer had tried on multiple outfits before departing. Standing sentry in the far corner of the room, also draped with clothing, was an ironing board. Gracing the wall above the headboard was a framed poster of Joan Benoit Samuelson running the New York City Marathon in 1988. Chloe immediately recognized the famous image from her childhood. After overcoming several significant obstacles, Joan had still managed to finish third overall. A Herculean feat and the start of a long and impressive journey. Samuelson's triumphs had inspired Chloe too, leading her to announce that she would one day be a world-famous long-distance runner. A pipe dream that had lasted all of one month before Chloe had found some other less taxing dream on which to focus. The poster made clear that Summer's love of running may well have begun with the Maine icon. Surrounding the poster, affixed directly to the wall, were dozens of numbered running badges from road races. The shadow of sadness darkened Chloe's thoughts as she realized that Summer had been killed while doing the very thing she loved. Life could be so cruel.

The bureau and nightstand were cluttered with textbooks and framed family photos. Chloe noticed that the framed pictures only included shots of Summer and her mother, or Summer and Taylor. There were none depicting all three of them. She wondered how long the Randalls had been divorced. As with the previous rooms, Chloe photographed the bedroom as she found it, pausing to examine a photograph of Summer and another young woman with their arms around each other's shoulders, wearing genuine smiles. The other female, who appeared to be of mixed heritage and nearly a foot taller than Summer, was dressed in a nurse's uniform. The background of the image was out of focus, but Chloe guessed that it had been taken outside on the campus of the Northern Light Hospital. Nearby was another photo of the two women. In the second photo, they were dressed in matching shorts and tank tops with road race numbers pinned to the shirts. Standing between them was a handsome man dressed in normal attire. Chloe wondered who the other woman was and how close she and Summer had been. Close enough to share news of a pregnancy? Perhaps. It was worth following up.

Chloe moved on to the closet. The bifold doors were already standing open, revealing that every square inch of space had been used. Clothing and boxes were literally stacked to the ceiling. Chloe realized she would have liked Summer. They were a lot more alike than she was comfortable with.

Brock parked his SUV in the nearly empty visitors' lot near the *Katahdin*. With Chloe busy searching Summer's apartment, Brock wanted to talk with Ronnie Libby, Summer's ex-boyfriend, sooner than later. If Libby and Summer Randall were still involved, even in secret, and Libby was responsible for another attack on her, finding out now before he had a chance to concoct an alibi would be key. Recovering or not, Libby wouldn't have been the first addict to revert to bad decisions.

Despite his reason for being there, Brock was captivated by the beauty surrounding the area. Brightly colored foliage dotted both sides of the shoreline as far as he could see. And the windswept whitecaps rolling across Moosehead Lake made it appear even larger than it already was, more like a small ocean. The *Katahdin* was tethered to the dock while the ongoing repairs were made. A single black-and-white smokestack adorned with the letter *K* protruded from the roof of the main cabin. As Brock drew nearer to the bright white turn-of-the-century vessel, he couldn't help feeling as if he'd walked back into another time. A better time, long before Summer Randall had drawn her first or last breath.

Brock reached the chain that hung between the railings at the far end of the metal gangplank meant to prevent visitors from boarding the boat. Dangling from the chain was a hand-painted wooden sign announcing that the attraction was closed. The sign swung in the breeze as if taunting him.

A gray-bearded man wearing work clothes and a ball cap appeared on the upper deck. "Help you with something, friend?"

"I hope so," Brock said as he fished his credentials from his coat pocket. "Detective Justice, state police. I'm looking for Ronnie Libby. I was told he works here."

"Ronnie, huh? Well, you picked the wrong day for that."

"Day off?" Brock said.

"Nope. He called in sick first thing this morning."

Brock returned the ID to his pocket. "Perhaps I could speak with you, then."

The man's eyes narrowed with suspicion. "What about?"

"I'm investigating the death of Summer Randall."

"I'll be right down."

Chloe stared into the wicker wastebasket standing on the floor beside the toilet. Lying atop a pile of discarded tissues was a plastic pregnancy testing stick. The strip indicated a positive result.

"So you did know," Chloe said aloud to an empty room, again feeling voyeuristic as she dug into the most private parts of Summer's life.

She pulled out her cell phone and snapped several more pictures. The discovery only confirmed that Summer Randall knew she was pregnant. The pregnancy may not have had anything to do with her murder. Then again, if Summer had shared her secret with the wrong person, the pregnancy may have had everything to do with why she was killed. After photographing the evidence in situ, Chloe removed both the testing stick and its empty cardboard container from the trash bin, placing both items into an evidence bag.

Dr. Isleborn had said that Summer was about eight weeks along in her pregnancy, long enough to have experienced symptoms like morning sickness. Chloe wondered if this was the first time Summer had tested herself or if it was simply the latest confirmation.

Chloe made a quick check of the medicine cabinet for further clues but found nothing of note. In fact, the only things contained therein were shaving cream, razors, toothpaste, and feminine hygiene products. Even the single bottle of painkiller was nothing stronger than ibuprofen. It was clear that Summer kept herself in excellent shape and had no maladies that would have required ongoing prescription medications.

She departed the bathroom and made another sweep of the bedroom. From this new angle, she noticed a charging cord hanging from an outlet directly behind the headboard. The cord wound its way up through the gap above the mattress and disappeared beneath the pillow. Chloe picked up the pillow and found a closed laptop computer hidden beneath it. Perhaps there was another way to find out if Summer had shared news of her pregnancy. Chloe grabbed another evidence bag and unplugged the laptop.

17

Wednesday, October 8, 3:00 p.m

The grizzled-looking man aboard the *Katahdin* turned out to be Charlie Fasulo, the restoration project manager and Ronnie Libby's boss. After being led aboard the boat to Fasulo's makeshift office space, Brock declined a coffee but watched as Fasulo prepared one for himself.

The ongoing restoration had exposed much of the boat's skeleton. Brock could see newly installed beams and sheathing where rot had likely gotten a foothold in the century-old vessel. The space smelled of freshly sawed lumber and marine varnish, reminding him of his father's camp in Blue Hill. Brock realized that Albert would have gotten a kick out of seeing it.

"Bad habit, this," Fasulo said as he sat across from Brock on an upside-down five-gallon bucket at a table constructed from sawhorses and a single sheet of plywood. "Gives me the shakes if I drink too much, but some days I can't concentrate without it."

Brock nodded his understanding. After pulling an all-nighter, he knew the feeling too well. He pulled out his notepad, turned to a clean sheet, then scribbled the date and time along with Fasulo's name and location of the interview.

"So, you've come to ask me about Ronnie Libby, huh? I hope he didn't have anything to do with what happened on Lily Bay Road last night."

"What makes you say that?" Brock said.

"You know Ronnie and Summer Randall had a history, right?"

"Tell me about that," Brock said, intentionally keeping his questions open-ended. When questioning witnesses, it was always better to let them talk, especially when you had one talking already.

"Not much to tell, really. Those two were high school sweethearts, and everything was going along great until Summer went off to college and Ronnie dropped out. Young Ronnie got in with a bad crowd. The drugs and booze really messed him up. I imagine you heard about what Ronnie did to her."

"Why don't you tell me in your words what happened?"

"Not to put too fine a point on it, Ronnie beat her up. Blackened her eye and busted her lip, and a couple of other things, as I heard it. Police locked him up immediately and charged him with aggravated assault. Ronnie was actually pretty lucky that one of the other reserve officers made the arrest and not Summer's father, Taylor. Guess you know he worked part-time for the local PD."

Brock nodded. "Heard there were threats made."

"Oh, yeah," Fasulo chuckled. "One thing about Taylor Randall, he says exactly what he means. Not a guy you want to get on the wrong side of, if you know what I mean."

Brock allowed Fasulo to chatter on while making the occasional note. He wanted to see how closely the details mirrored what Chief Leavitt and Taylor Randall had already told them.

"How long has Ronnie worked for you?" Brock said.

"Pretty much since the deal was made. His folks had a big hand in getting financing for the restoration and, as you already know, Ronnie is one of the craftsmen working on this beauty."

"Any trouble with him?"

"Ronnie? Not one bit. He's the most reliable worker I've ever had. Skilled too. Good with his hands. The *Kate*'s well on her way to next year's grand reopening."

"Does Ronnie get along with the rest of your crew?"

"Very much so. He and Saul are probably the closest. You'll want to speak with him. Saul and Ronnie attended high school together. I sent him a text. He should be here shortly."

Brock felt Fasulo's eyes on him as he scribbled another note.

"You said you wanted to talk to Ronnie about what happened last night. I hope that doesn't mean he had anything to do with Summer's death. I mean, I heard she died in a car accident. But then I heard something different on the news. Not sure what to believe on the news anymore. Maybe you can tell me which version is the right one."

Brock knew he needed to tread very carefully. He wasn't here to share information. He was here to collect it. "We're still trying to piece together exactly what did happen, Charlie. Can you tell me what time Ronnie clocked off yesterday?"

"Yeah, he left an hour early at four o'clock."

"That unusual?"

"No, not really. I always tell my crew that if they need an hour here or there, I won't be a stickler about it as long as they make it up on the other end. They get paid well for what they do here, and I expect them to pull their weight."

"Did he say why he needed time off?"

"He didn't, but I can tell you he seemed pretty excited about something yesterday."

"Don't suppose he shared what that was, did he?"

"Nope. But I could tell it was something he was looking forward to."

"You wanted to see me, Skip?"

Brock turned to see a new arrival standing in the doorway. The dark-haired young man looked to be in his early twenties, the same age as Ronnie Libby. He had a thin patch of hair above his upper lip that might have passed for a mustache if he were twelve.

"Yeah, come on in, Saul," Fasulo said. "Detective Justice, I'd like you to meet another member of my restoration crew. This is Saul Emmons."

Brock rose from his makeshift plastic stool and reached out a hand in greeting. "Brock Justice."

"Sorry about the sawdust," Emmons said as he wiped his sweaty palm across his plaid chamois shirt.

"No worries," Brock said.

"You a state trooper?"

"State police detective. I'm here investigating the death of Summer Randall."

"We were just talking about Ronnie," Charlie said before his attention returned to Brock. "Anything you want to know about Ronnie, Saul is your man. Thick as thieves, these two."

Brock caught the slightest flinch from Emmons at the comment. "That so?" Brock said, delivering his most disarming smile. "Have a seat, Saul."

18

Wednesday, October 8, 3:30 p.m

Penny Cumberland was fuming as she listened to Major Morgan kissing the proverbial ass of Congresswoman Randall. It began the moment Randall and her security guard, Jamal, stepped off her private jet onto the tarmac in Bangor, and it continued during the trip to Greenville. Penny was listening on speakerphone as she followed Randall's black Cadillac in her unmarked Ford. Jamal sat in front beside the driver of the Escalade while Morgan and Randall sat in the back discussing the murder and what steps were being taken to catch her daughter's killer. On those rare occasions when Penny could get a word in edgewise, she assured the congresswoman that the two case detectives had been up all night working every angle and chasing down every possible lead. While Morgan promised that MCU North would solve Summer's murder in short order.

Cumberland had two problems with Morgan's ill-advised guarantee. Firstly, she didn't care for a snake like Morgan speaking for her and her detectives. Secondly, nobody who had ever been tasked with solving a homicide would ever make such a callous and foolhardy assurance. The comment said everything there was to say about Morgan's lack of investigative experience. A promise to solve a whodunnit murder with no known witnesses to the crime was not only stupid, it also wasn't fair to plant such lofty expectations in the minds of Summer's parents.

Penny's primary detectives, however, were more than up to the task. Despite Brock's maddening irreverent streak and a tendency to be a hot dog, Justice was one of the most tenacious and skilled homicide detectives she had ever seen. And Chloe Wright, while still new to the role, was already showing all the signs that she would successfully follow in his footsteps.

"And I can personally vouch for Lieutenant Cumberland," Morgan said. "Penny is one of the best female commanders we have."

It was all Penny could do to not call Morgan out for the misogynistic comment. She wasn't even sure he was bright enough to comprehend what he had said.

"One of the state police's best commanders, right?" Randall said, apparently having picked up on the slight.

"Th-that's what I meant," Morgan stammered.

Penny grinned.

Bringing up the rear of their small motorcade was an unmarked Interceptor occupied by Detective Zimmerman. Penny had wisely decided to include him to help Brock and Chloe work the case. The positive optics of increasing the number of investigators from two to three were obvious, but the real reason Penny had brought in additional resources was because she guessed that the word "reward" was about to be spoken.

"Now, Major Morgan," the congresswoman said. "I'd like to discuss offering a reward."

The grin on Penny's face vanished. She hated being right.

They arrived in what consisted of Greenville's downtown shortly after three thirty. As their tiny procession turned onto Minden Street, Penny got her first glimpse of the news vans clogging up the street and nearby parking lots. As she had expected, all the local news channels were all represented. What she hadn't expected was to see crews from as far away as Boston, Massachusetts. She knew they were about to lose control of the case. Penny also knew something else, that Congresswoman Randall had likely arranged to have the out-of-state media contacted about her press conference. As bereaved about the loss of her daughter as Randall might be, she wasn't about to miss the opportunity to garner some sympathy from the voters. Penny hated thinking that way, but she had known far too many political animals to miss it.

Chloe locked the door to Summer's apartment behind her, then carried the evidence down the steps to her unmarked. She had reached the bottom step before realizing that someone had parked next to her. Standing beside a marked sheriff's cruiser was Deputy Evan Mathers.

"Hey, Deputy," Chloe said, fixing him with a smirk. "Are you following me?"

"Guilty as charged," Mathers said as he raised his hands in mock surrender. "Actually, I swung by the PSB and found out you were here. Didn't know if you needed me to check on anything for you."

"Does that line ever work?" Chloe said as she popped the hatch on her SUV and stowed the evidence in the back.

"Not yet. But you can't blame a guy for trying."

Chloe knew how pissed Brock would be if he found Evan hanging around, but given the nature of what they were investigating, they weren't really in a position to turn down help from a seasoned cop. And truth be told, Mathers wasn't exactly hard on the eyes.

She stood up and closed the hatch on the Interceptor, then made a show of stretching her back while she eyed the deputy.

"Heard the media are descending on this town like the plague," Mathers said. "In fact, they're already swarming around the station."

"Yeah, seems like word of the stabbing got out somehow. You know anything about that?"

Chloe studied Mathers's face while waiting for him to respond. The dark glasses made him difficult to read.

"If you knew me at all, you'd know I have an aversion to reporters. Probably something to do with the trial."

"But I don't know you, do I?"

"I'd like to change that if you're interested. I imagine you'll be around for a few days. Maybe we can share dinner or something."

"Not sure I'll have much downtime until we crack this case. Plus, I'm not sure my partner will be all that thrilled with the idea. Brock's not exactly your biggest fan."

"No, it's okay. I get it. You're probably right."

Mathers turned as if to leave.

"Why don't you give me your number anyway?" Chloe said, stopping Mathers in his tracks. "Just in case."

"Seriously?"

"I like to keep my options open, Deputy Mathers."

Brock had hoped that Saul Emmons would be more forthcoming about Ronnie Libby, especially since they had been purported by Charlie Fasulo to be "thick as thieves." Aside from confirming that Libby had been clean and attending meetings regularly, Emmons had very little to offer about his friend and coworker. Brock figured it had more to do with Emmons's distrust of cops than his lack of insight into Libby. The one thing Emmons had let slip was that Ronnie and Summer had started meeting up with each other again for coffee and "chats." Emmons said he didn't think they were keeping these meetings a secret, but Brock guessed that wasn't entirely true. He could only imagine how Summer's father would react if he'd found out.

"How long had Ronnie and Summer been meeting up?" Brock said.

"I don't know," Emmons said. "Couple of months or so, maybe."

Brock's thoughts drifted back to his conversation with Chloe. Isleborn had said that Summer was about eight weeks along in her pregnancy.

"I think it's all part of moving on," Emmons continued.

"What do you mean?" Brock said.

"Ronnie said that part of recovery is about righting wrongs. Seeking forgiveness from those you hurt by your addiction."

Brock maintained eye contact as he watched Emmons try to make sense out of something he'd undoubtedly learned secondhand from Ronnie. It was clear that Emmons didn't entirely grasp the concept any more than he could understand Ronnie beating up his ex-girlfriend. Brock wondered if these meetings were really about forgiveness or if Ronnie saw them as a way to rekindle whatever relationship he once had with Summer.

"Do you know if Ronnie and Summer met up yesterday?" Brock said.

Emmons exchanged an uneasy glance with Charlie before responding. "I'm not sure, but I think so."

"What makes you think that? Did Ronnie tell you he was meeting her?"

"He was planning to give her something."

"What was it?"

"Said he bought her a necklace."

Brock wondered if that gift was the reason Ronnie had left early the previous afternoon. And if it had been the reason, he couldn't help but wonder how that meeting had gone. From what little Brock knew about Alcoholics Anonymous, seeking forgiveness from those you've wronged had little to do with gifts of affection. Had Summer reacted badly to the offering? Had she shunned his advances? And if she had, could that have set everything that happened afterward in motion? Perhaps young Ronnie Libby had a motive for attacking Summer after all.

Penny pulled to a stop behind the Escalade on Minden near the PD in a spot just large enough to accommodate their mini motorcade. She had called ahead to Greenville Police Chief Leavitt, requesting that he cordon off the area in advance of their arrival. As she eyed the throngs of reporters and locals who had turned out to witness the press conference, she was glad she'd made the call.

Morgan hurried to keep up with Randall and her bodyguard as they walked toward the throng of reporters gathered in front of the fire department's bay doors. Penny allowed herself to fall several steps behind while she fired off a quick text message to Chloe and Brock.

Circus just got 2 town. Where r u?

Brock frowned as he read the text message from Cumberland. He had hoped that they would have a bit more time to interview Summer's friends before things got too crazy. He briefly toyed with the idea of ignoring her text, but he knew she was already at her wits end and now wasn't the time to lose her as an ally. He typed out a quick reply.

Searching for Summer's ex.

Chloe's response came less than thirty seconds later.

Just finishing up my search of the vic's apartment.

Brock watched the bubble of repeating dots dance across the screen of his phone, indicating that Cumberland was typing her reply. He only hoped that she wasn't planning on dragging them down to the presser. Every moment spent on optics was a moment not solving the case.

At last, Cumberland's message appeared on screen.

Brought Zim w/ me. Meet us @ the PD

Brock sighed. Having another set of hands would help them quickly cover more ground, but there were already far too many things happening that were out of his control, and he didn't like it. Beginning with Evan Mathers. The way Brock figured it, the only thing that could make matters worse was if Congresswoman Randall offered a reward for information.

Before Brock could respond, Cumberland fired off another text.

FYI, Randall offering a 10K reward.

19

Wednesday, October 8, 3:45 p.m

Brock and Chloe stood across the street watching the hastily prepared press conference taking place in front of the public safety building. Congresswoman Randall was accompanied by a formidable-looking bodyguard, Major Morgan, and Lieutenant Cumberland. Although Brock was less than pleased to see that Morgan had inserted himself into this circus, he wasn't exactly surprised.

As expected, a caravan of local media outlets had descended on the tiny town, each clamoring for a sound byte from the congresswoman they could use to lead the evening news broadcast. Minden Street was choked with vehicles, most belonging to out-of-town newspaper reporters or news network vans. Several of the latter had raised antennae in preparation for live broadcasts. Brock noticed a husky cameraman standing beside a Boston-based news van. He was arguing with a Greenville PD reserve officer about parking in a restricted zone. A three-ring circus for the Fourth Estate, Brock thought, though finding nothing remotely humorous about it.

"Did you expect all this?" Chloe said.

Brock sighed. "Yeah, this is just about what I envisioned."

"It looks more like a campaign stop than a public plea for help solving her daughter's murder."

"That's because it is. Nothing brings out the voters like a bereaved parent."

As Rhonda Randall addressed those in attendance, Brock surveyed the crowd. Standing behind the congresswoman in a show of solidarity were her ex-husband, Taylor, and several members of the local law enforcement community, including Chief Leavitt, Lt. Cumberland, Major Morgan, and Armand Pelletier, the sheriff of Piscataquis County. Randall's neckless bodyguard stood off to one side, looking particularly intimidating as his eyes scanned the crowd for threats. Brock couldn't help noticing that Evan Mathers was not in attendance. He wondered if the absence was because Mathers was busy handling a call or by design. As soon as Randall finished making her remarks, Lt. Cumberland separated herself from the fray and made a beeline toward Brock and Chloe.

"Here we go," Chloe muttered under her breath.

Brock nodded.

"Thanks for meeting me here," Cumberland said.

"Of course," Chloe said.

"I would have thought that our time might be better spent investigating the actual murder rather than being here for what amounts to nothing but a dog and pony show, LT," Brock said, earning a glare from Cumberland.

"Don't start, Detective," Cumberland cautioned. "I am not in the mood."

For a split second, Brock contemplated an inappropriate response but managed to rein himself in.

"Congresswoman Randall has requested an audience with both of you in Chief Leavitt's office," Cumberland said. "She would like you to bring her and Taylor up to speed."

"Of course," Chloe said.

Cumberland waited a beat as if Brock might protest. When he didn't, she said, "Now, what do I need to know before we meet with them?"

Brock and Chloe stood outside the closed door to Leavitt's office. Standing beside them was Randall's bodyguard, Jamal. Through the door came the sound of raised voices followed by several pleas for calm. The former belonged to Taylor and Rhonda Randall, each looking to place blame for what had happened to Summer squarely on the shoulders of the other. The latter voices belonged to Leavitt, Morgan, and Cumberland. Brock shook his head as he considered the awkwardness of their current situation.

"Not hard to see why they got divorced," Chloe said under her breath.

Jamal said nothing as he made eye contact with Brock. There was something in his expression that told Brock he had witnessed this dance before.

Brock considered the ease at which his own vows had been nullified. He wondered if it might have been more difficult had he and the former Carmen Justice had children.

"This never would have happened if she had come to live with me, Taylor," the congresswoman charged.

"Oh, that's rich, coming from you," Taylor shot back. "Like this couldn't have happened anywhere, even at UMO."

"That's another thing," Rhonda said. "Why didn't you press her to return to college?"

Brock wondered how much of what they were now witnessing had contributed to Summer's undoing. From what little they had managed to uncover so far, something drastic had changed in her life even before being attacked in the woods. The only question that remained was, could those two things be linked?

At last, the voices quieted, and the door to the office swung open. Brock and Chloe waited as the law enforcement contingent filed out one at a time until only the Randalls remained. Lt. Cumberland was the last one out the door. As she passed by Brock and Chloe, she mouthed the words, "You're up."

Brock paused to see if the congresswoman's security guard would be joining them inside.

Jamal shook his head. "All you, man. I'll be waiting out here."

Brock followed Chloe into the office, then closed the door.

Taylor Randall stood in the far corner of the room, anger and heartbreak radiating from him in waves. Congresswoman Randall sat in Chief Leavitt's chair as if she had commandeered the office and was now holding court with her subjects. Brock wondered if she wielded her congressional power in a similar manner or if this was simply her maternal instincts kicking in.

"Lt. Cumberland assures me that you two are the best homicide detectives she has," Randall said.

Brock noticed that there was an unmistakable edge to her tone. It was almost as if she were denigrating them. Like he and Chloe were the best Cumberland could do with limited resources.

"I'm sure I don't need to tell you how much I want to see my daughter's killer brought to justice," Randall continued.

Brock glanced at Taylor to see if he had caught the slight. His dour expression confirmed that he hadn't missed it.

"Congresswoman Randall," Chloe said. "I assure you that we will do everything in our power to try and bring Summer's killer to justice."

"Try?" Randall said, spitting out the word as if she had bitten into something bitter tasting.

Brock jumped in before Chloe said something she would regret.

"Detective Wright is correct. You have our word that we will do everything in our power to bring this case to a positive conclusion."

"I hope so," Randall said. "Now, how soon can we expect an arrest?"

Brock drew a deep breath, holding it for a moment before responding.

"It doesn't work that way."

"How exactly does it work?" Taylor said, speaking for the first time.

"It's not like television," Brock continued. "There is more to this than simply making an arrest. We want to find the person responsible, of course, but in order to build a case that will stand up to the scrutiny of a judge or jury, we also have to rule out all other possible suspects. We can arrest with probable cause, but there is a monumental difference between probable cause and the threshold of beyond a reasonable doubt. And that threshold is what we will need to formally charge and convict your daughter's killer."

"And exactly how long will that take?" the congresswoman said, glaring at him.

"As long as it takes to get it right," Brock said.

Taylor nodded his understanding.

"We expect to be kept apprised of *all* developments as they happen," Randall said, jockeying for a better position.

"We will update you as regularly as we can," Chloe said.

"What does that mean, *Detective*?"

Brock stepped in again. "It means we will provide you with updates when we are positive they won't compromise our investigation."

"Well, I have resources enough to assist you," Randall shot back. "And if ten thousand isn't sufficient to entice someone to come forward, I am more than happy to increase the amount."

Realizing that diplomacy wasn't working with this woman, Brock decided to lay all the cards on the table.

"With all due respect, we want to solve this case as badly as you want us to. And we want to see Summer's killer pay for what they've done. But we need to work this case our way, devoid of outside influences. While I know you believe your reward will help us catch them, it will also overload our resources chasing down bogus leads, which is what most of them will be."

Brock saw the congresswoman's eyes flash. It was clear that she wasn't used to being challenged.

"You're saying my reward won't help?"

"I'm saying that money will bring out the crazies. It always does. Money, and a chance at notoriety, some people simply can't help themselves. Anyone who really wanted to help would do the right thing and come forward without needing financial enticement."

"What would you have us do?" Taylor said.

"Nothing," Brock said.

"Nothing?" Randall said indignantly.

"Let us do what we do best," Brock said. "And don't talk to the media about this."

"Don't talk to the media?" Randall said. "Need I remind you I'm in the middle of a campaign right now?"

"Rhonda," Taylor said, clearly attempting to cut her off.

"What? It's true. Even if I agreed with what this detective is saying, I couldn't avoid the media if I tried."

"Then tell them you won't talk about Summer's murder," Chloe suggested. "Tell them you have full faith in the state police to get to the bottom of this. Can you do that much for us?"

She opened her mouth to speak, but Taylor beat her to the punch.

"We can. Thank you both for what you're doing for our little girl. Come on, Rhonda. Let's get out of their hair and let them get to it."

The congresswoman remained seated, glaring at Chloe. Her ire had clearly shifted again. While Brock appreciated Chloe having his back and standing up to the woman, he hoped she wouldn't pay a price for her outspokenness.

20

Wednesday, October 8, 4:30 p.m

The Randalls wordlessly departed, leaving Brock and Chloe alone inside Leavitt's office. Neither spoke as they tried to process the heated intensity of the last several minutes. Brock wondered how long it would take before the fallout from Randall made its way through the state police hierarchy to land on them with as much grace as a bird dropping. They didn't have long to wait before Cumberland stepped back inside.

"Well?" Cumberland said. "How did it go?"

"I'm surprised Congresswoman Randall didn't share any of her thoughts with you," Brock said. "She had plenty to say in here."

"Did something happen?"

"It was—intense," Brock said.

"How do you mean?"

"I mean, I'm used to the grief. That's nothing new. But the anger that those two people have for each other seems over the top."

"They are divorced," Cumberland said.

"So am I," Brock said. "But neither I nor my ex harbor any resentment toward each other."

"It's different when a child dies," Cumberland said. "The loss is just one more thing to blame on each other. Not all that different from the parents who use their children as cudgels during a custody battle. Did you impress upon them how the offer of a reward may lead to false leads?"

"We did," Chloe said.

"And we didn't sugarcoat it," Brock said. "Not sure it made any difference. Speaking of which, how exactly are we supposed to work this case and the tip lines simultaneously? Neither of us has slept since—well—since yesterday morning."

A knock at the door caused everyone to look up.

"Come," Cumberland said.

Chief Leavitt opened the door and stepped inside. "We're ready when you are, Penny."

"Thanks, Rich," Cumberland said before turning back to Brock and Chloe. "Ready to meet your tip line wrangler?"

The detectives found Jordan Zimmerman inside the fire bay of the public safety building, personally overseeing the tip line setup. Attempting to streamline the avalanche of tips that a ten-thousand-dollar reward would bring to the town of Greenville, Leavitt had arranged the installation of temporary phone extensions. Four dedicated lines were dropped down from the overhead beams to four workstations that were nothing more than eight-foot folding tables with phones. Detective Zimmerman was tasked with overseeing the operation, and Chief Leavitt assigned his reserves to staff the phones and record any information obtained on standard-format tip sheets. Calls received with anything resembling a possible legitimate lead would immediately be brought to the attention of Jordan Zimmerman. Anything else would simply go into a pile marked "Follow up."

"Impressive," Chloe said.

"Hey, don't look at me," Zim said. "This is all down to the chief here."

"Wish I could take credit," Leavitt said. "But this is Congresswoman Randall's doing. Hell, if I had the kind of clout to make this all happen, imagine what I could do for the PD."

"Anything yet?" Brock said as he watched two of the reserves speaking on their respective telephones.

"We've only received a half dozen calls so far," Zimmerman said.

"Once the nightly news airs Randall's presser, that number will spike," Cumberland said. "Can you handle this, Zim?"

"Of course, LT. Happy to help."

"And I imagine the two of you need to get some rest," Cumberland said.

"Or a shower at least," Brock said.

"And something to eat," Chloe added.

Cumberland's attention turned to Leavitt. "Can you help with overnight accommodations?"

"I already called the owners of the Moose Mountain Inn. They've reserved three rooms. I didn't know there would be four of you."

"It's okay," Cumberland said. "I'm not staying."

Brock looked at Zimmerman. "What about you?"

"Check in for me, if you wouldn't mind. And while you're at it, toss my go bag into my room."

Brock and Chloe followed Chief Leavitt in their respective vehicles to Rockwood Road. Before departing, Cumberland provided Brock with her state credit card along with a warning about what it was to be used for.

As they navigated through town toward the far side of Moosehead Lake, Brock realized that he was just beginning to feel the first tentacles of fatigue. He knew that the signs of exhaustion came in pairs. The physical part, obviously. But even more insidious were the tentacles that slowly and methodically wrapped themselves around the mind, strangling each and every link that made up the chain of thought until concentration became muddled. Despite the quantity of coffee he had consumed, and the adrenaline dump that came with catching a new homicide case, the body and mind eventually succumb to the need for rest. Brock knew he could shake off the physical exhaustion for a while longer, but the mental exhaustion was quickly becoming a problem.

Murder investigations consist of many moving parts. Things needed to happen in a specific order and in a specific way. Tired brains led to mistakes. And mistakes could unravel even the most well-constructed case. Justice might be blind, but the sharp eye of the legal system was unforgiving. In addition to the added stressors this homicide investigation came bundled with, Brock and Chloe had been hard at it since receiving the call the previous night, meaning that they were fast approaching forty hours without sleep. And though he was pleased to see that Chloe was still laser focused and showing no sign of slowing, Brock knew he was going to have to shut it down and soon. Whether he wanted to admit it or not, Zimmerman's arrival had been a godsend.

21

Wednesday, October 8, 5:00 p.m

The Moose Mountain Inn was situated on a wooded elevation on the west side of the lake about three miles outside of downtown Greenville. The burnt-orange two-story structure looked like the typical accommodations of every New England ski resort Brock had ever visited. Sporting cedar siding, exposed beams, a maroon metal roof, and fifteen guest rooms that faced the lake, the inn was perfect. Neither Brock nor Chloe cared all that much about the amenities, as they would only be using the rooms for what little rest they could manage, but it was away from town, and that meant quiet.

"State card, huh?" the desk clerk said as Brock handed him Cumberland's card. "You folks here about the murder?"

"Something like that," Chloe said.

"I gotta tell ya, we aren't used to things like that happening up here."

Brock decided against wasting the effort to point out that things like that can happen anywhere.

"Any idea who would want to do something like that to such a sweet girl like Summer Randall?"

"We can't really talk about an ongoing case," Chloe said.

"Sure, sure, I completely understand."

Brock and Chloe exchanged a glance as the clerk went back to working the computer.

"Chief Leavitt told the owners that you weren't sure how long you would be in town," the clerk said.

"He's right," Brock said.

"Is that a problem?" Chloe said.

"Well, we are in the middle of leaf peeper season here. As long as the weather holds, we'll stay pretty busy. Weekends we'll be full up, so if you want to make sure you don't lose your rooms, you should book the week."

"What if we don't end up staying that long?" Brock said.

"No worries," the clerk said, cracking a smile. "We have a free cancelation policy for state police detectives."

"Thanks," Chloe said.

After tossing Zimmerman's belongings into his room, Brock and Chloe retired to their own rooms to freshen up with a plan to meet up in one hour.

As he peeled off the clothes he'd been wearing for the past two days, Brock stared at the matching pinecone-and-evergreen pillowcases and comforter. The Hyatt Regency it wasn't. It was utilitarian, not fancy. Designed for folks who wanted to escape from the hustle and bustle of whatever world they lived in for the beauty of Northern Maine. A little peace and solitude as they enjoyed Maine's many outdoor pastimes. Be it boating or fishing on the lake, hiking, skiing, snowmobiling, or even investigating a murder.

Brock padded to the bathroom and checked the water temperature of the shower that he had previously turned on. Perfect. He stepped into the tub, pulled the curtain, and let the hot water work its magic.

An hour later, freshly dressed, showered, and shaved, Brock stepped outside and closed the door to his room behind him. Chloe was already standing beside her SUV waiting for him.

"Well, that's a refreshing change," Chloe said as he approached.

"What is?"

"The guy taking longer to get ready."

"Trust me, if I'd given in to the urge to crawl into that king-sized bed, I'd still be there."

On the recommendation of Chief Leavitt, Brock and Chloe drove to a place called the Dockside Inn and Tavern. They entered the dining room shocked to find Zimmerman sitting at a four-top next to a bank of windows overlooking the lake. He waved them over.

"What are you doing here?" Chloe said as they approached the table. "I thought you'd be knee-deep in leads."

"Me too," Zimmerman said as he took a sip of the amber-colored liquid contained in his pint glass.

"Don't tell me the calls dried up already," Brock said.

"Okay, I won't tell you," Zimmerman said.

"You're kidding," Chloe said.

"Nope. We had a steady stream of calls for about thirty minutes after you guys left. Then they trickled down to nothing. I think Congresswoman Randall may have overestimated the power of her reward. I don't know if either of you noticed, but there aren't enough people residing in the area to keep one phone line buzzing, let alone the four they put in."

"So, what are Chief Leavitt's reserves doing at the station?" Brock said.

"Well, I sent two of them home."

"And the other two?" Chloe said.

"They were playing cutthroat cribbage with a couple of the firemen when I left."

"Not helpful to the case," Brock said.

"Don't worry, I plan to check in again after we eat."

"So there was nothing promising at all?" Chloe said.

"Depends on what you consider promising," Zimmerman said. "One slightly intoxicated-sounding individual called to say he knew who killed Summer. He said, and I quote, 'It was the drunk driver who ran her down.'"

"Again, not altogether helpful," Brock said.

"Or insightful," Chloe added.

"Nope," Zimmerman said. "But you'll be happy to know that there's no shortage of crazies. We've got everything from illegal aliens to the more extraterrestrial variety."

"Great. ET phone home," Chloe said.

"Half of the callers were clearly certifiable, either looking for attention or free money. Most became angry when they were told that the money would only be paid if the information they were providing could be verified as correct and only if it led to the identification and conviction of the person or persons responsible for Summer Randall's murder. Apparently that was a leap too far."

Brock wasn't sure if he was more disappointed that the reward hadn't led to any helpful leads or pleased that it didn't appear to have made more work for them.

"There was one lead that might be worth following up on," Zimmerman said.

"And that was?" Brock said.

"One of the locals claimed to have seen a man hunting out of season in the woods where Summer was training. Some woman named Colello."

"What did Chief Leavitt have to say about that one?" Brock said.

"Haven't seen him since the tip came in."

"That's something that the warden service might be able to help us with," Chloe offered.

Brock nodded, making a mental note to follow up with the chief, both on the lead and the reliability of the caller. "Did she provide any contact information?"

Zimmerman shook his head. "Refused. But we did capture the number she called from."

"Good," Chloe said.

"Tell me again why they couldn't put us up here?" Zimmerman said as he gestured at their surroundings.

"Because you wouldn't get a moment's rest if we were staying here, Zim," Chloe said.

"Yeah, that's probably true."

Brock looked around the dining room at the people occupying the nearby tables. It was clear from the stolen glances that everyone knew who they were and why they were in town. He wondered if perhaps Summer's killer sat among them. If there was one thing he'd learned during his time investigating homicides, it was that people were very good at hiding their true feelings from the prying eyes of others.

"Penny for your thoughts?" Chloe asked Brock.

"I was just wondering who else might have known about Summer's pregnancy."

"The victim was pregnant?" Zimmerman said.

"Yeah," Brock said, "but we're keeping that close to the vest for now."

"How did her parents take the news?"

"We haven't told them," Chloe said.

"Jesus," Zimmerman said, nearly choking on his beer. "You guys think that's wise?"

"I don't think we have a choice," Brock said. "We couldn't manage to keep the stabbing a secret for one night."

"Good point," Zimmerman said. "You think that might be the motive behind the murder?"

"It's one of many possibilities," Brock said.

Their waitress breezed over from the next table. "All right now, who's hungry?"

"I am famished," Chloe said.

They each ordered the special, which came highly recommended by their waitress, though Brock had been monitoring the various meals as they were delivered to nearby tables, and even he had to admit everything coming out of the kitchen looked great.

"I honestly can't tell if I'm more hungry or tired," Chloe said.

"I'm both," Zimmerman said. "And at least I had the luxury of a good night's sleep last night."

"A good night's sleep," Brock said. "What's that?"

"Excuse me," a voice said from behind Brock. All eyes turned to face the middle-aged woman who had approached them from a table on the far side of the dining room. "I'm terribly sorry to bother you during dinner. I just want to let you know that we're here to help you in any way we can."

"Thank you," Chloe said.

"We really appreciate it," Brock said.

"Summer was like family to all of us in Greenville. It's so hard to believe something like this could really happen here."

Brock nodded, but like his fellow investigators, he was burdened with the knowledge that murder can happen anywhere. To anyone.

22

Thursday, October 9, 6:00 a.m

Brock managed about five hours of restful sleep, from nothing but sheer exhaustion, he imagined, but once the wheels and cogs inside his brain began spinning again, there was no stopping them. He rose before dawn and was up and out of the inn well before Chloe or Zimmerman. They had agreed to regroup at the PSB by eight o'clock, but Brock had a piece of unfinished business from the previous day that still needed doing.

Brock called Piscataquis County Sheriff's Department for a backup officer to accompany him to Ronnie Libby's cabin on the off chance that Libby wasn't feeling overly cooperative. It was a prudent move based on Libby's prior history of violence. What Brock hadn't counted on was that the backup officer they assigned would be none other than Evan Mathers.

"Looks like we are destined to work together again, ay, partner?" Mathers cracked as he stepped from the police vehicle.

"We aren't partners," Brock said. "I'm just here to question Ronnie Libby."

Mathers lifted both hands in surrender. "Whatever you say, Brock."

Mathers agreed to cover the back of the cabin while Brock approached the front door. As he waited for confirmation that Evan was in position, Brock couldn't help but be reminded of the last time they had worked together to try and take Terry Kirke into custody, and how badly that had turned out.

After knocking several times and receiving no reply from inside, Brock gave up and slid a business card between the doorframe and the storm door. He retreated to his vehicle as Mathers returned around the corner.

"No luck?" Mathers said.

Brock shook his head and pointed at Libby's Jeep. "Maybe he really is sick."

"Yeah, and maybe he's hiding out after offing his girlfriend."

Brock hesitated at the comment. "Speaking of which, you ever see Laura?"

"Laura?" Mathers said, intentionally feigning ignorance.

"You know, Laura Croxford, your girlfriend. The ex-girlfriend of Darrell Kirke, the guy you killed."

"You must mean Darrell Kirke, the guy I killed in self-defense. Saving your life, if memory serves."

"Not the way I remember it," Brock said. "Aren't you worried that she'll eventually rear her head and give you up?"

A disturbing grin crept across Mathers's face. One that Brock didn't care for one bit.

"First off, Laura doesn't have anything on me, because as you already know, I didn't do anything wrong. A jury of my peers said so. Secondly, and sadly, I hear tell Laura is no longer with us."

"What?" Brock said, unable to conceal his shock at the comment.

Mathers moved toward his cruiser and opened the door. "Oh yeah, I thought you might have heard. She drowned in a hotel bathtub a few months ago. I guess what they say about water and alcohol being a dangerous combo must be true."

Brock was speechless.

"Hey, let me know if you or Chloe need any more help. I'm always happy to lend a hand."

Brock watched as Mathers turned the cruiser around and headed back down the drive. He didn't know whether Evan was telling the truth about Laura or just trying to get a rise out of him. One thing he was sure of was that Evan was more than capable of murder. Brock himself had witnessed it firsthand.

23

Thursday, October 9, 7:30 a.m

Brock returned to downtown Greenville intending to drive to the public safety building a half hour early. But he knew if he ran into anyone associated with the press or the media, he wouldn't have time to check out Mathers's story about Laura Croxford. He pulled into the deserted lot of the Shaw Public Library and parked. Availing himself of the Interceptor's laptop computer, he conducted an online search for Laura Croxford. There were several links to Laura Croxfords outside of New England but nothing local at the top of the list. He changed the search parameters to include the state of Maine. This time his search yielded a result from the *Bangor Daily News*. Brock clicked on the link and was taken to a police blotter article dated July 12, 2025.

According to the reporting, police had been called to a Bangor area hotel early Saturday morning for a possible death in one of the rooms. The body of an adult female had been found by the hotel cleaning staff. Bangor police responded to the scene to investigate. Brock scrolled past an endless bank of pop-up advertisements looking for more information, but there was none.

Brock returned to the search results screen and scrolled down the page until he found another entry dated July 23rd. It was a follow-up piece identifying the deceased female as Laura Croxford, thirty-eight years of age, from Biddeford, Maine. According to police, the official cause of death was accidental overdose. Again, there was very little detail in the story. He returned to the search results and scrolled through multiple pages, but there were no other entries connected to Laura Croxford's death.

He sat back in the driver's seat and considered what this meant, only half watching as a school bus passed by. Evan had said that Laura drowned in a hotel bathtub, yet there was no mention of drowning in the articles. There could only be two explanations for this. The first was that he had reached out to someone at the Bangor police department for specifics. The second and more ominous possibility was that Evan had been present when Laura died.

Brock exited out of the search program and checked the time. It was twenty minutes until eight. Doing his best to put Evan Mathers out of his mind, Brock drove directly to the PSB.

He pulled into the visitors' lot, pleasantly surprised to find that Chloe's and Zimmerman's vehicles were already parked there.

"Wondered where you got off to," Chloe said as Brock stepped inside the lobby.

"Had some unfinished business from yesterday to take care of."

"Care to share with the rest of the class?" Zimmerman said.

"Ronnie Libby," Brock said. "Thanks to yesterday afternoon's dog and pony fiasco, I never made it up to his cabin."

"Geez, you could have let one of us know," Chloe said. "We would have gone with you."

"I had a county deputy meet me there," Brock said, intentionally leaving out the deputy's identity.

"Any luck?" Chloe said.

Brock shook his head. "Ronnie's Jeep was parked in the dooryard, but he didn't answer the door."

"Think he's avoiding us?" Chloe said.

"Or lying low inside," Zimmerman opined.

"I don't know," Brock said. "Maybe. It didn't look like anyone was home."

"Good morning," Leavitt said as he strolled in through the front door into the lobby.

"Morning, Chief," they said in unison.

"The early bird, right?" Leavitt said.

"Something like that," Brock said.

"Listen," Leavitt said. "After all the craziness from yesterday, I figured you folks would need a private place to set up your base of operations."

"That would be great," Chloe said.

"Follow me," Leavitt said.

The chief led them to the rear of the large bay where the Greenville fire trucks were stored, past the empty tip line tables to a steel security door at the center of a concrete block wall. Leavitt opened the steel-gray door and flicked on a bank of rocker switches, bathing the entire room in overhead fluorescent lighting.

"Will this work?" Leavitt said as they filed into the room.

"It's perfect," Chloe said, answering for all of them.

"It isn't much, probably nothing like you're used to, but it's got a lock on the door, a big whiteboard, a table, and plenty of chairs."

"What is this space?" Brock said. "Doesn't look like it gets much use."

"It doesn't. This building came with all the trappings of every other grant-funded project."

"Let me guess," Zimmerman said. "Emergency operations center?"

"Bingo," Leavitt said. "EOC it is. One of the many requirements for a newly built public safety venue was that we had an actual space to utilize in case of a major catastrophic event."

"You get many of those up here, Chief?" Chloe said.

"Haven't had one yet, knock on wood. But the room has all the dedicated communication lines you folks should need. And best of all, the door locks with a deadbolt, so no one will be in here snooping around. I figure after the leak about Summer being stabbed, you might need a bit of privacy."

"Much appreciated, Chief," Brock said.

Brock wasn't sure that he'd ever get used to the feeling that he was operating out of a suitcase. When he'd still been part of MCU South, working in York and

Cumberland Counties, everything they'd needed to conduct a thorough homicide investigation had been available within a short drive. Even returning home after a long day was more like a short commute, not a trip measured in hours. Being assigned to MCU North made every case feel like an away game.

"Bathroom's just down the hall," Leavitt continued. "And the ever-important coffee station is available to you twenty-four seven. There's always someone here drinking it, either the police or the fire side of the house. And allow me to apologize in advance for how terrible it is. We brought the coffeemaker with us from the old station."

"Good luck or nostalgia?" Zimmerman said.

"Maybe a little of both," Leavitt said. "And I'm sorry we weren't able to generate more leads for you folks yesterday. Guess I figured if we had four lines specifically for tips that somehow the lead you needed would magically appear."

"Not your fault, Chief," Zimmerman said. "And it's Zim, by the way."

"Detective Zim?" Leavitt said with a mischievous twinkle in his eye.

"Just Zim."

"Zim's our resident joker," Chloe said.

"Well, I'd imagine a sense of humor would come in mighty handy in your line of work."

Brock nodded his agreement.

"Anything else you can think of that you might need today?" Leavitt said. "Any meetings with the locals that I can help facilitate?"

"There is one thing," Brock said. "We received a tip from someone named Collelo who called about an illegal hunter in the woods where Summer was attacked. That ring any bells?"

"We do have a few poachers who operate around here. Did the caller give you a description?"

"She didn't," Zimmerman said.

"Don't suppose you know the caller, do you?" Chloe said.

Leavitt absently scratched his head. "Collelo, huh? Can't say as I recognize the name. They leave a number?"

Zimmerman shook his head. "No, but we captured it. I'll see if I can run it down."

"Sounds good. I'll reach out to the local warden and see if he can help you."

"Thanks, Chief," Brock said.

"Anything else?" Leavitt said.

"Think that's about it for now," Brock said. "Probably have a better idea where we need to direct our resources once we get set up."

"Okay, well, I'll be tied up at town meetings all day. We've got our annual leaf peeper events scheduled to open this week. Foliage season is kind of a big deal around here. It's the last influx of tourist money until the snow falls. You can reach me by phone or by radio if you need anything. Or my secretary, Isabelle, always knows where I am, even if I don't. Feel free to rattle her chain if you can't readily find me."

"Will do, Chief," Chloe said.

"Um, it's office assistant, not secretary, you Neanderthal," a voice said from the doorway.

All eyes turned to face the middle-aged woman wearing a dour expression standing just outside the door. "Please excuse Chief Leavitt, he wasn't born in this century."

"See what I mean?" Leavitt said.

"You must be Isabelle," Chloe said, sticking out her hand in greeting. "Chloe Wright."

"Isabelle Sanborn," she said. "Pleased to meet you, Detective."

"And these are my cohorts," Chloe continued. "Brock Justice, and Jordan Zimmerman."

"Gentlemen," Isabelle said with a nod. "Like the chief said, anything you need, just holler. Printer, copier, whatever."

"Thanks, Isabelle," Brock said.

And with that, Isabelle shoved Leavitt out the door to his first meeting.

"I'll chase down some mugs of java if you two want to get started on the murder board," Zimmerman said.

"Sounds good," Chloe said.

24

Thursday, October 9, 8:15 a.m

By the time Zimmerman returned with their coffees, Brock and Chloe had commandeered space on the table for their laptops and notebooks. They took turns writing the names of the players on the whiteboard, beginning with the victim, Summer Randall. Next to Randall's name was a large inkjet photograph taken from the Bureau of Motor Vehicles. Unlike most of the poor BMV images Brock had seen during his time with the state police, Summer's photo was actually flattering. The young woman staring back at them wore a smile as genuine and full of life as everyone had described. Based solely on her BMV photo, it wasn't a surprise that Summer had been so well liked by everyone in town. Everyone except for a killer.

"So, I got called in to pitch after you guys had already played a few innings," Zimmerman said as he sat down and sipped his coffee. "How about filling in some blanks?"

"What does that make you?" Chloe said. "The closer?"

"Ah, Kyra Sedgwick," Zimmerman cooed. "Man, I love that sexy Southern accent."

"You realize it's fake, right?" Chloe said. "The accent."

"Whatever. Don't ruin it for me."

Chloe laughed.

"Anyway, my point was, do you want to run down what we've got and who you've talked with so far?"

"I'll take that, if you want to keep going," Brock said.

"Sure," Chloe said.

Brock was about to begin when his cell phone rang with a call from Assistant Attorney General Gene Grover. Brock answered, putting the call on speakerphone.

"Good morning, all," Grover said.

"Morning," they said in unison.

"How'd you get so lucky to draw the short straw on this one, Gene?" Zimmerman said.

"It's a gift, Zim," Grover said. "Sorry I couldn't make it up there in person this morning."

"No worries," Brock said. "Your timing is perfect. We were just about to recap the investigation for Zim."

"Great. Let's have it."

"So, as you know, Chloe and I were called to respond to Greenville, more specifically Lily Bay Road, night before last for what at first glance appeared to be a vehicle-versus-pedestrian fatal motor vehicle accident. The victim, a local woman named Summer Randall, was found lying in the middle of the road by a passerby. The driver and only occupant of the truck that struck Randall was also a local, and repeat drunk driving offender, by the name of Jonathan Watters. After striking Randall, Watters's vehicle overturned and crashed into the woods at the edge of the roadway. Watters had to be extricated by members of the Greenville Fire Department. EMTs later transported him to Northern Light Hospital with what turned out to be non-life-threatening injuries."

"Geez, that's too bad," Zimmerman said with a smirk clearly showing beneath his immaculately trimmed Hercule Poirot mustache.

"My thoughts exactly," Chloe said as she added Watters's name to the board.

"Anyway," Brock continued. "As it turns out, Watters wasn't responsible for Summer's death, only for mangling her leg. According to the ME,

Summer died as a result of massive blood loss from a single stab wound to her lower abdomen, having nothing to do with the accident."

"Jesus," Zimmerman said with a wince.

"Yeah," Chloe said. "Exsanguination. Helluva way to die."

"If we end up charging someone with Summer's murder, those facts are gonna stir up a legal hornet's nest with the defense," Grover said.

"They certainly will," Brock said.

"And the ME is confident in this finding?" Grover said.

"Dr. Isleborn was very clear on the cause of death," Chloe said. "She said Summer had lost approximately forty percent of her blood supply."

"Where do we think the stabbing occurred?"

"In the woods less than a mile from where Summer was struck by Watters's truck," Brock said.

"Do we know what she was doing in the woods to begin with?" Zimmerman said.

"Training," Chloe said. "She was an avid runner, preparing for an upcoming 10K."

"So, the real question is, was the attack a random encounter, or was Summer specifically targeted?" Grover said.

"Exactly," Brock said.

"Have we recovered the murder weapon?" Grover asked.

"No," Brock said. "A K9 led us to the site of the attack but couldn't locate the knife."

"What do we need in the way of subpoenas or search warrants?" Grover said. "Cell phones, computers, anything?"

"We couldn't locate the victim's phone," Chloe said. "It wasn't on her person or in her vehicle, which was burglarized."

"The killer broke into her car too?" Grover said. "Now that is interesting. Any idea what they were after?"

"Not a clue at this point," Brock said. "Though we weren't able to locate a purse or pocketbook in her car or apartment."

"So it could be she interrupted a burglar breaking into her car?" Grover said.

"Maybe," Brock said. "Only problem with that is that she was attacked quite a distance from her car."

"Any evidence recovered from the vehicle?" Grover said.

"Yeah," Brock said. "I got word this morning that ERT found traces of blood inside her vehicle."

"Belonging to the suspect or the victim?"

"I'd say more likely the suspect, but we'll have to wait for the lab results."

"We did recover Summer's laptop from her apartment, so we'll need to get into that," Chloe said. "And we'll need whatever the cell provider can give us."

"Shoot me the affidavit whenever you're ready, and I'll give it the once-over. Anything sensitive you're holding back?"

Brock and Chloe locked eyes.

"Actually, yes," Brock said. "The victim was two months pregnant at the time of her death."

"Possible motive?" Grover said.

"We're considering it," Chloe said.

"Any idea who the father is?"

"Not yet," Brock said. "But we're holding that little detail back from everyone."

"Have Summer's parents been informed?" Grover said.

"We haven't told them," Brock said.

"Congresswoman Randall won't be happy when she finds out you held that back," Grover said.

"It's okay," Zimmerman said. "We haven't told Lt. Cumberland either."

"You sure about this?" Grover said.

"We can't risk any more leaks to the media," Brock said. "Besides, we don't want to tip our hand too soon if it turns out that the killer is the baby's father. We think holding that back might be a good way to get voluntary DNA samples as we interview potential persons of interest."

"For comparison purposes?" Grover said.

"More like elimination purposes," Chloe said.

"We'll tell them we found evidence at the scene and we need to rule people out," Brock said.

"Uh-huh," Grover said. "And you're referring to the blood in the victim's car?"

"I am," Brock said.

"Okay, I can probably sell that if I need to," Grover said after several moments. "Make sure they each sign and date consent forms. I don't want this coming back to bite us later."

"Of course," Brock said.

"And when you're ready, make sure Summer's parents are informed before the media. Congresswoman Randall's gonna blow a gasket as it is."

"Will do," Brock said.

"Okay, I gotta run to another meeting, but keep me posted and let me know if you need anything."

"Maybe you can help keep the press at bay," Zimmerman said.

Grover could be heard chuckling at the other end of the call. "I'm a prosecutor, not a miracle worker, Zim. Good luck."

25

Thursday, October 9, 9:30 a.m

After updating the whiteboard and bringing AAG Grover and Zimmerman up to speed, Brock decided to work on reconstructing the timeline of Summer Randall's last day. The work schedule Chloe had located in Summer's apartment indicated that she had worked a five-hour shift at the hospital from ten till three.

"Was she planning to run alone?" Zimmerman said as he studied the board.

"The calendar hanging on her wall said she was meeting Brit for a run at five thirty," Chloe said.

"Who's Brit?" Zimmerman said.

"Not a clue," Chloe said.

"Brittney LaRoux," Brock said as he flipped open his notebook.

"Who is Brittney LaRoux?" Chloe said

"She's a nurse I met yesterday at Northern Light," Brock said. "Brittney was supposed to meet up with Summer for a training run but had to cancel at the last minute. She lives with her elderly grandmother, who had taken a fall, and she had to run home to deal with that."

Chloe dug a photo from her briefcase and held it up. It was one of the pictures she'd located in Summer's apartment, depicting Summer and another woman celebrating after a road race. "She look anything like this?"

"That's her," Brock said.

"Who's the guy standing with them?" Zimmerman said.

"No idea," Brock said.

"Too bad we don't have Summer's phone," Zimmerman said. "Might fill in some of the gaps."

"LaRoux did show me a text thread between her and Summer," Brock said as he pulled up the photo he had snapped with his phone. "The last two messages from Brittney were her bailing on the run to assist her grandmother. The very last text was from Summer to LaRoux stating that she understood."

"Christ, doesn't anyone talk on the phone anymore?" Zimmerman said.

"Whatever, grandpa," Chloe said. "Is this where you give us the 'get off my lawn' speech?"

Brock laughed, despite his current mood. "She's got a point, Zim."

"Yeah, well, you'll see what I mean soon enough. This tech stuff will be our undoing. You wait."

"What time did LaRoux send the cancelation text?" Chloe said.

Brock checked the photo he had taken of the text thread.

"Four forty-five."

"And Summer's reply? What time was that?"

"Six oh one," Brock said.

"Twenty minutes or so before we believe the accident happened," Chloe said as she added the time to the board. "So she would have already been on her run."

"Meaning?" Zimmerman said.

"That Summer had her phone with her during the run," Chloe said.

Brock had been thinking a lot about Summer's missing phone. It was entirely possible that it was lying in the woods somewhere just off the trail, lost during the attack. It was just as likely that the phone had been taken by Summer's attacker. Was there something on the phone the attacker didn't want anyone to see? And if so, had she known her killer?

Brock knew they needed to remain methodical and resist the urge to jump to conclusions. Narrowing the scope of what might or might not be relevant to the investigation at this early stage was a recipe for disaster. Still, the missing phone, and what it might mean, would need to be considered as they moved forward.

"Let's try to get access to any recent contact that she had with the people we interview," Brock said. "We may not have Summer's phone, but we might be able to recreate it with interviews and cellular history from her provider."

"Good idea," Chloe said.

"What about Wheels?" Zimmerman said, referring to Detective Wheeler back at Troop E in Bangor. "He is the guru of all things electronic. Can't we get him working on a subpoena for her cell provider?"

"It's on my list of things to do today," Chloe said. "How do you want to split up the interviews?"

Brock looked at the growing list of names populating the whiteboard. "Why don't you and Zim take the hospital staff. Sounds like that's where Summer spent most of her time. Let's see if her friends and coworkers can shed some light on her final days."

"And you?" Zimmerman said.

"I still need to locate Ronnie Libby. And I want to speak with Taylor Randall again. The notification wasn't exactly the time or place to get any detailed information about what Summer might have been up to recently."

"You want one of us to go with you?" Chloe said.

"No, I figure Taylor might be more forthcoming if it's just the two of us."

Zimmerman chuckled. "What your partner is trying to say is that the victim's father might be more comfortable in a man-to-man setting."

"Sexist," Chloe teased.

"Where *was* Ronnie Libby yesterday?" Zimmerman said.

"I don't know. His boss told me that he called in sick."

"Coincidence?" Zimmerman said, raising and lowering his eyebrows in a Groucho-like fashion.

"I don't believe in coincidence," Brock said. "We also need to check in at this gym where Summer previously worked."

"Balance Gym," Chloe said. "Zim and I can take that."

"You think Summer quit or got fired?" Zimmerman said.

Before he could respond, Brock's cell rang with a call from Cumberland.

"The Dreadful One?" Zimmerman said.

"None other," Brock said as he rose from his chair and headed for the door. "I gotta take this. Everyone good on their assignments?"

"Don't worry about a thing, partner," Chloe said. "Zim and I are on the case."

26

Thursday, October 9, 10:30 a.m

Brock had never really understood the outdoor lifestyle, at least not beyond the one his father, Albert, had tried to instill in him and his older brother, Jacob. For Brock, the out-of-doors life began and ended at their family camp in Blue Hill. The long summers he and Jake had spent swimming in the lake, catching snapping turtles and writing their names in permanent marker on their shells before releasing them back into the water were the memories that made him smile, even though he and Jake had spent more time swamping the boat on submerged logs than actually marking up amphibians.

To Albert, recipient of the Legendary Trooper Award and legendary outdoorsman, the camp in Blue Hill and the wilderness surrounding it was the only life worth living. Brock's dad lived to hunt, fish, and snowmobile, and he did his best to jam as many of those pursuits into his sons' lives as he could. Albert Justice had never done anything halfway in his entire life. It didn't matter if it was chasing bad guys in his cruiser or tracking game in the Maine woods, Albert Justice was larger than life. Brock had grown up under the formidable shadow that his father cast. A shadow that haunted Brock to this day.

As he stepped through the entrance of Greenville Outfitters, Brock was overwhelmed by the sense of everything Albert. The heady smell of leather boots and gun oil hung heavily in the air. Everywhere he looked were symbols of living in the great outdoors. Hiking poles, crampons, tents, ultralight hammocks, fishing poles, and guns. There was no question that Albert Justice would have felt right at home here.

"Can I help you with something?" a youthful-looking blond salesclerk said as he approached Brock.

Before Brock could respond, a deeper voice resonated from behind the counter.

"I've got this one, Toby," Taylor Randall said.

"Yes, sir," Toby said as he nodded and moved away toward the other side of the store where several people were looking at footwear.

"Detective Justice," Randall said as Brock approached the counter.

"Mr. Randall."

Randall sported those same rugged good looks that Brock's father had. Sun-darkened skin and a chiseled jawline, and a full head of sandy-colored hair called to mind that timeless image of a Maine guide, like some model straight out of an L.L. Bean catalogue. But behind the outward appearance of first impressions, Taylor Randall had visibly aged in the past two days. At least it looked that way to Brock. Being informed that your only child was dead, long before her time, something no parent should ever experience, was hard enough to navigate without the added weight of murder. Brock couldn't imagine the thoughts that were undoubtedly running through the man's head. Questioning every decision that had led Summer to that moment in time. What if the Randalls hadn't gotten divorced? What if Summer had opted to live with her mother instead of in Greenville? Brock was far enough removed from the situation to know that none of those things would likely have changed a thing as far as Summer Randall was concerned. Sometimes life just wasn't fair. Dwelling on what-ifs was a guaranteed way to drive oneself crazy, or into an early grave. Brock knew that neither he nor Chloe could change what had already occurred, but they might be able to affect the outcome. Catching the person, or persons, responsible for Summer's untimely and cruel death and bringing some manner of closure to the Randalls and to the people who knew and cared for their daughter.

"Wasn't sure if I would find you here today," Brock said.

"Figured I'd be home grieving, did you?"

Brock had no idea how to respond to that, so he didn't.

"I've got a business to run," Randall said. "Regardless of what kind of shit life flings in my direction. I don't imagine your line of work is much different."

On that point, Brock couldn't disagree.

"I was hoping we might speak in private," Brock said.

"We can talk upstairs in my office if you want. Give me a second to get someone to cover the counter."

Chloe and Zimmerman entered the Northern Light CA Dean Hospital not knowing exactly who they were looking to speak with. Chloe had managed to find several framed photographs in Summer's apartment that showed her with various members of the hospital staff, including Brittney LaRoux, the nurse Brock had spoken to. Several of the photos featured Summer with those same people mugging it up for the camera at various road races. It was clear that her work friendships had carried over into her personal life. After introducing themselves to the woman manning the lobby check-in desk and explaining their reason for being there, they were told to have a seat and that someone would be right out to speak with them.

"Seems like a well-run facility," Chloe said, attempting to make conversation while they waited.

"Yeah, read up on it last night," Zimmerman said. "Only twenty-five beds. A far cry from the emergency-based medical monstrosities around Portland."

"Maybe," Chloe said. "But something tells me that the personal care is likely far greater. The patients probably feel more like they matter and less like a number."

Zimmerman nodded.

"Detectives?" a tall, slender man asked as he approached the waiting area. "My name is Ismail Tandor. I am the director of human resources for the hospital. I understand you have some questions about the staff?"

"We do," Chloe said as she and Zimmerman stood and repeated the process of identifying themselves. "We'd like to ask you some questions about one of your former employees, Summer Randall."

Chloe watched Tandor's grief reveal itself in his features.

"We were all shocked to learn of her death," Tandor said. "She was so young and vibrant."

Chloe and Zimmerman were both aware that they had garnered the attention of several others seated in the waiting area.

"Is there someplace more private where we could ask you some questions?" Chloe said.

"Certainly," Tandor said. "If you'll follow me."

27

Thursday, October 9, 10:40 a.m

Brock waited while Taylor Randall quickly removed several cardboard boxes of equipment from one of the chairs in front of his desk and relocated them to the floor. Everything in the cluttered office was designed to perpetuate the wide pine plank and log cabin feel of the place. The hunting and fishing motif continued from the sales floor on the main level to the office furnishings; even the deer antler wall lamps were camp rustic. As he studied the contents of the office, Brock half expected to see a carved wooden bear holding up a glass-top coffee table or a moose head mounted over the window.

"Please," Randall said, gesturing to Brock. "Have a seat."

"Thanks," Brock said as he sat across from the man.

"I don't suppose you've come to tell me that you've arrested the man responsible for murdering my little girl."

Brock chose his words carefully. Despite the obvious grief Taylor was suffering, there was also the occasional flash of anger behind those tired eyes. Brock needed to remember that this was the same man who lost his job as a police reserve officer after threatening Ronnie Libby for assaulting his daughter. He wondered what such a man might be capable of doing to the person who murdered that same daughter.

"I have not come here for that, Mr. Randall."

"Please, it's Taylor. And I know how this works. Don't sugarcoat things to try and placate me. I'd rather you just come out and tell me what it is. Or ask whatever questions you need to ask."

"Fair enough," Brock said. "When my partner and I asked you the other night if you knew of anyone who might want to harm Summer, you said no, but that wasn't entirely true, was it?"

Taylor stared at him, unblinking, as if sizing him up. "You're referring to Ronnie Libby."

"I am. I'm curious why you wouldn't mention something as relevant as her abusive ex-boyfriend?"

Taylor's eyes narrowed with suspicion. "Are you trying to tell me you think Ronnie is responsible for killing my little girl?"

"I am not trying to tell you anything," Brock said. "If you worked as a part-time cop, you know we have to examine every possibility."

"Well, if you know about Ronnie assaulting Summer, then I assume you also know I lost my job at the PD over what happened. Rich Leavitt fired me over the incident."

"The way I heard it was that you might have threatened Ronnie Libby."

"No 'might have' about it. I did threaten that little prick. And it wasn't an assault. Libby beat the shit out of the most important thing in my life. I'll never be okay with that."

Brock couldn't say that he wouldn't have reacted similarly if the proverbial shoe had been on the other foot. But Brock wasn't ready to let go of this line of questioning just yet. "It must be difficult to live and work in the same town as Ronnie."

"We do our best to steer clear of each other," Taylor said.

"But still, it is a small town," Brock countered.

Taylor nodded in silent agreement. Brock could see the muscles in the man's jaw flexing in anger.

"My ex spoke with the state medical examiner, Dr. Isleborn, and she said they will be releasing Summer's body in a couple of days so that we can begin planning her service. I assume you got whatever you needed from the autopsy."

"We did," Brock said, again trying to step lightly and cautiously. He knew how sensitive broaching the next subject might be.

"Then my daughter died as a result of the attack you mentioned?"

"Prior to being struck by the vehicle Jonathan Watters was operating, we believe Summer was attacked by an unknown assailant as she jogged through the woods."

"Attacked how?"

"Summer was stabbed with some type of edged weapon."

Tears flooded Taylor's eyes and spilled down his cheeks. The beaten man made no effort to wipe them away as he faced head on what Brock was telling him.

"And you have no idea who may have stabbed her?"

"Not yet. But it's early days. We are attempting to reconstruct Summer's last twenty-four hours. Who she talked to. Who she met with. What her plans were for later. It's important that we develop a complete picture of Summer's life and everyone in it. For instance, I wondered whether you might be able to tell me why she didn't return to UMO for the fall semester? It would seem as though she would want to finish her senior year at college."

Taylor let out a sigh of frustration. "I still don't know. She told me just before classes were supposed to start that she had decided to take some time off while she figured some things out."

"What kind of things?"

"She wouldn't say."

"Was she in a relationship?"

"I'm her father, which means I'm probably the last person she would share something like that with. You have kids, Detective Justice?"

Brock shook his head.

"You'd be more likely to get that information from her mother."

"I was under the impression that Summer and her mother weren't close," Brock said.

"Rhonda has her faults, her political motivations being the biggest, but she loves Summer as much as I do. Trust me, they still talked on the phone regularly."

"About?"

"Probably about all the things she couldn't tell me. Like her relationships." Taylor's eyes narrowed again. "Why exactly did you ask me if she was in a relationship with anyone? Did you find something?"

"No," Brock said. "But I have to ask. Was there any chance that Summer and Ronnie had gotten back together?"

"None. Summer knew I wouldn't allow it. Besides, she made a clean break with him."

But Brock wondered. How many domestic situations had he tried to intercede in to break the cycle of control and violence only to have the victim recant their testimony or give the abuser yet another chance. It was always the fault of something else, like substance addiction, or "He was stressed," or "Something I said or did set him off. He's not always like this. He has a gentle side." Brock had heard every excuse invented, but he'd never heard one that could justify the assault of a loved one. Love tended to cloud the judgment of even the most rational people. Brock wondered if maybe Summer had been seeing Ronnie on the sly. Maybe without either parent being aware. It was an angle that needed following up.

28

Thursday, October 9, 10:45 a.m

After speaking with Tandor, Chloe and Zimmerman were led to a private consultation room where they could interview any of the hospital staff they deemed important to the investigation. The first person they spoke with was Brittney LaRoux, a twenty-five-year-old full-time nurse who had met and befriended Summer during her hospital internship. The attractive brunette was visibly upset as she spoke to the detectives about the loss of her friend.

"It still doesn't feel real," Brittney said as she wiped the tears from her eyes with a tissue. "I can't help but think that this is all my fault."

"How so?" Chloe said.

"Summer and I work out together. It's one of the things that connected us. We trained at the same gym and ran the trails around Greenville. I can't tell you how many road races we've run together."

A fresh flood of tears welled up in Brittney's eyes as she fought to keep her emotions in check.

"How does that make her murder your fault?" Zimmerman said after a moment.

"Because Summer and I had planned to run together the night she was killed. I can't help but think that if I hadn't canceled, Summer might still be alive today."

"I'm not sure that's helpful to think like that," Chloe said. "You don't know things wouldn't have turned out exactly the same."

"You might have been attacked yourself had you been there," Zimmerman offered.

"You can't blame yourself, Brittney," Chloe said.

LaRoux nodded silently as she dabbed at the corners of her eyes with the tissue.

"How often did you and Summer train together?" Zimmerman said.

"Two or three times a week. It really depended on our scheduling at the hospital. Some weeks it was more and others less because we didn't always work the same shift. Or one of us might pick up an extra shift."

Chloe nodded and made a note. "Are you aware of anyone who might have wanted to harm Summer? Or any recent threats she may have received?"

LaRoux paused to consider the question. "None that I know of."

"Is that the kind of thing she would have mentioned to you?" Zimmerman said.

"Of course," Brittney said, as if surprised by the question. "Summer and I didn't keep secrets from each other. We were very close."

"You shared everything?" Chloe said.

"I'd say so. She was more like a sister to me than my own."

After they finished questioning Brittney, Chloe showed her several of the framed pictures she had removed from Summer's apartment, asking her to point out and identify any of the other people in the photos.

"That's Ivan Heiden," Brittney said as she pointed to a handsome young man standing with her and Summer.

"A mutual friend, I assume," Zimmerman said.

"Yes. Dr. Heiden is one of the primary doctors on staff here at Northern Light."

"Did he train with you and Summer?" Chloe said.

"No, nothing like that. He was there to cheer us on. He is a big runner, though. Ivan has run several full-length races in Boston and New York."

"Full length?" Zimmerman said.

"Yeah, you know, twenty-six-point-two miles. Marathons."

"People really do that to their bodies?" Zimmerman said, garnering a laugh from Brittney. "Heck, I only ran in the police academy because they made me."

"Ivan is a serious runner, not like me and Summer. We enjoy—enjoyed training for the 5K and 10K races around here. It's a great way to blow off the stress of the job and to stay in shape."

Chloe smiled. "Unlike my couch potato partner over here, I totally get that."

"Hey," Zimmerman said, feigning offense.

"You're a runner too?" Brittney said.

"Nothing like Dr. Heiden," Chloe said. "I'd say I'm more in the same camp as you and Summer. A recreational runner."

Chloe studied every nuance of Brittney's responses to their questions. Something about the way she looked when talking about Dr. Heiden gave Chloe pause. She was clearly enamored with the man. Chloe wondered if perhaps there was something more than a shared friendship between Brittney and the good doctor. Maybe even between Summer and Heiden.

"Was Summer seeing anyone?" Zimmerman said.

"I don't think so," Brittney said. "At least not in a serious way."

"What does that mean?" Chloe said.

"Well, the only person I know she'd been seeing on occasion was Ronnie Libby."

"Her ex?" Zimmerman said.

Brittney nodded. "I didn't think it was anything more than an attempt to rekindle their friendship. You know they both attended Greenville High, right? Ronnie was a three-sport athlete. They ran track and field together senior year."

"We know that Ronnie assaulted her," Chloe said. "Pretty badly by all accounts."

"Yeah," Brittney said. "Summer told me that Ronnie had gone down a bad road. He dropped out of college in his first year and began hanging around the wrong crowd and doing drugs. But he's been clean since that incident happened. Close to a year now."

"You think there's a possibility that Summer and Ronnie were romantically involved again?" Chloe said.

"I don't think so. She was pretty devastated after the assault."

Chloe waited to see if she would say more.

"I think seeing Ronnie was more about reconnecting. I do know Summer was afraid that her dad would find out about them seeing each other. Apparently, he'd made threats against Ronnie."

Chloe wondered how Taylor would react if he found out they'd been seeing each other again.

After Brittney departed, Chloe turned to Zimmerman. "What do you say we interview Dr. Heiden next?"

"And obtain a DNA sample?" Zimmerman said, grinning.

"Absolutely," Chloe said.

29

Thursday, October 9, 11:15 a.m

Brock departed from Greenville Outfitters satisfied with the new information he had received from Taylor Randall. The distraught father had been forthcoming about the threats he'd made against Ronnie Libby and the reason for his firing. It was also clear to Brock that Taylor hadn't known about Summer's pregnancy, or the subject would have come up.

Niggling around in the back of Brock's mind during his interview of Taylor Randall, taking up space he didn't have to spare, was the death of Laura Croxford. The disturbing conversation he had with Evan Mathers did little to dissuade the feeling that the ex-girlfriend of Darrell Kirke, and of Evan Mathers, had met her death not by accidental overdose but by drowning at the hands of another, taking to her grave damning information that would have given the jury pause about the questionable police shooting of Darrell Kirke.

Before Brock could decide his next move, his cell phone rang, displaying a number he didn't recognize. Brock answered anyway.

"Justice."

"Detective, this is Charlie Fasulo. We spoke yesterday at the *Kate*—uh—the *Katahdin*."

"What can I do for you, Charlie?"

"Wondering if you'd caught up with Ronnie Libby yet?"

"No, I haven't. Is he working today?"

"Actually, that's why I'm calling. Ronnie was here, but I sent him home."

"Was he still sick?"

"He was drunk."

Brock was halfway to the Libbys' cabin when he passed Deputy Mathers's cruiser traveling in the opposite direction. Several moments later, his cell phone rang again. Even without looking, he knew it would be Evan.

"Justice."

"I assume you're still looking for Ronnie Libby," Mathers said.

"You assume correctly," Brock said as his eyes shifted to Libby's Jeep parked unattended in a passing turnout. "Tell me you didn't just arrest him for OUI."

"Aw, you ruined my surprise. I'm on my way to the PD to book him and administer an intoxilyzer test."

Brock was beyond angry as he pulled in next to the Piscataquis County cruiser where Mathers was in the process of removing Libby from the vehicle. Brock barely managed to jam the transmission into park before jumping out of the Interceptor.

"What the fuck are you playing at?" Brock said as he marched toward Mathers with his hands clenched into fists.

"Not playing at anything, brother. Just doing my job. You should try it sometime."

Brock glared at his former partner while trying to think of reasons not to deck him. The presence of Ronnie Libby was the only thing holding him back. Before Brock could respond verbally or physically, Chloe and Zimmerman pulled into the lot.

"I see you found him," Zimmerman said as he and Chloe approached on foot.

"Not exactly the way I'd pictured it," Mathers said, breaking eye contact with Brock for the first time.

"Nice work," Chloe said.

"Thanks," Mathers said before his attention returned to Brock. "Now, if you don't mind, I've got to book and process my arrest."

Against his better judgment, Brock stood back and allowed Mathers to pass, leading a disheveled-looking Ronnie Libby into the PSB.

"What's gotten into you, Brock?" Chloe said as soon as the door closed behind Mathers and Libby.

"Yeah," Zimmerman said. "You look like you want to punch something."

"Not something," Brock growled. "Someone."

"You're pissed at Evan?" Chloe said.

"Very perceptive," Brock said.

"Hey, don't take it out on me, *partner*. We needed to talk to Ronnie Libby anyway."

"Evan just managed to locate him first," Zimmerman said.

"Is that what happened?" Brock snapped. "Funny, but it doesn't seem random to me. Evan knew I was looking for Libby."

"How could he have known that?" Chloe said.

"Because he was my backup this morning at Libby's cabin."

Brock paced back and forth inside the fire department garage bay as he waited for Mathers to finish with Libby. Several volunteer firefighters were busy checking equipment; each of them gave him a wide berth. Brock had been hoping for a noncustodial situation in which to interview Libby for the first time. Mathers's arrest had muddied the waters. Custody not only changed the nature of any interview that Brock might conduct with Libby, but the OUI arrest, depending on his level of intoxication, meant that Libby's ability to comprehend his rights might later be called into question by any savvy defense lawyer. In short, Mathers's decision to arrest Libby had dropped Brock right in it.

Chloe and Zimmerman, having only stopped by the station on their way to interview the owner of the gym where Summer had previously worked, had already departed. Brock felt bad about snapping at the two of them, but he was still pissed off at Mathers.

Brock had just checked the time again, wondering what was taking Mathers so long, when Mathers and Libby walked into the garage. Libby was no longer handcuffed.

"He's all yours," Mathers said.

"What are you talking about?" Brock said. "Aren't you charging him?"

"I'm releasing him with a criminal summons to appear in court next month."

Libby sheepishly held up his copy of the ticket.

"He's all yours," Mathers repeated.

"And the test?"

"Oh, he failed it. Blew a point-oh-nine."

Brock considered this. Libby's blood alcohol level, while technically over the state's designated limit of point-oh-eight, was prima facie evidence that he was too intoxicated to drive, but not so high that he couldn't understand his rights. Additionally, by releasing Libby with a summons, Mathers had removed custody from the equation.

"See you around, Ronnie," Mathers said before heading for the exit. "And remember, don't drive until you've sobered up, sport. See ya, Brock."

Brock ignored Mathers and turned his full attention to Libby. "We need to talk."

30

Thursday, October 9, 12:15 p.m

Chloe parked across the street from the Balance Gym in Greenville Junction. Before exiting the vehicle, she looked over at Zimmerman.

"You think we were right leaving the two of them alone?" she said.

"What?" Zimmerman said. "You think Brock would be dumb enough to get into a physical altercation with Evan Mathers?"

"The thought had crossed my mind," Chloe said. "There's definitely no love lost between those two. I think they each blame the other for their current circumstances."

"Well, whatever the issue is, Brock is all about working the case. He's not about to do anything to screw that up. He may be a hot dog at times, but he's like a hot dog with a bone when he's on the trail. Trust me, I know the type."

"I hope you're right," Chloe said as they both stepped out of the SUV.

Balance Gym was like any other workout facility Chloe had ever been inside, only smaller than the chain gyms. One side of the business was packed with rows of cardio machines while the other was dedicated to weightlifters and iron tossers. The gym's interior walls were painted in bright colors, making her wonder if there was a psychological component to the color scheme. Chloe had always loved working out and never once cared what shade the gym, or even her workout clothing, was. Training was training. It was all about sweat, gains, and the feeling of accomplishment.

Before they could get their bearings, a Lycra-clad buxom brunette hurried toward them.

"May I help you?" she said.

Zimmerman pounced. "I hope so."

"Are you looking to join our gym?" she said, immediately turning on the fake charm.

Chloe produced her credentials and held them up. "Actually, we were hoping to speak to the owner." She took some pleasure in seeing the woman's bleached smile falter as the possibility of adding two memberships to her monthly quota evaporated before her very eyes.

"You're looking for Chris Mitchell," she said, casting a glance toward the cardio end of the space where a muscular male wearing a green tank top and white shorts was putting an elliptical through its paces. "I'll check and see if he's free. May I ask what this is about?"

"We're investigating the death of a former employee," Chloe said.

"Is that the woman I read about in the paper? The one who was attacked in the woods?"

"It is," Zimmerman said.

"Oh, my God. It's so terrible to think that happened around here."

Chloe stared at the woman, waiting to see if her attention might return to the task at hand, but it didn't.

"Mr. Mitchell?" Chloe prompted.

"Oh, right. Be right back."

"I can't believe she reads the paper," Chloe said as she watched the shapely woman make a beeline toward the elliptical Mitchell was punishing.

"I wonder how much they charge for a membership?" Zimmerman said, never taking his eyes off the brunette.

"Easy there, Studly Do-Right," Chloe said. "You're married, remember?"

"I agreed to honor and obey, never said anything about not looking."

Brock decided to give Libby a ride back to the cabin. If there was one legal maneuver he had learned the hard way, it was that custody had more to do with the detainee's state of mind than actual intent of the detective conducting the interview. Thanks to Evan Mathers's ill-timed decision to strictly enforce Maine's traffic laws, Libby was stranded at the PSB with a blood alcohol level too high to safely operate a motor vehicle. And stranded could easily be manipulated by an experienced trial attorney to look like custody. Transporting Libby back to his residence for a chat negated the need for any Miranda warning.

"You coming in?" Libby said as Brock watched him open the passenger door.

Brock killed the ignition, then climbed out of the unmarked and followed Ronnie to the side door of the cabin.

"I'm gonna make myself a drink if you don't mind," Libby said as they stepped inside. "You want anything?"

"Actually, Ronnie, I'd rather you refrained from any more alcohol until after we talk."

Libby turned to him and frowned.

"I was told you had been sober since—well—since the incident with Summer."

"I'd say that ship has sailed, wouldn't you?"

Brock said nothing, waiting to see what Libby would do.

"All right. Then let's grab a seat at the table, and you can ask your questions."

They sat across from each other at the dining room table. Brock wondered if Libby could see the irony of their positioning, which was exactly the same as it would have been back at the PSB.

"Fire away," Libby said. "You want to know if I had anything to do with Summer's death, right? I'm the asshole who beat up his girlfriend, then dodged jail, thanks to a rich mommy, so I must have killed her, right?"

"Did you?" Brock said.

"Of course not. And yes, despite what you might think of me now, I was clean and sober for an entire year."

"What pushed you off the wagon?"

"It wasn't killing Summer, if that's what you're thinking."

"Then what?"

Libby wet his lips as he considered whether he wanted to answer Brock's question. It was a tick that Brock had seen many times when dealing with addicts. Especially alcoholics.

"Summer and I had started seeing each other again. Casually and on the sly."

"How long?"

Libby shrugged. "Couple of months. We had to be careful, though. She didn't want her dad finding out."

"Why was that?" Brock said.

"Because Taylor threatened to kill me after I beat up Summer. Lost his cop job over it."

"His job at Greenville PD?" Brock said. "I thought he was fired as part of the deal your mom helped facilitate."

Libby's lips tightened into a thin line. "Yeah, that's right. The district attorney decided it was more important that I get help for my substance abuse than go to jail."

"Lucky you," Brock said. "I've seen the pictures of what you did to Summer. You're lucky Summer wasn't my daughter."

Libby said nothing.

"Were you and Summer intimately involved?"

"That's none of your business."

"Where were you on the evening Summer was killed?"

"Visiting a friend."

"Who?"

"My AA sponsor."

"Name?"

"Maybe you haven't heard, but they call it Alcoholics Anonymous for a reason. Especially the anonymous part."

"So, you have no alibi?"

Libby let out a prolonged sigh. "Look, all I know is her first name. She goes by Candy."

"Candy? Is that her real name or a moniker?"

Libby shrugged again.

"What time did you meet with Candy?"

"I don't know. I drove to a seven thirty meeting in Monson. Then Candy and I went to get coffee and talk."

"What time did you get back to Greenville?"

"I didn't come directly back, okay? I went drinking instead."

"Sounds like a real successful meeting," Brock said. "Your boss said you left work early that day. Why was that?"

"I had some personal shit to take care of."

"What kind of personal shit?"

"I don't think that's any of your business either."

"Okay. What happened that day that made you quit after a year of sobriety?"

"I don't want to talk about it." Libby abruptly stood up from his chair. "Are we finished here?"

Brock wanted to push harder, but he still needed Libby's cooperation. He reached into his suit coat pocket and removed a DNA swab kit and a consent form.

"What is that?" Libby said, eyes widening.

"It's a swab kit for a DNA sample."

"Why would you need my DNA?"

"We're taking DNA from everyone we talk to about this case."

"Why?"

"To rule out involvement in the attack on Summer. You just told me that you were out of town when it happened. This is a real simple way to eliminate yourself from suspicion. You do want to help us catch Summer's killer, don't you?"

"Fine," Libby said as he scribbled out his signature on the consent form, then began to roll up his sleeve.

"It isn't a blood test, Ronnie. I just need a swab from inside your mouth."

Libby shook his head. "Whatever. Let's just get this over with."

Brock slipped a pair of nitrile gloves from his pocket and worked his hands inside them. He followed the instructions printed on the kit to the letter, thoroughly swabbing the interior surface of both cheeks inside Libby's mouth with the oversized Q-tip. After sealing and marking the sample, Brock returned the kit to his pocket.

"Thank you for your cooperation," Brock said as he pushed his chair back and stood. "One more question."

"What now?"

"When was the last time you saw Summer Randall?"

"I'd like you to leave now."

31

Thursday, October 9, 12:30 p.m

Chloe and Zimmerman followed Mitchell into a small office tucked behind the reception desk where a bouncy blond teen was checking in a middle-aged gym member.

"Take a seat," Mitchell said as he opened a bottled water and took a long swig.

Chloe sat down beside Zimmerman and waited for Mitchell to sit at his desk. The man looked like something straight out of a workout video. In fact, he reminded her of the P90X guy, whose name she couldn't immediately recall. He was ripped but not large. She couldn't imagine that Mitchell's body mass index even came close to ten percent. Though his tank top was soaked with sweat, Mitchell's hair was still styled to perfection. She wondered how much product he used to keep it looking like that through a strenuous workout. His teeth looked capped, and his fingernails were professionally manicured. A heady mixture of perspiration and aftershave emanated off his body. Mitchell was like a walking billboard for the business.

"How many gyms do you own?" Zimmerman said. "I assume this is a chain business."

Mitchell took another long pull, nearly emptying the bottle before answering.

"Five at present. Though we are looking to add a couple more in the area around Greater Portland."

"We?" Chloe said. "You have partners?"

"My wife, Emily, comes from money. She provides the financial resources while I provide inspiration and perspiration."

Chloe recalled having met a few people whose egos could match that of Mitchell, but not many.

Mitchell tossed the empty bottle across the room in a high arc before it clattered into a nearly empty plastic recycle bin. "Okay, now that we got the niceties out of the way, why exactly are you guys here?"

"We're investigating the murder of Summer Randall," Chloe said.

"I heard about that. Horrible. But what does that have to do with me?"

"We understand that Summer worked for you part-time as a personal trainer," Zimmerman said.

"Yeah, she did the last couple of summers during her time off from college."

"We understand that she stopped working for you fairly recently," Chloe said. "Do you mind telling us why?"

"No idea," Mitchell said.

"See, that's interesting," Zimmerman said. "Because the way we heard it, you let her go."

Mitchell said nothing as he crossed his arms across his chest. Chloe could see he was intentionally flexing his biceps in a lame attempt to be intimidating.

"Perhaps we could take a look at her personnel records," Chloe said. "That would probably help clear this up."

"I, uh, didn't keep them," Mitchell said after a moment's consideration.

"Why not?" Zimmerman said.

"Don't know. Didn't seem to be much point in it after she left."

"Was she a bad employee?" Chloe said.

"No, not at all. The customers all liked her. And she wasn't exactly hard on the eyes. But I wouldn't exactly call her an employee anyway."

"No?" Zimmerman said. "What would you call her, then?"

"She was only seasonal, and most of what she received for working here was access to all of the benefits of a full gym membership."

"Sort of like a barter system?" Chloe said.

"Exactly," Mitchell said.

"Did you have a personal relationship with Summer?" Chloe said, dropping a well-timed bomb.

"What?"

"Seems like a pretty straightforward question, Mr. Mitchell," Chloe said. "Do you need me to repeat it?"

"No. I heard you, and the answer is no. Like I said, I'm married."

Zimmerman turned to Chloe. "It's so nice to meet a young man who still believes in the sanctity of marriage, isn't it?"

Mitchell fixed Zimmerman with a frown that didn't need interpreting.

"I couldn't help but notice you don't wear a wedding ring," Zimmerman said, continuing to press.

"I handle weights and gym equipment every day, Detective. Wearing a ring is a good way to lose a finger."

"Sound thinking," Zimmerman mocked.

"Where were you on the evening of October 7th?" Chloe said.

"I don't remember."

Having expected his answer, Chloe removed a DNA kit from her inside pocket and held it up.

"What's that?" Mitchell said, his Adam's apple bouncing nervously.

"It's a DNA test kit," Chloe said. "We're asking everyone we talk with who is connected to Summer to submit a sample."

"Why?"

"We found trace evidence at the scene of the crime that we know doesn't belong to Summer Randall," Zimmerman said as he slid a consent form across the desk.

"We're taking samples to eliminate everyone from suspicion," Chloe said. "Don't you want to be eliminated?"

Mitchell swallowed again as he stared at the testing kit.

"Look, maybe Summer and I did have a brief thing, okay? But that doesn't mean I had anything to do with her murder."

"No one said you did, Mr. Mitchell," Chloe said, doing her best to project innocence. "Giving us a sample will rule you out as a suspect."

"What about the—you know?"

"The sex you had with Summer," Zimmerman said, poking Mitchell hard with a metaphorical stick.

"If my wife finds out, I'll lose everything."

"Probably should have thought of that before hooking up with one of your employees," Chloe said. "All we're concerned with is finding Summer's killer. If you weren't involved, you have nothing to worry about."

"Yeah," Zimmerman said. "Last I checked, we aren't the marriage police."

"Fine," Mitchell said. "How long will this take? I gotta shower and get back out there."

Chloe beamed a big smile as she opened the kit. "It'll only take a second, Mr. Mitchell."

32

Thursday, October 9, 1:30 p.m

Brock departed Libby's cabin with more questions than answers. Though he hadn't expected much in the way of cooperation from the man, especially after Mathers had taken him into custody on what amounted to a borderline operating under the influence case. Brock understood the danger impaired drivers posed to the public, but this was a murder investigation, and Mathers knew damn well that he was only making Brock's job harder by locking up Ronnie Libby.

On the plus side, he had the partial name of Libby's alibi and sponsor and, even more importantly, Ronnie Libby's DNA.

Still fuming about Mathers, Brock had traveled less than a mile before placing a call to the only Bangor homicide detective with whom he had a history, Detective Ginger Dashofy. Her cell phone and office numbers were still programmed into his contact list. After thinking about how long it had been since they last spoke, he decided on her office number. To his great disappointment, the call went directly to her voicemail. Following her prerecorded greeting, Brock left a brief message, intentionally devoid of too many facts on the off chance that someone else ended up listening to the message.

It took Ginger less than five minutes to return his call.

"Hey, stranger," Ginger said. "Imagine my surprise at getting a voicemail from the fabled Detective Brock Justice."

"Call screening?" Brock said.

"Always. Especially yours."

"Been a long time."

"That's an understatement. Heard all about your transfer up to the williwags last spring. I figured for sure that I'd hear from my old pal as soon as he arrived up in my neck of the woods."

"Yeah, sorry about that, Ginger. Things weren't exactly going too good for me at that point. I should have reached out."

"Damn right you should have."

Her words scolded him, but the tone of her voice made clear that she wasn't really pissed.

"So, now out of the blue I get a cryptic message asking for a favor. If either one of us was still pushing a cruiser, I might think this was one of those calls where someone was looking for a traffic ticket to be fixed."

"Except that would be unethical, Detective Dashofy."

"Not to mention illegal," Ginger said with a laugh. "Okay. So, tell me about this favor you need."

Brock explained that he'd learned of the sudden passing of a woman named Laura Croxford and that it had occurred inside the city of Bangor. "Any chance one of your ilk caught that particular unattended?"

"What makes you think it was an unattended death?" Ginger asked.

"I guess I figured because the paper used those magical words 'unexpected death.' And she was only a young woman."

"Why does it feel like there's a lot more to your request than you're telling me?"

"It's complicated," Brock said.

"It always is with you, Justice."

"So, do you know who caught the case?"

"It just so happens that I did. My partner and I got called out to a local hotel for what might have been an accidental drowning."

Brock felt the hairs prickle at the back of his neck. How likely was it that Evan Mathers would know about the sudden death of a woman that he probably hadn't had any contact with since leaving the state police? Additionally, how could he have known the manner of her death unless he'd either been given a heads-up or had firsthand knowledge? Both possibilities made Brock extremely uneasy.

"And did it turn out that way?" Brock asked at last.

"Oh yeah, she drowned all right. In the hotel tub. Had elevated levels of opioids and alcohol in her system. The medical examiner ruled the death accidental."

Brock said nothing as he digested this new information.

"Why do I get the feeling that you're about to ruin my day?" Ginger said.

"I don't suppose you'd be willing to meet me and share copies of whatever you've got on the case?"

There was a long pause at the other end of the line, and Brock began to wonder if he'd lost the connection.

"You still there?"

"I'm here," Ginger said. "May I ask why you're asking all these questions about a case that we already cleared as accidental?"

"It's a long story. One that would be better shared in person."

"Uh-huh," Ginger said. "When were you hoping to meet?"

"I'm actually in Greenville at the moment, investigating a homicide."

"You know I love you, Brock, but I'm not driving to Greenville just to have you dump all over one of my cases."

"It's not like that. I swear."

"Where have I heard that before? Oh yeah, every asshole I ever dated then broke up with."

Brock let the comment slide. "I could meet you tonight, somewhere between here and Bangor if that works."

"What time?"

33

Thursday, October 9, 3:30 p.m

Brock met up with Chloe and Zimmerman back at the Greenville PSB. State police ERT member Clayton Veilleux was expected to drop by within the hour to pick up whatever samples they had obtained for processing. Each of them recounted their interviews with Dr. Heiden, Chris Mitchell, and Ronnie Libby.

"So, we got samples from all three?" Brock said.

"You sound surprised," Chloe said.

"May have had something to do with the fact that we held back that Summer was pregnant," Zimmerman said with a grin.

"However it happened, they all freely provided samples and signed consent forms," Chloe said. "Besides, we still have blood that needs to be matched from Summer's vehicle."

"Did Mitchell or Heiden admit to being intimate with Summer?" Brock said.

"Heiden didn't," Chloe said. "Told us he hadn't dated any of the nurses."

"What about Mitchell?" Brock said.

"I'd say that's a big ten-four," Zimmerman said. "And he's afraid his wife, a.k.a. Sugar Mama, is going to find out."

Brock knew that their methods would most likely be challenged in court, but all three men had willingly signed consent forms before allowing their DNA to be taken for comparative testing. He knew the men would do anything to avoid being connected to the crime. And the fact that they had actually found blood inside Summer's burglarized vehicle meant that they were looking for more than just a paternal match to Summer's unborn child. It was a maneuver that most trial attorneys referred to as legal sleight of hand.

"I am surprised to hear that none of the three mentioned any knowledge of Summer being with child," Zimmerman said.

"I think Summer may have only recently found out herself," Brock said.

"I agree," Chloe said. "The discarded test kit I found in her wastebasket seemed to indicate that she was still hoping it wasn't true."

"Any luck on Summer's emails or cell phone records?" Brock said.

"The subpoena has been sent to her provider," Zimmerman said. "Wheels tells us he has a contact at the telecommunications company who may be able to put a rush on it."

"And the emails?"

"I just sent the affidavit to Grover," Chloe said. "Waiting to hear back before we find a local judge to sign off on the warrant. Wheels is going to talk me through getting into the hard drive as soon as we have legal standing."

"Good," Brock said. "Feels like we're finally beginning to make some headway."

"Now if we can just get Clay to get these samples analyzed and compared quickly," Zimmerman said.

"Anything new from the tip lines?" Brock said as he looked through the door at the four unmanned tables inside the garage bay.

"Nada," Chloe said.

"How would we even know?" Brock said.

"Worry not, young Jedi," Zimmerman said. "Each of those lines has been forwarded to the Piscataquis County Comm Center. Any hot leads come in and we'll be notified immediately."

Brock wasn't surprised that nothing had come from the exercise generated by Congresswoman Randall's shortsighted attempt to grab the reins of their investigation into her daughter's murder. But he was surprised the calls had dried up so quickly. There was a time when ten grand would entice a boatload of crazies to show themselves. Either inflation had made the reward irrelevant or there were fewer crazies in the world than Brock thought. He was betting on the former.

"Got a hot date?" Chloe said.

"What are you talking about?" Brock said.

"You keep checking the time. Figured you've got someplace to be."

Brock glanced over at Zimmerman. He was wearing a Cheshire Cat grin.

"If you must know, I'm meeting up with an old friend for dinner."

"Good," Zimmerman said. "That means I get to pick where we eat tonight."

"How do you figure?" Chloe said.

"Um, because I'm senior to you, and I want pizza."

"Guess I know what I'm having tonight," Chloe said, her attention returning to the murder board.

They all turned to the sound of Clayton Veilleux's knuckles rapping on the metal doorframe of their makeshift office.

"Heard you guys might have something for me."

34

Thursday, October 9, 7:30 p.m

The town of Dover-Foxcroft, formerly a prosperous mill town where everything from woolen cloth, wood siding, and pianos were once manufactured, is the largest populated community in Piscataquis County. Of course, boasting the largest population takes on an entirely different meaning in the northern half of the Pine Tree State. The name came into being following the 1922 merger of neighboring towns Foxcroft and Dover. Separated geographically by the Piscataquis River, the oddly named municipality had long since fallen out of favor with investors as automation became the norm, jobs moved overseas, and repurposing became the name of the game.

Detective Dashofy was already waiting for Brock when he walked into the East Main Street pizzeria. The aroma of basil, tomato, and garlic permeated the air of the overly warm establishment. Ginger sat alone at a corner table with her back to the wall, a typical position for anyone working in the field of law enforcement longer than six months. As both detectives knew, officer survival trumped everything. She greeted Brock with a wave and gestured to an empty seat.

"I was beginning to wonder if you might stand me up, Justice," she said as she treated Brock to a warm embrace.

"Never," Brock said as he slid into the chair across the table from hers. "Getting away turned out to be more difficult than I thought."

"Sneaking away, don't you mean?" she said, giving him a sly smirk.

"That too."

"Have you eaten yet?"

"No, and I'm starving."

"Good. Then let's get our order in before they close the kitchen."

"It's only seven thirty," Brock said. "I thought this place stayed open until nine."

"Yeah, when there are actual customers. Look around you. You're in the sticks. Pat's Pizza closes early in these parts," Ginger said, attempting her best Downeast accent.

Ginger flagged down the waitress as Brock quickly surveyed the offerings on the menu. He was pleasantly surprised to find the food choices were nearly identical to the locations in and around Bangor. As a bachelor, one of Brock's go-to locations for takeout was Pat's Pizza. When it was his turn, he ordered a large pizza topped with ground beef, green peppers, and Greek olives along with a Diet Pepsi.

"A large?" Ginger said. "Are you really going to eat all that?"

"I didn't plan to, but since I'm currently living out of my suitcase in a Greenville motel, I figured I might be able to manage breakfast and lunch out of the leftovers."

"Sound thinking."

They spent the time waiting for their food to take care of the small talk and catch up. Ginger told him that she had followed the Evan Mathers trial closely, but the outcome had left her conflicted. She was pleased to see Mathers cleared of what she imagined was a nearly impossible split-second judgment call that went badly, but she also knew the fresh hell that awaited Brock following his testimony against a fellow trooper.

"I didn't envy you for finding yourself in that situation," Ginger said.

"Yeah, I hear that a lot," Brock said.

She paused before speaking again. Her expression told Brock she was holding something back.

"What?" Brock said.

"If you could do it over again, I mean now that you've seen how it turned out, would you?"

Brock didn't hesitate before answering. "I wouldn't do a thing differently. What's right is right."

Ginger stared at him as she sipped soda from a straw. "Gotta admire a man of principle. That's becoming a rare commodity these days."

"You wouldn't have done the same thing?" Brock said.

"I don't know that I could answer that until I'd seen what you saw. By the way, I see the rumors about you are true."

"What rumors?"

She pointed at the unadorned ring finger of his left hand.

"Yeah," Brock said. "Turns out working homicides wasn't conducive to a solid marriage."

"Why I never took the plunge," she said with a wink.

Their food arrived just as Brock was about to broach the reason for their clandestine meeting. Both detectives dug in without fanfare.

"So, tell me what's got you all hot and bothered about my accidental death by drowning case?" Ginger said as she pulled a thin file folder from her bag and slid it across the table.

Brock finished chewing his bite of pizza before he answered. "I don't believe it was an accident."

"How could you possibly know that?"

"Because I believe the victim may have been blackmailing Evan Mathers."

Ginger's jaw went slack. "Mathers again? You're not serious."

Brock spent the next twenty minutes filling her in on what he knew about Laura Croxford and about her unknown relationship with Evan Mathers. Ginger listened quietly while picking at several of the rogue pepperoni slices scattered around her plate. When Brock had finished sharing as much information as he was comfortable sharing, he sat back and waited for her to respond.

"Well, that's quite a story, Brock. And to be honest, I wasn't sure what you were going to tell me, but a murder certainly wasn't on my radar." She let out a deep sigh, as if trying to figure out how much deeper she wanted to get dragged into whatever this was.

"How much of what you're telling me came out at the trial?" Dashofy said.

"None of it," Brock said.

"Tell me you're kidding," Ginger said, wide-eyed.

Brock shook his head. "Wish I was."

"You didn't tell anyone about Evan's relationship with Kirke's girlfriend? Not even the prosecutor?"

"Oh, I told them. The prosecutor didn't want to muddy the waters with the jury. He felt the better strategy was to keep to the facts."

"Those being?"

"Evan shooting an unarmed Darrell Kirke after he had surrendered his weapon. Any mention of an alleged relationship between Mathers and Croxford by me would constitute hearsay and likely be explained away by the defense as nothing more than Croxford operating as a snitch for Evan. It wasn't like I had actual proof that they were sleeping together."

Ginger pushed the remnants of her meal away as she digested what he had told her.

"It seemed like a good strategy at the time," Brock said.

"Until Evan was found not guilty," Ginger said.

"Yeah, until then."

"I still don't understand how they wouldn't already know about the connection between Evan and this woman. The state police still require confidential informants to be registered, right? There had to be a CI file and some vetting that took place."

"Croxford was an off-the-books informant."

"Jesus, how stupid is that?"

"Maybe. But it happens."

"Still, the state police fired Evan, right?"

Brock shook his head. "That was my understanding. I've since learned that he was allowed to resign in good standing."

"That's bullshit," Ginger said. "Christ, he may have killed a guy in cold blood over a woman."

Brock laid his hand over the file folder. "Not just a woman. This woman. Laura Croxford."

Dashofy shook her head in disgust. "Why did I ever return your call? I don't need this crap in my life, Justice."

"I haven't told you the best part," Brock said.

"Oh goody. There's more?"

"Evan is now working for the Piscataquis County Sheriff's Department as a road deputy."

"You're kidding. How is it that Evan's certification wasn't pulled by the criminal justice academy?"

Brock shrugged. "Politics?"

"God, I hate that word," Dashofy said.

"Tell me about this investigation," Brock said. "Did you or your partner have any doubts about Croxford's death being accidental?"

"Come on," Dashofy said. "You know better than that. A good investigator always has doubts. We look for things that other people miss or happily accept on blind faith."

"And?"

"And truthfully, it did bother me that Croxford would drive all the way up to Bangor to stay at a second-rate hotel alone. Most people come for the gambling and stay at the Hollywood Casino or somewhere close by."

"But not her?"

"No. It would have made more sense to me if she had been planning to meet someone there."

"But she didn't?"

"Not that we could find. And believe me, we looked. The only fingerprints we found in the entire room belonged to the victim. The vodka bottle, the mixer, the bathroom. Even the television remote."

"Wasn't that in itself a little odd?" Brock said.

"What do you mean?"

"I mean, how clean do they keep rooms at a second-rate hotel? Seems to me that there would be prints other than Laura's on everything."

"From other customers, you mean," Dashofy said absently as the idea sunk in.

"Bingo. What about calls or texts on her phone? I'm assuming you located her cell."

"We did. There weren't any texts pertaining to her Bangor trip, but there were several calls to and from a burner phone. No voicemail messages."

"What about security video from the hotel?"

"The only working camera was in the lobby. Croxford checked in alone."

"In other words, it would have been relatively easy for someone to lure her up to Bangor using a burner phone, get her drunk and drugged and unable to defend herself, and drown her in the tub, right?"

"Must be nice to be able to sit there and speculate like that about my case. Only problem I see is you don't have any proof that it was murder. Nor do you have any proof that Evan Mathers had anything to do with what happened to her."

"Not yet."

"Brock, listen, you know I love you. And you know I think you're one of the most dedicated detectives I've ever had the pleasure to work with."

"Here comes the 'but,'" Brock said.

"I think you might not be seeing things clearly. Look, I get it. You're pissed that Evan got away with a bad shoot. Those incidents make all of us look like crap. Not to mention making it a hundred times harder to do our jobs. But it feels to me like you're taking it personally that he wasn't found guilty at trial. Like it's some reflection on you."

"It does reflect on me, Ginger. They questioned my recall during the trial. Used the fact that I was seeing a shrink following the incident to imply that I might not have seen what I thought I saw. You know how it works. I was required to be cleared by a department-sanctioned psychologist before I could return to active duty. The defense theory was a complete fabrication. I know what I witnessed that day. I saw Evan Mathers gun down an unarmed man. A man who was sleeping with Mathers's girlfriend."

"A fact that they wouldn't let you testify to," Ginger said.

Brock said nothing. He couldn't tell if she was playing devil's advocate or if she too thought he was crazy.

"Are you two all set?" the waitress said. "We're getting ready to close up for the night."

Brock looked around, surprised to find the entire dining room empty.

"Sorry about that," Brock said. "Guess we lost track of time."

"No problem. Would you like separate checks?"

"Just one," Ginger said before Brock could respond.

"How about a box for your leftover pizza?" the waitress said as she eyed Brock's remaining slices.

"That'd be great."

"Be right back."

"You don't have to do this," Brock said.

"I know I don't," Ginger said. "I'm doing it because I want to."

"Thanks."

"Look, I'm not saying that you might not be one hundred percent right about everything. Maybe you are. Maybe Evan did shoot that Kirke guy on purpose. Maybe he even had a reason to want Croxford dead so she couldn't go public with his secret. Even if he couldn't be tried again for manslaughter, she certainly could damage his reputation by going public. Even put an end to his law enforcement career."

"Not to mention the legal ramifications of having every defense attorney in Maine filing motions to have his cases overturned," Brock said.

"Look, Brock, the problem I'm having is that I've got nothing that validates what you're telling me about their relationship, nor do I have any evidence to link Evan to her death."

"What if I learned something that would cause you to take another look at this case?" Brock said. "Would you consider reopening it?"

Ginger glanced at the check, then handed it back to the waitress along with a credit card. She waited for the woman to depart before answering. "Maybe. It would depend on what you had. And I couldn't promise to reopen it, not officially, anyway. My boss would have to give the okay for that."

Brock nodded his understanding while he boxed up his remaining slices. He knew all too well how pissed Lt. Cumberland would be if she found out he was moonlighting on the Randall case to chase down something that was long over and done with, at least as far as the Bangor police were concerned.

"And honestly, I'm not sure I want to dive into the shitstorm that something like this could kick up. You're talking about my career, Brock. And my reputation. I mean, not to be cruel about it, but look what your courtroom testimony did to your career."

There was nothing in her reasoning that Brock could argue with. His decision to testify against a fellow trooper had come at an extremely high price. Derailing his rising star in the world of Southern Maine homicide investigation and getting him transferred to the northern reaches of nowhere. His marriage, already on shaky ground, had ended due in large part to the stress of the shooting aftermath and the trial. He had lost untold law enforcement friends and still read the suspicion in the face of every cop he met. Brock knew he was asking Ginger to stick her neck out for him, based on nothing more than a gut feeling that Evan had been involved in Laura Croxford's untimely death. And, as he'd learned the hard way, following the jury's not guilty verdict, being right did nothing to protect you from public perception or the politics of policing.

"Do you have anything more than a suspicion that Evan Mathers was involved in this woman's death?" Ginger asked.

Brock paused to consider his next words carefully. He knew he was already on thin ice with her. He didn't want to give her a reason to shut him out completely.

"Didn't you wonder how I knew about Croxford's death in the first place?" Brock said after a moment.

"Truthfully? I hadn't given it a lot of thought. How did you find out?"

"Evan told me."

For a long moment, Ginger didn't respond. "He tell you anything else?"

"Yeah. He knew the cause of death was accidental drowning."

Ginger's eyes widened. "We never made that information public."

"Exactly," Brock said.

35

Friday, October 10, 7:30 a.m

Brock awoke exhausted. Upon returning to the Moose Mountain Inn the previous evening, he had spent several hours looking over the Croxford case file and taking notes. Reaching out blindly to kill the alarm on his cell phone, he only managed to knock it off the nightstand onto the floor. As usual when working on a murder investigation, or in this case, two separate murder investigations, his brain didn't allow for anything even close to a good night's rest. He dreamt about everything from Laura Croxford's drowning to the shootout with the Kirke brothers, to Summer Randall fleeing through the darkened woods for her life. As is frequently the case in dreams, the three unrelated incidents merged into one. But in the light of day, the intertwining made zero sense.

Brock quickly showered and dressed for the day. A check of his go-bag confirmed that he was running dangerously low on clean socks and underwear. If they didn't break the Randall case open soon, he would need to hit the nearest clothing store or see if the inn had a washer and dryer on site.

He arrived at their makeshift headquarters at the PSB to find Chloe, Zimmerman, and Chief Leavitt already gathered there. Brock wasn't sure he liked the idea of Leavitt getting eyes on the murder board. Seated among the investigators enjoying a cup of coffee was a new face Brock hadn't seen before. Brock was even less happy that a stranger was privy to their work.

"Good morning, sunshine," Zimmerman joked. "Nice of you to join us."

"Sorry I'm late," Brock said, catching Chloe's look of disapproval. It was clear that she hadn't bought his story about meeting a friend for dinner. Chloe wasn't stupid. She'd likely ascertained that he was moonlighting. Clearly she didn't approve.

Brock's attention turned to the middle-aged man dressed in a khaki uniform seated at the head of the table.

"Brock, I'd like you to meet Wilber Labbe, long-time warden service investigator," Chloe said.

"Brock Justice," he said as he leaned over the table and offered his hand.

"Pleased to meet you, Detective," Labbe said as he solidly gripped the offering with a dry and callused hand, precisely what Brock had expected of a seasoned outdoorsman.

Chief Leavitt jumped in to offer up an explanation for Labbe's presence. "Will has been patrolling this area of the state for as many years as I've been in law enforcement. He returned my call late yesterday with some information he thinks might be relevant to Summer's murder."

"Do tell," Brock said.

Labbe cleared his throat before speaking. "Not sure if it's related to your case or not, but I thought it might be worth mentioning. We've been having a problem with poachers operating in this area."

"Poachers?" Brock said.

"Yeah, some backwoods folks who feel that the state laws on hunting don't apply to them. Hunting game, specifically deer, out of season. We've got a few up in this area who like to work the woods between Lily Bay and Kokadjo, where I understand Summer Randall was running."

"Hunting around the hiking trails doesn't exactly sound safe," Zimmerman said.

"It isn't," Labbe said. "Even during hunting season."

"Any idea who these poachers are?" Chloe said.

"Actually, I do," Labbe said as he dug a crumpled piece of paper from the pocket of his field jacket and handed it across the table to Chloe. "Here are the most likely suspects. All three men have at least one conviction for hunting out of season and a few other hunting-related crimes."

"And you're thinking what?" Zimmerman said. "That one of these desperados got caught by Summer hunting out of season and they killed her for it? Sounds a little extreme, doesn't it?"

"You familiar with the jail time or the hefty fines associated with some of these crimes, Detective?" Labbe said.

Zimmerman shook his head. "Can't say as I am. I must have missed the tree-hugger courses during basic training at the academy."

Labbe smirked at the comment before firing back. "Probably the same week they were teaching you how to stop a car on the highway."

"Ouch," Chloe said.

"Touché," Zimmerman said.

Brock immediately knew he was going to like working with Warden Labbe.

"It does sound like a bit of an overreaction," Chloe said as she handed the names to Brock. "Killing a witness to illegal hunting."

"If you're thinking like a normal person," Labbe said. "But some of these folks depend on these illegal methods to keep food on the table. To them it is literally life and death. They don't believe they have to live by the laws of the state."

"You're talking about sovereign citizens?" Brock said as he copied the names and relevant information into his notebook.

"Some of them definitely fit that bill," Labbe said. "With others, though, it's more of a distrust of their fellow man. One of the names I included on that list, Peter Bragg, is a decorated war hero. Local boy who served his country. Three tours in the Middle East."

"That sounds like a good thing," Chloe said.

"You'd think so," Labbe continued. "But Bragg came back a broken man. Now he mostly keeps to himself whenever possible. Kind of an antisocial hermit. I'm not saying he had anything to do with killing Summer Randall, but I am saying he might be worth a look."

"And you know where to locate these men?" Brock said.

Labbe nodded. "I do. Matter of fact, I might be able to do you one better than putting you in touch with them."

"How's that?" Zimmerman said.

Chief Leavitt weighed in again. "Will is also an experienced pilot."

"If you want, I'd be happy to fly you around the area, give you a bird's-eye view of the woods where Summer was attacked as well as its proximity to the compounds where these guys reside."

"That would be great," Chloe said enthusiastically. "When can we go?"

36

Friday, October 10, 8:30 a.m

"Where were you last night?" Chloe said as their impromptu meeting with the game warden broke up and she and Brock shuffled to the kitchen for coffee.

"I was just following up on a couple of leads," Brock said.

"Leads on the Randall case?"

"Um, yeah," Brock replied absently.

"Oh, I thought you were meeting a friend for dinner."

"That too."

"Which ones?"

"Which ones what?"

"Leads," Chloe said. "I'd like to know so we don't duplicate our efforts."

"Don't worry about it," Brock said as he poured himself a cup of coffee from the carafe. "These leads weren't on our list."

"You're freelancing again, aren't you?"

"I'm not, okay?"

"I need to know your head is in the game, Brock," Chloe said. "I know you, and I know you've got a hard-on for Evan Mathers. Just tell me you're not up to something to try and get him canned from his current job."

"Do me a favor, Chloe. Let it go, okay?"

Chloe stared at him, unblinking. "You do realize we're partners, right? I mean, the last time we worked a case, it seemed like you had some trouble grasping that particular concept, right up until the time I saved your ass."

Brock had always had trouble with the idea of trust and sharing the load when it came to investigations. And that same close-to-the-vest mentality had nearly cost him his life at the hands of someone he thought he could trust. But change is hard. Breaking a habit that he'd had since being hired as a trooper was near impossible.

"Just know that since we are partners, like it or not, we need to be able to trust each other," Chloe continued. "If you go off on some tangent instead of keeping your eye on the prize, it won't just be your ass on the line. Zim and I are in this with you."

Brock opened his mouth to say something he would most likely regret, when Warden Labbe stuck his head around the corner.

"Who's ready for a bird's-eye view of some fantastic foliage?"

"I am," Chloe said enthusiastically.

Brock couldn't help wondering how much of their conversation Labbe had overheard.

Twenty minutes later, they were at the Greenville Forestry Seaplane Base preparing for takeoff.

"This is quite a plane," Chloe said as she buckled in on the passenger side of the cockpit.

"She's my baby," Labbe said. "Cessna 185F Skywagon. We've been through a lot together."

"How fast can she go?" Chloe said.

"Well, she's rated for one seventy-eight, but she cruises pretty nicely at about a hundred and sixty knots."

"Wish my unmarked was capable of that," Chloe said.

"It sure would help your response time," Labbe said.

"How many planes do you guys operate?" Brock said from the back seat, where he sat next to Zimmerman.

"If by 'you guys' you mean the Maine Warden Service, we have three fixed-wing aircraft."

"I would think you'd need more than that given the area you have to cover," Zimmerman said.

"More planes would mean more pilots, which of course means more money. Storage, repairs, training, it all costs extra. The good thing about these planes is that they are adaptable for different seasons."

"How do you mean?" Chloe said.

"At the moment, we are bobbing up and down in the waters of Moosehead Lake, but change out the landing gear and we could just as easily be sitting on a remote airport tarmac or taking off from a snowfield with skis."

"Didn't realize these things were so versatile," Brock said.

"Kind of like having three planes in one," Labbe said as he throttled up the engine. "Just an FYI, things could get a little bumpy today. We got a stiff breeze coming out of the northwest."

Brock looked over at Zimmerman, who had grown quiet. The senior detective had a death grip on the seat cushion, and his face had taken on the colorless pallor of a corpse.

"You okay, Zim?" Brock said, shouting to be heard above the engine noise.

"Just ducky," Zimmerman shouted back unconvincingly. "I love to fly."

At Labbe's signal, the deckhand untethered the plane from the dock. Labbe used the rudder pedals to steer them out into the dark choppy waters of the lake. Brock was amazed at how blue the sky was, Prussian colored with only a few wispy clouds racing past the lake. Bright sunlight reflected off the brilliant red and gold leaves of the deciduous trees along the shoreline as far as they could see. After clearing the first set of marker buoys, Labbe throttled up again. Brock could tell by the difference in pitch of the three-hundred-horsepower engine that this time the warden meant business. Water sprayed the side windows as the pontoons glided surprisingly smoothly through the waves. In less than a minute, the Cessna had pulled free of the lake's grasp and soared skyward.

Brock grinned as he caught another glimpse of Zimmerman. The detective's eyes were squinted shut, and his hands had curled into talons. Perhaps the flight would be fun after all.

Labbe handed each of them a pair of Bluetooth headsets. Each was equipped with a microphone that allowed them to communicate with each other without the need to holler to be heard above the engine noise.

"If you all look down to our left, you'll see Moose Bay," Labbe said. "Up ahead of us is Deer Island."

"This is such a beautiful area," Chloe said.

"It truly is," Labbe agreed. "Autumn makes it even more magical, but no matter the season, I've been blessed to work this region for as long as I have. It's hard to believe that an attack like the one on Summer Randall could really happen here."

Brock agreed, but deep down inside he knew, as they all did, that evil, even in the outer reaches of Maine's natural beauty and tranquility, was alive and well. There was never any geographic escape from it. Wherever humans reside, so does the dark side of their nature.

Labbe continued in a straight path directly above the lake, ascending to a thousand feet. "Off to our right is Lily Bay State Park and Lily Bay itself. See that sliver of water off in the distance?"

"I see it," Chloe said.

"That's First Roach Pond and Kokadjo beyond that."

"What's the big mountain in the distance?" Brock asked.

"That, Detective Justice, is Mount Katahdin. Maine's tallest mountain. She's a beauty, isn't she?"

"I'll say," Chloe said.

"Gets her name from the Penobscot Indians. 'Katahdin' literally means 'greatest mountain.' Those Native Americans really had a gift for understatement."

Brock checked on Zimmerman, who was keeping silent. His ashen color hadn't improved, but he had relaxed his death grip on the seat.

"Won't be long now before Katahdin is covered in snow," Labbe said.

"But it's only the first week of October," Brock said.

"Winter comes early at this latitude, son," Labbe said. "Not to mention altitude. The peak of Katahdin is approximately one mile above sea level."

Brock gazed out over the wooded landscape while wondering how much longer before the first snow coated the ground in Greenville, obliterating any evidence they might have missed pertaining to the murder of

Summer Randall. He thought about the falling leaves he'd seen as he drove along Moosehead Lake the previous day. That same leaf drop portended the time running out in their window to solve this case.

"Earth to Justice," Chloe said, her voice breaking through Brock's reverie.

"Sorry," Brock said. "What was that?"

Labbe chuckled into his mouthpiece. "I said, did you want to see more of the area, or did you want to focus specifically on the locations of the men on the list I gave you?"

"I'd like to get a look at those properties to see how close they're located to where we believe the attack occurred."

"You're the boss," Labbe said as he banked the Cessna slightly to the right.

37

Friday, October 10, 9:30 a.m

"If you look straight down along the right shoreline of the lake, you can see Lily Bay Road winding its way from the lower bay up toward Kokadjo," Labbe said.

"I can see the area where we found Summer's body," Chloe said. "Looks like it isn't far from State Park Road."

"Good eyes, Detective," Labbe said. "That is the main access road to Lily Bay State Park."

"Where are the hiking trails that Summer was running on?" Brock said. "I can't see them."

"You wouldn't be able to make those out, not from up here, anyway. Not until the leaf drop picks up some. Eventually, the forest canopy will be thin enough that the running trails will be every bit as clear as the roads."

Brock sighed as he considered their conundrum. Too early in the fall season for good visibility from the air, but right on the cusp of the ground being covered in snow. Neither condition would be helpful in solving the case.

"How are you holding up, Zim?" Chloe said as she turned in her seat to look at him.

"Your friend have an aversion to flying?" Labbe chuckled.

"To crashing," Zimmerman said, his voice devoid of humor.

"Well, you're in good hands, Detective Zimmerman," Labbe said. "I've only had one bad landing in twenty-five years of flying."

"Why doesn't that make me feel any better?" Zimmerman groaned.

Labbe's attention returned to the scenery below them. "If you look to the area north of the woods where the running trails are located, you can just make out the thin threads of the ATV trails where they cut through the woods. Those are the trails the guys on my short list of poachers use to get around."

"Why wouldn't they just use the roads?" Zimmerman said. "Don't most of them drive pickups?"

"Too easy to get caught transporting illegal kills," Labbe said. "Nothing will get a warden's attention quicker than a pickup dripping blood from its payload. Especially when the truck is driven by a known poacher."

"Makes sense," Brock said.

"Then how do they transport the deer or whatever?" Zimmerman said.

"ATVs. Once they kill the animal, they field-dress it on site, then strap it down to the front or back of the ATV and transport it through the woods to their slaughterhouse."

"So, there might be evidence of a fresh kill somewhere near the place we believe Summer was attacked," Chloe said.

"Could be," Labbe said. "If any of these desperados were out hunting illegally that night, it's entirely possible," Labbe said.

"How would we locate something like that?" Brock said.

"Easiest way is to let the birds show you," Labbe said. "Crows, turkey vultures, any of the birds that feed on carrion will often circle the area from above."

"What about the hunters?" Zimmerman said.

"What about 'em?" Labbe said.

"Do they just wander around willy-nilly looking for animals?"

"Maybe at one time, but these days hunters have gotten tech savvy. They avail themselves of game cameras, calls, and bait to see where the big deer are located."

"Sounds like cheating to me," Chloe said.

Labbe laughed again. "Young lady, I believe you just defined poaching."

As they continued over the northeast side of the lake, Labbe pointed out the compounds of the poachers he had previously identified. By Brock's estimation, only two of the usual suspects lived close enough to the woods in question to warrant checking them out. But short of a witness putting one of them on site at the time of Summer's attack meant they would be relying on the cooperation of both men, not evidence. In other words, they had no stick to hold over them. And barring an ill-advised admission from one of the men, unlikely given their frequent contact with law enforcement, there would be no way of obtaining the probable cause necessary for a warrant to search either premises.

"You see that clearing right below us?" Labbe said. "The one with the big steel Quonset hut?"

They all nodded.

"That is the Bragg compound. The war vet I told you about."

"Is he the most likely to have been hunting in the area where Summer was attacked?" Chloe said.

"Well, he is a nearly constant offender," Labbe said. "He never stops trying to outsmart us, and he never stops hunting."

"Is he the most intelligent of the names you provided?" Zimmerman said.

"By far," Labbe said. "And trust me, he knows his rights. Ought to. He's been through the legal system enough."

"You think he'd be willing to speak to us?" Chloe said.

"Only one way to find out."

38

Friday, October 10, 11:30 a.m

After completing the aerial tour of the lake, specifically the area surrounding Lily Bay State Park, Warden Labbe swung the Cessna around and returned to the dock. As he had previously cautioned, the wind speed had increased since they took off from the lower bay. The landing was a bit tricky, as he had to fight to keep the wings level to the surface of the water. After a few bumpy attempts, Labbe was able to set the pontoons down into the waves. As he steered toward the dock and cut back on the throttle, he checked in on everyone.

"Everybody hold their breakfast down okay?" Labbe said.

"Mine's still here," Brock said.

"Mine too," Chloe laughed.

"What about you, Detective Zimmerman?" Labbe said.

"Just let me know when we're tied up to the dock."

The deckhand was awaiting their arrival as Labbe slid up beside the launch. The young man made quick work of tying off the plane. Labbe cut the engine on the Cessna and removed his communication headset.

"Welcome back to terra firma, Detectives," Labbe said. "We hope you enjoyed your flight."

"I have no words," Zimmerman grumbled.

It was well past noon by the time they rejoined Chief Leavitt at the Dockside Inn and Tavern for lunch.

"How was your aerial tour of our little hamlet?" Leavitt said after they had each placed their orders with the waiter.

"It's one of the most beautiful places I've ever visited," Chloe said. "And I grew up in The County."

"I'm not sure everyone is in agreement on that point," Labbe teased.

"No," Zimmerman said. "Greenville is picturesque as long as you're viewing it from the ground."

Labbe chuckled as he hoisted his tumbler of soda. "I'll drink to that."

"You're not a fan of flying either?" Brock said.

"Didn't used to be," Labbe said. "One of my old flight instructors used to say: 'If God had meant for man to fly, he would have given us wings.' I think he may have pilfered that particular line."

"Who said that?" Chloe said.

"Icarus," Zimmerman grumbled.

"Actually, I think it was Bishop Milton Wright," Labbe said with a chuckle.

"Who?" Chloe said.

"The father of the Wright brothers," Brock said.

"Any thoughts on that list of poachers?" Labbe said.

"Yeah," Brock said. "Based solely on his proximity to the running trails and what we know about him, I'd say Peter Bragg might be our best lead to chase down."

Zimmerman weighed in. "Yeah, even if he wasn't hunting in the area, he might know something that he'd be willing to share with us."

"While I wouldn't count him out for knowing something, I wouldn't hold out too much hope that he'll be helpful," Labbe said.

"Any suggestions on how we might best approach him?" Brock said.

"It really depends on what kind of mood you catch him in," Labbe said. "There was the man I knew before his three tours in the Middle East, and there's the one I know now. Trust me when I tell you that those two men bear almost no resemblance to each other."

All eyes turned as their waiter approached holding a precariously overloaded tray of delightful-smelling entrees.

"Who had the tuna melt with fries?"

"Right here," Chloe said.

After they'd eaten and the waiter refilled their drinks, they sat looking out across the lake, watching as several seaplanes arrived for the long weekend.

"Good thing you got a spot at the docks before they filled up," Chloe said.

"I'll let you in on a little secret," Labbe said with a wink. "The warden service always has a spot."

"Good to know people in high places," Zimmerman said.

"Somebody's feeling better," Brock said.

"And all it took was putting both feet on the ground," Zimmerman said.

"How many planes do you normally get coming in during foliage season?" Chloe asked Chief Leavitt.

"Normally? A dozen or so. Nothing like the International Seaplane Fly-In festival we had here last month. There were around fifty or so that stayed for the entire event. COVID really put a damper on things for a couple of years. We just started to get our feet back under us last year when we had about thirty-five. Hopefully the leaf peepers will turn out in droves this year."

"And we don't care how they get here, do we, Chief?" Labbe added.

"That, we don't," Leavitt said. "Autumn provides a much-needed financial boost to the area. Places like Greenville thrive on the tourist dollar, and we only get so many chances a year. Even the weather seems to be cooperating so far."

Brock didn't want to shatter the bonding that appeared to be taking place, but they still had a case to solve and murderer to catch, and Labbe had handed them a very probable new lead.

"So, Warden, what are your thoughts on the best way to approach Peter Bragg?" Brock said.

"Sounds like the best way would be very carefully," Zimmerman quipped.

"Yup," Labbe said. "Can't argue with that sentiment. Not one bit."

"We are planning to talk to each of the men on your list of poachers, though, right?" Chloe said. "I mean, I know you think Bragg is the most likely to know something, but we don't want to look like we're unfairly homing in on him."

"Chloe's right," Brock said. "If we're going to do this, we want to cast a wide net. The lead is the poaching, not one individual poacher. If we can tell each of the people on that list that we're talking to everyone, they'll be far less likely to raise a fuss about us targeting them."

"I agree," Labbe said. "I still think you should start with Bragg, but talking to all of them is a far better strategy. As for how to make the approach, I think it might go better if I do it and take one of you with me. Too many cops show up and Peter's liable to get jittery."

"And believe you me," Leavitt said. "You do not want to make this guy nervous."

"I'll go with you," Chloe said.

"Why you?" Zimmerman said.

"Because I'm charming and far less threatening than either of you."

"I'm wounded that you find me even remotely threatening," Zimmerman said.

"She's right, though," Brock said. "Given your bad jokes, you're likely to get everyone shot."

"Okay, then," Labbe said. "Sounds like it's settled business. Chloe and I will take a ride up to see Bragg within the hour."

"What about us?" Zimmerman said.

"We'll be stationed right around the corner," Brock said. "If anything seems off, you give us a shout on the radio, and we'll come on the double."

39

Friday, October 10, 1:30 p.m

Forty-five minutes later, Chloe and Warden Labbe rolled into Peter Bragg's dooryard. Located off Scammon Road near Upper Wilson Pond, the property—or compound, as Labbe referred to it—consisted of a two-story rough plank–sided structure that Chloe assumed was the main living quarters, the large gray Quonset hut they'd seen from the air, and several wooden outbuildings of various sizes. The compound was bordered on all sides by dense forest consisting of maples, birches, and evergreens. The dooryard immediately surrounding the buildings was mostly razed gravel and weeds. Chloe wondered if Bragg's main consideration was more about keeping a low-maintenance property or an open sightline, especially given his history of lawbreaking.

"That's Bragg right there," Labbe said as they drove up the dirt incline toward a man hosing mud from a green-and-black all-terrain vehicle. Aside from turning his head slightly in their direction, the man made no other movements that might have caused Chloe any concern.

Bragg was tall and athletically built with close-cropped brown hair. He wore dark glasses with reflective lenses, green-and-black camouflage BDU pants, an untucked plaid chamois shirt, and Corcoran jump boots. His attire made him look like he had either just returned from a combat mission or was about to head out on one.

"I never asked," Chloe said, keeping her eyes on Bragg. "Does this guy live alone?"

"Far as I know," Labbe said. "At least I've never seen anyone else here."

Labbe braked to a stop about thirty feet from Bragg, kicking up a cloud of dust that slowly drifted past them.

"Let me get out first and make the initial approach," Labbe said. "No point in spooking him unnecessarily. He'll recognize me, but he has no idea who you are."

Chloe's portable radio crackled. "You guys arrive yet?" Brock's voice said through the static.

"Just pulled into the dooryard," Chloe said. "Bragg's here, and we're about to make contact."

"Be careful," Zimmerman's voice interjected.

Chloe rolled her eyes for Labbe's benefit as she keyed the mic. "Yes, Dad."

She paused a beat for Labbe to exit the truck before following. Bragg kept his focus fixed in their direction while maintaining the stream of water blasting at the ATV. Chloe scanned the property, looking for anything that might be considered a threat. The axe leaning against a nearby woodpile. The homemade game targets near the edge of the tree line, each with several arrows still protruding from them, were a clear indicator that Bragg was proficient with a bow. One thing was clear to Chloe: if they ever had to take this guy into custody, he was more than capable of resisting and of putting up one hell of a fight.

"Afternoon, Pete," Labbe said, greeting the man with a wave.

"Warden," Bragg said as he released the sprayer, stopping the stream of water, and turned his body to face them head on.

As Chloe eyed the fixed-blade hunting knife sheathed to Bragg's belt, she couldn't help but recall Dr. Isleborn's description of the murder weapon.

"What's up?" Bragg said.

"Wondered if you might have a spare moment to chat?"

Bragg nodded his head in Chloe's direction. "Who's she?"

"This is a detective friend of mine, Chloe Wright."

"Warden detective?"

"State police," Chloe said.

Bragg's eyes narrowed. "What do you want with me?"

Chloe knew despite Labbe's laid-back, grandfatherly approach to this situation, if things were about to go sideways with Bragg, now was the time.

"We need to chat with you about the death of Summer Randall," Chloe said.

Brock had parked in a gravel turnout off Scammon Road about a half mile from the private drive that led to Bragg's compound. After donning his ballistic vest and state police raid jacket, Brock nervously paced back and forth beside the unmarked Ford while awaiting the next radio contact with Chloe or Warden Labbe. He eyed the dark clouds moving in above them and wondered if they were a sign. He had never wanted a cigarette more in his entire adult life than he did at that moment.

"What do you think's happening?" Zimmerman said, perched on the passenger seat with the door open.

"I don't know, do I?" Brock snapped.

"Hey, brother, relax. No need to bite my head off. I'm worried about them too, ya know."

"Sorry," Brock said. "It's just—we shouldn't have let her go in there alone."

"She isn't alone. She's got Warden Labbe with her."

"A crusty old warden isn't going to be much help if some real shit goes down, Zim."

"Um, that crusty old warden has been facing down armed hunters in these woods longer than you or I have been on the job, amigo. Besides, he's the only one of us that has a history with this guy. If Bragg does decide to cooperate, it will be because Labbe interceded on our behalf."

"And if he decides not to?"

Before Zimmerman could respond, a burst of static came through their portable radio speakers. Both men froze. There was no audible transmission accompanying the static, only the carrier signal.

"Goddammit," Brock said as he hurried around to the driver's side of the SUV.

"Give it a sec, Brock. You don't even know that was them."

Brock's cell phone chimed as he reached for the door handle.

It was a single line of text from Chloe.

All good. Bragg is talking 2 us.

40

Friday, October 10, 1:40 p.m

"Yeah, I heard about that woman getting killed by a drunk driver," Bragg said. "And I heard the cops arrested the guy responsible."

"That isn't how Summer Randall died," Chloe said.

A wave of confusion passed over Bragg's sun-weathered features. "But I read it in the paper."

"As usual, there's much more to the story, Pete," Labbe said.

"Summer was attacked *before* she ran out into the roadway and got hit," Chloe said. "We think she may have been trying to flag the driver down for help."

"Attacked by who?" Bragg said.

"That's what we're trying to ascertain," Chloe said.

"What does any of this have to do with me?" Bragg said as his eyes shifted between them.

"I told Detective Wright that you and I have a bit of history together, Pete," Labbe said.

Bragg grinned, but Chloe didn't see any warmth in the gesture.

"If by history you mean me breaking the law and you busting me for it, then yeah, we have history."

"Two sides of the same coin," Labbe continued.

Bragg nodded in agreement.

"Where were you between six and ten o'clock Tuesday night?" Chloe said, intentionally leaving the time window wider than she needed. She saw no sense in making it too easy for him.

"You think I attacked this Randall woman?"

"I don't know, do I? But I still need to ask."

"If you're targeting poachers, I'm not the only one who hunts these woods," Bragg said. "Maybe you should check with Joe Levasseur up in Kokadjo."

Chloe recognized the name as one of the men Labbe had included on the list. "According to Warden Labbe here, nobody knows these woods and what goes on around here better than you."

"I was right here that night. At home watching television with Rosie until we turned in."

"Rosie?" Chloe said, glancing in Labbe's direction. "I was under the impression that you lived alone."

Bragg put a finger and thumb to his lips and gave a sharp whistle. Almost instantly, an aging Labrador retriever loped around the far corner of the house and trotted slowly in their direction.

"Rosie?" Chloe said.

"You state folks don't miss a trick, do ya?" Bragg said.

"So, Rosie's your only alibi?"

Bragg leered at her. "Guess if I'd known I'd need an alibi, I could've requested human company."

Chloe looked to Labbe for help. They had absolutely nothing on Bragg to suggest that he'd been involved in any way with Summer Randall's death, and he knew it. Unless they found something to implicate him, they were dead in the water with this new lead.

"Don't suppose you know anything that might help us, would you, Pete?" Labbe said.

Chloe studied Bragg's face. It appeared that he was trying to decide whether or not he wanted to cooperate with them. Or perhaps throw them off his property.

"Look," Chloe said. "I get it. You don't want anyone from the government telling you what to do. And you certainly don't want us to snoop around your land or your home. But we both know that I have a job to do. And that job is to see to it that the person, or persons, responsible for the attack on Summer Randall are brought to justice."

"Your point?" Bragg said after a long moment.

"My point is that you have a history of breaking the law around here."

"Laws I don't recognize," Bragg said.

"They are still the laws of this state. For all I know, Summer might have seen something she wasn't supposed to."

"And for that I attacked her?"

"It's a line of investigation we need to run down," Chloe said.

"It's a ridiculous line," Bragg scoffed.

"Be that as it may, the quicker we uncover the truth, the sooner we'll be able to pack up and get out of everyone's hair. But neither I nor my fellow investigators are going anywhere until we've solved Summer's murder."

"I already told you I had nothing to do with her murder."

"Then you have no reason not to assist us in finding out who did," Chloe persisted.

"And where are these fellow investigators you mentioned?"

"Parked right down the road, waiting to see how this meeting goes."

Bragg averted his eyes from Chloe to look at the warden.

Labbe grinned. "She isn't lying."

Bragg's attention returned to Chloe. He was clearly perplexed by her candor. And her stubbornness. It was something she had grown accustomed to.

"Are you always so direct, Detective Wright?"

"I grew up with three older brothers, Mr. Bragg. Direct is the only way I know to be."

Something seemed to loosen inside Bragg. For the first time, he responded with a genuine smile. After a long moment, he spoke. "What do you need from me?"

Chloe radioed Brock and Zimmerman, telling them it was okay to approach the compound. Both men remained unconvinced that nothing untoward was happening until they saw Chloe and Labbe standing in the dooryard with Bragg.

"Well, I'll be," Zimmerman said as Brock parked beside the warden's truck.

"You'll be what?" Brock said.

"Looks like your partner actually managed to charm this badass."

"For now," Brock said as he killed the engine. "Let's see if this shaky détente actually holds before we cut the cake."

Following the introductions, Bragg led the four investigators on a short tour around his property. Everywhere they looked, there were indications of a life lived for hunting. Brock saw freezers for meat, an armorer's shop, a bullet press for reloading, spare targets, even an indoor firing range. The tour included everything but the main house.

"What about your home?" Brock said at last.

"What about it?" Bragg said.

"May we see inside?" Chloe said.

"Got a warrant?" Bragg said, looking directly at Labbe as he said it.

"You know we don't, Pete," Labbe said.

"Then I guess the tour is over."

41

Friday, October 10, 4:45 p.m

Taylor Randall sat behind the wheel of his pickup in the lot of the Shop 'n Save, staring at the store's front exit doors. The Indian Hill business complex, consisting of the supermarket, a wilderness outfitter, gift shop, and gas station, sat at the crest of a steep hill like a gateway overlooking Moosehead Lake. The building that housed the supermarket more closely resembled an airplane hangar than a grocery depot, lacking much of the charm normally associated with the fancier façades of chain supermarkets in the more populous areas of Maine.

Taylor had strategically picked his parking spot after following Saul Emmons from the docks at Moosehead to the Shop 'n Save. As he sat waiting for the young man to return to his car, the drizzle had gotten heavy enough to warrant turning the wipers on intermittently. He drummed his fingers impatiently atop the steering wheel as he repeatedly checked the time on the dashboard clock. It had been nearly twenty minutes since Emmons had entered the store, and Taylor began to wonder whether he had been made. It didn't seem likely, as he had been careful, hanging back several car lengths until he figured out exactly where Emmons was headed.

Having previously been a coach, Taylor had known Saul Emmons ever since his days as a Laker at the Greenville Consolidated School. Following Emmons's high school graduation, Taylor had several interactions with him in his capacity as a reserve Greenville police officer. The incidents had been little things, like possession of alcohol by a minor. As far as Taylor knew, the young man had never gotten into any real trouble. And Emmons had always been respectful during their interactions. But Taylor knew Emmons was more than just a coworker of Ronnie Libby; the two men were also close friends. Taylor figured if something had been going on between Summer and Ronnie, Emmons would know about it.

He was pondering his next move when Emmons exited the store carrying several plastic bags. Taylor donned his Red Sox ball cap, then stepped out of the idling truck to intercept Emmons on the way to his car.

"Mr. Randall," Emmons said, clearly surprised to see him.

"Hey, Saul," Taylor said. "You got a second?"

"Not really," Emmons said, taking a step to one side as if he might circle around Taylor. "I gotta get home and start dinner. My girlfriend is expecting me. It's my night to cook."

Taylor stood his ground, preventing Emmons from moving any closer to his vehicle. "No worries, Saul. This will only take a minute. I just want to talk."

Emmons's eyes darted nervously back and forth, as if he were trying to decide whether to bolt back inside the store or call out for help, but there wasn't a single pedestrian in sight. Taylor reached out with his left hand and opened the passenger door on his extended cab.

"Hop in, son. Get out of the rain."

Taylor stood for a long moment, intentionally holding Emmons's gaze while waiting for him to give in. Finally, the young man accepted his fate and moved toward the cab of the truck and climbed inside. Taylor slammed the door, then quickly circled around to the driver's side and joined him.

"There we are," Taylor said as he removed his cap and set it on the dash to dry. "Beats standing out in the rain, huh?"

"I want to tell you how sorry I am about Summer, Mr. Randall," Emmons said.

Blindsided by the comment, Taylor felt some of the fight leak out of him. He had been doing his best to channel his grief into rage. Something to hold onto that would keep him moving forward to find the person responsible for killing his little girl and making them pay. And here Emmons was, acting all sympathetic. Taylor steeled himself for what he had to do. Sympathy would not dissuade him from the task at hand.

"Thank you, Saul. That means a lot. I'll be sure to pass your condolences along to Summer's mom."

"W-what did you want to talk about, Mr. Randall?" Emmons said, his voice cracking as he stuttered nervously.

"I wanted to ask you about Ronnie Libby."

"What about him?"

"Had my daughter and Ronnie been seeing each other again?"

Taylor watched Emmons's eyes widen ever so slightly. It was a clear tell. Emmons hadn't been ready for the question and was now struggling to come up with an answer that wouldn't betray his friendship or any promise he may have made to Libby.

"I don't—"

Taylor held up a hand, cutting Emmons off mid-sentence. "Please, whatever you do, don't lie to me, son. I don't think I can handle that. Not from you. Were they seeing each other again?"

Emmons's gaze fell to the floor of the cab as if he might have discovered something interesting rolling around on the mat. After a moment, he gave a barely perceptible nod.

Taylor sighed. He should have known. This was his fault. He should have kept a closer eye on Summer. He supposed it had been inevitable that they might try and rekindle whatever they had before the assault.

"Ronnie's not the same guy he was, Mr. Randall," Emmons said in an ill-advised attempt to justify the secret. "He really cared about Summer."

Taylor's rage came storming back as his mind conjured up the police photographs of Summer's bruised and battered face and split lip following the drunken beating Ronnie had inflicted on her. The images would forever be etched upon his brain. There would be no forgiving something like that. Not ever. No father could.

After a moment, Taylor's attention returned to Emmons. "I heard Ronnie left work early the evening Summer was killed. Don't suppose you know where he went?"

"Mr. Randall, p-please. I don't—"

Taylor placed his muscular left forearm atop the steering wheel and leaned over the console toward Emmons, causing the young man to flinch ever so slightly.

"Where did Ronnie go when he left work that day?"

Emmons's shoulders slumped. "He went to the jewelers to pick up a necklace he'd bought for Summer. He was planning to give it to her that night."

42

Friday, October 10, 5:15 p.m

Taylor drove away from his meeting with Saul Emmons seeing red. He had no clear vision as to his next move. Subconsciously he squeezed the padded steering wheel until his fingers were purple, as if it were Ronnie's neck. He hadn't imagined that Summer would go behind his back to see Ronnie Libby again, against his wishes, but clearly she had. Even so, he could forgive his only daughter anything. More problematic was the fact that Ronnie Libby had dared cross him. Taylor had made clear in no uncertain terms exactly what would happen if he ever caught Ronnie near his daughter again. Apparently young Mr. Libby hadn't taken the threat seriously.

As Taylor drove through the rain without a clear destination in mind, he couldn't help but wonder what had happened when Ronnie presented his daughter with the necklace. Emmons claimed not to know. He said Ronnie had missed work the next day. Called in sick. Summer hadn't been wearing the necklace when she was attacked in the woods, and no necklace had been recovered by the police. Had Summer turned down Ronnie's advances to move their relationship forward? And if she had, did it cost her her life? Had Ronnie snapped after being rebuffed? Is that why he skipped work the next day? Taylor realized that all of this was entirely possible. And it was far more probable than Summer being attacked by some random person while running through the woods where she had trained hundreds of times before.

Prior to departing from Indian Hill, Taylor impressed upon Emmons his wish that their meeting and conversation remained a secret. Emmons readily agreed, but the kid was scared. Saul likely would have agreed to anything in order to get out of the truck and as far away from Taylor as possible. Taylor wondered how much time he had before Emmons spilled their conversation to Ronnie Libby, or his girlfriend, or to one of the state police detectives. Taylor knew he needed to act on this information quickly. What wasn't clear was how he should act on it.

Brock felt the cell phone vibrating inside his jacket pocket. He removed the phone and saw that it was Detective Dashofy.

"Hey, Ginger," he answered. "Didn't expect to hear from you so soon."

"That makes two of us. I'm still not happy that you dragged me into this shit show of yours."

Brock said nothing, but inside he was pleased that she was agreeing to help and was confident that she had found something.

"Are you available to meet up again tonight?" Ginger said.

"Of course. Did you find something?"

"I'm not doing this over the phone, Brock."

"Fair enough. Pat's Pizza in Dover-Foxcroft?"

"No. I'm not meeting you in public again. And I'm not buying you dinner. This won't be a social call. I have something to give you. What you do with it is up to you."

Brock's mind began conjuring up all sorts of possibilities. "All right. Where and when do you want to meet?"

"Nine o'clock in the lot of the Dover-Foxcroft Dollar Tree on West Main. Know where that is?"

"No, but I'm sure I can find it. Thanks again, G—"

Ginger had already hung up.

Brock was about ten minutes late getting to Dover-Foxcroft. Tardiness hadn't been his plan, but he had gotten a late start from Greenville as they finished up contacting the men on Labbe's list. He had sent Ginger a text saying that he was running late, but she hadn't responded. She had sounded shaky on the phone, and he was worried that she might just up and leave.

With some trepidation, he turned into the nearly deserted lot of the Dollar Tree. Parked facing him at the far end of the lot under a burned-out sodium arc light was Ginger's unmarked. Brock killed the headlights on his SUV as he pulled up next to the driver's side of her vehicle and lowered his window.

"I'm not used to all this cloak-and-dagger," Brock said, attempting to lighten the mood.

Ginger's expression was stoic. "Don't make light of this, Brock. This is my ass too."

"Sorry," Brock said. "I know what I'm asking of you."

"Do you? You testifying against Evan in open court didn't do anything good for your career. But you did what you thought was right, and any cop worth a damn, regardless of what they might say publicly, has to respect that. But my involvement in this is an entirely different thing. I don't work for the state police. And I'm not internal affairs."

"But you *are* a homicide investigator," Brock countered. "And it is your job to look into suspicious deaths, right?" Brock hoped he wasn't pushing too hard. Whatever it was Ginger had found, she could just as easily drive away with.

"Don't try to shame me into doing the right thing, Justice. I'm not some asshole you can use reverse psychology on. I get it. And I get that I owe it to the victim in this case."

Brock still wasn't sure that she wouldn't just drive off, but he took the fact that she had called Laura Croxford the victim as a positive sign. He decided to wait and let her make the next move.

Ginger's eyes met his. "I am so far off the reservation on this it isn't funny, Brock. This case was already cleared as accidental. I'm working without a net, without supervisory approval. Hell, even my partner doesn't know what I'm up to. Fuck, I've still got eight years to go before I can collect my pension. If you can't prove that Evan had anything to do with this woman's death, we will both be screwed if this gets out. You do understand that, right? What I'm risking by even being here?"

Brock nodded. "I do. And you're right. If there was any other way to do this without involving you, I would. Believe me. But I need your help."

Brock watched as she reached into the console to retrieve something. Ginger held up a small rectangular piece of plastic. Brock recognized it as a computer thumb drive. Ginger held onto it for a long moment before turning to face him and extending her hand.

"Here," she said.

He accepted the drive before she could change her mind.

"Before we decided that Croxford was alone in the hotel room and died as a result of accidental death, we collected surveillance video from the hotel and from the surrounding businesses. You know, checking boxes."

Brock nodded.

"Anyway, after her death had been determined to be accidental, these videos went right into property as part of the case."

"Nobody reviewed them?"

Ginger frowned and shook her head. "Only the hotel lobby video, and I own that. I had no reason to review them. At least I didn't until you reached out."

Brock stared at the drive in his hand.

"You'll need to review what's on there for yourself. I've included all the written reports as well as the video files. If you find anything noteworthy, contact me directly. No one else. Got it?"

"Got it," Brock said as he slipped the black-and-red thumb drive into his pocket. Realizing for the first time exactly what he had. And exactly what she was risking by bringing it to him. He turned back to Ginger.

"Thank you," he said.

She started the unmarked and shifted the transmission into drive. "Fuck you, Brock."

As he watched her drive away, he wondered if the bridge he had just destroyed could ever be repaired.

43

Friday, October 10, 9:25 p.m

Evan Mathers sat hunkered down inside his personal vehicle parked at the curb just down the street from the Dover-Foxcroft Dollar Tree. He was pretty sure that Brock hadn't realized he was being followed as he tailed him into town from Greenville. Evan had kept close tabs on Brock since their conversation regarding the death of Laura Croxford. Mathers had known something was up when Brock departed Greenville at night unaccompanied by either Chloe Wright or Jordan Zimmerman. He didn't need to be a rocket scientist to know that Brock was meeting someone unrelated to the Summer Randall case. At first, Mathers wondered whether he might be wasting his time tailing him out of town on a wild goose chase. Perhaps Brock was just hooking up with someone nearby to blow off a bit of mid-investigation steam, but the location of the meeting told him that this was something else entirely and perhaps he'd been right to follow Brock.

As the minutes dragged on, Mathers lit up a cigarette and rolled down the window. He'd been part of enough surveillance details to know better than to leave the car running. There was nothing that would make a target notice you quicker than dash lights or a plume of exhaust smoke rising from the rear of a parked car. He also knew the glow of a burning cigarette could give him away, but it was far less obvious, and Evan was addicted to nicotine. He simply couldn't help himself.

As the time dragged on, and his cigarette burned down to a stub, Evan began to think that maybe he'd been wrong. Maybe Brock was having a late-night tryst in the back of someone's vehicle. Either his own or of the vehicle belonging to whomever he'd met. Evan was toying with the idea of becoming a pedestrian and taking a stroll past the Dollar Tree when he caught the reflection of headlights moving across the lot toward the exit. The vehicle wasn't Brock's, though clearly it was an unmarked police vehicle. If there was one thing cops and bad guys could easily spot, it was unmarked cop cars. This was partly due to the lack of imagination on the part of most law enforcement agencies, and to the bulk purchases that neighboring departments take part in, providing discounts for large orders of a single model of vehicle. And once you've seen the next generation of police vehicles, it is impossible not to be on the lookout for them everywhere.

The operator of the unmarked Ford appeared to be a dark-haired woman. She barely glanced both ways before driving out of the lot and turning in his direction. Evan tossed the remnants of his smoke and lifted his cell phone. He zoomed in on the vehicle as it neared, snapping several photos of both the registration plate and the driver's face as she passed by. She looked vaguely familiar, but he couldn't put a name to the face. No matter, he thought. He would run a query on the plate and find out which agency she worked for, though he was pretty sure it was Bangor. And if it was the Bangor Police Department, as he suspected, the woman behind the wheel was likely one of the detectives who worked Laura Croxford's death.

A second vehicle appeared at the parking lot exit. This time it was Brock's SUV. After a moment, Brock turned and headed in the opposite direction. There was no question now, not in Evan's mind, anyway. Brock was meddling in Laura's death investigation. Evan sighed. He should have kept his big mouth shut. He'd said too much to Brock. Hell, he'd practically bragged about knowing Laura was dead. Even the cause of her death. His only hope now was that he hadn't fucked up in some way. Left something incriminating behind. He knew there were no surveillance cameras outside the hotel. Hell, he'd picked the location of the meeting for that very reason.

Laura had checked in using her own name and credit card, and as far as the hotel staff were concerned, she'd been alone when she died. Unless he'd inadvertently left some kind of transient evidence behind, like hair or fibers, there was no way Brock or whoever the woman was would be able to connect him to Laura's death. Besides, the medical examiner had already ruled the death an accidental drowning. Case closed.

As Evan started the car, he lit another cigarette. It was nearly time for him to go on duty for the overnight shift. After a moment, he pulled away from the curb and turned to head toward home. The way he reasoned it, assuming the woman driving the other car was a Bangor detective, only three things could have come from Brock's meeting with her. Either she had nothing and told Brock so, or she had something she told Brock about, or she had given him something tangible. Something Brock might be able to act on. Evan stopped for a blinking red traffic signal. He waited for a pickup to pass through the intersection while trying to decide his next move. If he was right and Brock was moonlighting on the investigation into Laura's death, Brock wouldn't share whatever he'd learned with the other members of his team. Evan had worked alongside Brock long enough to know he was a creature of habit. Brock played things close to the vest, not trusting anyone. But if there was one person he might confide in, it would be his new partner. Perhaps it was time to pay another visit to Chloe Wright.

44

Friday, October 10, 10:30 p.m

Ronnie Libby sat alone on the couch, staring at the television screen. He hadn't felt like himself for the past several days. It seemed that each twenty-four-hour cycle had been accompanied by a gut punch that he couldn't recover from. It started with Summer rebuffing his offer of more than friendship. Him losing his temper again. And the end of his sobriety. It was all just too much.

He leaned forward and opened the box that held the gold necklace he had purchased for Summer. He removed the glimmering piece of jewelry. Hanging from the thin chain was a small golden heart. It was beautifully rendered; even Summer had admitted that much. He still couldn't understand why she had turned it down. Turned him down. They had been meeting in secret for several months, and things seemed to be going so well. They had talked through many things, including his substance abuse issue and what it had led him to do.

He had apologized to Summer repeatedly following the assault, but she had told him only one thing mattered to her, that he seek help and get sober. And he had. He had done everything she had asked. The sponsorship. The twelve steps. The meetings. Ronnie had done all of that and more. He didn't understand how she could no longer care about him. How could she just give up on him like that? And how had he misread her intentions so badly? Now she was dead. Everything he had been working toward was gone. What was the point?

He tossed the necklace onto the table and leaned back into the couch cushion. His red eyes returned to the television screen. Following Summer's rejection, Ronnie had fallen into a bottle, drinking until he vomited. He called in sick to work the following day. In the afternoon, he picked up the phone and called Candy, his sponsor.

"Addiction isn't something you can cure," Candy had told him. "We all carry it like luggage. And occasionally life can place obstacles in our way that make us fall from the sobriety wagon and even momentarily forget how good a sober life can be. Falling is one thing, but you've got to climb back up and never be afraid to ask for help. That's why I'm here, Ronnie."

He had heard the words, even attended a meeting, but none of it changed the way he was feeling. Lessened the guilt he was carrying.

A knock came from the kitchen door that opened onto the side porch. He checked the time on his cell. Ten thirty. Who would be stopping by at this hour?

Ronnie got up and crossed to the kitchen. He flicked on the outside light, then opened the door. Standing atop the landing was a figure dressed all in black. The outfit even included leather gloves and a black balaclava. Before he could react to the threat, the figure was on him, forcing their way into the kitchen and delivering several devastating punches to Ronnie's face, knocking him backward onto the floor. The punches were bad enough, but the impact to the back of his head as he struck the hardwood floor sent black spots dancing across his vision. As he struggled to recover, he saw his assailant turn, shut the door, and turn off the porch light before their attention returned to him.

"Please," Ronnie pleaded as he struggled to regain his feet. "Take whatever you want from the cabin. I won't stop you. This isn't even my property."

"I'm not here to rob you, Ronnie," a familiar voice hissed before delivering a hard kick to Ronnie's ribs, forcing the air from his lungs.

The pain was beyond description, and Ronnie was pretty sure he heard the crack of bone somewhere in the distance. As he fought to draw breath, the figure moved forward, straddling him. They leaned down, and with one gloved hand, they grabbed Ronnie by the hair and jerked his head up roughly until it was nearly perpendicular to his chest. The next punch shattered Ronnie's nose cartilage and sent blood cascading down his face. It was the last thing he remembered.

45

Friday, October 10, 10:55 p.m

Brock returned to his room at the inn and immediately walked to the desk and inserted the memory stick into his laptop. While waiting for the computer to boot up, he kicked off his shoes and stripped down to his boxers and T-shirt to make himself comfortable. He had barely gotten settled at the computer before he heard a sharp knock at the door. He walked over and peered through the peephole to see Chloe standing there with her hands on her hips, looking pissed off. For a half second, he considered ignoring her in hopes that she would go away, but he knew she had something on her mind, and she wouldn't leave until she had shared it with him. He unlocked the door and opened it.

"Hey, partner," Brock said, recognizing the futility of his words even as he spoke them.

"Partner?" she spat. "Is that how you see this relationship? Was there some sort of reboot that I missed?"

Brock sighed deeply, then stepped back from the doorway. "If you're planning to yell at me, could you at least do it inside so the rest of Greenville won't have to bear witness?"

"Gladly," she said, marching past him into the room.

"Look, I've obviously done something to upset you," Brock said. "Spare me the drama, and just tell me what it is."

"I should think it would be more than obvious," Chloe said. "Wasn't it you who gave me that speech about going all in on a case? 'An investigator can't give fifty percent, Chloe. Not if they expect to solve a homicide.' That was you, wasn't it? Because it certainly sounded like you."

Brock nodded, aware of his own hypocrisy.

"Well, then maybe you can explain to me what investigation you've been freelancing on, because it's obvious it's not connected to Summer Randall's murder. If it were, you'd have shared it by now."

Brock waited to see if she was finished. As upset as Chloe was, he wanted to make sure he gave her a chance to fully make her point before he responded. Even though she was directing her ire at him, Brock couldn't help but be pleased that he had been paired with someone as capable and tenacious as Chloe Wright. She was fearless, intelligent, and had already saved his butt once in the short time they had been partnered. He wondered whether things in MCU South might have turned out differently had they been partners when the Kirke shooting had occurred. Chloe certainly held much higher ethical standards than Evan Mathers.

"Well?" Chloe said as she plopped down in the middle of the small sofa and crossed her arms.

"I was waiting to see whether you had finished," Brock said.

"Don't be an asshole, Brock," Chloe warned. "I'm serious."

"I know you are. It's just that you caught me by surprise. And you're right. I have been moonlighting on the Randall case, something I told you never to do."

"Why? I keep thinking thank God Zim is here, or you'd have left me to work this on my own."

Brock felt the first pangs of guilt at that comment. She was right, he had taken his eye off the ball. And maybe it was because Lt. Cumberland had assigned Zimmerman to help them. Or maybe it was because Mathers felt like unfinished business. The truth was it was all about seeing Mathers again.

"You're right, Chloe. I guess I have done that, and it isn't fair. But there's more to what I'm doing than you know."

"Then tell me all about it."

"I can't."

"Why the hell not?"

"Because I'm trying to protect you."

"I don't need your protection, Brock. Just tell me the truth."

46

Friday, October 10, 10:55 p.m

Saul Emmons drove into the darkened dooryard of Ronnie Libby's cabin and parked his Toyota beside Ronnie's Cherokee. There were several lights burning inside the cabin, and Saul assumed Ronnie was still awake.

He had been worried about Ronnie anyway, but since his unplanned meeting with Taylor Randall, guilt had now crept into the mix. Saul certainly hadn't intended to give up Ronnie's rendezvous with Summer, but the intimidating nature of Taylor and the way he had trapped him outside of the supermarket hadn't made keeping the secret easy. Saul only hoped that Ronnie would forgive him, and that Taylor wouldn't do anything stupid now that he knew. Prior to driving over to the lakeside property, Saul had left a voice message on Ronnie's cell phone, requesting that he call him back. No call ever came, and Saul was anxious.

He stepped out of his vehicle and approached the cabin on foot. He was halfway to the side porch when he noticed that the cabin door was ajar. The hair on the back of Saul's neck bristled. Something was wrong.

"Ronnie," Saul called out. "You in there?"

He waited a second before mounting the steps. "Hey, Ronnie. It's Saul.

Are you home?" It was a stupid question, and he knew it. Ronnie's Jeep was in the driveway, and he lived alone, where else would he be?

Saul reached the porch and moved toward the open door. After calling out Ronnie's name again, he reached out and shoved the door open.

"Hey, Ronnie, I'm coming in to—"

Saul's words caught in his throat at the sight before him. Ronnie Libby's body, or what looked like Ronnie's body, was lying motionless face up on the kitchen floor beside the island. Ronnie's face was covered in blood, as was the hardwood floor around him.

"Oh my God," Saul said as he rushed toward him. "Ronnie, can you hear me?"

There was no reply. His friend was either unconscious or dead. Saul knelt beside him and grabbed Ronnie's wrist to check for a pulse. For several panicked seconds, he was unable to find a pulse. At last, he located one. The pulse was weak, but Ronnie was alive. At least for the moment. Saul reached into his pocket for his cell phone to call for help but came up empty. He had left his phone in the car.

"Hang on, buddy," Saul said. "Okay? I'm gonna get you some help. Hang on."

Saul rose to his feet and sprinted outside.

Brock was sitting on the edge of the bed, trying to decide whether or not to share what he was working on with Chloe, when someone began pounding on the door to his hotel room.

"What now?" Brock said.

Brock opened the door and found Zimmerman standing there.

"I can't find Chloe, but—"

"I'm right here, Zim," Chloe said from behind Brock, cutting him off.

Zimmerman's gaze shifted from Chloe back to Brock.

"This isn't what you think," Brock said.

"None of my business," Zimmerman said as he held up his hands.

"What are you doing here, Zim?" Chloe said as she moved to the door.

"There's been a development."

"What development?" Brock said.

"They just found Ronnie Libby's body at the family cabin. Someone beat the ever-loving crap out of him."

"Is he alive?" Brock said as he turned and grabbed his shirt and pants off the bed.

"Just barely. They've transported him to the hospital. Chief Leavitt and one of his men are at the cabin now, waiting on a county crime scene tech."

"Holy crap," Chloe said.

"Where do you want me?" Zimmerman said.

"Why don't you head over to the hospital," Brock said. "Chloe and I will go to the scene."

"You got it," Zimmerman said. "I'll let you know what the doc says."

47

Friday, October 10, 11:30 p.m

If Brock hadn't already known the way to the Libbys' camp, the cluster of blue and red strobes would have made finding it easy. Zimmerman had told them that Chief Leavitt and one of his officers were holding the scene, but Brock counted at least four police vehicles parked in the dooryard. He recognized Leavitt's unmarked vehicle immediately, and he knew the black-and-white pickup was used by Greenville PD's reserve officers. The two remaining marked units belonged to the Piscataquis County Sheriff's Department, and Brock was pretty sure he knew to whom at least one of them belonged.

"You know this isn't finished, right?" Chloe said as Brock pulled to a stop. "I want to know what you're up to."

"Let's just worry about this case for now," Brock said. "I promise I'll fill you in as soon as I can. Let's go."

They both climbed out of Brock's SUV as Evan Mathers approached them on foot.

Mercifully, they only had to listen to Mathers's arrogance for a second or two before Chief Leavitt interceded to bring them up to speed.

"What happened here, Chief?" Chloe said.

"That's a good question, Detective," Leavitt said. "The county dispatcher received a panicked 911 call from Saul Emmons just before twenty-three hundred hours."

Brock recognized the name of Ronnie's coworker from his interview with him at the *Kate*.

"Emmons requested an ambulance at this address for a man barely breathing."

"Did Emmons say what happened?" Chloe said.

"The county dispatcher said he was pretty shaken up and couldn't provide much in the way of details."

"I spoke to the dispatcher too," Mathers said. "She seemed to think that Emmons may have driven here to check on Libby and found him like this."

"Did she ask why he felt the need to check on him?" Brock said.

"She did not," Mathers said.

"Where is Emmons now?" Brock said.

"He's at the station talking to one of my reservists," Leavitt said.

"And he's covered in blood," Mathers added.

Brock looked at Chloe. "Let's get a detailed statement from Emmons. And from the reserve officer too. I want to know what he did and what he touched while at the scene."

"What *she* did," Leavitt interrupted. "My reserve is a woman. Officer Donna Sinclair."

"I stand corrected," Brock said. "Would you get a statement from Officer Sinclair about what *she* did and observed?"

"Keys," Chloe said, holding out her hand and giving him a smirk.

Brock handed her his keys.

"I'll let you know," Chloe said as she hurried toward Brock's Interceptor.

Brock turned back to Leavitt and Mathers. "I want a look at the scene."

"Right this way," Leavitt said.

Brock moved into the open doorway of the cabin, looking past the crime scene tape that someone had strung up around the perimeter of the home. He exchanged nods with the Piscataquis County evidence tech, who was covered head to toe in Tyvek and toting a large digital camera. The kitchen showed indications of either a fight or an attack having occurred there. Several wooden barstools lay on their sides in front of the kitchen island. They appeared to have been knocked over during whatever had taken place here. A large puddle of blood coated the hardwood floor at the room's center, the outer edges of which had been smeared. Brock presumed that some of the visible smears and shoe prints had been made by the responding EMTs as they quickly evaluated and prepped Libby for transport. Lifesaving measures always trumped police investigations; it was one of the things that made successfully investigating homicides so difficult.

"It took the Northern Light ambulance folks about ten minutes to arrive on scene," Leavitt said. "As you can see from the amount of blood, Ronnie was in pretty rough shape when they got here. They did what they could on site, then transported him to Northern Light. Reserve Officer Sinclair got here before me, and I arrived just as the EMTs were preparing to leave. We did the best we could to secure the scene and made the call to county for backup and an evidence tech."

As Leavitt continued to speak, Brock took note of the discarded wrappers scattered about the scene from the various disposable lifesaving paraphernalia used by the first responders. The Maine State Police, like many of their sister agencies, were fond of referring to EMTs and firefighters as evidence eradication units. While Brock understood the primary need to save lives above all other considerations, the detritus left behind at crime scenes often hindered the investigation that followed. Footwear impressions and fingerprints left behind would need to be compared to the footwear and prints of each of the responding EMTs to eliminate them as possible suspects. Whatever remained unidentified in this case would most likely belong to Libby's assailant, or to Saul Emmons.

"We'll need names and contact info for everyone who enters the scene, Chief," Brock said.

"Of course. I'll get someone on it straight away."

Brock studied the kitchen door latch and handle. Neither had been damaged, indicating that Ronnie Libby had either left the door unlocked and was taken by surprise when his assailant entered the cabin, or he knew his attacker and let them inside. The other possibility was that he had opened the door without checking to see who was outside. Regardless, it was clear that the attacker's intent had been to inflict as much physical damage to Libby as possible. And based solely on the blood-spattered scene, it appeared they had succeeded.

Brock's cell rang with a call from Zimmerman.

"What's the update on Libby?" Brock said by way of a greeting.

"Ronnie's still among the living. At least he was when he left here."

"Left there? Where is he now?"

"They LifeFlighted him to Bangor."

Brock knew Zimmerman was referring to the medical helicopter transport company LifeFlight. He also knew it meant that Libby was in very bad shape if the Northern Light Hospital couldn't patch him up.

"Any idea as to the extent of Libby's injuries?" Brock said.

"Let's just say it's gonna be one hell of a repair bill to get him out of the shop," Zimmerman said.

"I don't suppose the doc gave you any idea about his chances of pulling through?"

"You know how doctors are. When it comes to predictions, they're more like weather guessers than meteorologists."

Brock was about to ask what that meant when Zimmerman translated his own puzzle.

"Dr. Heiden said Libby's got a lot going for him. He's young, fit, and healthy. At least he was prior to this beating."

"So it's a maybe?" Brock said.

"That's all Heiden's willing to commit to. Want me to head over to Eastern Maine Med?"

"I don't think we have a choice," Brock said. "If Libby dies, this becomes our homicide."

"Okay. I'll contact you when I have something."

As Brock ended the call with Zimmerman, he turned to look through the doorway at the bloody scene where the county evidence tech was still snapping photos. One thing was certain, Ronnie Libby was their best hope at a witness to whatever had happened here. They needed him to pull through.

Chloe found Officer Sinclair and Emmons seated across from each other in the PSB interview room with the door standing open. Emmons was bent over the table, working on his written statement.

"Detective," Sinclair said upon seeing Chloe in the doorway.

"Can I talk to you out here for a second?" Chloe said.

"I'll be right back, Mr. Emmons," Sinclair said as she stood and moved into the hall.

Chloe led Sinclair down the hall far enough to avoid having Emmons overhear their conversation.

"How's Ronnie?" Sinclair asked.

The question made Chloe pause for a split second. The usual question would have been "How's the victim," but in a town as small as Greenville, most of the residents knew each other. She wondered whether it was simply the norm or if there might be more to the familiarity.

"I'm still waiting for an update," Chloe said.

Sinclair nodded. "Somebody beat him up really badly. That might be the worst I've seen since I've been on the job."

"How long have you worked as a reserve?" Chloe said before she could stop herself.

"Almost six months," Sinclair said proudly.

"Stay in this job long enough, you'll see worse," Chloe said. "Trust me."

The confidence in Sinclair's expression seemed to wither.

"You know why I'm here, right?" Chloe said.

"In case Ronnie Libby dies?"

"That would certainly change things," Chloe said. "But regardless, Ronnie is still a suspect in Summer Randall's murder."

"Does that mean you're gonna kick me out of my interview of Saul Emmons?"

"Not at all," Chloe said, hoping to soften the blow. "But I am going to play a part in it now, okay? We'll do it together."

"Okay," Sinclair said, though her tone indicated that she was less than pleased with the idea. Chloe totally understood the feeling. It was much like her days working the road as a uniformed trooper whenever one of the state detectives came in and shoved her to the side. She knew it was necessary, but she still sympathized with the young officer.

"What has Emmons told you so far?" Chloe said.

48

Saturday, October 11, 12:15 a.m

Brock retreated to Leavitt's vehicle to give the evidence tech a chance to finish processing the scene and to get away from Evan, who was working on the incident report via the mobile reporting terminal inside his own cruiser. The less communication he had with the former trooper, the better. He retrieved his phone and checked the time. It was after midnight. Cumberland wouldn't be pleased about being bothered at this time of night, but Brock knew she would be more upset if he didn't inform her of the latest development. He scanned the recent call list on his cell until he found her number, then tapped the screen.

A half dozen rings later, a groggy-sounding Cumberland answered the phone. "This better be good," she croaked.

"Good morning, Lieutenant," Brock said, intentionally altering his voice to sound cheerier than he felt. "Did I wake you?"

"Cut the crap, Justice. Just tell me what you've got."

Brock quickly brought her up to speed. Aside from the occasional clarifying question, she let him speak. He knew Cumberland was likely taking notes to accurately recall the details in the morning when she would have to pass the information on to Major Morgan, her boss.

"LifeFlight to Bangor doesn't sound good," Cumberland said after Brock had finished. "What do we think Ronnie Libby's chances are?"

"Zim says the Northern Light doc won't commit one way or the other."

"Typical," Cumberland growled. "And do we still like Libby for the Randall murder?"

"We haven't been able to rule him out. With his history, he remains a suspect."

"And do we have any idea who may have done this to Libby?"

Brock had some definite ideas, but the last thing he wanted to do was accuse Taylor Randall without any proof.

Whenever inside information was shared with superiors, there was always the chance that someone higher up the hierarchal food chain would leak the information to someone in the press to give the appearance that they were in the know. The last thing Brock needed was for Morgan to go off half-cocked and screw up their case. Or worse, to publicly cast Taylor Randall in an unflattering and unfair light. As Brock knew too well, those kinds of accusations could haunt an innocent person for the rest of their lives.

"I do," Brock said. "But none I'm willing to share just yet."

"Fair enough," Cumberland said after a brief hesitation. "Where are your fellow detectives?"

"Zim is on his way to Bangor, and Chloe is taking a statement from the guy who discovered Libby."

"Okay," Cumberland said with a sigh. "Anything else I should know?"

Her question gave him pause. Was Penny simply covering all her bases, or had she somehow found out about Brock poking around into Laura Croxford's death?

"Nope, that just about covers it," Brock said, choosing his words carefully. While it wasn't exactly a lie, it was an omission he might have to answer for just the same.

"Okay. Let me know if anything changes."

Chloe sat beside Officer Sinclair. Though she had clearly taken over the interview, she did allow Sinclair to ask the occasional question. The young reservist seemed to be a natural at interviews, never asking a leading question. Chloe wondered what Sinclair did for a living when she wasn't working for the Greenville PD.

As soon as she sat down, Chloe had Saul Emmons back up and tell the story from the beginning. She compared his recounting of the events to what he'd already written in his partial statement. It was clear to Chloe that the one glaring omission was why Emmons had been trying to reach Ronnie Libby in the first place. And why Ronnie's failure to respond to his phone calls rose to the level that required him to drive all the way to Libby's cabin in the middle of the night.

Chloe waited for Emmons to finish speaking before painting on a concerned expression, as if she were a newscaster about to deliver some disturbing information.

"It must have been quite a shock to find your friend like that, Saul. Is it okay if I call you Saul?"

Emmons nodded. "Yes. And it was. I still can't believe it."

"Saul, Officer Sinclair and I really appreciate you coming in here and helping us like this. I know it's late, and you're probably exhausted from everything that has happened tonight. Ronnie is lucky to have a friend like you. I do still have a few questions, though, if that's okay."

"Of course," Emmons said, having no idea that he was walking into a trap.

"What was it that you needed to talk to Ronnie about?"

"I'm sorry," Emmons said with a confused expression on his face. "What do you mean?"

"Well, you said you telephoned him around—" Chloe paused to check her notes against Emmons's statement for effect. "Here it is. You said you left him a voicemail at around seven thirty and that he never called you back. Then you phoned again around nine but didn't leave a message when he didn't answer your call. What were you calling him about? It must have been pretty important for you to drive all the way to Ronnie's cabin in the middle of the night. I mean, that must be, what, four or five miles one way, right?" Chloe turned to Sinclair for confirmation.

"At least," Sinclair said.

Chloe's attention returned to Emmons. His expression had changed again. It was clear that he realized what she was doing, and that there was no getting around it. "So, what was it that was so important that it couldn't wait until you saw Ronnie at work tomorrow?"

Emmons shrugged. Chloe could see the perspiration forming on his upper lip.

"Did it have anything to do with him being attacked?"

Emmons broke eye contact and began running the fingers of his hand over the surface of the table.

"You need to tell us the truth, Saul," Chloe said. "What happened last night?"

49

Saturday, October 11, 1:30 a.m

An hour later, after the evidence tech had finished with the scene, Brock was allowed inside the Libby's cabin to do a walk-through. He donned a pair of Tyvek booties to keep his footwear from becoming biohazards. Up close, the evidence told the story of the savage beating that had taken place there only hours before. It was clear that the attacker had made it personal. There was more to this than a simple break-in gone bad.

The blood on the floor had begun to dry, and as it did, the color shifted from deep crimson to brown. Within the blood, Brock could see multiple sets of footwear impressions left behind. He turned to the county evidence tech, who was packing up his equipment and preparing to head to the hospital.

"We got samples of the blood for testing?"

"Yup. I took samples from various points in case there is blood here that belongs to the suspect."

Brock nodded, although he would have been surprised if there was any blood besides Ronnie Libby's. Everything appeared to indicate a surprise attack.

"And you'll make sure we get a copy of the list of all the first responders who entered the scene," Brock said. "I want to eliminate their impressions as soon as possible so that we know which ones were made by the suspect."

"I'm on it," the tech said. "I'll be stopping by the Northern Light Hospital on my way to Bangor."

"Thanks," Brock said before turning his attention to the television in the next room. It was still on, just as it had been when they first arrived. Brock walked into the living room and turned the TV off. He looked at the couch directly opposite the TV, surmising that Libby had likely been sitting there when the attacker arrived at the cabin. As Brock walked over to the couch, his eyes fell upon the coffee table where an empty jewelry box sat beside a gold heart-pendant necklace. Brock snapped a picture of the necklace and its position before picking it up. The jewelry looked brand new. And it looked like something Libby might have purchased for someone special. Someone like Summer Randall.

"Is this case yours now?" Evan Mathers said from the doorway.

"Guess that depends on whether or not Libby dies," Brock said matter-of-factly.

"Don't worry about procedure, Brock," Mathers said. "Believe it or not, there are other departments besides the staties that know how to work a case."

Brock returned the necklace to the table, then turned to face him. "I guess you'd know better than anyone."

The smirk disappeared from Mathers's face, and there was a flash of anger in his eyes. It was the first time Brock had seen this from him. He was pleased to have finally hit a nerve with the former trooper. It meant the man was capable of emotion after all. Evan might well be a murderer, maybe even twice over, but at least he wasn't a complete sociopath.

"I'll email the JPEGS along with my supplemental report and findings, everything I have, to you and Detective Wright as soon as I can," the tech said. "It may be late afternoon or tomorrow night by the time I get everything together. You'll have to swing by the lab at the sheriff's department if you want high-res pics. I'll copy everything to thumb drives."

"I appreciate it," Brock said, finally breaking eye contact with Mathers.

"Anytime. I'll grab the vic's clothes while I'm at the hospital too. And, assuming they let me anywhere near Libby, I'll try and get photos of his injuries and maybe some swabs from his hands and fingernails on the off chance he fought back."

"Sounds good," Brock said as he surveyed the scene again. It didn't look like Libby had put up much of a fight, if any. Brock turned back toward the door. Mathers was gone.

As Brock watched the two sheriff's department vehicles roll up the dirt drive, he realized that Chloe still had his unmarked. He had no way to get back to town. His eyes found the young reserve officer standing on the porch.

"Looks like we've both been abandoned," Brock said.

"I'm used to it," the officer said with a chuckle.

Brock wasn't. He was contemplating his next move when he heard gravel crunching under the tires of an approaching vehicle. It was Chloe returning with his SUV. She parked near the cabin and hopped out.

"Looks like you need a ride," Chloe said as she looked around at the empty dooryard.

"Emmons give you anything useful?" Brock asked.

"Oh yeah," Chloe said with a grin. "Hop in, sailor, and I'll tell you all about it."

Brock turned back to the reserve officer still guarding the scene. "You need anything before we take off, officer? I didn't get your name."

"Hastings, sir. Leo Hastings. And I'm all set for now."

"Okay. Thanks for helping out, Leo," Brock said.

"Anytime, sir."

As Chloe drove them toward the inn to retrieve her vehicle, she recounted the entire conversation with Saul Emmons while Brock listened intently. He couldn't tell if her anger with him had passed or if she was just distracted by the attack on Libby.

"The first time he struggled was when I hit him with the most obvious question," Chloe said. "Like why was he calling Ronnie Libby to begin with? And what was so important that it couldn't wait until morning?"

"How did he respond?" Brock said.

"At first he tried to portray it as no big deal, but eventually he came clean. Apparently Taylor Randall was lying in wait for him as he left the grocery store this afternoon after work."

Brock checked the time on the dash clock. "You mean yesterday afternoon, right?"

"Jesus, is it that late already? Anyway, Randall coerced him into his truck and made him give up that Ronnie and Summer had been meeting in secret against his wishes."

Brock could only imagine Taylor's reaction to that unwanted news.

"I mean, it isn't like we weren't already thinking about Randall for the beating," Chloe continued. "But Saul spilling the secret might have pushed him right over the edge."

Brock sat quietly as he thought it through.

"What are you thinking?" Chloe said.

"I'm thinking if Ronnie Libby is responsible for Summer's death, Taylor may have single-handedly made it impossible for us to prove."

"Tell you something else," Chloe said as she turned into the parking lot of the inn. "If Taylor really did this to Ronnie, Congresswoman Randall's gonna shit a brick. So much for avoiding negative press, right? Nothing worse than having your ex-husband turn out to be a vigilante."

"Except for becoming a murderer," Brock said. "Change of plan. Turn around."

"Where are we going?"

"To pay Taylor Randall a visit."

50

Saturday, October 11, 1:45 a.m

The porch light was lit as Chloe pulled into the driveway and drove toward the darkened house. Brock wasn't surprised to find the yard empty. Taylor's pickup was nowhere to be found.

"Looks like the light is on and nobody's home, partner," Chloe said.

"Careful," Brock said. "You're beginning to sound like Zim."

"The horror," Chloe said. "Where do you think he's holed up?"

"Don't know," Brock said as his mind worked the problem. "Maybe he's out establishing an alibi."

"Makes sense," Chloe said. "That's what I'd be doing if I was involved in beating someone nearly to death. Any ideas?"

"Let's not make it harder than it has to be," Brock said. "Drive over to the store."

"You really think he'd go there?"

"No, but unless you have any better ideas, that's the only other place we know he's connected to."

They arrived at the Greenville Outfitters supply store fifteen minutes later to find every light inside the store blazing.

"What the hell?" Chloe said. "It looks like they're open."

"Not at two in the morning, they're not," Brock said.

Chloe parked the Interceptor across the street, and they approached the entrance to Taylor's store on foot.

"Hang back a little," Brock said. "I want to see what's happening inside before we announce our presence."

They both stood back from the plate glass windows, watching for several minutes as two employees walked back and forth inside the store. They were too far away to positively identify, but the larger of the two figures looked like it might have been Taylor.

"What do you think?" Chloe said. "Is one of those people Taylor?"

"Only one way to find out."

They moved to the front door, and Chloe rapped on the glass with Brock's keys. After several moments, one of the employees hurried toward the door and unlocked it.

"Help you?" the young man said as he stuck his head through the partially opened door.

"Toby, right?" Brock said, recognizing the employee as the one who waited on him, thinking he was a customer. "Detective Justice. I was in here the other day to talk to your boss."

"Oh yeah," Toby said. "I remember you."

"This is Detective Wright," Brock said.

"Pleased to meet you, ma'am."

Brock fought back a grin as he exchanged a glance with Chloe. He knew how much she hated being called "ma'am." Said it made her feel old.

"Is Taylor Randall here?" Chloe said, the irritation clear in her tone.

"Yeah. We're doing the semiannual inventory. You wanna come in?"

"That's the general idea," Chloe said.

Toby let them in, then relocked the doors behind them. "Come on. He's out back."

They followed the young man toward the back of the store where they found Taylor Randall standing in front of a wall of shelves, holding a clipboard. Brock took note of his clothing and general appearance, but there was nothing to indicate that he might have been involved in a recent altercation.

"Detectives," Taylor said with a look of surprise on his face.

"Mr. Randall," Brock said.

"You have some news about Summer's murder?"

"No," Brock said. "Nothing new that we can share, anyway. We're still working the case."

"What can I do for you?"

"We need to ask you some questions," Chloe said. "Is there someplace we can talk?"

Taylor addressed his employee. "It's okay, Toby. Why don't you keep working, and I'll be back to help you shortly."

"Okay, Mr. Randall."

Toby returned to the front part of the store while Brock and Chloe followed Taylor upstairs to his office.

"So, how can I help you?" Taylor said after they were seated.

"Where were you last night between six and eleven?" Brock said.

Taylor's eyes moved back and forth between the detectives. "You're serious?"

"Yes, Mr. Randall," Chloe said. "We are."

"Okay. Let me think. I closed the store about six o'clock, give or take. Drove home, had supper, and was back here by nine to start working on the inventory with Toby."

"Did you leave the store at any point after nine?" Brock said.

"No. Why would I?"

"And Toby," Chloe said. "Has he been here all night too?"

"Yes. And if you don't believe me, you can ask him yourself."

Brock nodded at Chloe. She got up from her chair and departed the office.

"What exactly am I supposed to have done?" Taylor said. "You're treating me as if I've committed a crime."

"Ronnie Libby was assaulted in his home several hours ago."

Brock studied Taylor's reaction to see if he'd give anything away. His eyebrows arched in surprise, but there was no real emotion associated with the gesture.

"Well, I can't say as I'm surprised. Ronnie runs with a rough crowd."

"He was nearly beaten to death, Mr. Randall. He's currently at the hospital in Bangor undergoing surgery."

"And you're telling me this why? You think I had something to do with it?"

"Did you?"

"Of course not. Why would I?"

Brock remained silent as he studied Taylor's expression. His years as an investigator had instilled in him the importance of silence. Suspects often can't handle the stress that comes with silence. They try to fill the void to relieve the tension, sometimes talking for the sake of it, much like a child who knows they've been caught red-handed but isn't ready to give up.

"Look, I've been here all night, okay? Toby will verify that. I'm sorry that Ronnie Libby got the shit kicked out of him, but that doesn't make me a suspect, does it? I thought you were trying to solve Summer's murder. Isn't that what you and your partner are supposed to be doing? Not harassing a grieving father."

"You're right, Mr. Randall. That is what we're supposed to be working on."

"Good. I'm glad we're in agreement on that."

Brock let Taylor's words hang there for a minute, creating the illusion that Randall had gotten the upper hand before pouncing.

"Tell me, when was the last time you spoke with Saul Emmons?"

51

Saturday, October 11, 2:30 a.m

"You think Taylor did it?" Chloe said as they drove away from the store and headed back toward the inn. "I mean, the alibi that kid is giving him could be phony as hell. He does work for him, after all. He wouldn't want to lose his job, right?"

"I'm not sure," Brock said. "But if it wasn't Taylor, then he may well have gotten someone to do it for him. You should have seen his face when he found out we'd talked with Saul Emmons."

"It also means he lied about going directly home after closing the store," Chloe said.

"Yes, he did," Brock said.

"How did he explain being at the supermarket?"

"Said he stopped by to pick up something for supper and just happened to run into Emmons."

"You believe him?"

"Not for a second."

Brock knew nothing good would come from bringing Taylor down to the station for a formal interview. If he didn't lawyer up immediately, at the very least his ex-wife would raise holy hell that the state police were targeting the homicide victim's family. And he knew all too well how that would play with Lt. Cumberland. But he also knew how badly this whole thing was likely to go with Ronnie Libby's parents. If they didn't already suspect Taylor, they would soon enough.

As Chloe turned into the parking lot of the inn, the screen of Brock's cell phone illuminated with a text message.

"Update from Zim?" Chloe said.

"Yup," Brock said. "No update on Ronnie Libby, but his parents just arrived, and they're wild."

"Great," Chloe said. "I assume you're planning to drive to Bangor."

"I am. Can't leave Zim hanging out there like that."

"You want me to drive you?" Chloe said.

"No," Brock said. "I appreciate the offer, but one of us should try and get some rest, or tomorrow is going to be a bust."

"You mean today, don't you?"

It took Brock the better part of two hours to make the eighty-mile drive to Northern Light Eastern Maine Medical Center in Bangor. On the way, he filled the SUV with fuel and himself with caffeine; it was the only way to keep things running. After getting a quick update from Zimmerman, Brock found a private space not far from the ER and led the Libbys to it. Brock figured taking the lead as liaison would give Zimmerman a much-needed break from the ongoing drama while keeping their conversation private and away from prying eyes.

"You know who did this, Detective Justice," Mrs. Libby snapped. "It was Taylor Randall. Why haven't you arrested him?"

"Because we don't know that he was responsible," Brock said calmly, attempting to defuse the situation.

"Don't you?" Mr. Libby said. "Who the hell else would it be? Taylor obviously blames our son for what happened to Summer. I demand you arrest him. He'll talk."

"Mr. Randall has an alibi," Brock said. "Detective Wright and I spoke with him a couple of hours ago."

"Of course he does," Mrs. Libby said. "Taylor knows everyone in town. He could get anyone to back him up. Meanwhile my boy may—"

Brock watched Mr. Libby move toward his wife and wrap an arm around her as she began to wail in agony at the thought of losing her only child. For a moment, Brock was glad that Ronnie had been flown out of Greenville. The last thing any of them needed was for the Libbys to confront Taylor Randall.

As soon as she recovered, the Libbys returned to the ER waiting area. Brock followed at a distance. He found Zimmerman sitting alone reviewing some paperwork. He looked exhausted. The Libbys sat on the opposite side of the room like outcasts.

Brock motioned for Zimmerman to follow him.

They walked down the hallway until they were out of earshot of the Libbys.

"How did it go?" Zimmerman said, intentionally keeping his voice low.

"Not good," Brock said. "They're looking for someone to blame."

"And they want us to arrest Taylor, right? Alibi be damned."

"Pretty much," Brock said.

"Yeah, they were pretty pissed off to find me sitting here," Zimmerman said. "Accused me of doing nothing."

Brock looked around, surprised to find that the sheriff's office wasn't represented.

"Piscataquis County evidence tech still around?" Brock said.

"He and Deputy Mathers just left," Zimmerman said. "The tech asked me to tell you that he got what you asked for."

"Good," Brock said, happy that at least something had gone right. "Did the doctor give you any idea how long it would be before we'd know anything?"

"Nope," Zimmerman said. "I caught a glimpse of one of the emergency room techs, but nobody has given me an update yet."

As if by uttering those few words Zimmerman summoned an answer, a doctor, still attired in his surgical scrubs, shuffled down the hallway toward them. He looked as tired as Brock felt.

"How is our son?" Mr. Libby said, his voice cracking.

Brock turned to see the Libbys standing behind them. Mr. Libby still had an arm around his wife. It was difficult to tell whether he was comforting her or trying to prevent her from collapsing.

"Tell me my boy is alive," Mrs. Libby pleaded.

The doctor reached up and removed the surgery cap from the top of his head. "Your son is alive, Mr. Libby. But I'll be honest with you. He has suffered some very serious injuries."

The doctor's words unleashed a fresh flood of tears from Mrs. Libby.

"How soon can we see him?" Mr. Libby said.

"I'm afraid I can't give you an estimate on that. We are keeping him in a medically induced coma for now. His body needs time to heal. I've done as much as I can to stabilize him. Probably as much as any hospital could do given his condition."

"Will my Ronnie make it?" Mrs. Libby said, forcing the words out.

"That's out of my hands. Your son's recovery—"

"Ronnie," Mrs. Libby interrupted. "His name is Ronnie."

"Ronnie's recovery depends entirely on him. Ronnie is young, fit, and strong. Those things are all in his favor. But he suffered a serious assault."

"Exactly what are the extent of his injuries?" Mr. Libby said, causing Brock to cringe.

Brock had learned from experience that it was far better not to ask a question if you weren't fully prepared for the answer. He was confident, given the condition of the crime scene, that neither of the Libbys were prepared.

"Your son—Ronnie has sustained several cracked ribs, a concussion, a broken nose and jaw, both of which will require additional surgery to repair properly. We've managed to stop the internal bleeding, but his liver and spleen are also damaged."

"Jesus," Zimmerman whispered, echoing Brock's very thoughts on the subject.

Mrs. Libby broke down completely and slumped to the hallway floor, where she began to wail loudly. Mr. Libby made no effort to console her this time. Brock could see the man was too broken to be of any use to her.

Zimmerman approached Mrs. Libby and knelt down and wrapped her in a hug. Brock was worried how the aggrieved woman would react, but she gave in and rested her head on the detective's shoulder. After several long uncomfortable moments, Zimmerman whispered something to Mrs. Libby, then helped her to her feet and led her toward the exit. Mr. Libby stood there looking at Brock. He seemed unsure of what he should do next.

Brock approached him and touched him on the upper arm. "Mr. Libby, why don't you go be with your wife. We've got this."

Libby looked up. His eyes were blank and watery, as if all emotion had departed from his body.

"Go on," Brock prompted again.

Libby slowly turned away and shuffled through the exit doors.

"Any idea who did this?" the doctor said after the Libbys were out of earshot.

"We're working some leads," Brock said, giving the standard textbook response that required absolutely nothing to back it up. "Having looked at Ronnie Libby's injuries up close and personal, can you tell whether or not more than one assailant was involved?"

"That really isn't my area of expertise, but if I had to guess, I'd say no more than one or two. Most of the damage appears to have been inflicted by punches from a closed fist, maybe gloved, based on the flecks of black leather I found in several of the facial wounds."

"Right-handed or left?" Brock said.

The doctor paused as if considering this for the first time. "Most of the injuries were on Ronnie's left, so most likely you're looking for a right-handed assailant."

"Anything else?" Brock said.

"The torso injuries are a combination of punches and kicks. The kicks look to have been delivered by something along the lines of a work boot, maybe. I would guess something with a steel toe."

"Any chance of obtaining a tread pattern?" Brock said. "Something we might be able to match?"

"Your evidence guy snapped a few photos of the contusions, and I turned over the specks of leather I mentioned to him as well. Again, that's not really my area."

"Understood," Brock said.

"The overnight staff will continue to monitor Ronnie's vitals throughout the night. I'll be back in the morning for my regular shift. We may know more at that time."

"Thanks, Doc," Brock said.

And with that, the doctor departed back down the hallway.

Zimmerman returned alone.

"How is she?" Brock said.

"A hot mess," Zimmerman said. "They're both in shock."

"You look exhausted, Zim. Why don't you take off and get a couple hours of sleep."

"That sounds grand to me," Zimmerman said. "What about the Libbys?"

"I'll check on them," Brock said. "You go ahead and take off. Let's plan to meet back at the PSB by nine."

"Works for me," Zimmerman said. "See you in a few hours. I'll bring the coffee."

"Night, Zim," Brock said.

Zimmerman raised a hand as he walked away.

52

Saturday, October 11, 6:30 a.m

Shortly after 4:00 a.m., Brock retreated to his SUV parked outside the hospital, hoping to get some shut-eye of his own. He'd managed less than two hours of sleep before the wail of an approaching ambulance ripped him from his uncomfortable slumber behind the wheel.

Insomnia and exhaustion were the typical and pervasive symptoms that accompanied every murder case Brock worked on. This one, however, was particularly problematic, as his mind was tasked to work through three cases simultaneously. Summer Randall had been murdered, stabbed then chased through the woods until she bled out and was struck by a drunk driver. Laura Croxford may well have been murdered, and it was likely that her death had been at the hands of a dirty cop, but Brock still needed to prove it. In addition to all that, Ronnie Libby, a prime suspect in Summer's murder, now lay in a hospital bed fighting for his very life, and whether he managed to hang on would make the difference between his attacker being charged with elevated aggravated assault or murder.

Brock opened the door to the SUV and stepped out onto the dew-covered pavement. The air was thick with humidity, and the fog rising from the Penobscot River made everything appear dreamlike, including the flashers on the ambulance that had woken him as it pulled up to the emergency doors. He paused to stretch his stiff neck and back as he gazed around the nearly deserted hospital parking lot. He checked the time on his cell, then headed toward the entrance.

Once inside, he checked the waiting area for the Libbys, but they were nowhere to be found. He imagined they had departed sometime during the early morning hours to a nearby hotel to get a few hours of rest themselves. Brock wasn't surprised. The only thing worse than sleeping in an unmarked police vehicle was sleeping in a hospital waiting area.

"You're still here."

Brock turned to find a middle-aged hospital security guard approaching.

"Barely," Brock said.

"I'm Cliff Johnson, by the way," the guard said. "We never got properly introduced last night."

"Brock Justice."

"Pleased to meet you, Detective. You must be looking for the Libbys. They left here shortly after you did."

Brock nodded. "I've got to get back to Greenville, but I was hoping to get an update on their son before I left."

Cliff looked around to make sure no one was listening in. "You didn't hear it from me, but Ronnie Libby is still among the living. His monitors are still making all the proper beeps and boops, and the nurses have been fussing about with him all night. He's being well looked after."

"Thanks," Brock said.

"Someone really tuned that kid up, huh?"

Brock nodded at the understatement.

"You want me to give you a call if anything changes?" Cliff said.

Brock cocked his head to one side, surprised at the offer.

Cliff grinned. "Retired Atlanta detective. I get it. Thanks to HIPAA and those goddamned lawyers, it's nearly impossible to get a straight answer nowadays."

Brock knew he was referring to the Health Insurance Portability and Accountability Act, a federal law designed to protect the privacy of patients. But like most legislation, even those passed with good intentions, the overly burdensome restrictions made it infinitely harder for healthcare providers and first responders to carry out their duties.

Brock scribbled the number to his cell phone on the back of a business card and handed it to the guard. "Thanks again," Brock said.

"Don't mention it."

Brock retreated to his SUV to find the low-hanging blanket of fog had begun to lift. He was already dreading the long trip back to Greenville in morning traffic, and fog would only make it worse. His stomach began to protest loudly as soon as he was on the road. Unable to remember the last time he'd consumed anything nutritious, Brock headed toward the closest Dunkin' he could find.

He made the eighty-mile trip back to Greenville in just under two hours. Aside from polishing off an extra-large black coffee, some of which he managed to spill on himself, and a bacon-and-egg breakfast bagel, Brock's trip was uneventful.

He drove through town straight to the inn and was pleased to see that both Chloe and Zimmerman had already departed. He entered his room and peeled off his wrinkled clothes on the way to the shower.

Twenty minutes later, Brock walked from the bathroom clean and refreshed. The sleep deprivation clung to him like a weighted vest, but like any good investigator, the work ahead kept driving him forward.

As he dressed for the day, his eyes fell upon his laptop still sitting atop the desk where he had left it the night before. The thumb drive containing the Laura Croxford death investigation still protruded from the computer. He'd barely gotten a look at the incident report before Chloe barged in on him. And he'd nearly forgotten about it given last night's drama and the attack on Ronnie Libby. He sighed, realizing that his side project would have to wait.

53

Saturday, October 11, 9:00 a.m

As expected, Chloe's unmarked was parked unattended in the side lot of their temporary headquarters. Despite all the trouble that had led him from Troop A to Troop E and MCU North, Brock realized that he had lucked out when he drew Chloe Wright as a partner.

"Decided to sleep in, huh?" Chloe teased as he entered their makeshift office.

"Funny," Brock said. "Did you manage any sleep at all?"

"Figure I got two and a half solid hours before the case took over my brain again," Chloe said. "I've been here since six or so. Wanted to get down a few ideas I had before they drifted away."

"Care to share?" Brock said.

"Grab yourself a coffee first. I made some fresh."

"Thanks," Brock said. "You're a lifesaver."

Brock scoured the kitchenette for a mug that would at least pass for clean. The closest thing he could find was a dark blue ceramic mug embossed on one side with a gold Greenville PD badge. After rinsing it out several times with the hottest water he could manage from the tap and wiping it dry with a paper towel, Brock filled it with coffee from the carafe, then returned to the conference room. Chloe was standing at the whiteboard, updating the information.

"Any word from the hospital?" Chloe asked as Brock sat down at the table.

"Ronnie Libby made it through the night," Brock said.

"Guess we can call that a win," Chloe said as her attention returned to the board.

"And we haven't had too many of those yet," Brock said before taking another sip of the hot coffee. "Libby's parents were already there when I arrived."

"How badly did that go?"

"About like you would imagine. They were pissed that we hadn't locked up Taylor Randall already."

"Did you mention he has an alibi?" Chloe said.

"They didn't want to hear that. Speaking of which, where's Zim?"

"He's chasing down the EMTs from last night for statements."

"Good," Brock said as he perused the murder board.

The murder board was the same in almost every investigation. The photo of the victim, in this case Summer Randall, normally graced the top of the display, as if they were the head of some organized crime syndicate, followed by photos and relevant information of every known suspect and witness. As detectives continued to work the case, and new information was discovered, the designation of each player could change. Witnesses might become suspects, or vice versa, as the case progressed and more became known. In this case, Taylor Randall had gone from simply being a witness and the victim's father to a suspect in the attack on Ronnie Libby. Libby himself remained a suspect in Summer Randall's murder. Regardless of the case complexity, an organized murder board could help to minimize confusion and show the facts and links more clearly.

As Brock studied the board, he noticed the addition of a new face. This one belonged to Toby Lonegan, Taylor Randall's employee and the only person able to provide his boss with an alibi for the time they believed Ronnie Libby had been attacked in his home. Brock knew, as they all did, that Taylor's alibi still needed to be fleshed out. As an employee, Lonegan had every reason to cover for his boss. His relationship to the most likely suspect in the attack didn't mean he was lying, but it did mean that his account was worthy of a hard look. Hell, for all they knew, Lonegan himself might have given Ronnie the beating for Taylor, which would mean that Taylor was actually providing him with an alibi. Brock had learned long ago that when it came to investigating murder, it was always best not to take anything at face value. Albert had always said, "Trust but verify." Brock didn't know where that sage advice had originated, but he knew it hadn't come from Albert Justice.

"So, let's hear these ideas of yours," Brock said at last.

"Okay," Chloe said as she dropped the marker in the tray at the base of the whiteboard and turned to face Brock. "I've been thinking. We've been handed many of the theories we are currently running down, right?"

Brock nodded and took another sip of coffee.

"What if the motive for this has nothing to do with half-crazed combat veterans or shunned ex-boyfriends?"

"Abusive shunned ex-boyfriends," Brock said.

"I stand corrected," Chloe said.

"Okay, let's hear it," Brock said. "What other motive do you have?"

"Summer's pregnancy still bothers me. I had a scare myself when I was about her age."

"And?"

"And it was the most terrifying thing I could imagine at the time. I mean, I had a plan about how my life would go, and becoming a mother wasn't part of that plan."

"What did you do?" Brock said before he could stop himself. "Never mind. I shouldn't have asked you that. It's none of my business."

"No, it's okay. I am the one who brought it up. In my case, it hadn't happened. I wasn't pregnant, just late. But Summer was pregnant, and she knew it. The testing kit I found in her trash confirms that she knew."

Brock still wasn't sure where she was going with this. "So, what are you thinking?"

"I'm thinking she told someone. I know what a heavy burden something like that can be, and Summer wouldn't have been able to deal with that on her own. She would have brought someone into the fold."

"Assuming you're right, who do you think she would have told? The father?"

"Not necessarily," Chloe said. "Honestly, most men are shit when it comes to just listening. You guys want to try and fix everything."

Brock recalled having heard his ex-wife say something similar during an argument.

"And if I were Summer, the last person I would confide in, at least until I had a better handle on what I was going to do, would be the baby's father."

"Then who?" Brock said.

"In my case, I went to my closest friend."

Brock's eyes drifted to the whiteboard and the photo of Summer standing with her arm around nurse Brittney LaRoux.

"LaRoux already told us she was Summer's closest friend. Trained together. Ran marathons together. Hell, they even worked together."

"I guess that makes sense," Brock said as he nodded his agreement. "You want to approach her together?"

"No, I think I'll take this one myself."

"Who's hungry?" Zimmerman said from the doorway of the conference room as he held up a bag from the Greenville Grinds café.

"Is that what I hope it is?" Brock said, his mouth watering with the thought.

"You mean three of the biggest, sweetest cinnamon buns in the entire state?" Zimmerman said as he opened the top of the bag and inhaled deeply.

"Don't tease," Chloe pleaded. "I'm starving."

"Better grab a boatload of napkins, then," Zimmerman said.

After they'd finished devouring their pastries, Chloe and Brock filled Zimmerman in on their earlier conversation. They also discussed strategy going forward.

"Can't argue with your feelings about LaRoux," Zimmerman said. "I can't imagine what getting that news would be like from Summer Randall's perspective, but it sounds like you're on to something, Chloe."

"By all accounts, they were best of friends," Brock said.

"You want help talking with her?" Zimmerman said.

"Brock already offered," Chloe said, shaking her head. "Thanks, but I think she's more likely to be forthcoming if it's just me."

Zimmerman turned to Brock. "You're the primary on this, amigo. What would you like me to focus on today?"

"I need you to camp out at the hospital to monitor Ronnie Libby."

Zimmerman groaned. "I was afraid you'd say that. After last night, the last thing I want to deal with is more family drama."

"Can't be helped," Brock said.

"Plus, you know there will be visitors," Chloe said. "I'd like to know who comes to see Ronnie and how they react to your presence."

"What, you think the suspect is just gonna walk in and confess to me?" Zimmerman said.

"No, but guilty people do and say stupid things," Brock said, coming to Chloe's defense.

"So do people in mourning," Chloe added. "In that setting, you're more likely to catch people with their guard down."

"So, you want me to play the compassionate detective?"

"I was thinking more along the lines of Uncle Zim," Brock said.

"And if you really want to sell it, you should pick up some more of those sticky buns," Chloe chuckled.

54

Saturday, October 11, 10:05 a.m

It was after ten o'clock by the time Chloe walked through the main entrance of the Northern Light Hospital. She hadn't bothered to contact Brittney LaRoux ahead of time because she wanted her visit to catch the nurse by surprise. Chloe only hoped that she was scheduled to work.

As she neared the nurses' station, Chloe realized she was in luck, catching a glimpse of LaRoux exiting one of the rooms.

"Hey, Detective," LaRoux said. "If you're looking for Ronnie Libby, he's not here."

"I know," Chloe said. "Two of our detectives went to Eastern Maine Med last night."

"His injuries required far more care than we're equipped to provide here," a voice said from behind Chloe.

"Dr. Heiden," Chloe said. "I didn't see you standing there."

"I would have treated Ronnie here if I could have," Heiden continued.

"I understand," Chloe said.

"I just got off the phone with the attending physician, and while I can't give you any specifics, I can tell you that the standard course of treatment, assuming he remains stable, is to try and bring Ronnie around in the next day or two. The last time he was conscious, he was very agitated and confused. No one wants him in that state. He could injure himself further by thrashing around."

"Thanks for that, Doc," Chloe said.

"You're welcome, Detective."

Chloe watched Heiden move down the hall toward the far end. She guessed he was making his normal rounds to check on all the patients. Chloe turned, surprised to find LaRoux still standing there.

"I was wondering if you've made any progress on Summer's case?" LaRoux said.

"We are making progress," Chloe said. "But there is still a lot to do. Speaking of which, I wonder if you might have a minute to speak in private?"

"Can I?" LaRoux said to the woman manning the duty station.

"Go, but don't be long. We're short-staffed as it is."

Chloe watched the duty nurse's expression turn grim as she realized what she had said. She hadn't meant to be callous, but everyone knew why they were short-staffed, and it was because Summer Randall was dead.

"I'm sorry," the duty nurse said.

"I'll only keep her for a minute," Chloe said. "I promise."

Brock stepped outside the public safety building to grab a fresh notebook from his unmarked when he nearly collided with Warden Labbe.

"Hey, Warden," Brock said.

"Hey, yourself," Labbe said. "Things are still pretty heated around here, I see. Heard about Ronnie Libby being attacked last night."

"Yeah, we're still trying to figure out who might be behind that."

"The running theory is that it's connected to Summer Randall's murder. Course, I don't subscribe to that kind of scuttlebutt. It's facts that make the law enforcement world go 'round, am I right?"

"Right you are," Brock said.

"I'm sure you know that Ronnie ran with a rough crowd when he was still drinking. Could be someone held a grudge."

"Someone besides Taylor Randall, you mean," Brock said.

"Like I said, Detective, I don't get involved in rumors and such."

"That's good to hear," Brock said. "Is there something I can do for you, Warden?"

"Actually, I'm here because there might be something I can do for you."

"Oh?"

"We just got a call from a concerned citizen about seeing someone removing game cameras along Scammon Road." Labbe pantomimed air quotes with his fingers as he said the words "concerned citizen." "Said the guy was dressed in camouflage."

"You think it's legit?" Brock said.

"Who knows. But I knew you guys were interested in Peter Bragg's ongoing poaching, so I thought you might like to take a ride out there with me."

"What makes you think it's Bragg? You gave us a list of poachers."

Labbe grinned. "Call it a hunch."

"Let's go," Brock said.

Chloe and Brittney LaRoux sat outside in the warm sunshine on a wooden bench beside the hospital. The grassy alcove, where most of the hospital employees took their breaks during nice weather, offered protection from the wind. It was clear she didn't want to talk about Summer's secret with anyone.

Chloe watched as the nurse fumbled with a cigarette and lighter until finally she got it lit. The nurse held the pack up to Chloe.

"You want one?"

"No thanks," Chloe said. "I don't smoke."

"I know," the nurse said. "I shouldn't either. Not something you expect from a medical professional, huh? It is a nasty habit and hasn't done a thing for my wind when I'm in training. I should probably quit."

"I imagine every profession has its vices," Chloe said. "Stress?"

"You can't imagine," LaRoux said after exhaling a plume of bluish smoke.

But Chloe could imagine it. She'd seen Brock continue to struggle with his nicotine addiction, and she knew if she ever took up the habit, she likely wouldn't be able to stop.

"How long had you known?" Chloe said.

"About Summer's pregnancy? She told me the day before she was—the day before she died. She said that she hadn't told anyone else, because she didn't know what she wanted to do about it."

"You mean keep it or terminate it?"

LaRoux shrugged. "I don't know. We didn't really have a chance to discuss it in any detail. We had planned to grab a drink after our training run, but I had to cancel because of a personal matter with my gran."

"Your grandmother?" Chloe said.

"She suffers from dementia. It's still in the early stages, but I live with her so that she can maintain her independence for as long as possible. But every once in a while she gets confused, and I, well, I have to get home to be with her."

"Completely understandable," Chloe said. "It must be difficult with a job like yours."

LaRoux nodded. "I have a home healthcare nurse on speed dial for those times when I can't get away."

"Did you cancel your run with Summer because something happened?"

"Gran got confused and had a fall."

"I hope she wasn't injured," Chloe said.

"No. More embarrassed than anything, but I can't help but wonder what would have happened if I had been with Summer in the woods that afternoon, instead of running home to be with my gran. Maybe Summer would still be okay. Maybe she'd still be alive?"

Chloe watched a single tear roll down the nurse's cheek.

"There is no way you could have known. Besides, if you'd been out there instead of tending to your grandmother, you might both have become victims."

"I guess," LaRoux said as she wiped the tear from her face with the back of her hand.

"Did Summer tell you?" Chloe said.

"Tell me what?"

"Who the baby's father was?"

LaRoux shook her head. "Like I said, I never got the chance to ask her any questions. I figured she'd tell me more after our run. Guess I just figured it was Ronnie Libby's."

"What makes you say that?" Chloe said.

"Like I told you, she'd been seeing Ronnie again. But she was keeping it a secret."

Chloe was beginning to see a pattern when it came to Summer Randall and her secrets.

"A secret from who?" Chloe said.

"Everyone, I guess. But mostly her dad."

"Taylor?"

"Yeah. She was afraid Taylor would kill Ronnie if he found out."

55

Saturday, October 11, 11:05 a.m

Brock scanned his side of the road from the passenger seat of Labbe's pickup as they motored along Scammon Road. His view was limited to a blur of passing trees and the occasional swampy clearing. Knowing full well how much wardens enjoyed mucking about in the outdoors, Brock decided to err on the side of caution, grabbing the Bean boots out of his unmarked before they departed from the PSB. He had no idea what Labbe was dragging him into, but he had already been warned by Lt. Cumberland that she would not be paying for any more of Brock's ruined dress shoes out of the Troop E budget.

Everything inside the truck seemed to rattle and squeak as it rolled along the country road, causing Brock to wonder how long the vehicle had been assigned to Labbe.

"I would have thought they would've assigned you something a bit newer," Brock said. "You know, with your seniority."

"Ha," Labbe said. "Seniority sounds suspiciously like long in the tooth."

"I might have gone with seasoned," Brock said.

"That's me," Labbe said. "Truth is, I like this old girl. The newer vehicles are all plastic and computer chips. It's ridiculous. You can't do anything without something breaking. Give me an old Chevy any day."

"Aren't you afraid they'll force you into a newer model eventually?"

"Nope. Provided the repairs don't start costing more than a new one. Besides, at this point, if they force me into anything, it will be retirement."

Brock figured he had a point.

"See anything yet?" Labbe said.

"Not sure what I'm looking for," Brock said.

"Hang on a sec, and I'll show you."

Warden Labbe pulled off the pavement into a small dirt turnout on the side of the road. He killed the engine, then opened the door and jumped out. Brock followed suit, grabbing his boots from the passenger-side footwell as he exited.

"Good idea," Labbe said. "Those fancy clodhoppers probably won't do you much good in the mud."

"Yeah," Brock said. "I figured that out the hard way."

As soon as Brock finished changing his footwear, he tossed his dress shoes inside the cab and locked the door.

"Follow me," Labbe said as he started down the steep embankment into the scrub brush below.

Brock struggled to keep up, once again surprised at just how nimble the veteran warden seemed to be. It was clear that the man loved his job and loved the outdoors in a way that reminded Brock of his father, Albert.

Labbe continually looked down as if unsure of his footing, but that wasn't what the wily old warden was focused on.

"Fresh prints," Labbe said, pointing at a patch of matted grass across the top of a hummock.

"How did you know that this is where the caller spotted the guy dressed in camouflage?"

"I didn't," Labbe said. "But if you're an experienced poacher, there are only so many good hunting spots along Scammon Road."

"And this is a good one?" Brock said, struggling to avoid losing his balance and slipping into the standing water of the bog.

"Good for hunting. Not so good for walking. Come on."

Chloe exited the hospital's main entry doors and was headed back across the parking lot toward her unmarked when a woman flagged her down.

The woman, dressed in street clothes, appeared to have been walking toward the hospital before turning in Chloe's direction. Sporting shoulder-length salt-and-pepper hair, she looked to be at least two decades Chloe's senior and several inches shorter.

"Can I help you with something?" Chloe said.

"No, but I think I might be able to help you. You're one of the detectives who's been asking about Summer Randall, right?"

"That's right. I'm Chloe Wright."

"Nice to meet you, Chloe. Nancy Higgins. I work here as a full-time nurse."

"Then you must have known Summer, right?"

"Of course. Everybody knew Summer. We loved her. Such a sweet young woman. Nothing like some of the young'uns we get here."

Chloe hadn't spoken with the woman before, nor could she remember seeing the name Nancy Higgins on any of the statements already taken.

"Have you spoken with any of the other detectives?" Chloe said.

Higgins shook her head. "I've been off on PTO since last week. You couldn't have interviewed me even if you wanted to."

"Do you have time now?" Chloe said.

Higgins checked her watch. "Well, I'm scheduled to go on duty in twenty minutes. Is that enough time?"

"Hop in," Chloe said, gesturing toward the Interceptor.

56

Saturday, October 11, 11:35 a.m

As they neared the far edge of the clearing where the bog met the woods, Labbe stopped to examine something on one of the tree trunks. Brock foolishly lifted his eyes from the ground to see what the warden was up to and lost his footing. His right leg plunged down at least two feet deep into the stagnant water of the bog, releasing an odiferous combination of sulfur and something even more unpleasant from beneath the depths. Brock pinwheeled his arms, barely maintaining his balance as the chilly water quickly seeped inside his boot, soaking his sock.

"Shit," Brock said.

Labbe turned back to face him. "You okay?"

"Just dandy," Brock said. He grabbed a hold of a nearby stump with both hands and dragged himself up and out of the water, the mud nearly pulling his boot off in the process.

"Nice boots. But they aren't much good if you submerge them. You'd do well to get yourself something a bit taller, like these Wellingtons."

"Thanks," Brock said. "I'll try and remember that."

"Happy to help."

"What did you find on that tree that's so interesting?" Brock said as he plopped down on a dry patch of ground and began to unlace the boot.

"See here on this swamp maple where the moss is missing and compressed slightly on this side of the trunk?"

Brock peeled off his sodden sock and wrung it out as he looked to where Labbe was pointing. "I guess," Brock said. "I wouldn't have noticed it."

Labbe fixed him with a knowing grin. "That's because you're not a warden."

"Okay, I'll bite. What caused that?"

"The strap of a game camera, most likely. Probably belonging to the guy the anonymous caller saw down here."

"A poacher moving a game camera, then? To another location?"

"Maybe. Or maybe he was just taking it down so that I wouldn't find it. By now, word has gotten out that we've been poking around."

"You're referring to Peter Bragg?" Brock said.

"Or one of the other poachers du jour. It's like they have their own little network. Trust me, son, as soon as word got out that Summer Randall had been murdered, and not simply run over by a drunk driver, all of my usual suspects got nervous. How many times have you tripped over a crime while investigating one that's totally unrelated?"

Brock couldn't argue the point. It happened more often than people thought, making him wonder what that said about the human condition that it was so easy to trip over unrelated crimes. He replaced his damp sock, then pulled on his boot and quickly laced it. He stood up and watched as Labbe moved around behind the tree and looked back toward Scammon Road.

"What are you doing?" Brock said.

"I'm trying to get the camera's view from where we're standing."

"What will that tell us?"

Labbe's head appeared from behind the tree, a mischievous glint in his eyes. "Might not tell us a damn thing. Or it might be the thing that solves your case."

Brock turned and looked back across the bog the way they had come. The only thing standing between them and the road was a hundred or so feet of stagnant water, protruding grassy mounds, and chest-high scrub growth. While the roadside bog might make for good poaching, Brock couldn't see how it could possibly help them find Summer Randall's killer.

Zimmerman sat in a chair in the hallway across from Ronnie Libby's room. He'd positioned himself in such a way that he could watch the comings and goings of the medical staff as well as any visitors who approached the nurses' station.

The chair was one of those unpadded, formfitting plastic seats with curved metal legs that was popular in most medical facilities that he had visited. Zimmerman had been sitting there for over an hour, and his lower back had begun to protest. He wondered if maybe the chair manufacturers were colluding with the medical field in order to bring them more patients.

The door to Libby's room was closed, but Zimmerman could still hear the faint beeping of the equipment used to monitor Ronnie's vitals. He wondered if Libby, even in his current state, was aware of the sound.

"Detective?"

Zimmerman looked up from the magazine he was reading to see one of the nurses. "Can I help you?" he said.

"There's someone here who would like to speak with you," the nurse said as she gestured toward the nurses' station, where a young blond woman dressed in a blue windbreaker and jeans stood by herself.

Zimmerman pushed himself up from the chair and followed the nurse down the hall.

"I'm Detective Zimmerman," he said. "I understand you wish to speak with me."

"Candace Issacson," she said.

"Nice to meet you, Candace," Zimmerman said. "What did you want to talk about?"

Issacson looked around nervously. "Can we talk somewhere in private?"

The nurse who had approached him was now standing behind the counter at the nurses' station. "You're welcome to use the cafeteria," she said, pointing down the hall.

"Thank you," Zimmerman said.

57

Saturday, October 11, 12:15 p.m

Deputy Evan Mathers checked in at the Greenville Police Department using the ruse that he was looking for an update from the state police detectives. Leavitt's secretary, Isabelle Sanborn, had informed him that Detective Wright was at the hospital and Zimmerman had gone to Bangor to check on Ronnie Libby.

"What about Brock Justice?" Evan had asked.

"He's out following up on a lead with Warden Labbe."

Evan thanked her before driving straight to the inn where he knew the detectives were staying. Having done a bit of sleuthing himself, he had been able to confirm the identity of the woman Brock had met in Dover-Foxcroft as none other than Bangor Police Detective Ginger Dashofy. Dashofy was one of the two detectives who had been assigned to investigate the unattended death of Laura Croxford. Evan wasn't a big believer in coincidence, but even if he had been, this was a bridge too far.

He turned into the lot of the Moose Mountain Inn and parked at the curb directly in front of room number eight, Brock's room. The location was perfect, on the ground level and as far away from the office as he could get.

As he had hoped, the housemaid was still working. Evan spotted her pushcart parked in front of an open door several rooms down from Brock's.

"Excuse me," he said, poking his head in through the open door.

"Oh my God," the cleaning woman said, clutching her hands to her chest.

"I'm so sorry," Evan said. "I didn't mean to startle you."

"It's okay," she said after taking a moment to compose herself. "What can I do for you, officer?"

Evan decided to forgo the title correction. The sooner he was in and out, the better.

"I feel like such an idiot," he said. "I'm supposed to leave something for one of the state police detectives, but I forgot to bring the room card and can't get in. I don't suppose you could—?"

Evan cut himself off mid-sentence. He could see by the woman's expression that she was about to turn him down. Maybe even send him down to the manager's office, someplace he had no intention of going.

"You know what? Never mind. I shouldn't even ask. It's just that we've been working on this murder case, and I—"

This time the woman interrupted him. "That poor Randall girl?"

Evan nodded, keeping his expression grim. "Yes. It's so sad. Sounds like everyone loved Summer."

The housemaid dug into the pocket of her apron and walked toward him. "Which room do you need access to?"

"Number eight," Evan said as he moved to let her pass by. "I can't thank you enough for this. You're an angel."

Zimmerman realized that despite requesting to speak with him, Ms. Issacson was still on the fence about sharing whatever information she had with the police. He decided to splurge on a cup of coffee, thinking that a small gesture of goodwill might at least get things moving in the right direction. Candace sat down at a vacant table in the far corner of the room while he went to make the purchase. He kept one eye on the skittish young woman as he stood at the register paying for the coffees, half expecting her to bolt.

"Here you go," Zimmerman said as he handed her the cup. "Cream and two sugars."

"Thank you, Detective Zimmerman," she said in a barely audible voice.

"Don't thank me yet. Have you ever tried cafeteria coffee?"

She grinned.

"And it's Zim," he said as he removed the lid from his cup and took a sip. "At least that's what my friends call me."

"Thank you, Zim. My friends call me Candy."

"Now, what can I do for you, Candy?"

She didn't respond right away. He could tell she was still processing what she wanted to say, and how to say it. He remained quiet. If she was half as conflicted about coming forward as she appeared, the last thing he wanted was to spook her.

At last, she placed the cup on the table and looked directly at him. "I have information about Ronnie Libby that might help you."

"Okay," Zimmerman said. "I'm all ears."

"I know everyone thinks Ronnie had something to do with killing Summer Randall. But—he didn't do it."

"How do you know?"

"Because at the time Summer was killed, Ronnie was with me."

Once he was safely inside Brock's room with the door closed, Evan removed a pair of nitrile gloves from a small black pouch on his duty belt. Carefully he worked his hands into the gloves, then turned and locked the deadbolt. The room had already been cleaned and the bed made, and the strong smell of disinfectant emanated from the bathroom. He scanned the room from where he stood at the door. He wanted a mental image of where everything was when he first entered. A quick and thorough search was what he had planned, but not so haphazard that he left some trace that he'd been snooping around.

He approached the writing desk, where a laptop sat open with a darkened screen. He knew it was entirely possible that whatever Detective Dashofy had given to Brock, he might be carrying it with him, but Mathers was betting not. If he were in Brock's shoes, there was no way he would tote around evidence from a case that had nothing to do with the one he was currently working. If Zimmerman or Chloe found it, how would Brock explain it? No, it was far more likely that Brock had hidden whatever it was somewhere inside the room.

Aside from the laptop, the desk was clean, and the drawers were bare. Likewise, the wastebasket on the floor beside the desk was empty. Evan knew that one problem with having the cleaning staff beat him to the room was that there was no chance of gleaning something useful from the trash. A balled-up piece of notepaper, a business card or phone number, something he could use. He had made enough cases against bad guys to know that nobody gives enough thought to what they throw away. Not even cops.

Evan moved into the bathroom. Despite the amenities contained within, there was virtually nowhere to hide something. He knew Brock was smarter than that, but Evan checked inside the toilet tank anyway. After coming up empty, he returned to the room and checked the closet. A pile of dirty clothes lay on the closet floor. On the hangers were several dress shirts and a pair of blue jeans. He searched inside every pocket, but there was nothing to find but lint. Even the small room safe was standing open, unused.

That fucking Boy Scout probably even locks his weapon in the trunk safe of his unmarked, Evan thought.

He got down on his hands and knees to look under the bed but was thwarted again. The bed was the type without a box spring—just a mattress that sat on a solid wooden platform. He slid his hands under the mattress anyway, carefully lifting it to look underneath. Again, he found nothing. He re-tucked and smoothed the bedding that had come loose during his inspection, then rose to his feet again. Maybe he'd been wrong about Brock's meeting with the Bangor detective. Maybe the meeting was about another case entirely. Or perhaps the two of them were seeing each other on the sly. If they were, perhaps he might be able to use that to his advantage.

"You're a bad boy, Detective Justice," Evan said to the empty room.

He was halfway to the door, thinking that he'd been wrong about everything, when he stopped and turned toward the television. It was a midsized flat-screen TV, the kind that could be hung on a wall or mounted to a plastic base. This flat-screen sat on a base. Evan grabbed onto the top of the television frame at its center and carefully tilted the entire unit backward. There under the hollow plastic base was a black-and-red thumb drive lying atop a manila envelope along with several sheets of notepaper. Evan removed his phone and photographed the position of the items before touching them. He knew the picture would allow him to at least approximate their locations.

He carried the items over to the desk and turned on the lamp.

Written across the front of the envelope was a 2025 BPD case number. Below the number was the name Laura Croxford. Inside the envelope was the entire death investigation, or at least what there was of it. Evan sighed deeply. He had nothing available on which to examine the drive except Brock's laptop. He pressed on the computer's built-in mouse pad and brought the screen to life. The computer was locked.

Dammit, he thought.

He looked down at the drive again, already knowing that whatever was on it would not be good. Not for him, anyway. He pushed it aside and picked up the sheets of notepaper. The handwriting on the paper was Brock's. Evan recognized it immediately. He'd seen more than his fair share of Brock's scribbling during the trial preparations with his attorney. There were two pages of penned notes that consisted of a list of times. Each entry was followed by a brief description of something that happened at that time. Brock had used the initials *EM* in several places instead of writing out Evan's complete name.

As his attention returned to the computer screen, he had a thought. He wondered if Brock was savvy enough to change his password. It was widely known that most road troopers used their unit number, the number on their registration plates, as a password. One they wouldn't forget. Evan typed in Brock's number from memory: 1213. He hit enter. The screensaver disappeared, and the home screen appeared. Evan grinned as he inserted the thumb drive into a USB port on the side of the laptop.

He waited a few seconds for the drive to boot up, then clicked on the icon. The screen filled with several rows of files contained on the drive. Some folders were labeled as containing documents, while others contained photos. But the folder that got his immediate attention was labeled "Videos."

Brock had Warden Labbe drop him back at the PSB to retrieve his Interceptor and change socks before checking in with Chloe and Zimmerman. Brock bumped into the chief's secretary while walking to his vehicle.

"I don't suppose Deputy Mathers caught up with you, did he?" Sanborn said.

"Didn't know he was looking for me," Brock said.

"Maybe not you specifically, but he stopped by here earlier looking for a case update. I told him you were out with the warden and that the other detectives were at the hospitals."

"Nope, we never connected," Brock said, doing his best to hide the pleasure he was feeling about it.

"Well, I'm sure he must have talked to Detective Wright or Zimmerman."

"I'm sure you're right," Brock said. "Anyone else stop by?"

Sanborn shook her head. "Just Evan."

"Thanks," Brock said, picking up on her familiar use of Mathers's given name and wondering how close they were.

58

Saturday, October 11, 1:55 p.m

Evan scanned the files contained within the video folder. Each file had the name of a business typed below it. He knew the detectives would have collected any nearby surveillance footage on the off chance that the death they were investigating turned out to be something other than a suicide or an accidental death. He knew there hadn't been any security cameras at the hotel, at least not outside the lobby. It was the reason he'd picked it in the first place. But the restaurant where he'd parked the rental apparently did have exterior cameras. He moved the cursor over the file marked "Denny's" and clicked on it.

As he began to watch the footage recorded by Denny's exterior camera, Evan realized he'd made a big mistake, a rookie move. He looked at the time and date stamp in the lower corner of the screen and toggled ahead until it was near the time he was interested in. He watched the screen for several minutes until he found what he was looking for. The rental car and the hooded figure getting out of it, then walking in the direction of the hotel.

Evan sat back in the chair and tapped his fingers on the desk as he thought about his next move. It was too late to do anything about it now. And what did they really have on him? A coincidence? So he happened to grab something to eat at the local Denny's. And his dinner just happened to coincide with an intoxicated and drugged woman drowning in a hotel bathroom next door. So what? And yes, he'd rented a car. The last time he checked, it wasn't a crime to lease a vehicle. If that's all Brock and Dashofy had, then he had nothing to worry about. Any first-year trial lawyer could get him off. That flimsy shit didn't come close to probable cause. Even if Brock had shared his suspicions with Dashofy, suspicions weren't evidence. But still.

Evan froze to the sound of a car door closing right outside the room. He realized that he had been here for far too long. And getting caught inside Brock's room would be impossible to explain. Not to mention the additional ammunition it would give Brock to use against him. At the moment, Brock looked like a bitter ex-partner who couldn't let go of the idea that Mathers had been found not guilty. Even some of Brock's fellow state police detectives were still siding with Evan. The last thing Evan wanted was to be the reason that situation changed.

He exited out of the file, unplugged the flash drive, and picked up the notes. Quickly he returned everything to their previous location beneath the base of the television, even double-checking the photo he had taken to approximate locations of each item. When he was satisfied, he lowered the TV onto the stand. He returned to the desk and switched off the lamp. Evan scanned the room one last time before unbolting the door and stepping outside. He peeled off the gloves and shoved them into his rear pants pocket. Walking as if he belonged there, he exchanged a wave with the housemaid. He wondered if she would say anything to Brock, but as he scanned the lot crowded with people checking in, he realized it was more likely she'd forget all about it.

He climbed back inside the cruiser and fired up the engine. He'd found what he'd been looking for. Evidence that Brock really was looking to jam him up again. And in truth, it was Evan's own fault for bragging about Laura's death. He shouldn't have done it. But there was just something about Brock Justice that brought out the worst in him. As he drove out of the lot onto Route 15, Evan considered how much of a problem the involvement of Detective Dashofy might be. Brock already had a reputation for being a dog who refuses to give up the bone. Dashofy, on the other hand, was an unknown quantity. One that could present a serious problem.

59

Saturday, October 11, 2:05 p.m

Brock drove to the inn on Rockwood Road and parked in the only open space near his room. He grabbed his dress shoes from the floor behind the driver's seat, then headed toward the door to his unit. He inserted the room's electronic key card and waited for the lock to turn green. He heard the click of the lock disengaging before he turned the handle and opened the door.

He flicked the switch for the floor lamp, then dropped his shoes on the carpet. He was bending down to remove his boots when something made him freeze in place. The faint aroma of burnt cigarette smoke hung in the air. If there was one thing a nicotine addict knew well, it was the siren call of tobacco. He stood erect and drew the Heckler & Koch .45 from its holster, holding it firmly in both hands at the low ready position. Either someone other than the housemaid, who didn't smoke, had been in his room, or they still were. Brock moved to his right toward the bed to give himself some cover should the need arise. There were only two places to hide in this unit. The closet or the bathroom.

Brock stood very still for close to a minute, listening for even the slightest sound. He heard nothing. No creaking of the floor, no nervous breathing, nothing. He raised the gun slightly and moved around the bed toward the bathroom, avoiding the closet completely. He stayed against the far wall, away from both doors, planting one foot in front of the other. As the bathroom slowly came into view, Brock could see it was empty. That left only the closet. He turned his attention to the door as he stood next to the adjacent wall. He reached out with his left hand and turned the knob slowly until he was sure the latch was clear of the strike plate. Brock whipped the door open and stepped back with the barrel of his gun pointed inside the closet. No one was hiding inside. Nothing but a few items of clothing on the hangers and a small pile of dirty clothes on the floor.

As he holstered the semiauto, his gaze moved to the television. He crossed the room in three long strides and tilted the screen back. The evidence was still there. Exactly as he had left it. He lowered the TV back onto the shelf, then turned to study the room. The smell of nicotine was still present but very faint. A smoker had definitely been inside his room, he was sure of it. The only question remaining was who? A different member of motel cleaning staff than the one he had met? Or Deputy Evan Mathers?

A text message from Chloe ripped Brock from his thoughts.

Where R U? Zim has news.

Brock's heart sank as he considered the possibility that Ronnie Libby might have succumbed to his injuries.

On my way back to the PSB. ETA 5.

C U there.

Much to his dismay, Brock strolled into the conference room to find Chloe and Chief Leavitt seated at the table across from Evan Mathers.

"There he is," Mathers said.

Brock glared at him but wisely kept his thoughts to himself.

"Heard you were out with Warden Labbe," Leavitt said. "Find anything useful?"

"Yeah," Brock said as he pulled out a chair and sat down. "Wellingtons are better in deep water than Bean boots."

"I'm almost afraid to ask," Leavitt chuckled.

"Don't," Brock said. "What's the status on Libby?"

"We've got Zim on speakerphone," Chloe said, gesturing to her phone lying on the table.

"Young Ronnie's still with us," Zimmerman said. "At least for now."

Brock felt some of the tension let go.

"Doctor said there's been no change in his condition," Zimmerman continued. "But the more time passes, the greater his chance at recovery."

"Zim found out something interesting, though," Chloe said. "Tell him."

"It appears that Ronnie might not be a viable suspect in Summer Randall's murder after all. I spoke to a woman named Candace Issacson. Evidently she is Libby's AA sponsor."

Candy, Brock thought to himself. He had totally dropped the ball on following up Libby's alibi.

"According to Issacson, Ronnie called her all distraught, asking to meet early evening the night Summer was killed."

"How early?" Brock said.

"She says they met up in Dover-Foxcroft for coffee around seven and talked for more than three hours."

"Then there's no way Ronnie could have stabbed Summer Randall," Mathers said.

Brock ignored Mathers's comment. "How did we happen to run into this Candace—?"

"Issacson," Zimmerman said. "She came to the hospital to check on Ronnie after she heard about the attack. Asked the duty nurse if there was a detective she could speak to."

"You believe her story?" Brock said.

"Yeah, I do. She was really conflicted about sharing Ronnie's personal stuff with me, which is why she hadn't come forward before now. Apparently, young Mr. Libby is still infatuated with Summer, enough so that he wouldn't heed Candace's warnings about avoiding relationships during the first year of addiction recovery."

"She confirmed that Ronnie had been meeting in secret with Summer,"

Chloe said. "The reason he reached out to her that night was because Summer had refused to accept the necklace Ronnie bought her."

The heart-pendant necklace, Brock thought.

"Candace said he really took it hard," Zimmerman said. "Not in an angry way, but it sorta decimated him. He was afraid he'd go get drunk."

Brock looked up at the whiteboard as he considered this new revelation. He noticed Issacson's name had been added to the case as a witness. But was she reliable?

"Did Candace tell you which AA chapter she and Ronnie belonged to?" Brock said.

"She did," Zimmerman said. "I don't think it has a formal name or anything, but they meet twice a week at some old meeting house in the town of Monson. According to her, Ronnie has been attending meetings since the assault case with Summer. Hasn't missed a single one."

"Let's follow up with the leader of that chapter, then," Brock said. "I want to find out more about Issacson and if the group leader shares her high opinion of Ronnie Libby."

"You got it," Zimmerman said.

"Are you still at Eastern Maine Med?" Brock said.

"No, I'm headed back to Greenville, where I can be of more help."

"Okay," Brock said as he turned his attention to Evan. "What about you, Deputy? Do you have anything helpful to share, or are you just here to data mine?"

"Brock," Chloe said. "That's totally uncalled for. Evan's just trying to help."

"It's okay," Mathers said. "I'm used to it. If you want me to leave, just say so."

"We do not," Chloe said. "Do we, Brock?"

"I guess not," Brock said. "Does that mean you've discovered something that will help?"

"Not yet," Evan said as he fixed Brock with a knowing smirk. "I'm still conducting my background research."

Both men locked eyes for a long moment before Chloe broke the impasse.

"Well, I have news," Chloe said. "I had a long conversation with a nurse named Nancy Higgins."

"Higgins?" Brock said as he scanned the list of hospital employees.

"I don't remember speaking with anyone by that name," Zimmerman said.

"We haven't," Chloe said. "She just returned from vacation, flagged me down as I was leaving the hospital this afternoon."

"And?" Brock said.

"And, according to Nancy, the good Dr. Heiden has been warned several times for fraternizing with members of the staff," Chloe said. "Apparently, that is frowned upon in medical circles."

"He's been banging the nurses, in other words," Zimmerman said.

"Real nice, Zim," Chloe said.

"What?" Zimmerman said. "I'm just saying what you're all thinking."

"Anyway," Chloe said. "It appears that Heiden may have lied to us when he said he wasn't in a relationship with any of the staff members."

"Was he seeing Summer?" Evan said.

"No," Chloe said. "He wasn't, at least according to Higgins, and it sounds like she has her finger on the pulse of everything that goes on at Northern Light."

"So, who was the doctor seeing?" Brock said.

"Summer's best friend, Brittney LaRoux."

"Then she lied too," Zimmerman said.

"Probably because she didn't want to get the doc in trouble," Leavitt said.

Brock studied the whiteboard, focusing on the names of the hospital employees. Assuming Nurse Nancy was right, Northern Light Hospital had as many secrets as Summer Randall herself.

"What do you think?" Chloe asked Brock.

"I think it's time to pay another visit to the good doctor."

"I'm still not clear on something," Evan said. "Why would Heiden's secret relationship with LaRoux matter? It's not like he was seeing Summer Randall, right?"

"That's a good question," Chloe said as they all turned to look at the photo depicting all three of them following a road race.

Mathers's portable radio chirped with static a moment before the voice of the dispatcher called his unit number.

"Seven thirty-eight, are you available for a call?"

"Ten-four. What do you have?"

"Seven thirty-eight, respond along with fire rescue for a ten fifty-five PI on Route 201 near Newton Field in Jackman. Receiving multiple calls stating serious injuries."

"En route," Evan said into the shoulder mic as he jumped out of the chair and headed for the door. "I'll check in with you guys later."

60

Saturday, October 11, 2:35 p.m

Evan Mathers had barely left the conference room before Chief Leavitt piped up with something to add.

"I'm sorry to bother you all with this," Leavitt said. "But I need to share something with you. Is this a good time?"

"Of course, Chief," Chloe said.

"What's up?" Brock said, his curiosity now fully piqued.

"Um, I received a call from one of my reserve officers this morning. His name is Leo Hastings, and he's been an asset to this department. I hired him just before the start of the summer tourist season. He's done an outstanding job for us."

"Why do I get the feeling I'm not going to like this?" Zimmerman said.

"Because you're not," Leavitt said. "Hastings just informed me that he was working the early shift last week when he received a report from the county dispatcher that a couple of tourists had called in a report of a suspicious male lurking about in the woods off Lily Bay Road."

"And?" Brock said, attempting to hurry the chief along. "Did he make contact?"

"Well, that's the thing. He informed me that he never responded to check out the report."

"That's just great," Zimmerman's voice shot back from the phone speaker. "You mean to tell me that we've been killing ourselves to double-check alibis and statements of everyone who might have had a reason to kill Summer, and the suspect might simply be some vagrant creeper hanging out in the woods? Someone we didn't even know about?"

Leavitt said nothing.

"Did Hastings say why he didn't respond?" Brock said.

"Told me it was a busy evening and he didn't want to get tied up walking through the woods and unable to respond to something serious."

"What did he do?" Chloe said.

"He said he acknowledged the call, then waited about fifteen minutes before radioing to the dispatcher that the suspect was GOA."

"Goddammit," Zimmerman said, echoing Brock's very thoughts.

"Where is Hastings now?" Brock said.

"He's supposed to report to me by three this afternoon. I told him that you guys would want to speak with him."

"Oh, I'd like to do more than speak to him," Zimmerman said.

"Chief Leavitt," a voice called out. Everyone turned to see Isabelle Sanborn, Leavitt's office assistant, standing in the doorway.

"What is it, Isabelle?" Leavitt said.

"It's your three o'clock. Officer Hastings is waiting in your office."

"I'll take this," Brock said as he rose from his chair. "Chloe, I need you to follow up with county dispatch. See if we can get audio from the actual call and the identity of the caller."

"You got it," Chloe said.

"I'm almost to Dover-Foxcroft now, if you need me to stop by and grab anything," Zimmerman said.

"Thanks, Zim," Chloe said. "I'll let you know."

"Okay," Zimmerman said. "And if you need any help working the kid over, let me know. I can be there in thirty minutes."

"Leo is a good kid," Leavitt said. "He's just young and naïve."

"Detective Zimmerman is kidding," Chloe said. "Aren't you, Zim?"

"Only half kidding," Zimmerman said.

Brock found Hastings seated with his back to the door in one of the visitor chairs in Leavitt's office. The reserve officer, dressed in civilian clothes, turned his head as they entered. He looked nervous.

"Detective Justice, this is Reserve Officer Leo Hastings," Leavitt said.

Hastings quickly stood and extended a hand in greeting.

"Officer Hastings," Brock said, ignoring the gesture to keep the young man off-balance. He'd already decided to play the fatherly role during their interaction. Chief Leavitt would decide the punishment to be meted out, but Brock needed the full picture of what they were dealing with and how bad Hastings had screwed their case. "Have a seat."

After a moment, Hastings lowered his hand and sat.

Brock turned the one empty visitor chair in the room to face Hastings directly, then sat down. Chief Leavitt commandeered the seat behind the desk.

"I remember you from last night," Brock said. "At the scene of the attack on Ronnie Libby."

"Yes, sir," Hastings said.

"I understand that you have something to share that might be relevant to our murder investigation," Brock said.

Hastings looked at the chief before turning to face Brock directly. "Yes, sir," he said. "I think I may have messed up."

"That just might be the understatement of the century," Leavitt said.

"Why don't you take us through what happened," Brock said.

"The caller didn't leave a name," the dispatcher said.

"What about a number?" Chloe said. "Certainly the 911 system would've captured the number."

"Would have, if they had called in on the emergency line," the dispatcher said. "Unfortunately, they called in through the Greenville switchboard and were automatically transferred to county dispatch when no one answered."

"Chief Leavitt mentioned that the caller was a tourist," Chloe said. "How do you know that?"

"I pulled and listened to the tape as soon as the chief called. Would you like to hear it?"

"Please," Chloe said.

"Give me a minute, and I'll put it on speaker for you."

"Thanks," Chloe said.

"Piscataquis County Dispatch Center," the call taker answered.

"Hello, I'm calling to report a suspicious person. A man in the woods off Lily Bay Road in Greenville."

Chloe scribbled a note that the caller's voice sounded female.

"Okay," the call taker said. "Is anyone in immediate danger?"

"What? No. I mean, I don't think so. Maybe."

Chloe could hear the caller whispering to someone in the background. It sounded like the caller may have covered the phone with their hand.

"Where are you calling from, ma'am?" the call taker said. "Can you still see the man?"

"Um, no. We left and headed back to our car."

"Can I get your name?"

"I really don't want to get involved. We're not even from around here. I just wanted someone to know."

"Where were you when you last saw the man?"

"We just left the woods off Lily Bay Road. The hiking trails. I don't know what they are called."

"Can you tell me what was suspicious about the man's behavior?"

"He looked like he didn't belong there. Like, he wasn't hiking or anything. Just hanging out and watching us."

"Can you describe what the man looked like?"

"He was dressed in dark-colored clothing, kind of shabby, and he had this weird look on his face, like he might have been under the influence of something. He just creeped us out."

"Can you give me any more detail? Like height or weight, skin color, or approximate age?"

"He was light-skinned. Not too old. Look, I've gotta go. I just wanted to let you know."

"Can you answer a few more questions?"

"I'm sorry. I don't want to get involved."

The caller could be heard disconnecting.

"That's it?" Chloe said.

"The call taker couldn't call back, as the call came through Greenville PD," the dispatcher said.

"How soon after the call did county put out the information?" Chloe said.

"Less than five minutes. Officer Hastings was assigned by radio to investigate the report. It was a pretty active evening. Normally we would have placed a call like that on the lower end of the priority list, but Hastings was already in the area, as he'd just cleared a traffic stop."

"What was the end result?" Chloe said.

"Hastings acknowledged the call by radio and said he would be checking. He cleared the call approximately fifteen minutes later, saying that the 10-39 subject was GOA."

Chloe considered the facts as they were presented. Even if Hastings had gotten his lazy butt out of the cruiser and walked into the woods, the furthest he could have gotten was seven minutes in before he would have to turn around and walk back. Seven minutes was hardly long enough to traverse anything more than a quarter mile, even if he had been on the correct path.

"Have there been any similar calls recently?" Chloe said.

"I can run a query if you want."

"That would be great. Also, any chance you could email me a printout of the call information and an MPEG of the radio traffic and phone call?"

"Certainly," the dispatcher said. "Give me about fifteen minutes, and I'll send everything out."

"Thanks," Chloe said before providing her with the email address.

"Do you mind if I ask you a question?" the dispatcher said.

"Shoot," Chloe said.

The woman paused for a moment as if trying to find the right words. "Is Officer Hastings in some kind of trouble?"

"Let's just say I don't think he'll be in the running for officer of the month anytime soon."

61

Saturday, October 11, 4:35 p.m

Brock sat at the conference room table with Chloe and Zimmerman, listening for the second time as the recorded phone call played over Chloe's laptop. He scribbled notes as he listened.

"Okay, I'm good," Brock said after the second playback was finished.

"What do you think?" Chloe said.

"I think Leo Hastings just handed a fantastic alternative suspect theory to the defense, assuming we can't make a solid case against Summer Randall's killer."

"Exactly what I told her," Zimmerman said.

"Did the dispatcher happen to mention whether there had been any similar reports recently?" Brock said.

"I asked her that, and she ran a query for us. According to the county database, there haven't been any calls like that since June," Chloe said.

"Was the June report a similar description?"

"No," Chloe said. "And that one actually was investigated. Turned out to be a couple of kids lighting off firecrackers."

"How about the phone number?" Zimmerman said. "Can we try calling it?"

"Can't," Chloe said. "The number wasn't captured. It came through the Greenville switchboard nonemergency number."

"Of course it did," Zimmerman groaned.

"What are you thinking?" Brock said. "Burner?"

"Maybe," Zimmerman said. "Or it might be legit, and the caller just didn't want her name associated with making the call."

Brock nodded as he considered it.

"It is strange that a call like that would come in just before a woman gets attacked on those very trails," Zimmerman said.

"True," Chloe said. "Maybe those women really did see a weird dude out there."

"Or maybe someone was setting up the attack," Brock said absently.

"Who else is hungry?" Zimmerman said. "I could eat the ass end of a—"

"Please don't finish that thought," Chloe said.

"Why not?" Zimmerman said, feigning innocence.

"Because I'm starving, and if you say what I think you're about to say, I won't be able to eat."

"Let's go," Brock said.

The detectives headed toward Moosehead Lake on foot, deciding to walk to dinner, as the temperature was still very mild.

"I gotta admit, this is a pretty little town," Zimmerman said.

"You've never been here before?" Brock said, surprised. "I figured a County boy would know all these out-of-the-way places."

"You know, contrary to what you flatlanders think, we don't all know each other up here in The County."

"Flatlanders?" Brock said with a chuckle.

"What would you call someone from Southern Maine?" Zimmerman said.

"Hey, I spent my childhood summers in Blue Hill."

Chloe chimed in. "Doesn't count."

"Why not?"

"She's right, Justice," Zimmerman said. "Summers don't count. Coming north for a couple of months each year doesn't make you a real northerner any more than spending every summer on Nantucket makes you an islander."

"And Blue Hill is hardly The County," Chloe added.

"I stand corrected," Brock said. "I am a flatlander."

They turned left onto Pritham Avenue.

"Where to?" Zimmerman said as he rubbed his stomach. "How about The Stress Free Moose? I could really go for a Reuben sandwich."

"We just went there the other night, Zim," Chloe protested.

"Yeah, because you didn't want pizza."

"I was thinking Dockside," Brock said. "But I'm open to anything. Chloe, why don't you decide?"

"Well, if it's up to me, I say we go to the Dockside Inn and Tavern."

"Because?" Zimmerman said.

"Because it's dockside, Zim. Sits on a big lake you might have heard of."

"Yeah, Zim," Brock said. "Even this flatlander has heard of Moosehead Lake."

62

Saturday, October 11, 5:30 p.m

Inside the restaurant, all the window seats were taken. The increased activity in town, both vehicle and pedestrian, was becoming more apparent by the day. Brock guessed that what passed for congestion in Greenville was due to a combination of it being the weekend along with the normal autumn influx of leaf peepers.

"The Dockside Inn and Tavern sits on a big lake you might have heard of," Zimmerman said in a poorly executed falsetto that was supposed to sound like Chloe.

"Hey, I didn't know they'd be this busy," Chloe said.

"You folks okay with sitting outside?" the hostess said. "I do have a couple available tables on the deck near Rowboat Joe's. Some people think it's a little chilly out there."

"Chilly?" Zimmerman said. "Lady, we're all hardy Mainers. It doesn't get chilly until the thermometer hits zero. And what, pray tell, is Rowboat Joe's?"

"Our seasonal outside bar."

"Now you're talking," Zimmerman said.

"I'll take that as a yes on the deck," the hostess said with a laugh as she picked up three menus. "Follow me."

She led them outside to a four-top at the far end of the deck. The table afforded them an unobstructed view of the steamboat *Katahdin* and the lake beyond.

"Is this okay?" the hostess said.

"Perfect," Brock said. "Thank you."

"Of course. Your server will be right over to take your drink order."

"Thanks," Chloe and Zimmerman said in unison.

"Look, Zim," Chloe said as she glanced at her menu. "They've got pizza."

"Wonder if it's as good as Jamo's?" Zimmerman said.

"Only one way to find out," Brock said.

"Whatever, flatlander."

They ordered drinks, then studied the menu in silence. Brock knew they were all thinking about Summer's murder. It was all any of them, except for Brock, had been able to think about since first arriving in town. Brock's own thoughts were evenly split between the Randall murder, the death of Laura Croxford, and the attack on Ronnie Libby. While Croxford may have been playing a dangerous game of blackmail with an equally dangerous ex-trooper, her death at the hands of Evan Mathers was no less deserving of Brock's attention than the death of Summer Randall.

He wondered what would have happened if he'd defied the prosecutor's wishes and mentioned Evan's relationship with Kirke's girlfriend during the trial. Would the jury have come to a different verdict? Would they have found Mathers guilty? No, the truth was that the judge would very likely have declared a mistrial after Brock uttered those ill-fated words. No such details had ever been shared with the defense, and Brock wouldn't have been able to prove the allegation anyway. He wasn't sure which thing angered him the most. The fact that Mathers may have gotten away with two murders or that he was dividing Brock's time, keeping him from giving one hundred percent of his effort to catching Summer's killer.

"You all ready to order?" the waiter said, snapping Brock back to the here and now.

Zimmerman ordered first, choosing to go with a loaded steak bomb pizza and a side of buffalo wings. Chloe chose the sweet chili salmon. Brock ordered last, opting for the bourbon steak tips with mashed potato.

"Would anyone like a refill?" the waiter said.

Brock raised his glass. "I'll take another Diet, please."

"Just ice water," Chloe said.

"Of course," the waiter said before turning to Zimmerman. "And you, sir?"

"I'll try the Maine Beer Company draft special," Zimmerman said.

"The Peeper. Short or tall?"

"Let's make it a tall."

Chloe waited until the waiter had departed before commenting. "Beer, Zim?"

"What?" Zimmerman said. "I'm off duty."

"And your weapon?" Brock said.

"Locked safely in my trunk safe. Off duty means off duty, Cochise."

"Fair enough," Chloe said as she gazed out over the lake. "Just look at that."

The setting sun was perched atop the distant foothills, bathing the trees on the opposite shore in its golden glow and refracting across the waves of Moosehead Lake like spilled diamonds. Once again, Brock wondered how Summer Randall could have met such a brutal and senseless death in a place as beautiful as this.

Chloe brought the conversation back to the case. "Thoughts on Hastings?"

"I have some thoughts," Zimmerman said.

"He's young," Brock said.

"That's no excuse," Zimmerman said. "He should know better."

"You never cut any corners when you were in uniform, Zim?" Chloe said.

"None that resulted in someone getting killed."

"You're assuming that the suspicious person those women saw in the woods was responsible for what happened to Summer," Chloe said.

"Maybe he is," Zimmerman said.

"And maybe he isn't," Brock said, wondering if perhaps the man the caller had described could have been one of the poachers Warden Labbe had mentioned. Her description didn't sound much like Peter Bragg, but Brock knew the recall of most witnesses was at best unreliable, and often colored by bias.

The waiter returned with their drinks.

"Ah, an ice-cold draft beer," Zimmerman said before taking a long pull.

"Any good?" Brock said.

"It's fabulous."

63

Saturday, October 11, 9:00 p.m

They were back at the inn by nine. Zimmerman headed directly for his room with explicit instructions that he was not to be disturbed unless the world was about to end. Brock and Chloe chatted in the parking lot for a few moments.

"I need to check in at the hospital," Brock said.

"I already did," Chloe said.

"Recently?"

"On the drive here. No change in Ronnie's condition. Serious but stable, the nurse said."

Brock guessed that was at least something. As much as he disliked Ronnie for what he had done to Summer Randall, he could hardly wish him dead. Unless, of course, Ronnie was responsible for killing her.

"What are you thinking?" Chloe said.

Brock briefly toyed with the idea of filling Chloe in on the latest developments concerning Evan Mathers and the possibility that he had snuck into his room, but then decided against it. He knew the more she learned about Evan, the more difficult it would be for her to act normal around the former trooper.

"Just wondering if Libby will ever be able to tell us who attacked him."

Chloe nodded in agreement.

"What about you?" Brock said. "Any thoughts?"

"I'm beginning to worry that we might not solve this one, partner. In a town this small, where everyone seems to know everybody, how could someone do something like this to that young woman? I mean, by all accounts, everyone loved Summer."

"Not everyone," Brock said.

"You don't really believe she was killed by some drifter hanging out in the woods?"

"If you're asking me how likely I think that is, I'd say highly unlikely."

"But not impossible?" Chloe said.

"No, not impossible. There's just something to the way in which she was killed that feels personal to me."

"Like she was hunted then pursued through the woods?"

"You grew up hunting," Brock said. "Did you ever wound an animal and not kill it?"

"Once," Chloe said after a moment. "I shot a doe, but it wasn't a clean shot. Missed the heart."

"What did you do?"

"My brothers and I tracked her through the woods for hours. The animal was badly wounded, but somehow she found the strength to keep moving. I remember following the trail of blood and feeling like a monster."

"What happened?"

"Just before dark, I found her hiding in a thick copse of evergreens. She was still alive but barely. My oldest brother talked me through putting her out of her misery."

"I'm sorry," Brock said.

"No, it's okay. I had to learn. It's all part of hunting. That final shot was me ending her suffering."

As Brock tilted his head back and looked up at the stars, he wondered if Summer's killer had been thinking the same thing when he chased her into the path of an oncoming vehicle.

It was nearly nine thirty before Brock was settled in for the night. He was so tired that the bed looked like the most comfortable thing he had ever seen, but he knew if he gave in to the impulse to crawl under the covers and lay his head on the pillow, he wouldn't sleep. Not when he still had the thumb drive from Dashofy to review. He retrieved his notes and the drive from their hiding place and carried them to the desk. After plugging in the drive and booting up his laptop, Brock got to work.

The previous night's interruption had kept him from getting much beyond the unattended death report. As he perused the file folders, his eyes fell upon the one marked "Videos." He opened the folder and saw video files from a half dozen businesses, including the Bangor hotel where Laura's death had occurred. He pulled up the hotel on the computer's GPS application and studied the layout of the surrounding block. He was operating on the assumption that if Evan had killed Croxford, he wouldn't have parked in the lot of the hotel for fear of being seen and of having his registration number recorded somewhere. No, Brock thought it far more likely that Evan would have parked nearby and approached Croxford's room on foot. He returned to the video folders and, after a moment, clicked on the one titled "Denny's." It seemed like the best choice given its close proximity to the hotel and how busy the restaurant chain usually was regardless of the time of day.

As Brock opened the video, he was pleased to see that the file included a player that allowed him to view it without the need to download something to his computer. The file was large and, assuming the time and date stamps were correct, covered the night of Croxford's death from the time that she checked in until the first officers arrived on scene the following morning. Brock scrolled right to the time of check-in, 8:00 p.m. As he suspected, the Denny's lot was a busy place. The camera covered the entire side of the building and parking lot that bordered the hotel property, where Brock figured much of the restaurant's business came from. After watching people endlessly come and go, Brock located the playback speed control and sped up the playback until it was running at ten times the speed of the normal playback rate. Cars came and went from the lot at a comical speed, and the people walking to and from the restaurant moved like two-legged bugs high on cocaine.

Brock kept his focus on the people and their vehicles, looking for anything out of the ordinary while the time counter ticked off the minutes. According to a supplemental file written by Detective Dashofy, the medical examiner placed the time of death between 9:30 and 11:00 p.m., which meant that if Mathers had parked in the Denny's lot, there would be two chances to locate him on the video. He continued through the video until his eyes grew heavy. He was growing bored, and nothing was jumping out at him. Maybe he was wrong. Maybe Mathers hadn't used the Denny's lot as a ruse. And maybe he had nothing to do with Laura Croxford's death. Except Brock didn't believe that. Not for a second. He'd seen with his own eyes what Evan was capable of the moment he gunned down Darrell Kirke.

Brock was about to exit from the player when something caught his eye. He paused the playback at 11:55, then dragged the cursor back on the timeline several minutes and resumed playback at normal speed. A dark-colored sedan that he couldn't recall having seen previously sat backed in to the far edge of the lot as far away from Denny's as possible. At first, all Brock saw was the flash of the vehicle's marker lights, indicating that someone had pressed a keyless remote to unlock the doors. He studied the entrance to Denny's, hoping to get a good look at the driver, but no one was exiting. The next thing Brock saw was the sedan's headlights pop on as the vehicle pulled out of its spot. Where did the driver come from? Brock backed the video up again, but this time he focused on the car, not the restaurant. Several seconds after the marker lights flashed, he noticed a dark figure approaching from the direction of the hotel. Whoever it was wore a hood pulled up over their head and kept their face low. Brock paused the video at the point that the figure opened the driver's door of the sedan. As he stared at the image, he thought about what he was looking at. The vehicle had been backed in, something most people don't bother to do. But a cop does this without thinking about it. The quick getaway is hardwired into all first responders. And whoever this was hadn't come from Denny's. Hadn't been a patron of the restaurant. They had come from the direction of the hotel where Laura Croxford had drowned, less than an hour after the ME said her death might have occurred. Time enough to remove anything incriminating from the scene, Brock thought.

No longer sleepy, Brock restarted the playback, this time hours before. He wanted to see when the sedan first arrived in the Denny's lot. And he wanted a better image of the driver.

64

Sunday, October 12, 6:30 a.m

Dawn broke above the horizon in the form of a flaming red sun, bathing everything in blood-like shades of crimson. In less than half an hour it was gone, swallowed up by a front of dark, foreboding clouds. Brock had been keeping one eye on the forecast throughout the week in the hopes that the television weather guessers were wrong and their incredible spell of good weather would hold on a little longer. Despite the dazzling beauty that Maine's autumn foliage often provided, it was an inevitable truth that bouts of heavy rain and drizzle would soon put a damper on autumn's glory.

Brock always looked forward to the start of the fall season when the impossibly bright red leaves of the swamp maples made their debut like the opening salvo of the stunning forest tapestry yet to come. But like everything in life, beauty fades quickly, and the first leaves to transform were also the first to depart. The stiff October winds that typically accompanied the rain snatched the red from the trees almost overnight, leaving only russet and gold leaves behind. Brock knew as miserable as the driving rains and standing puddles would be, they also made any outdoor searches for evidence leading to Summer Randall's killer infinitely more difficult.

Brock met Chloe and Zimmerman at eight thirty at the Greenville

Grinds. Though the PSB conference room was where their investigation centered, the small café was quickly becoming their morning base of operations. He wasn't sure if it was due to the intoxicating aroma of freshly baked pastries or because the locals allowed them their refuge. Brock gazed around the room at the scattering of tables, but nobody there gave them a second look. And yet, aside from the recent arrivals, most of the townsfolk knew who they were and exactly what they were doing in Greenville.

"Thought I'd hit the store today," Zimmerman announced, breaking Brock's mini trance.

"Groceries?" Chloe joked. "I would have thought the restaurants were enough for you."

"Ha ha," Zimmerman said. "No, I need socks and underwear. I didn't pack for a prolonged adventure."

"That's a good idea," Brock said. "I'm afraid my allotment of clean undergarments is also dangerously depleted."

"Typical," Chloe said, rolling her eyes.

"Why typical?" Zimmerman said. "How is it you haven't run out of clean clothes?"

"Because I'm a woman. I actually plan when I pack."

"I planned," Brock offered, though he knew it sounded like a lame protest.

"Me too," Zimmerman said.

"No, I mean actually gave some thought to what I might need," Chloe said. "The number of days. What the weather might be. And extras for any unseen emergencies. I'm not talking about grabbing everything that might fit into a gym bag and calling it good."

"I thought that was planning," Zimmerman said.

Brock, who knew Chloe was right, said nothing.

"Anyone manage sleep last night?" Chloe said.

"A little," Brock lied.

"I slept like a baby," Zimmerman said.

"It was probably those tall pints you had with supper," Chloe said.

"Nothing like a fresh Maine microbrew," Zimmerman said.

"Here you go," Jean Prescott, the owner, said as she delivered three plate-sized sticky buns to their table.

"It's like you know me," Zimmerman said.

"Relax, Romeo," Prescott said, displaying the ring on her finger. "I'm spoken for."

"So is Zim," Chloe said.

After Prescott departed, Brock steered them back to the investigation. "We need to think of something that will move this thing forward."

"Like what?" Zimmerman said. "I feel like we're not making any real progress. We have as many suspects now as we did when we started."

Chloe swallowed the mouthful of cinnamon bun she was chewing before weighing in. "Actually, if you count yesterday's revelation about the guy lurking in the woods, we've expanded our pool of suspects by one."

"I feel like we're missing something here," Brock said. "Something we don't even know to ask about."

Zimmerman didn't bother to swallow his food before responding. "We need to find the nosey parker. In a town this small, that's where we'll get our answers."

"Despite my training officer's lack of table manners, I think Zim has a point," Chloe said. "Someone in this town knows the secrets of these people we've been speaking with, and that's who we need to find."

"Any idea who that might be?" Brock said.

"Actually, I might," Chloe said. "I plan to check in with Wheels on the electronic searches, then go from there."

"Any word yet on the DNA?" Zimmerman said.

"I've got a call in," Brock said. "I don't know what else I can do to speed this process up."

"Who knows," Chloe said. "Those results might not move us any closer to the killer."

"Yeah, but they might at least rule some people out," Brock said.

"I think I'm gonna poke around the gym again," Zimmerman said. "Muscles McMitchell was really worried about his wife finding out he'd been shagging the help. Maybe I can make him nervous enough to get his tongue wagging."

"It can't hurt," Brock said.

"What about you, Brock?" Chloe said.

"Thought I might reach out to Warden Labbe again."

"You really think there might be something to the game cameras being removed?" Zimmerman said.

Brock shrugged. "Seems to me that the surveillance is better in the woods than right here in town. Maybe it's time to start shaking a few trees."

There was one tree in particular Brock wanted to shake. Peter Bragg.

65

Sunday, October 12, 8:30 a.m

Chief Leavitt had just plunked himself down in the chair behind his desk when he heard someone rapping on the open door to his office. He looked up to find Reserve Officer Leo Hastings standing in the doorway. Hastings wore his civilian clothes and a downtrodden expression.

"You wanted to see me, Chief?" Hastings said.

"Come in, son," Leavitt said, gesturing to one of the visitor chairs in front of his desk. "Take a seat."

Leavitt took a sip from his coffee mug as he formulated his next words. He was pleased to see the look of contrition on the young man's face. It boded well for any future he might have in law enforcement.

"I wanted you to have a night to think about what you've done, Officer Hastings," Leavitt began. "I hope you know how much trouble you have caused for the state police detectives."

Hastings nodded in silence.

"Investigating a murder is very different from most other crimes. Not only do they have to prove beyond a reasonable doubt who is guilty of the murder, they also must disprove that any others could have committed the crime. Do you understand?"

"I do."

"Now I know that many of the calls we respond to are nuisance calls, or wild goose chases. I'm sure that even in your short tenure, you have found this to be true. But ignoring a call for service from someone worried about a suspicious man lurking in the woods isn't the kind of call you can blow off. Ever. We're not talking about a barking dog complaint here. You get me?"

"Yes, sir."

"I know you couldn't have known that a woman would be killed only a few days later in those same woods, but that isn't the point. The point is the people of this town expect us to do the job they pay us for. To keep them safe and to follow up on anything suspicious."

Hastings said nothing. It pleased Leavitt to know that Leo knew when to keep his inexperienced mouth shut and simply listen.

"Worse than blowing off a call for service in my town was lying to the dispatcher about it. You told her that you'd handled the call. That's the kind of thing that can come back to haunt a man. Don't know whether you noticed, but the law enforcement community has taken a beating as of late. The only thing any of us has is our credibility. Lose that and you've got nothing. A good reputation is like virginity. Once lost, it doesn't come back."

Hastings nodded again.

"My first thought was to simply fire your ass and be done with it. But I got a visit from Deputy Mathers."

For the first time, Hastings raised his eyes to look directly at the chief.

"He tells me that you've got what it takes to be a good cop down the line. Says you did a nice job this summer, even when the tourists and seasonal crowd came to town. And God knows some of them aren't the easiest of folks to deal with. I know you're young and impulsive, probably not all that different from what I was like when I started on the job. But you're on thin ice here. Good cops may be hard to find, but shit bums are a dime a dozen. You're not a shit bum, are you, Officer Hastings?"

"No, sir, I'm not."

"That's good to hear. I've decided to give you another shot. A written reprimand will be placed in your employment jacket, but you won't be suspended or fired."

"Thank you, Chief."

"You're lucky you've got an experienced officer like Mathers in your corner. You could learn a thing or two from him."

"Yes, sir."

"Now get out of my office before I change my mind."

Hastings stood. "Should I plan on covering my next shift, sir?"

"Is your name on the schedule, Officer Hastings?"

"It is."

"Then I expect to see you out there answering calls and patrolling the town."

"Thank you, sir."

Leavitt watched as Hastings beat a hasty retreat from his office and down the hall. The grin Leavitt had been hiding was now on full display.

Chloe was reaching for her cell to call Detective Wheeler when it began ringing.

"Speak of the devil," she said. "I was just about to call you."

"How goes the battle out there?" Wheeler said. "Sounds like you guys have your hands full with this one."

"And then some," Chloe said. "Tell me you're calling with some good news. We could use it."

"Don't know if it's good or not, but I definitely found some interesting things."

"Okay, shoot."

"Well, there was nothing unusual on the phone records I got from her provider. As you would expect, most of the back-and-forth are calls to her places of employment, Northern Light, the fitness place, though those stopped a few months ago, her father and mother, and someone named Brittney LaRoux."

"She's a close friend and hospital coworker of Summer's," Chloe said.

"Okay. That makes sense, then."

"Anybody else?"

"Yeah, there were a bunch of phone calls with Ronnie Libby. He's the guy who got beat up, right?"

"Right. Libby is still one of our suspects in Summer's murder."

"Well, that's an interesting twist. You guys got a vigilante dispensing some homegrown justice up there?"

"It isn't out of the realm of possibility," Chloe said as she pictured Taylor Randall's face the night she and Brock notified him of Summer's death. "How about emails or finances?"

"Nothing eye-opening in her email history, but I did find a few interesting things in her banking records."

"Oh?"

"Yeah, there is a deposit for five grand that appeared out of the blue two months ago."

"A deposited check?"

"No. That's the thing. It just shows up as a cash deposit. A month later, there is another unexplained deposit for two grand. Then one week before she was murdered, there was another two-thousand-dollar deposit. Was Summer doing something on the side that no one knew about?"

"That's a good question," Chloe said. "Not that we are aware of. Summer was still working at Northern Light as a nursing intern, and that wouldn't explain the amount or the payment method."

"And her job at the gym, um, Balance Gym?"

"No way," Chloe said. "Besides, she left that job a—"

"Couple of months ago?" Wheeler said, finishing her thought.

"Yeah, you don't think...?"

"That someone was paying her off? Who knows. The timing is definitely suspect. There were no such deposits prior to the five thousand at the beginning of August."

Chloe stared at her notepad. Could Summer have been blackmailing Chris Mitchell to keep their affair quiet? Had that been the reason he let her go? Could Summer have been carrying Mitchell's child? Had she told him about the pregnancy? Did she demand even more money?

"You still there, Chloe?" Wheeler said.

"Yeah, sorry, just thinking about motive. Good work, Wheels."

"Anything I can do."

Before Chloe could respond, her cell phone displayed another call coming in.

"I gotta let you go," Chloe said. "Talk later."

Chloe ended the call with Detective Wheeler and accepted the incoming call.

"Detective Wright."

66

Sunday, October 12, 10:30 a.m

Brock was walking down the back hallway of the PSB wondering whether Ginger Dashofy would act on the information he'd left on her voicemail when he heard Chloe's voice emanating excitedly from the conference room. He rightly assumed that she was on the phone to someone, as he could only hear her half of the conversation. She hung up as he entered.

"What's up?" Brock said.

"You're never going to believe who that was," Chloe said. "I just got off the phone with Summer's cellular provider. Someone just activated her cell phone."

"Holy shit," Zimmerman said from the doorway behind Brock.

"Have they managed to locate it?" Brock said.

"Yup," Chloe said as she moved toward the wall map they had been using to plot out the investigation. She drew a circle covering the area the provider had given to her. "Right here."

The circle encompassed a small area northeast of Greenville. At the center of the circle was the pin designating Peter Bragg's compound.

"Holy shit," Zimmerman repeated. "That's Bragg's place."

"Who else knows about this?" Brock said.

"No one," Chloe said.

"Good," Brock said. "We'll need to handle this correctly."

"What do you mean?" Chloe said. "Her phone is clearly on Bragg's property. Someplace where it has no business being. Let's get a warrant and go get it."

"I agree with the warrant," Zimmerman said. "But Brock's right. We can't just march up there and demand entry. Not with what we know about Bragg. Christ, at a minimum there could be a standoff."

"Then what do you suggest?" Chloe said.

"We contact the TAC team and bring them in on this," Brock said.

The disappointment was etched on Chloe's face. "There's no reason we can't do this ourselves."

"Bringing in the TAC team is the right move, Chloe," Zimmerman said.

"Fine."

It took the better part of two hours before Lt. Holmquist, the tactical commander, and a handful of his people arrived in Greenville. By then Chief Leavitt and several of his on-duty reservists had been brought up to speed. Chloe had been in contact with AAG Gene Grover and was putting the finishing touches on the affidavit to search Bragg's property, allowing them to seize Summer's cell phone and any other evidence relevant to the murder of Summer Randall.

"Everyone clear on how we'll do this?" Brock said to a room of collective nods. "Chief Leavitt informed us that Bragg comes to town twice a week to resupply."

"He's regular as clockwork," Leavitt said. "Every Saturday and Wednesday."

A flattop Piscataquis County deputy standing near Evan Mathers spoke up. "How do we know Bragg won't vary his schedule?"

"We don't," Holmquist said. "But given his history and known PTSD symptoms, I'd rather chance taking him down in a parking lot on his way to a disabled vehicle than risk a standoff on his property. That's his home base. It's likely fortified, and maybe even booby-trapped. Trust me, that is the last place we want to confront Peter Bragg."

"We'll set up along the route Bragg will take into town and in various spots around Greenville, allowing us to monitor him without tipping him off, but do not engage," Brock said. "Eyes and ears only."

Holmquist followed up. "Once Bragg is spotted, we'll wait until he's left his vehicle unattended, at which point Smitty will disable it. We'll wait until Bragg has left the supermarket, minimizing the potential for any hostages. My team will take him down either in the parking lot or inside his vehicle."

"Is everybody clear on how we do this?" Brock said. Again, every attendee nodded.

"Hopefully, he'll realize the situation and surrender peacefully," Holmquist said.

"Hopefully," Zimmerman muttered. "Best-laid plans and all that."

"Not helpful," Brock said as he turned to face the senior detective.

"I'm just saying."

Brock's attention returned to the group. "Any questions or concerns?" No one raised a hand. "Okay, everyone assigned to this detail uses the tactical frequency only."

"Good luck," Leavitt said.

"This is total bullshit," Leo Hastings said to Evan Mathers as they stepped outside of the public safety building and walked toward their respective vehicles. "This Bragg guy might have been a badass soldier in Afghanistan, but he isn't Rambo."

"Maybe not," Mathers said. "But you're already on thin ice with Chief Leavitt. The last thing you want to do is disobey a direct order. This is a team sport, kid. Bad things happen to hot dogs."

"I guess," Hastings said. "I just want my first big arrest, you know?"

Mathers chuckled and patted the young officer on the back. "Yeah, I know. Don't worry, your moment will come."

67

Sunday, October 12, 1:30 p.m

Leo Hastings sat in his cruiser parked in a turnout along Lily Bay Road, running radar. Traffic on the road was light, as most everyone was either shopping downtown or boating on Moosehead Lake. Hastings was still ruminating about being left out of the plan to take down Bragg when the dash-mounted radar emitted a tone indicating an approaching vehicle. Hastings glanced at the digital display and saw that the vehicle's speed was thirty-eight miles per hour. The posted speed limit was thirty-five. The unwritten policy of the local police agencies was that they didn't bother pulling anyone over for a speeding infraction unless the offending vehicle was traveling at least fifteen miles per hour above the posted limit. Hastings was about to press the radar's hold button and go back to sulking when he did a double take. The approaching truck belonged to Peter Bragg. Hastings picked up the briefing sheet that the state police had handed out and confirmed the registration number on the maroon F-250.

As the truck passed, Hastings made eye contact with the driver. It was definitely Bragg. The vehicle's speed never varied as it passed by Hastings's location and continued toward Greenville. He locked in the speed of thirty-eight. The red digital display flashed like a warning beacon. Hastings had heard other more seasoned officers talk about their make-or-break moment. The decision that made their entire career. As he watched Bragg's pickup shrink into the distance, Hastings couldn't help but think he was watching his own career disappear right along with it.

What if this was his one chance to be the hero? The only opportunity he might ever get to arrest a murderer? He looked back at the flashing number. Three over was chickenshit, but technically it was still a moving violation. A Title-29A speeding infraction. Bragg was in fact speeding, and that three miles an hour above the posted limit was all the articulable suspicion Hastings needed to pull him over. Besides, he'd taken an oath to uphold the law. And Peter Bragg was breaking one.

Hastings shifted the transmission into drive, then floored the accelerator, sending gravel flying out behind the cruiser. As the drive wheels found purchase on the asphalt, Hastings flicked on the blue strobes and siren. It was time to chisel the name Leo Hastings into the annals of Maine police history.

"Well, that didn't take long," Chloe said to Brock as he slid into the driver's seat of his unmarked Ford and handed her a cardboard to-go cup of coffee.

"What do you mean?" Brock said.

"I mean one of the Greenville officers just called in a pursuit."

"You've gotta be shitting me," Brock said. "Now? Tell me it isn't that Hastings kid."

"Leo Hastings it is, and the vehicle he's chasing is registered to Bragg."

"Goddammit. Where are they?"

As if in answer to the question, static broke over the radio, immediately followed by the sound of a siren. "Greenville one three," the county dispatcher said. "Your twenty?"

"Inbound on Lily Bay approaching Shoals Road."

"His call sign is thirteen?" Brock said.

"Yup," Chloe said.

"I knew that kid was trouble."

"Hyped up too," Chloe said. "You can hear it in his voice. Bad combo."

"Greenville One."

"Go ahead, Chief," the dispatcher said.

"Find out the speed of his pursuit."

"Ten-four, Chief," the dispatcher said. "Greenville one three, car one is requesting your speed?"

Brock knew exactly what Leavitt was doing. It was standard procedure for the supervisor, or in this case the chief, to obtain enough information to decide whether or not to allow the chase to continue. It wouldn't matter who Hastings was chasing, or even why, the priority now was whether or not the pursuit might endanger anyone else on the road. And with the pursuit heading toward town, and a possible murderer behind the wheel, the smart call was to terminate the pursuit before someone got hurt. Or worse.

"Should we head that way?" Chloe said.

Brock shook his head. "Let's wait and see where it goes. We're in a good position here."

"Greenville one three," the dispatcher called again. "Your status?"

Brock and Chloe stared at the base radio while awaiting a response, but no response came. The seconds ticked by, but the radio remained silent. They both knew every cop monitoring the tactical channel was on high alert.

"Unit one three," the dispatcher tried again.

"Something's wrong," Brock said as he put the SUV in gear. "Hastings should have responded by now."

As Brock turned onto the main road, the dispatcher came on the radio again.

"Greenville One."

"Go ahead," Leavitt said.

"We're receiving multiple calls for a vehicle rollover on Lily Bay Road."

Brock's heart sank in his chest.

"You think—?" Chloe began.

"You know it is," Brock said as he activated the emergency lights and siren.

"Greenville One," the dispatcher said.

"Go ahead," Leavitt responded.

"Caller says it's one of ours."

"Shit," Chloe said.

"Start EMS," Leavitt said. "And show me en route."

68

Sunday, October 12, 1:45 p.m

Brock brought the Interceptor to a hard stop on the right side of the roadway, parking directly behind a marked Piscataquis County unit. Brock and Chloe jumped out and ran toward the overturned Greenville cruiser. Smoke was pouring from the underside of the vehicle, and Brock could see Evan Mathers trying desperately to free Leo Hastings through the driver's side window.

As Brock and Chloe approached the twisted hunk of sheet metal that once passed for a police car, a flicker of flame appeared from inside the rear wheel well.

Brock circled around to the passenger side of the unit, hoping that he might have better luck reaching Hastings. Chloe disappeared around the driver's side.

Brock reached through the broken window and unlocked the passenger door. He jerked the door open, then pushed himself partially inside. Hastings was unconscious, hanging upside down like a bat. Mathers was struggling with the seat belt buckle.

"It won't release," Mathers yelled.

"Here," Brock said as he slid a survival knife from his front pocket. After a moment's apprehension, Brock flicked it open and handed it to Mathers.

"Help me hold his torso up," Mathers said.

The passenger compartment was quickly filling with smoke, reducing visibility to near zero as Brock crawled further inside the vehicle. Kneeling on the headliner, he wrapped Hastings's upper body in an awkward embrace.

"Ready," Brock yelled.

"Here goes," Mathers said as he began sawing through the seat belt webbing.

Brock gently lowered Hastings's body, taking extra care not to injure him further. There was no way of knowing whether the officer had sustained a spinal injury, but one thing was certain, if they couldn't remove him from the vehicle, he wouldn't survive the flames.

Brock struggled with Hastings's dead weight as he slowly backed out through the passenger door opening. He was almost through when Hastings's gun belt caught on the console.

Brock felt hands pulling at him from behind.

"We gotcha, partner," Chloe said as she and Mathers tugged at him again.

"Hang on," Brock yelled. "His gun belt is hung up. I gotta get it off him."

Brock coughed out the last words. He didn't want to think about what he might be inhaling. The air inside the SUV was a noxious cloud, choking him and stinging his eyes. The visibility had been reduced to no more than a few inches, and Brock's eyes were watering so badly he couldn't keep them open. Working only by feel, he scrambled to locate the keepers holding Hastings's belt in place. The first two were easy, as they were located at the front of his belt. The two rear keepers were harder to reach. After a long moment, Brock found and tore the Velcro loose. The last thing holding the gun belt in place was the plastic buckle. Brock unhooked the buckle, freeing Hastings's body at last.

"Now," Brock said, choking out the word.

With help from Chloe and Mathers, Brock was finally able to pull Hastings from the burning wreckage. They half carried, half dragged Hastings's body to safety before other first responders arrived and took over. Brock's legs were like rubber as he plopped down against a tree trunk and began coughing, trying to clear his lungs.

"You okay?" Chloe said.

"Give me a minute," Brock managed as he waved her off.

What was left of the Greenville police unit was fully engulfed now, and the heat was intense. With help from Chloe, Brock regained his feet and moved further away before collapsing to a seated position on the ground again. The air was filled with a cacophony of approaching sirens.

"Here," Mathers said as he handed Brock a bottled water.

Brock opened the bottle and drank. He coughed half of it back up, before rolling over on his stomach and retching up a small puddle that appeared to be a mixture of coffee and water.

"Easy with that, partner," Chloe said. "Maybe try sipping it."

Brock rolled back onto his butt and took a small sip. The cool water helped ease the burning sensation in his throat.

"How's the kid?" Brock managed after a minute.

"He's alive," one of the paramedics said as he knelt next to Brock. "He's being prepped for transport to the hospital."

"What about—?"

Before Brock could finish the thought, another paramedic placed an oxygen mask over his mouth and nose.

"I'll have to remember that one," Chloe said before giving Brock a playful wink.

69

Sunday, October 12, 2:30 p.m

Brock sat on the diamond plate step of one of the town fire trucks, watching as they quickly knocked down the flames coming from Hastings's cruiser. Whatever else the kid was, he was one lucky SOB, Brock thought. The oxygen was working. His head felt clearer, and the coughing had nearly ceased.

Chloe approached him with another bottle of water. "How're you feeling, partner?"

Brock removed the mask. "Better. Thanks for pulling me out."

"I had help," she said, gesturing toward Mathers, who was standing about fifty feet away next to Chief Leavitt. "Couple more seconds and that might not have ended well for anyone."

"Where's Bragg?" Brock said before another coughing fit overtook him.

Chloe removed the mask from Brock's hand and returned it to his face.

"They are searching for him now," she said. "His pickup was abandoned about half a mile from here. Flat tire."

Brock's attention shifted as Chief Leavitt approached them.

"Chief," Chloe said.

"You doin' okay?" Leavitt said to Brock.

Brock lowered the mask again. "I'll live."

"Thank you both for saving Leo's life," Leavitt said.

"It was a team effort," Chloe said.

"Well, however it happened, I'm just happy you're all okay."

"Any word on Bragg?" Brock said.

"Not yet," Leavitt said. "I'm afraid he may have made it back home."

Exactly what we were trying to avoid, Brock thought. What should have been an easy op had turned into a worst-case scenario. They would be lucky to make it out of this mess without further casualties.

"I apologize for my officer's impulsiveness," Leavitt said.

Brock said nothing. All eyes turned to watch as Holmquist approached.

"Any word, LT?" Chloe said.

"Just got word from one of my spotters. Bragg made it back to his compound."

Brock shook his head in disgust.

"Now what?" Leavitt said.

"We do it the hard way," Brock said, his attention returning to Holmquist. "What do you need from us?"

It took less than twenty minutes for them to establish a perimeter around Peter Bragg's compound and set up a nearby command post. Lily Bay Road was barricaded at each end to prevent vehicle traffic from driving into harm's way. Brock and Chloe were joined by Zimmerman at the CP while Leavitt drove to the hospital to check on Hastings.

"How did it go with Cumberland?" Zimmerman asked as Brock pocketed his phone and stepped inside the mobile unit.

"About like you'd expect," Brock said. "She's on her way here."

"That should be fun," Chloe said.

"Any contact?" Brock said.

"He's not picking up," Holmquist said. "But we've spotted him inside one of the outbuildings. We're tightening the perimeter, and I've repositioned two snipers to cover the exits. He's contained for now."

Brock checked the time, trying to estimate how many hours of daylight were remaining. The last thing they needed was for Bragg, a seasoned hunter and trained soldier, to slip through the cracks. Things were already bad, but nightfall could make them a whole lot worse.

Lt. Cumberland arrived an hour later, and she wasn't happy.

"Is this Officer Hastings alive?" Cumberland said by way of a greeting.

"According to the hospital, he suffered some bruises and lacerations, but he'll be fine," Brock said.

"We'll see about that," Cumberland said. "Depending on how things play out here, Hastings may receive a few more injuries."

"Penny," Holmquist said as he stepped out of the trailer.

"Thanks for your help with this fiasco, Mark," Cumberland said.

"Of course."

"What do you need from my end?"

"Nothing I can think of at this point. I've got several other team members on the way. We're trying to make contact with Bragg. No luck as of yet, but we're prepared to wait him out as long as it takes."

Cumberland turned to Brock and Chloe. "How sure are we that this Bragg guy is our killer?"

"We're not," Brock said.

"The only thing we know for sure is that he is in possession of the victim's cell phone," Chloe added.

"It's been missing since the night she was killed," Brock said. "How Bragg came by it is anybody's guess."

Zimmerman stuck his head out of the trailer. "We just made telephonic contact with him."

70

Sunday, October 12, 4:30 p.m

The bespectacled tactical team communications specialist turned to look at Holmquist and sighed in frustration as Peter Bragg hung up on him for a second time. Brock and the others were all crammed into the far end of the command post, listening in.

"He keeps hanging up. He's convinced that the police are setting him up."

"Given the reckless manner in which Reserve Officer Hastings handled things, I can see why he might feel that way," Zimmerman said.

"Do we know exactly what happened that led up to the chase?" Cumberland said.

"Hastings decided to play hero rather than stick to the plan," Chloe said. "He tried stopping Bragg for a speeding violation. Thirty-eight in a thirty-five."

"What the hell?" Holmquist said.

"It gets worse," Zimmerman said.

"What could be worse than that?" Cumberland said.

"It looks like Hastings tried to force Bragg off the road with his cruiser."

"No wonder he thinks we're out to get him," the comm specialist said.

Brock considered their options. Bragg was a decorated soldier having served three tours in the Middle East. If there was one thing they might be able to use to gain his trust, it was another veteran.

"Anyone here serve in the Middle East?" Brock said.

"I was stationed stateside," the comm specialist said.

"Why?" Cumberland asked Brock.

"Because Bragg doesn't trust anybody, and we need to find a way around that to get him to talk to us."

"What are you proposing?" Holmquist said. "Did you serve?"

"No, but my brother did."

"How does that help us?" Zimmerman said.

Cumberland weighed in before Brock could answer. "Because his brother was killed by a roadside IED."

"Sorry," Zimmerman said. "I didn't realize."

Brock saw the wheels turning inside Holmquist's head.

"That might just work," Holmquist said at last. "It's as close as we can get to a shared experience that Bragg will identify with."

"He can't do any worse than I've done," the communications specialist said. "Let me try and get Bragg on the horn again."

"I'm sorry about your brother," Bragg said. "I know firsthand how bad something like that can fuck a guy up."

"I'm sure you've seen worse," Brock said.

"Still, none of that changes anything, does it? Why should I believe anything you say? I was trying to help when that cop ambushed me. Fucker tried to run me off the road."

The anger and betrayal Bragg felt were clear in his tone.

"What do you mean you were trying to help?" Brock said.

"Just what I said," Bragg barked into the phone. "I found that phone, and it was dead. I brought it back to my place and charged it. As soon as I saw the girl's face on the screen saver, I knew who it belonged to."

"Why didn't you contact the police?" Brock said.

"Why do you think I was headed into town?"

Brock exchanged a knowing glance with Chloe. She nodded, then pulled out her cell phone and stepped from the trailer. If Bragg was telling the truth, the cell service provider should have contacted them again to say the phone was on the move.

"You said you found the phone," Brock said. "Where exactly?"

71

Sunday, October 12, 5:30 p.m

"Are you kidding me right now?" Cumberland said. "I didn't agree to any of that."

"The lieutenant is right," Zimmerman said. "How do we know Bragg isn't just setting you up?"

"I don't think he operates that way," Brock said.

"Oh, and you're an expert in how this guy operates now?" Cumberland said. "After a ten-minute phone call?"

"Mind if I weigh in on this?" Holmquist said.

"By all means," Cumberland said. "Maybe you can talk some sense into my overzealous investigator. I don't seem to be able to."

"Actually, I was about to say that I think Brock may be right."

"Some ally you turned out to be," Cumberland said. "You're both crazy."

"I don't think so. This guy has had numerous run-ins with law enforcement, right? And the only time he acted aggressively was when Hastings tried to run him off the road. I think he operates by a moral code. If he thinks Brock is being square with him, then I think he'll surrender."

"And if you're both wrong?" Cumberland said.

Chloe stepped back inside the trailer.

"Well?" Brock said.

"Bragg was telling the truth," Chloe said.

"What are you talking about?" Cumberland said.

"The phone company confirmed Summer Randall's cell was on the move. Headed toward Greenville."

"Why didn't they notify us?" Zimmerman said.

"Someone dropped the ball on that end," Chloe said. "They figured that we only wanted to know when and where it went live."

Holmquist exchanged a glance with Cumberland, who raised her hands in surrender. He turned his attention to Brock. "Let's get you suited up."

As Brock walked along the long dirt drive that led into Bragg's compound, he knew he was being foolhardy, even without Cumberland's assessment, but he also knew that there was something about Bragg's involvement that made him seem sincere. The man might well suffer from PTSD from his time overseas, and he clearly had issues with authority, at least so far as Maine's hunting laws were concerned, but neither made him a killer. By all accounts, at least according to Warden Labbe, Bragg was intelligent and cunning. Not the kind of guy who would risk activating the dead cell phone of a murder victim, especially if he was responsible for the murder.

And if he needed more proof to bolster his theory about Bragg's innocence, the cell phone provider's confirmation that they had tracked the phone away from its original GPS coordinates in the direction of Greenville tended to support Bragg's assertion that he was bringing his find to the police. But there were questions that still needed answering. Questions that only Bragg could answer. Had he stumbled over the phone by accident while hunting in the woods illegally? Or had he discovered the phone by some other means? Brock wanted the chance to sit down across from Bragg and ask these questions face-to-face. Based on the overzealousness of at least one of Leavitt's men, Brock wasn't confident that there would be a way to end this standoff without Bragg, or worse, one of his fellow cops getting injured or killed.

Yes, he was needlessly putting himself in harm's way, but the payoff to their investigation, assuming he was successful in getting Bragg to surrender peacefully, seemed worth the risk. If not for Summer Randall's parents, then for Summer herself. A dead man with a cell phone could literally be the death of the case.

"You sure you know what you're doing?" Chloe said from back at the CP, her voice emanating clearly from Brock's earpiece.

"Not really," Brock said, keeping his eyes straight ahead.

"Then why do it?"

"Maybe I'm just feeling invincible after we pulled Hastings out of that burning wreck."

"That isn't funny, Brock."

"I know. Just trying to lighten the mood."

"What if Bragg's just baiting you in for the kill?"

"To what end? What would he gain from killing me, Chloe? He's not stupid. He knows that shooting me would be paramount to suicide. And if that's what he has in mind, he could have done that on his own without me."

Brock heard Chloe sigh.

"Besides," Brock continued. "Do you really think Bragg would stab Summer in the woods?"

"I don't know him, do I?"

"Over what? Because she caught him poaching deer out of season? If that was his motivation, then why hasn't he tried to kill Warden Labbe?"

Chloe didn't answer.

"Okay, I can see the compound now. I gotta concentrate."

"I'll be right here listening, partner. Be careful."

As Brock reached the clearing, he could see two of the TAC team members stationed at the far corners of two of the buildings. Both men had a bead on the front of the Quonset hut where Bragg was pinned down. Brock knew there were snipers he couldn't see from his vantage point, as well as officers covering the structure's rear exit.

"I have eyes on Justice," one of the team members radioed. "Two hundred feet out and closing."

Brock swallowed nervously. He was trying hard not to think about how exposed he was as he neared Bragg's location.

"One fifty out," the TAC team member said.

Brock wished he'd stop doing that. It was beginning to feel like a countdown to his own execution. His stomach was in knots as he walked slowly and steadily toward the steel enclosure. The steel overhead door was closed, as was the casement door to the right of it, but the casement door had a window. A window that Bragg might well be using at that very moment to target him.

"Seventy-five feet," another voice said over the radio.

Brock wasn't sure how comforting it was to know that so many highly trained armed cops were monitoring his position. None of that would keep him alive if Bragg went back on his word and fired on Brock. His temples were throbbing as blood raced through them. Cumberland was right. This was stupid. He never should have suggested it.

"That's far enough," a voice said from somewhere nearby. The voice belonged to Peter Bragg.

Brock stopped walking.

"Okay, Bragg," Brock said. "I've kept my part of the bargain."

"What guarantee do I have that one of the half dozen cops with weapons trained on me won't open fire as soon as I step outside?"

For the first time, Brock realized the flaw in the plan. Bragg had a point. And Brock had no idea what orders Holmquist had issued to his men. Brock wondered what he might do in their shoes. He had a pretty good idea.

"Peter, why don't you let me approach the building? You surrender to me, and I'll handcuff you and walk you out."

"Absolutely not," Holmquist's voice spat out of Brock's earpiece. "You will not go inside that building, Brock. Do you hear me?"

Brock ignored him. Though Holmquist outranked him by at least two steps, he wasn't Brock's immediate boss. Besides, it wasn't his ass hanging out here to get shot off, it was Brock's, and Brock alone would decide how to play this.

"Put down your rifle, open the door, and stand just inside. I'll walk to you and shield you until I've placed you in cuffs."

"Dammit, Brock," Holmquist said. "Are you trying to let him take you hostage?"

"What do you say, Peter?" Brock said, ignoring Holmquist once again.

"All right," Bragg said.

Brock continued forward one careful step at a time. He was only fifteen feet from the door when it opened. Brock stopped again. The Quonset hut was too dark inside for Brock to make out even a vague shape. He continued to stare into the darkness until his eyes began to adjust. He could just make out the barrel of a long gun off to the left. It was pointed downward at a forty-five-degree angle.

"Lose the weapon, Bragg," Brock said. "Or I can't protect you."

"Take out your handcuffs," Bragg said.

Brock removed the cuffs from the left side of his belt and held them up. For a long moment, nothing happened. At last he saw the barrel of the rifle shift until it was horizontal. Brock's breath caught in his throat. If Bragg was planning to kill him and go out in a blaze of glory, now was the time. Slowly Bragg's torso moved into view as he bent down and placed the gun on the floor.

"Okay, I'm unarmed," Bragg said.

Brock moved forward until he was blocking the doorway and the sightline of any snipers.

"Turn around and get down on your knees," Brock said.

Bragg complied with his hands raised.

"Place your hands behind your head and interlace your fingers."

Again, Bragg complied.

Brock drew a deep breath and held it as he moved through the doorway.

72

Sunday, October 12, 5:45 p.m

True to his word, Bragg surrendered peacefully, and Brock handcuffed him without incident. Brock led him from the Quonset hut and handed him over to the custody of two of the TAC team officers.

"Where is the cell phone?" Brock said as one of the officers thoroughly searched Bragg.

"Right front pocket," Bragg said.

"Got it right here," the officer said as he removed the phone from the pocket of Bragg's pants and handed it to Brock. The illuminated screen depicted the image of Summer Randall that Bragg had described.

Brock pocketed the phone and addressed Bragg. "And you'll provide us with the location you found it?"

"I can give you more than that," Bragg said.

"Where do you want to interview this guy?" the other tactical team member said.

Brock considered this. The public safety building was the most convenient option, but it really wasn't a secure facility. It didn't even have a holding cell. If they were going to do this right, the Piscataquis County Sheriff's Office was the smart move.

"Take him to the SO," Brock said.

"Charges?"

"Let's start with driving to endanger, leaving the scene of a PI accident, and creating a police standoff. I'll fill out the rest of the booking sheet when I get there."

"Roger that," both officers said.

The dooryard was suddenly flooded with marked and unmarked police vehicles. Chloe jumped out of her Ford and hurried toward Brock.

"I'd be pissed at you if I wasn't so happy to see that you're okay," she said. "God, you can be pigheaded sometimes."

"I prefer headstrong," Brock said.

"Speaking of pissed," Chloe said. "Here comes Penny Dreadful, and she doesn't look happy."

"What's new?" Brock said as he scanned the property. "We need to get that search warrant affidavit finished and get ERT in here. Also, we need to contact Grover with the update. Get his input on the search parameters."

"I'll take care of that," Chloe said. "Any idea what we're looking for, besides the murder weapon?"

"Any physical evidence associated with the murder of Summer Randall," Brock said.

"What about computers and digital evidence? If Warden Labbe was right, Bragg had game cameras everywhere."

"That too," Brock said.

"In other words, the standard all-encompassing boilerplate legalese," Chloe said.

"I'll know more after I speak with Bragg," Brock said.

"Detective Justice," Cumberland barked. "I need a word."

Brock nodded and held up an index finger.

"Right now, Brock," Cumberland said.

"Suddenly, the idea of writing another search warrant doesn't seem so daunting," Chloe said. "Good luck, partner."

Brock sat quietly in the passenger seat of Cumberland's SUV while she read him the riot act. He wasn't all that excited about the fact that it was happening in front of the other officers. And in a fishbowl, no less.

"You may not comprehend the weight of responsibility that comes with being the commander of Troop E, but let me assure you it is substantial. And one of those responsibilities is making sure that my people are playing by the rules and not acting in a cavalier way that would harm them or their coworkers. Like playing fast and loose with your life. Do you have some kind of a death wish?"

"Look, I got Bragg out safely," Brock said, regretting the words as soon as they passed his lips.

"Your success doesn't erase the foolhardy nature of the shit you just pulled. Things could just as easily have gone the other way. And if you had gotten shot, guess whose fault that would be?"

Cumberland's piercing tone increased several octaves, and he knew it was due to his ill-contrived comment.

"I warned you that I wouldn't tolerate that 'do as you please' crap you were known for at MCU South. We're a team up here, Brock. This isn't the NBA. You don't get to play glory boy at the expense of the rest of us. Not if you want to keep working for me, anyway."

Brock started to open his mouth to respond but thought better of it. This wasn't a discussion.

Cumberland's cell phone chimed with an incoming text message, momentarily breaking the tension. She ignored it for a long moment as she continued to glare at Brock. At last she lifted her phone to check it.

Brock, grateful for the break in the lieutenant's diatribe, sat watching in silence as several members of the tactical team walked past wearing smirks on their faces. No cop could resist witnessing a first-rate ass chewing.

Brock turned his attention back to Cumberland as he watched her fingers fly across the screen.

"Where are you taking Bragg?" Cumberland said as she switched gears. "The PSB?"

Brock shook his head. "Given Bragg's history, I figured he'd be easier to secure at the Piscataquis County Jail in Dover-Foxcroft. Why?"

"Because the major is asking."

"Tell me Morgan's not coming up here again," Brock groaned.

"An armed standoff? Tactical team callout? Of course he is. You just blew this thing up. Not only is he en route, he's planning a press conference."

"To talk about what? Bragg is only a person of interest at this point. We haven't charged him with anything to do with the Randall murder. You've got to get him to back down, LT."

Cumberland whipped her head around. "Have you forgotten how the chain of command works, Detective Justice? Major Morgan doesn't work for me, but *you* do. You work the case and let me worry about the political stuff. Got it?"

"Got it."

"Now, get out of my car before *I* shoot you."

73

Sunday, October 12, 6:00 p.m

Brock left the scene in the capable hands of his fellow Maine state troopers. Bragg's compound would remain locked down until the search warrant was obtained and executed. He telephoned Chloe en route to the county jail.

"How'd it go with Penny?" Chloe said.

"She thinks I've got a death wish."

"Huh, wonder where she got such a crazy idea?"

Ignoring her comment, Brock stayed on point. "What did Grover think about the search?"

"Gene said we need to be careful about casting too wide a net. All we have at this point is the victim's cell phone in his possession. Summer wasn't killed at his compound. She was killed in the woods and chased onto the road."

"What about the digital files from his game cameras?"

"Again, he wants a narrow focus. It would help if Bragg gave up the location where he found the phone. And how he happened to find it."

Brock recalled the comment Bragg made immediately following his arrest, indicating that he might have more information. "Let's see what he'll give me."

Located on Court Street in the mill town of Dover-Foxcroft and tethered to a two-story courthouse with a brick façade, the Piscataquis County Jail looked like virtually every other small corrections facility around the Pine Tree State. Protruding from the center of a sloped shingled roof was a bright white cupola complete with a copper dome and weathervane. It was the quintessential colonial-style architecture of New England. Shoehorned inside the structure was the sheriff's office, jail, and emergency communications center.

Brock parked in the visitors' lot. He was pleased to see that there was no sign of the impending chaos that would soon accompany Major Morgan's arrival. The last thing this investigation needed was additional public exposure. Successful murder investigations were all about managing external distractions and anything that pulled control of the case away from investigators. And from the outset, the Summer Randall murder had had more than its share of distractions. Beginning with the unusual nature of her death. It was almost as if the killer hoped to muddy the waters surrounding the cause of death. Brock hated the lack of control he was feeling. It was like having a lead in the fourth quarter of a football game, then watching the lead slowly eroded by mistakes. While there is no such thing as a perfect murder investigation, even one well executed can only survive a few mistakes before falling apart.

"May I help you, Detective?" the dark-haired deputy manning the front desk said as Brock showed him his credentials.

"I'm here to question a prisoner," Brock said.

"Did you call ahead?"

"It's okay, Mitch," a voice said from behind Brock.

Brock turned to see the sheriff himself strolling down the hall toward him.

"Been expecting you, Justice," the sheriff said as he extended a hand. "Armand Pelletier."

"Sheriff," Brock said.

"Your people just dropped off Mr. Bragg. You sure don't waste any time."

"I don't have time to waste," Brock said.

Pelletier turned his attention to the counter. "Mitch, help this man check in his weapons."

After taking care of the administrative procedures and securing his gun and ammo in a locker, Brock followed the sheriff into the secure area of the jail directly to the interview rooms.

Sheriff Pelletier unlocked the door to interview room one and led Brock inside. The room was strictly no frills. One scarred and dented rectangular steel table sat in the center of the room surrounded by four thinly padded metal chairs. Brock eyed the upper corners of the cement block walls, spotting what appeared to be fire sprinklers and emergency lighting. Both were commonly used to conceal cameras and microphones.

"Are these rooms monitored?" Brock said.

"Yup. And recorded. Nothing too fancy, I'm afraid, but it does a fair job with the video portion."

"And the audio?" Brock said, knowing it was the most important aspect of any interrogation.

"Excellent-quality audio. We might not have the personnel here right now to burn you a copy of the interview before you leave, but we can take care of that next week."

"That's fine. Thanks."

"Can I get you anything before you start?"

Brock shook his head. "I think I'm good. I just need Peter Bragg."

"I'll have him brought down here straight away."

74

Sunday, October 12, 7:00 p.m

Two Piscataquis County jail deputies escorted Bragg into the room. He had already been outfitted in the standard jail jumpsuit and sneakers. Bragg's wrists were handcuffed in front to a leather belt, and his ankles were shackled by a short chain. The leg restraints had the effect of hobbling him, requiring him to take short, shuffling steps to avoid face-planting on the concrete floor.

Bragg acknowledged Brock with a nod as the deputies led him to the chair across the table from Brock and sat him down. One of the handcuffs was removed before being inserted through a metal ring mounted atop the table. The handcuff was reattached to Bragg's wrist, securing him to the table and preventing him from being able to attack Brock, should he feel the need.

The first deputy turned and stepped back into the hallway while the second addressed Brock.

"We'll be right outside if you need anything."

"Thank you," Brock said.

Neither Brock nor Bragg uttered a single word until the deputies had departed and closed the heavy steel door behind them.

"Wasn't sure how long it would take you to get here," Bragg said.

"I work the priorities first," Brock said as he flipped open a fresh notebook and recorded the location, time, and date of Bragg's interview. Following that, he removed a single sheet of paper from his cloth briefcase upon which the Miranda warning had been preprinted.

"I'd think you'd know that by heart," Bragg said with a grin.

"Likewise," Brock said.

Bragg's grin withered. "Guess that's fair."

"We do this so the attorneys can't say you didn't receive the proper warning."

"Or that I didn't understand it, right?" Bragg said.

Brock paused a moment to take the man's measure. "You were an MP?"

"Indeed I was, Detective Justice," Bragg said. "I read those rights to more of my fellow soldiers than you would believe."

Brock got down to business, reciting each warning verbatim and waiting until he received a verbal acknowledgment from Bragg before continuing.

"Now, Mr. Bragg, keeping all those rights in mind, do you wish to answer questions at this time?"

Bragg shrugged. "Why not?"

Brock scribbled Bragg's response at the bottom of the sheet. After that he added the words: *Subject unable to sign due to being restrained.* Brock slid the sheet of paper back inside the portfolio protruding from his briefcase.

"Mr. Bragg, would you explain how you came into possession of Summer Randall's cell phone?"

Chloe sat staring at the blinking curser on the screen of her laptop while she awaited AAG Grover's response from the other end of the call. As she had previously cautioned Brock, Grover was worried that a judge might find the search too broad in its scope. The more they limited the items to be searched for, the greater chance they had of obtaining the judge's approval.

Grover cleared his throat before speaking. "So, it looks like you want to search for video files directly related to Mr. Bragg's illegal poaching hobby, is that right?"

"Yes, in addition to evidence that Mr. Bragg or any of his possessions, to include the knife, contain even trace amounts of blood belonging to the victim."

"The blood makes sense. Though, if he is an active hunter, you're liable to find blood everywhere on his property and belongings. Summer Randall's blood, if there is any, will be like looking for a needle in a haystack. My real problem with this warrant is the broadness of your electronic request to search and seize. If this guy keeps video files of all his illegal hunting spots, it might be too invasive for our purposes."

"We don't care about his poaching activities," Chloe said. "We only want to grab the footage, if it exists, that captures something related to Summer Randall's murder."

"I understand that, and I think the judge will likely understand that as well, but you may find evidence of additional crimes totally unrelated to the stabbing of Summer Randall."

"I guess that's likely," Chloe said. "But as I said, we aren't looking to enforce any wildlife or hunting laws against Peter Bragg. Only evidence directly and narrowly related to the murder of Summer Randall. Anything else deemed to be outside of our law enforcement authority and scope will be returned."

"To either Bragg or his attorney?"

"Yes."

"You should add that caveat to the affidavit. That will substantially narrow the scope of any evidence seizure. In other words, it will guarantee to the judge that you aren't on a fishing expedition against Bragg."

Chloe nodded and began adding the additional language to the affidavit to search.

"Any other areas of concern?"

"No. It all looks good. Nice work. Send me the amended copy when you're finished, and I'll give it one last look."

"Thanks, Gene."

75

Sunday, October 12, 8:00 p.m

Brock filled several pages in the new notebook even though the interview was electronically recorded. If he'd learned one lesson along the way, it was never trust that something electronic won't break down during an interview. If his notes were comprehensive enough, he would still be able to accurately recall the details of their conversation.

"You said you were in the process of bringing the phone to the Greenville public safety building."

"I was," Bragg said. "The next thing I know, I've got a police vehicle bearing down on me with emergency lights flashing."

"Why didn't you just pull over and hand the phone to Officer Hastings?"

"Because I hadn't done anything wrong."

"According to Hastings, you were speeding."

Bragg raised an eyebrow. "Is that what he told you? Trust me, I wasn't speeding. Felt like a setup from the get-go. That kid was on me so quick I figured you must have been tracking the phone."

Brock resisted the urge to confirm Bragg's suspicion. "What happened next?"

"Hastings moved to pass me, and I thought maybe he was just on his way to a call. That is, until he tried to force me off the road."

"He drove into your vehicle?" Brock said.

"Like a NASCAR driver on a mission."

"What did you do?"

"What could I do? Like I said, the whole thing felt like a setup. And I wasn't about to let this crazy-ass cop run me into a tree."

"So you drove him off the road instead?"

"Pretty much. He wasn't a very good driver, as it turned out."

"You realize Officer Hastings nearly died when his cruiser caught fire."

"Yeah, well, that wasn't my intention. He was fine when I left him. I didn't realize I had a flat tire until after I turned around to head back to my place."

"You ditched the truck?"

"Had to. I knew there would be other cops coming. I double-timed it through the woods to the compound. You already know the rest."

"Tell me again how you located Summer's phone."

"After you and your partners came to my place with Warden Labbe, I realized that I might have captured the murder on one of my game cameras. Or at least something important in the aftermath. I followed the news reports on the murder and did a bit of recon of the area myself. After that, I removed a dozen or so cameras and brought them back to my compound to review the digital footage. That's when I found a couple of things of interest."

"One of those cameras led you to Summer's phone?"

"Yes."

"Do you still have the footage?"

Bragg hesitated before answering Brock's question, as if he might be wondering if he could leverage the footage against his charges. Brock half expected Bragg to lawyer up at that point, but instead he nodded. "I do."

"Where is it?" Brock said.

Penelope Cumberland stood beside Major Morgan while he held court with the local media for the second time in a week. Though many of the usual outlets showed up for his impromptu dog and pony show, this time no out-of-state networks were present. She imagined it had more to do with the absence of Congresswoman Randall than any reflection on waning public interest in the murder of Summer Randall. Or perhaps, like her, the reporters weren't big fans of Morgan's less-than-charming personality.

"In addition to a litany of reckless driving charges, connected to the near death of a Greenville police officer, we have every confidence that we will uncover indisputable evidence of Peter Bragg's direct involvement in the murder of Summer Randall."

Penny resisted the urge to shake her head at Morgan's callous and ill-timed comments concerning Bragg's guilt in connection to Randall's murder. And she knew how wild Brock and Chloe would be when word reached them. Egocentric administrators like Morgan were creatures of habit. And when it came to trying cases in front of television cameras, those creatures were no better than a legion of ambulance-chasing lawyers, especially when there was a professional interest at stake. She knew Morgan was concerned with one thing and one thing only: becoming the next colonel of the Maine State Police. Peter Bragg and Summer Randall were merely the foundation footings of what he hoped was his successful campaign to be MSP's next top dog. As much as Penny wanted to see this case brought to a successful conclusion, she half hoped that Bragg turned out to be innocent of the murder, leaving the wannabe colonel with egg streaming down his face and his dream of promotion up in smoke.

As soon as Morgan had finished speaking, a half dozen reporters shouted over each other, vying for attention like gulls squawking for fries. The major maintained his stoic expression as he pretended to make a random selection from the crowd. Finally he pointed to one of his regular contacts with the *Bangor Daily News*. Penny had heard the rumors that the striking young blond reporter had been involved in an ongoing affair with the very married Major Morgan.

"You have a question, miss?" Morgan said as he pretended not to know her name.

"Dawn Miller, *Bangor Daily News*. Can you tell us what led your detectives to Peter Bragg in the first place?"

Morgan exchanged a quick glance with Cumberland. She responded with an almost imperceptible headshake.

"I'm afraid I can't comment on any specific details of the ongoing investigation, Dawn. But I can tell you that we expect to be releasing more to you over the coming days. Thank you all."

76

Sunday, October 12, 8:20 p.m

As Brock drove away from the Piscataquis County Jail, he saw Morgan and Cumberland standing near a throng of reporters and television news vans. Morgan was doing exactly what he wanted, regardless of the negative impact it might have on their investigation. Brock wondered if Cumberland had even tried to stop him.

He had been on the road less than five minutes before his thoughts returned to the death of Laura Croxford. Brock checked his phone to see if Ginger had responded to his message yet, but there was nothing. He'd given her the times and the registration number of the vehicle parked at Denny's, but Dashofy hadn't sent him a text or left a voicemail. Was she still pissed at him, or was Brock simply barking up the wrong tree with Mathers's involvement?

Before he could pocket the phone, it vibrated with a call from Chloe.

"How did it go with Grover?" Brock said.

"I think I've addressed all of his concerns," Chloe said. "I just emailed him the revised version."

"Concerns?"

"Like I told you, Gene was worried about the wide scope of the search."

"What are we left to search for?" Brock said.

"Blood belonging to the victim, electronic evidence as it directly pertains to the crime of murder, and the edged weapon used to stab Summer."

"In other words, he doesn't want us going fishing," Brock said.

"Correct. He said that given Bragg's known criminal history surrounding illegal hunting, we'd be better going to a judge with a narrower focus. If we find anything relevant to our case not included in the original affidavit, we can always file an addendum."

Brock couldn't disagree with Grover's logic, but he was worried about the amount of time all of this would take. If they were wrong about Bragg, every second spent on him was time wasted, allowing the real killer to better cover their tracks and avoid detection.

"I've been on the phone with Warden Labbe too," Chloe said. "He told me that Bragg might have game cameras all through those woods off Lily Bay Road. This search could literally take a week or more."

"Not necessarily," Brock said.

"What do you mean by that?" Chloe said.

"You still at the public safety building?" Brock said.

"Yeah. Zim is helping me look up stuff. Why?"

"I'll fill you in when I get there."

"I don't know about this, Brock," Grover said over the speakerphone. Both Chloe and Zimmerman wore pinched expressions on their faces as they reviewed the signed consent forms sitting on the conference room table. "I mean, the warrant is already written. And you know better than anyone that consent can be withdrawn at any time."

"That's just the problem," Brock countered. "We don't have a lot of time. As it is, the trail is nearly a week old. One of our prime suspects is in the hospital after being beaten within an inch of his life. And now a certain state police major has practically told the whole world that we've arrested the man responsible for murdering Summer Randall."

"That's Major Malfunction to you," Zimmerman quipped.

"While I agree that none of those things are helpful," Grover said. "They are also out of our control. The only thing we can control is to keep doing things by the numbers. And that means going through the court for our evidence process. There is no point in making Fourth Amendment challenges easier for Mr. Bragg's defense counsel."

"Haven't you successfully tried murder cases where consent was given by a suspect?" Chloe said.

"I have," Grover said. "But I try to avoid it whenever possible."

"What about the DNA swabs we've been collecting?" Brock said. "Those have all been taken by consent."

"That's only because we needed a sample to match the blood found in Summer's car and the fetus's DNA profile. And matching DNA doesn't necessarily make the baby's father the murderer. But this is different. Whether Bragg is involved in Summer's murder or not, there is no reason not to go through the court on this one."

"What about remote access?" Chloe said.

"What do you mean?" Grover said.

"Just what I said. Bragg has given us permission to access his computer and his video storage systems to include the cloud. Anything connected to an online source can be accessed remotely. What if someone really is trying to set up Bragg to take the fall for this murder? It wouldn't be that hard for someone with knowledge to hack his system and remove any damning files that exist."

"I hate to buck the system," Zimmerman said. "But I think these two may be onto something. Hacking gives this thing a whole new urgency."

They all waited for Grover to respond. Brock could hear pages turning from the other end of the call. He knew, as they all did, that Gene was looking for a relevant case that covered their current quandary. After several long moments, Grover returned to the phone.

"Okay, I think I found a ruling that would tend to support your argument. I still don't like the idea of taking what amounts to an early peek at video files we would eventually find under the search warrant."

"But?" Brock said hopefully.

"But if Bragg signed those willingly—"

"He did," Brock said. "On camera, no less."

"If he told you exactly where to find the files, then I guess I'm okay with it. But I still want you to proceed with getting the warrant approved by a magistrate."

"We're on it," Chloe said.

77

Sunday, October 12, 10:45 p.m

The evidence response team members argued with Brock about him entering Bragg's home before they had a chance to examine everything. If Bragg had killed Summer Randall, then any trace amount of her blood, assuming it was even present, would be easy to overlook entirely. In the end, the ERT agreed to allow Brock to enter by stipulating that he wore a complete Tyvek suit, covering him head to toe.

Almost instantly upon entering the cabin, Brock began to sweat profusely. The thin vinyl material trapped his body heat inside. Armed with the access codes Bragg had given him, Brock went right to the computer station and booted up the instrument. The video files were like everything else inside the cabin, organized to the point of ridiculousness. Each of the downloads contained within the main storage file were listed by date and location. Brock stared in wonder at row upon row of files. There had to be thousands. Bragg's poaching hobby had become an obsession. He wondered if it was Bragg's way of coping with life after the military.

Brock visually scanned the folders and their designations according to the directions Bragg had provided to him. Brock shook his head as he performed a quick count of the downloads. In the week following Summer's murder, Brock estimated that Bragg had downloaded file footage captured from at least fifty different cameras. He thought back to his recent visit to the bog with Warden Labbe and the evidence of a recently removed camera. Could Bragg have moved or repositioned that many cameras? It was possible, Brock thought. But considering that Bragg had only been spotted once while doing it was impressive.

Brock felt beads of sweat forming on his face and rolling down his back. He resisted the urge to wipe away the perspiration with the sleeve of his suit, knowing that he wasn't there to add evidence, only to recover it.

Nearly five minutes after sitting down at the computer, Brock finally located the video file in question. The file was labeled: D15 10-6-25. Brock double-clicked the icon and watched as a media player launched from the hard drive. According to the counter, the clip was three minutes and fifty-eight seconds long. It was recorded on the evening of Summer Randall's murder at approximately eight thirty p.m. The camera was listed as D15, a designation that meant nothing to Brock. Bragg had told him that D15 had been located in a bog along Scammon Road not far from Lower Wilson Pond. Brock pressed play and watched as the MPEG scrolled forward. He immediately recognized the location as the bog that he and Labbe had visited. Based on the point of view captured, Labbe had been right about where the camera had been mounted. The perspective from the back edge of the bog allowed a wide view of Scammon Road, encompassing the turnout where Warden Labbe had parked his truck. Though the camera recorded in color, the captured image was visibly muted due to the low lighting. Approximately fifteen seconds into the video, a dark-colored midsized SUV pulled into view and stopped in the turnout. The vehicle had come from the camera's right, meaning it had been traveling inbound on Scammon Road away from Mount View Trail, the location where Brock had located Summer Randall's car, heading toward downtown Greenville.

Ten seconds after stopping, the headlights were extinguished and the dome light came on as the driver opened the door and stepped from the SUV. In the brief glimpse allowed by the inside light, Brock could see the dark silhouette of a single figure moving away from the vehicle toward the bog. It was impossible to make out any detail from the distance recorded by the camera, but it was clear that the driver was carrying something. As the figure moved out of the trees into the clearing at the edge of the bog, they were partially illuminated by the ambient lighting of twilight spilling over the trees from the west. The figure appeared to be wearing some type of head covering. Brock studied the image, trying to make out whether it was a knit hat or perhaps a hood. The figure paused for just a second, turning both right and left before throwing something overhanded into the bog.

Brock froze the image and sat back in the chair. According to Bragg, after removing the camera from the bog and studying the captured video, he returned to the bog hoping to retrieve whatever had been discarded by the driver of the SUV. That item was Summer Randall's cell phone. Bragg said he'd located it lying atop a grassy hummock.

Brock pressed play and watched the remainder of the video. The figure moved back toward the SUV, then climbed inside. The dome light activated once again as the door was opened. The lighting didn't provide any more detail of the figure, but Brock did notice two things. The first was that the SUV appeared to be empty inside, meaning that the driver was the only occupant. The second thing he noticed was the top of the driver's head in relation to the roof of the SUV. If they could identify the make and model of the vehicle, they would have an approximate height for the suspect. It wasn't the kind of evidence that would make a positive identification in the eyes of the court, but it was something.

Brock removed the flash drive Chloe had given him from his pocket and inserted it into the side port of Bragg's computer. He knew the file already existed on the cloud server but wanted to make a copy in case something happened to it. As soon as the file was copied, Brock ejected and pocketed the flash drive.

Brock exited the program and the online file server, then powered down the computer. He stood up, took a quick look around, then headed for the door.

78

Monday, October 13, 8:45 a.m

"That's a 2014 Toyota 4Runner Trail," Zimmerman said after watching the video for the second time.

Brock, Chloe, Zimmerman, and Chief Leavitt were huddled around Chloe's computer in the conference room of the Greenville public safety building, watching the video that Brock had copied from Bragg's files.

"How could you possibly know that?" Chloe said. "It's nothing but a silhouette."

"Because I owned one," Zimmerman said.

"And from this low-light video, you can positively identify the model and year?" Brock said in disbelief.

"Of course. They only made three models of the 4Runner in 2014. The SR5, the Trail, and the Limited. We owned the Trail."

"How can you tell the difference?" Leavitt said.

"Easy. The Trail had a more aggressive look to the front end. And it had a hood scoop. Neither one of the other models came with a scoop."

"Functional?" Brock said.

"Of course not. But it looked pretty badass."

Chloe turned to one of the notebooks they had been compiling on the case.

"What are you looking for?" Brock said.

"I just want to double-check something. We ran registration checks for every one of our suspects in this case, but I don't recall seeing a single Toyota 4Runner in the mix."

They waited while Chloe skimmed through the printouts from the Bureau of Motor Vehicles.

"Well?" Zimmerman said.

"Nothing."

"Well, maybe it's an older vehicle that they haven't registered but still own," Brock opined.

Chloe shook her head. "Can't be, because I requested every vehicle ever registered to each person."

"In the state of Maine?" Zimmerman said.

"Well, yeah. Where else would I check?"

"Zim's right," Brock said. "If any of our suspects moved here from out of state, they may not have reregistered the vehicle in Maine."

"That would be a crime if they're still driving them," Chloe said.

"So's murder, but that doesn't seem to have dissuaded anyone," Zimmerman said.

"And we're positive that the object our mystery driver tossed was Summer's cell phone?" Leavitt said.

"Not positive," Brock said. "But confident. Bragg said that after he watched this clip, he went back to the bog to try and locate whatever had been discarded, and he located the cell phone."

"How do we know that was the only thing they tossed?" Zimmerman said.

"We don't," Brock said.

"We still don't have the murder weapon," Chloe said. "We need to go back to that spot and have another look."

Brock's attention was pulled away by the ringing of his own phone.

"Justice."

"Detective Justice. This is Assistant District Attorney Brendan Bains from the Piscataquis County District Attorney's Office calling about the Jonathan Watters OUI case. I wonder if you might have a moment?"

"It was my understanding that Watters is a county case," Brock said. "Not sure I can help you with that, Mr. Bains. I am investigating the stabbing death of Summer Randall, the woman Watters hit."

Zimmerman rolled his eyes.

"That is exactly why I need to speak with you, Detective. I was contacted by Mr. Watters's attorney, Henry Gifford. They are looking to make a plea deal."

"I'm sure they are," Brock said. "But as I said, it isn't my case. I'm tied up on a murder."

Brock was about to end the call when Bains responded.

"Gifford claims his client has information relative to your murder investigation that he is willing to share."

After ending the call with Bains, Brock placed a call to Assistant Attorney General Grover and set the phone to speaker mode, allowing Chloe and Zimmerman to weigh in.

"You think it's legit?" Grover said. "Or is Watters just pulling everyone's chain?"

"Don't know," Brock said. "I only met Watters briefly at the hospital. Not the most amiable person I've ever met, but I guess that doesn't mean anything."

"Any idea what he's going to tell you?"

"None. But I know he's going to try to leverage whatever he says to get his charge reduced from elevated aggravated OUI to something lesser."

Brock had known all along that the facts of this case would present a problem for either the AG's office or the county DA or both. The ambiguous nature of Summer Randall's death and injuries sustained as a result of being struck by Watters's vehicle were always going to rear their heads.

"Well, having Watters plea out wouldn't hurt my feelings at all," Grover said. "Watters's involvement has already muddied the waters, no pun intended, when it comes to prosecuting Summer's killer."

"A killer we have yet to identify," Chloe said.

"True," Zimmerman said.

"As far as I can see, listening to what he has to say doesn't cost us a thing," Grover said. "Any deal offered will have to come from the DA's office, which has nothing to do with us. Watters is either pulling everyone's chain or he knows something that could help us solve this case. How soon can they set up a meeting?"

"I told Bains I'd phone him back after we spoke with you," Brock said.

"I think it's worth the time. Tell Bains we're willing to listen to what Watters has to say."

79

Monday, October 13, 11:45 a.m

ADA Brendan Bains's office was barely large enough to accommodate two people and a desk. As a result, the decision was made to conduct the meeting in the Piscataquis County District Attorney's second-floor conference room.

The air was stuffy and about ten degrees higher than what Brock would have deemed comfortable. Brock, Chloe, and Grover sat on one side of the long table while Jonathan Watters and his attorney, Henry Gifford, sat opposite them. The moments ticked by slowly in the uncomfortable silence normally associated with high-stakes negotiations. Brock was beginning to wonder if something had gone wrong when ADA Bains finally strolled into the room.

"My apologies for keeping you all waiting," Bains said. "Had a last-minute issue to deal with."

"Nothing to do with my client's deal, I hope," Gifford chuckled in an obvious attempt to lighten the mood. It fell flat.

"No, nothing like that. A completely unrelated issue. Thank you all for agreeing to meet to discuss this."

"Where is the representative from the sheriff's office?" Grover said, echoing Brock's very thought. "I would have thought they would also be represented."

"I have spoken to the deputy assigned to the accident as well as Sheriff Pelletier himself, and they have agreed to defer the final decision on this matter to my office."

Brock knew that politics was playing a part in what was happening here. In Maine, both district attorneys and county sheriffs are elected positions. And whenever there is a less than desirable case connecting them, the preferred outcome is always the one that is least harmful to their bids for reelection. Whether anybody would admit it or not, Jonathan Watters's OUI motor vehicle accident was a giant pile of excrement on the prosecutorial side of the house. The facts of the case made it impossible to win. On one hand, the DA could try and charge Watters with elevated aggravated operating under the influence for the injuries he caused when he drove drunk and struck Summer Randall. The end result would most likely be that Watters's attorney, with absolutely nothing to lose, would take the case to trial, effectively rolling the dice on what would be his client's third OUI conviction in ten years, making it a felony offense even without the aggravating factors of the accident and injury to Summer Randall. But the trial would be messy, and there was always the chance that a jury might let their emotions dictate their findings, causing them to disregard the medical examiner's finding that Summer had died as a result of her stab wound. If that happened, Watters could theoretically receive up to thirty years in prison, and Brock and Chloe would lose out on the opportunity to learn what Watters knew about the murder. But successful or not, they would only succeed in casting doubt and possibly destroying the case against Summer's real killer, the person or persons who stabbed her and then chased her through the woods to her ultimate death. On the other hand, they could agree to reduce the charges in order to obtain a plea deal on the OUI charge in hopes that Watters and Gifford would simply go away, clearing the way for the murder case to go forward unencumbered by a disputed cause of death. Neither option would endear the district attorney's office or Sheriff Pelletier to the community.

With a smug grin painted upon his face, Gifford weighed in. "So, as I've already discussed with District Attorney Bains—"

"Assistant District Attorney," Bains corrected.

Gifford waved the correction away like a bothersome fly before continuing. "My client is willing to provide the state with important information pertaining to the murder of Summer Randall in exchange for having the elevated aggravated OUI charge reduced to a more reasonable simple OUI."

"I wouldn't say there was anything simple or reasonable about a third conviction for operating under the influence, Mr. Gifford," Chloe snapped. "Or running over a pedestrian. That still makes your client a menace in my book."

Brock glanced over at Chloe, surprised by her comment. He could clearly see the anger in her flushed face. He gave her a look that said, "Cool it."

"Like it or not, Detective Wright, that is the offer. If you don't want my client's help in solving the murder of Summer Randall, we'll be more than happy to take our chances at trial."

"That's not necessary," ADA Bains said quickly. "I'm sure the AG's office and the state police appreciate your client's willingness to assist in their investigation."

Gene Grover spoke for the first time. "I think I'll reserve my appreciation until we hear what it is that Mr. Watters has to offer."

Brock fought back a grin at the comment. With a single sentence, Grover had just put three people in their respective places. There was a reason the man specialized in trying homicide cases for the state.

Gifford turned his head toward Bains. "Do we have a deal or not, Brendan?"

"We do."

"Good. I'll expect it in writing before we leave here today."

"You'll have it."

"I'm glad that's settled," Grover said before turning his attention to Watters. "Now, what can you tell us about the murder of Summer Randall?"

"A woman?" Chloe said. "He's saying the killer is a woman?"

Brock, Chloe, and Grover had retreated to a conference room to discuss Watters's revelation in private.

"He didn't actually say that," Brock said.

"No," Grover said. "What he said was the first person he saw immediately following the accident was a woman wearing a hoodie."

"So, what do you think about his deal?" Chloe said.

"I think it's not quite the same as identifying Summer's killer, like he promised," Grover said. "But clearly it is an interesting development. You've spent an awful lot of time collecting DNA samples for comparison purposes in an attempt to discover the identity of the biological father of Summer's baby."

"And to match the blood found in her car," Brock corrected.

"That too," Grover said. "But my point is maybe you've been looking in the wrong place."

"I still think her pregnancy is the strongest motive we've got," Chloe said, attempting to defend her theory of what happened. "And I think Watters would say anything to get out of the predicament he's put himself in."

"Maybe," Brock said. "But Summer's pregnancy was always only one possible motive for the murder."

Chloe's head whipped around. "What? You're saying you believe a single thing that comes out of Jonathan Watters's mouth?"

"Not necessarily," Brock said. "But we do still need to keep an open mind."

"Brock's right," Grover said. "We have to look at this from every angle. Watters's word may not be worth a thing, but now that he's gone on record, his testimony will be fair game to any defense attorney who gets assigned to represent Summer's murderer. And if that defendant does end up being a man, Watters's testimony will be like firing a torpedo into the side of the state's case. The jury only needs reasonable doubt."

"Not even the whole jury," Brock said. "One person could stymy the entire thing."

"I still don't trust Watters," Chloe said. "He could have come forward with this supposed information at any time, but he waited until he could use it to cut a deal. He's nothing but a self-serving piece of shit."

"Watters may be the world's biggest piece of shit," Brock said. "But it doesn't mean he's not telling the truth about what he saw."

"And he could just as easily have told us he saw a man wearing a hoodie," Grover said. "The deal was up for grabs no matter what he told us. Face it, the DA wanted a way out of this mess, and Watters and Gifford gave him one."

"And dropped us right in it," Brock said.

80

Monday, October 13, 1:30 p.m

"Way to have my back," Chloe said as they drove away from the Piscataquis County Courthouse. "I thought at least *you'd* agree with me."

"I wasn't taking sides," Brock said. "I'm just trying to be pragmatic about what we have at this point."

"Well, congratulations, *partner*. You succeeded."

Brock caught the extra emphasis Chloe gave to the word "partner." Somehow she was always capable of making that word sound derogatory. He drew in a deep breath and let it out slowly, giving himself time to formulate his response. He knew Chloe was pissed at him for not taking her side, but it was clear that she was allowing her anger toward Watters, and the frustration she was feeling about not having caught Summer Randall's killer, cloud her normally sound judgment. He wondered if Chloe felt a more personal connection to Summer than she would admit.

"It wasn't about having your back, Chloe. I don't trust Watters, or his attorney, for that matter, any more than you do, but that doesn't mean he's lying about what he saw. Think about it. You remember the last murder we worked together? Remember how many people lied to us? But eventually we got to the truth. Hell, the only thing that doesn't lie is physical evidence. That's homicide investigation 101."

Chloe turned her head to look out through the side window. Brock wasn't sure if she was trying to formulate her own response or if she was simply giving him the cold shoulder. His ex-wife had been an expert at not communicating when she was pissed at him. One thing was certain, they needed to regroup and figure out the best way forward.

It was late afternoon by the time they arrived back at the PSB to find Zimmerman FaceTiming with Detective Wheeler.

"Wheels," Chloe said. "We've missed you around here."

"Hey, Chloe. It's nice to be missed."

"I was just telling Wheels that we may need help going through some of Bragg's electronic storage," Zimmerman said.

"There is so much here," Brock said. "This guy recorded everything. I think he knew the area better than anyone, including the wardens."

"Any idea what else we might be searching for?" Wheeler said.

"Not a clue," Zimmerman said.

"The SUV that we saw in the one clip Bragg gave us might be a good start," Chloe said. "None of the people close to Summer Randall have a 4Runner registered to them."

"The clip with the figure tossing the phone?" Wheeler said.

"Yes," Brock said. "While we can't say for sure that it was Summer's phone being discarded in the video, Bragg did tell us that is where he recovered it. Said he went down to the bog to remove the game camera because the area was getting too hot with law enforcement prowling around after the murder."

"And did he review the video, then go back down and find it?" Wheeler said.

"Yes. According to Bragg, after he viewed the footage, he returned to the bog to try and find whatever had been discarded. That's when he says he found the cell phone lying on top of a grassy hummock in the middle of the bog and picked it up."

"And the time and date stamp on the video put it shortly after the murder," Chloe said.

"It might also give us at least the direction that the killer was fleeing," Zimmerman added.

"How so?" Wheeler said.

"Because there are only two direct routes back into Greenville," Brock said. "And one of them was blocked by first responders working the accident."

"Okay, that's helpful," Wheeler said.

"The video isn't the best because of the low light and the distance it was taken from, but it gives us a place to start."

"Maybe you can work your magic and clean it up for us?" Chloe said.

"I'll do my best," Wheeler said.

"We need to check that bog for the murder weapon too," Brock said, thinking out loud.

"I can organize a search using the ERT guys if you want," Zimmerman offered.

"Thanks, Zim," Chloe said.

"What about the rest of the files and Bragg's computer?" Wheeler said.

"I'll run those over to the barracks mañana, amigo," Zimmerman said.

"Thanks," Wheeler said.

Zimmerman disconnected from the call with Wheeler, then turned to Brock and Chloe. "So, how did the meeting with the attorneys go?"

Before either one of them could answer, Brock's cell phone buzzed with a call. He grabbed it hoping that it was Ginger Dashofy getting back to him about his discovery, but the number displayed wasn't a number he recognized.

"Justice," Brock answered.

"Detective Justice. This is Cliff Johnson calling from Eastern Maine Medical Center. Not sure if you remember me. We spoke a couple of days ago."

It took a moment for the name to register as the former Atlanta police detective turned security guard who had offered to keep them apprised of Ronnie Libby's condition. "Hey, Cliff," Brock said. "Any update on Libby?"

"That's why I'm calling. Thought you'd want to know, Libby has regained consciousness."

81

Monday, October 13, 4:30 p.m

Brock and Chloe departed for the hospital in Bangor, leaving Zimmerman to his own devices. They located Libby's surgeon in the hallway not far from Libby's room. Doctor Chesbrough was less than pleased to see them.

"I hope your being here is merely a coincidence," Chesbrough said. "And not someone on my staff reporting back to you on my patient's condition, which is a clear violation of HIPAA privacy rules."

"I'm not sure what you're implying," Brock said, feigning innocence. "We just stopped by to check on our victim's condition."

"I'm not implying anything. I'm saying it is more than a little convenient that you two would show up right after Mr. Libby regained consciousness."

"He's conscious?" Chloe said. "That is good news."

The doctor's eyes narrowed with suspicion.

"Has he said anything?" Brock said.

"Not about the attack. Though he is able to speak."

"May we see him?" Chloe said.

"Normally I wouldn't allow visitors at this stage. Mr. Libby has a long way to go if he is to make a full recovery."

"Will he?" Brock said. "Make a full recovery?"

"The patient has suffered a great deal of trauma. His body and his brain are still healing and likely will be for some time."

"We won't stay long," Brock said.

The doctor eyed them both. His expression was doubtful.

"I'll give you five minutes. But I don't want you doing anything to agitate him, okay?"

"Scout's honor," Chloe said, holding up three fingers.

As the doctor departed down the hall, Brock and Chloe entered Libby's room.

"I didn't know you were a Scout," Brock said.

Chloe winked. "I wasn't."

Ronnie Libby was lying in the hospital bed, looking like he had gone five rounds with a front-end loader. He was on his back, his torso slightly elevated by the uncomfortable-looking contraption. Protruding from the hospital johnny were all the usual wires and tubes tethering him to the bank of monitors beside the bed. Brock couldn't help but be reminded of his own recent hospital stay when he'd been treated for a gunshot wound.

Libby's body was partially covered in a clean sheet and blanket. His eye sockets were purple, as was the skin of his taped broken nose. Stitches crisscrossed his swollen face, and his right arm was wrapped in a cast. And it was clear that Ronnie would be in dire need of major dental work if he ever hoped to smile again without scaring anyone.

Libby's bloodshot eyes shifted toward Brock and Chloe as they neared the bed. Brock heard the pace of the heart monitor increase slightly as they approached.

"What do you want?" Libby said, although with the damage to his mouth, it came out sounding more like "Whatdaywha?"

"Hey, Ronnie," Chloe said, taking the lead. "We just stopped by to see how you were doing."

Libby did his best to scowl, but it fell short. His eyes shifted back toward the opposite wall.

"I don't suppose you know who did this to you," Brock said.

Libby moved his head slightly side to side, and his eyes closed briefly. Brock imagined it was due to the pain that even the slightest movement caused him. He wondered if Libby had any idea how ironic his current condition was, given what he had previously done to Summer.

"How many attackers were there?" Chloe said.

Libby held up his left hand, extending the index finger.

"Did you get a look at your attacker?" Chloe continued. "Can you describe them for us?"

"Ski mask," Libby said. Again, his words were muddled. "Dark clothes."

Brock nodded.

"How did they get inside the house, Ronnie?" Brock said.

"Forthed their wee."

Brock heard the pace of the beeping increase yet again. He glanced at the monitor and saw that Libby's pulse rate was at 89 and rising.

"Can you tell us anything that might help catch the person who did this to you?" Chloe said. "Did they say anything?"

A piercing alarm sounded from the wall monitor as Libby's pulse eclipsed 100 bpm. Brock watched Libby's eyes roll back in their sockets, and his body began to convulse.

The door burst open, and two of the hospital staff hurried into the room.

"He's having a seizure," one of the attendants said.

"You two need to leave, right now," the other said before slapping the wall-mounted help button with an open palm.

Brock and Chloe retreated into the hallway across from the door as several nurses hurried past them. Brock turned and came face-to-face with Dr. Chesbrough.

"I warned you both," the doctor said. "Mr. Libby is off-limits to the police as of right now."

"Just the police?" Brock said before he could stop himself.

Chesbrough paused in the doorway to glare at Brock. "All visitors."

"That went well," Chloe said as she and Brock crossed the parking lot toward the unmarked Ford.

"I hadn't really expected he'd be happy to see us," Brock said. "I'm pretty sure he holds us partially responsible for what happened to him."

"If anyone is responsible, it's him for beating up Summer," Chloe said.

Brock agreed.

"Do you still think Taylor Randall is responsible for the attack on Ronnie?" Chloe said.

"It's the most obvious answer," Brock said. "Either he had someone else tune Ronnie up, or he did it himself, then got one of his employees to give him an alibi."

"You think that alibi can hold up to pressure?" Chloe said.

"Only one way to find out," Brock said, knowing full well to which employee she was referring.

82

Tuesday, October 14, 12:45 p.m

Chloe and Zimmerman were parked in a lot just down the street from Greenville Outfitters, Taylor Randall's store. Chloe had backed the Interceptor between a box truck on one side and a large pole-mounted sign on the other. Looking to the right underneath the sign and above the boxwoods allowed them an unobstructed view of Randall's pickup parked at the curb.

"You really think he'll leave for lunch?" Zimmerman said. "I don't want to be sitting out here on a fool's errand, not when there is a case that needs solving."

"He'll head out shortly," Chloe said. "Trust me."

"What makes you so sure?"

"First, because he's a creature of habit. He leaves for lunch everyday between one and one thirty."

"And the other reasons?"

"He knows we're watching his every move since the attack on Ronnie Libby. He wouldn't do anything to draw more attention to himself. Not now."

"Guess that makes sense," Zimmerman said.

"Of course it does," Chloe said. "I learned from the best."

She may have been assigned to learn the ropes of homicide investigation from Brock Justice, but seven years prior, fresh out of the Maine Criminal Justice Academy, Chloe, like all new recruits, had been assigned a field training officer. Someone who would teach her the ins and outs of law enforcement. Her FTO had been none other than Jordan Zimmerman.

"How do we know the kid we want to lean on is even working right now?" Zimmerman said.

"Because I had Taylor provide me with a copy of the weekly work schedule."

"Smart."

Chloe caught Zimmerman checking his cell. "Did they find anything yet?" she said, referring to the ERT bog search for the murder weapon.

"No, it's not Veilleux," Zimmerman said. "It's the missus checking in."

"How's Mrs. Zimmerman these days?" Chloe said.

"Clever as always."

"Sounds like a story there."

"Oh yeah. You know how I've been wanting a new gas grill for the back deck?"

"You even knew the model you wanted. Did she buy it for you?"

"Not hardly. And I intentionally left sales flyers lying around that featured the summer sales. She just tossed all of them in the trash without so much as a second look."

"Maybe you're being too subtle, Zim."

"It gets better. So, I figured if I started forgetting to cover the grill, it wouldn't take long before the burners began to rust out and she'd want a new one. They're already past their due date."

"That didn't work either?"

"Nope. Guess what she bought me last week?"

"A new grill cover?"

"A four-pack of replacement burners."

Chloe couldn't contain her laughter.

"That's right. Laugh it up, missy. Let's see how good you are at this game when you get hitched."

"If and when that ever happens, I'll be sure and watch out for the gas grill trap."

"Here he comes," Zimmerman said.

Chloe checked the time on the dashboard clock. 1:25. "Right on time."

They watched as Randall walked to his pickup, then climbed inside. Less than a minute later, his truck had disappeared around the block.

"Where do you think he's headed?" Zimmerman said.

"Home or the local diner. Either way, we've got forty-five minutes before he returns."

"Then let's not waste it."

The store was nearly empty as Chloe and Zimmerman entered. Typical small-town shop, Chloe thought. When the restaurants filled up, the retail stores emptied. Another hour or so from now, it would revert back to shoppers.

They found Taylor's alibi seated behind the counter, scrolling a social media feed on his cell phone.

"Does the boss know you do that while you're at work, Toby?" Zimmerman said.

"He's not here right now, and you're my only customers." Lonegan's attention shifted to Chloe. The recognition showed in his eyes, followed by disappointment. "I remember you from the other night. You're not here to buy anything, are you?"

"'Fraid not," Chloe said. "Why? Do you work on commission?"

"Not entirely, but yeah. If you wanna speak to Mr. Randall, he's at lunch."

"Actually, it's you we want to chat with," Zimmerman said.

"And now looks like a good time," Chloe said after scanning the empty store.

"You do know how much trouble you would be in if we found out you were lying to cover for your boss?" Chloe said.

"I told you the truth," Lonegan said. "We were both here conducting inventory that night. You saw us."

"Doesn't mean your boss didn't step out while you kept working," Zimmerman said.

Lonegan said nothing.

"You heard what happened to Ronnie Libby that night, right?" Chloe said.

"Of course. Everyone in town heard about it. How is he?"

"Much improved," Zimmerman said.

"In fact, I stopped by to see him in the hospital yesterday," Chloe said. "Looks like he's gonna pull through."

"I wonder what he'll tell us about his attacker," Zimmerman said as he leaned in close to Lonegan.

Chloe noticed the telltale swallow as Lonegan's Adam's apple bounced up and down. He was nervous. The walls were closing in around him, and he knew it.

"You sure you don't want to revise your statement to Detective Wright?" Zimmerman said. "It's always best to get out in front of these things."

"Look, I really need this job, okay?" Lonegan said. "Mr. Randall isn't a guy you want to cross."

Now it was Chloe's turn to lean in to the young man's space. "Was Taylor actually here with you all night, Toby? Or is it possible he could have stepped out without your knowledge?"

Lonegan's eyes darted back and forth between the detectives, and he wet his lips with his tongue.

Zimmerman slapped the counter hard, startling the young man. "Tell us the truth, Toby."

Lonegan's eyes fell to the floor. Chloe knew he was beaten.

"Did you lie to us the other night?" Chloe said softly, easily sliding into the role of good cop.

Lonegan nodded. "Not intentionally. I didn't have eyes on him the entire time, okay? I spent the first few hours working downstairs, listening to music on my earbuds while I worked. I guess he could have stepped out without me knowing."

"What time did you finish downstairs?" Chloe said.

"Ten thirty-ish. It could have been as late as eleven. When I went up to work the second floor, he was still at it. But, yeah, he could have left and come back."

Chloe paused for a minute, thinking back to the night Ronnie Libby was attacked. She and Brock had pulled up directly across the street from the store. She tried to visualize what things looked like from their vantage point, but all she could remember was looking through the front showroom windows, trying to see who was inside.

"Any more questions you want to ask our cooperative new friend here, Detective Wright?"

"Where does Mr. Randall park when he's at work?" Chloe said.

"Right out front. He always arrives first in the morning. It's a loading zone he kind of uses as his own personal space so he doesn't have to park in the lot. Doesn't want his truck getting banged up by customers."

Chloe exchanged a glance with Zimmerman. He looked confused.

"What?" Zimmerman said.

"I'll tell you on the way."

83

Tuesday, October 14, 1:45 p.m

Brock was catching up on his supplemental reports at the PSB when his cell phone rang with a call from Chloe. Once again, he was disappointed to find it wasn't Ginger calling.

"How'd you make out?" Brock said, skipping past the usual pleasantries.

"Taylor's alibi just fell apart," Chloe said.

"Lonegan gave him up?"

"Not exactly, but he couldn't account for Taylor's whereabouts from eight thirty that night until as late as eleven. Said he was working on an entirely different floor with music blasting through his earbuds."

"That doesn't give us Taylor as the attacker," Brock said. "But it's enough to bring him in for questioning."

"Zim and I are headed out to find him now. There's one more thing that I hadn't thought of until we questioned Toby again. The night of the attack, do you remember seeing Taylor's truck when we first pulled up to the store?"

Brock thought for a moment. "I'm not sure."

"Well, I remember. And it wasn't there. If Taylor had parked in his usual spot out in front, it would have blocked our view of the inside."

"So where was it?"

"Toby told us he parked out back that night. By the loading door."

"Were they unloading something?" Brock said.

"No. They were only there to do the inventory. Taylor could have snuck out through the delivery door, driven to the Libbys' camp and back without Toby being any wiser."

"You think the kid was in on it?" Brock said. "Supplying him with an alibi on purpose?"

"I don't think so. He's not the most attentive employee I've ever met. Zim and I caught him surfing social media when we got there this afternoon. What do you want us to do with Taylor when we find him?"

"See if he'll come voluntarily to the PSB."

"And if he won't?"

"Convince him."

As Brock ended the call with Chloe, his cell rang again. He answered it without bothering to check the caller ID.

"Justice."

"Brock, it's Clay."

"Tell me you found something," Brock said.

"I think we found the knife."

Brock studied the whiteboard, looking specifically for gaps that needed filling. He knew connecting Taylor Randall to the elevated aggravated assault on Ronnie Libby would be a big win, but it wouldn't get them any closer to identifying Summer's killer. He also knew what a shitstorm it would create with Congresswoman Randall if they ended up charging Taylor. She would raise holy hell with anyone who would listen about police overreach. Brock wasn't worried about Lt. Cumberland. She had worked cases and would understand; she wouldn't be happy about it, but she would understand. Major Morgan, however, was an entirely different animal. He would only be concerned with the optics, especially given that he was planning on the congresswoman's endorsement for the colonel's job at year-end. Brock knew Morgan would be livid.

Finding the bloody knife in the same location as Summer's cell had been a big piece. Oftentimes the murder weapon was impossible to locate, leaving a big hole in the prosecution's case. The only trouble with this find was that there were no fingerprints found on the weapon, leading Brock to believe that the killer had most likely worn gloves.

Something about the knife bothered him. Dumping the phone and the knife felt like a misdirection. After all, they hadn't located the killer's clothing, which would mean that they discarded them in another location. So why not dump everything at the same time? The killer couldn't have been concerned with getting pulled over that night, as most every first responder in the area went to the site of the accident. None of them would have had any reason to be searching for a murderer. At that point, Summer's death was still thought to be a fatal vehicle-versus-pedestrian accident. Something about it didn't make sense. And why take the cell phone in the first place? They'd found nothing incriminating on it.

Brock was wrestling with a thought that might have explained the killer's actions when his phone chimed with a text message. It was Chloe.

10-46. 10-19 to PSB.

Brock's eyes widened. Chloe and Zimmerman were en route to the PD, and Taylor Randall was under arrest.

84

Tuesday, October 14, 2:45 p.m

Brock stood in the open bay door of the fire department, watching as Chloe and Zimmerman led a handcuffed Taylor Randall from the unmarked Ford toward the PSB. Chloe said something to Zimmerman, at which point he continued on, leading Randall toward the main entry doors, while Chloe headed in Brock's direction, grinning from ear to ear.

"What happened?" Brock said. "I thought you were just going to bring him in for questioning."

"Spontaneous utterance," Chloe said. "He was just exiting his house when Zim and I pulled into the dooryard. Before we could tell him why we were there, Taylor told us he'd heard that Ronnie was awake and talking."

"Who did he hear that from?" Brock said.

"Who knows. He was a reserve here. And I'm sure he has friends at the hospital."

Brock nodded. "So, what did he say that made you arrest him?"

"He said, 'I guess I should have finished the job.'"

Brock watched as Zimmerman opened the door with one hand and led Taylor Randall inside the PSB with the other. Just before Randall disappeared inside, he turned his head in Brock's direction, making eye contact.

There was no remorse in his expression. In fact, Randall looked satisfied with himself for very nearly having killed Ronnie Libby. Brock hoped for Randall's sake that he was right about Ronnie being Summer's attacker. But something nagging inside Brock said he wasn't.

Following the booking, Randall agreed to answer questions. After a brief discussion, it was decided that Chloe should conduct the interview, as she seemed to have the best rapport with him. Zimmerman sat in on the interview as second detective.

Chloe sat down directly across the table from Taylor Randall, occupying the exact same chair she had nearly a week prior on the night that Summer died. She used the recorder application on her cell phone despite the fact that the room was equipped with an audio and video recorder. Brock told her it was better to be safe and make a second copy than to need it and not have it. Chloe looked over at Zimmerman, who had moved his chair around to the end of the table to monitor the proceedings. He nodded to her that he was ready.

Chloe followed the step-by-step procedure of reading the entire Miranda warning to Taylor Randall, obtaining a verbal acknowledgment of understanding after each section had been read.

"Now, Mr. Randall, having each of those rights which I just read to you in mind, do you wish to answer questions at this time?"

Randall nodded.

"I need a verbal response from you, sir," Chloe said.

"Yes," Randall said. "I'll answer your questions."

Chloe began her line of questioning at the night Summer had died, leading Taylor step by step until he reached the point at which he'd decided to attack Ronnie Libby.

"When did you decide to assault Ronnie Libby?" Chloe said.

"I'm not sure there was one particular point," Randall said. "It was just something floating around in the back of my head after finding out Summer had been murdered. I was ninety-nine percent sure that it was

Ronnie who killed her. And truthfully, I still felt guilty about not exacting revenge on him for the beating he gave her a year ago."

"We were told you lost your position here at the Greenville Police Department over threats you made against Ronnie."

"I did. Guess it makes sense that I couldn't be expected to provide security to a community while issuing threats against its residents, right?"

Chloe nodded.

"Anyway, Ronnie never served any jail time for what he did to Summer. They made some kind of bullshit plea agreement and checked him into a program for his substance addiction. Part of the deal was that I lost my certificate of eligibility to continue to be a law enforcement officer."

Chloe waited to see if Randall had more to say on the subject before bringing him back on point. He didn't.

"Tell me about the night of the attack," Chloe said. "Did you ask Toby Lonegan to participate in any way? Or to provide you with an alibi?"

"No. Tobias is a good kid, but not very reliable. I wouldn't have dragged him into this, anyway. Honestly, the overnight inventory just seemed like the perfect cover. I had already been thinking about it for a few days. I figured I'd be able to sell the alibi better if it looked like I'd been at the store the entire time."

"What happened?"

"Once I knew Lonegan was busy on the main floor, I snuck out through the loading doors, where I had intentionally parked that night. I powered my phone down in case anyone tracked it later, then drove directly to the Libbys' cabin on Moosehead Lake. I parked at the end of the drive just out of sight from the roadway, then walked to the cabin. I put on leather work gloves and a ski mask; guess you'd call it a balaclava. When I got onto the porch, I could see Ronnie inside. I waited a few minutes to make sure he was alone. I banged on the side door and saw Ronnie get up. As soon as he opened the door, I pounced. I knocked him back onto the floor. You know the rest."

"Did you use any weapons during your attack on Ronnie, Mr. Randall?"

"No. Just my fists. And my boots."

"Any idea how many times you struck him?"

"I don't remember. Twenty-five. Fifty? I just remember seeing my beautiful Summer's face and what he had done to it. Not once, but twice."

"Was your intent to kill Ronnie Libby?"

"I don't know. Maybe."

"What happened next?"

"I left. Walked back to my truck. Put all my bloody clothes into a trash bag and tossed the bag in the dumpster out behind Woody's."

"Woody's?"

"Woody's Bar and Grill on Industrial Park Road. I knew nobody there would give me a second look. After that, I drove back to the store and washed up."

"How long were you out of the store that night?"

"Forty-five minutes, tops. You guys showed up a couple of hours later."

"Anything else you want to add, Mr. Randall?" Chloe said after glancing over at Zimmerman.

"Same thing I told you before we came here. If that piece of shit did kill my little girl, then I'm sorry I didn't finish the job."

"And if he didn't?" Zimmerman said, speaking for the first time.

Taylor Randall said nothing for a long moment. "Then I guess I'll take that lawyer now."

85

Tuesday, October 14, 4:15 p.m

Brock entered the fire department garage bay where Clayton Veilleux was busy processing Taylor Randall's pickup. The confession seemed to wrap up the attack on Ronnie Libby, but Brock had learned long ago not to take anything for granted. Taylor Randall had lied to them before about where he was that night, not to mention the lie of omission regarding Ronnie Libby the night Summer died.

The interior lights were off inside the garage, but Brock could see the black light shining from inside the cab of the pickup. He circled the truck and found Veilleux kneeling at the open driver's door. He appeared to be examining the driver's side footwell.

"Any luck?" Brock said.

"Not until now," he said. "The truck's been cleaned. I'm sure that's not an accident."

Brock was sure it wasn't either.

"So, what did you find?"

"This." Veilleux directed the black light toward the floor mat. Brock clearly saw what appeared to be two partial boot prints glowing on the carpeted mat.

"Blood?" Brock said.

"That would be my guess. It's certainly glowing like blood."

Brock knew Veilleux had sprayed Luminol on various surfaces inside the truck. It was the preferred method for detecting blood and bodily fluids. Luminol interacts chemically with the heavy metals found in blood.

"If this is blood, and it turns out to be Libby's, then you've got him."

Brock nodded.

"How did the interview go? Did he lawyer up?"

"Surprisingly, he didn't. At least not until the end."

"So he confessed to the attack?"

"He did. Says he acted alone. Have you found anything that would contradict that?"

"I haven't."

"Thanks, Clay."

"Anytime. And I'm sorry I didn't have better news on the knife recovery. I'll let you know as soon as I know whether or not the blood belongs to Summer."

Brock returned to the conference room, where he found Chloe and Zimmerman talking with AAG Grover by speakerphone.

"Sounds like you've wrapped up the attack on Ronnie Libby pretty well," Grover said. "The spontaneous utterance, the arrest, even the Mirandized confession all look airtight."

"Brock just walked in," Chloe said.

"Hey, Brock," Grover said. "Anything from the truck search?"

"Veilleux found two partial bloody boot prints on the driver's side floor mat."

"Which would seem to support Randall's confession," Grover said.

"Nice work, young lady," Zimmerman said.

"Thanks," Chloe said as she looked at Brock. "Only one problem."

"What's that?" Grover said.

"We still don't know who killed Summer Randall."

Zimmerman volunteered to accompany Deputy Evan Mathers to the Piscataquis County Jail to book Taylor Randall for the elevated aggravated assault on Ronnie Libby. Brock and Chloe remained at the PSB to regroup.

"We've missed something," Brock said.

"I know," Chloe said. "But I feel like we've been really thorough to this point."

"We've still got a motive problem," Brock said.

"Not if it was simply a random attack on a woman running through the woods," Chloe said.

"Well, if that's true, we've got an even bigger problem in that we don't have any leads."

Chloe sat back in her chair and sighed as she studied the whiteboard.

"What we really need are the DNA results," Brock said. "Maybe you could try bugging them again."

As if by uttering those very words Brock had conjured up a result, Chloe's cell phone rang. She checked the caller ID.

"That's just spooky," Chloe said.

"What is?" Brock said.

"It's the state lab." Chloe answered the call, putting it on speaker as she set the phone down on the table. "Hey, Connor. Tell me you've got good news."

"As a matter of fact, I do. One of the samples you sent matched the fetus sample supplied by the ME's office."

"Don't keep us in suspense," Chloe said. "Who's the father?"

"Ivan Heiden."

"Dr. Heiden?" Brock said, sounding as surprised as he felt.

"I guess," Connor said. "You didn't specify what any of the donors did for work."

"No, I get it," Brock said. "I'm just surprised."

"Same here," Chloe said. "I was beginning to think it might be Chris Mitchell, the guy from the fitness place. That is, assuming it wasn't Ronnie Libby himself."

"And the blood found in Summer's car?" Brock said.

"Unfortunately, it didn't match any of the samples you submitted," Connor said.

"Damn," Chloe said, echoing Brock's own thoughts.

"Hey, you're still batting five hundred," Connor said.

But Brock knew it wasn't good enough. If the blood found in Summer's car belonged to someone other than Dr. Heiden, it meant they couldn't link him to the murder. It also called into question Summer's pregnancy as a motive.

"Thanks for putting a rush on this, Connor," Brock said.

"Anytime."

Chloe had no sooner ended the call with the lab than Brock's cell rang.

The caller ID read Lt. Cumberland. After a moment's hesitation, Brock answered it.

"Hey, LT."

"Have you completely lost your mind? You arrested the victim's father?"

Brock bit his tongue. He knew Cumberland was unaware of the recent developments concerning the Libby assault, mostly because he hadn't bothered to update her yet.

"Would you mind telling me what exactly you charged him with?" Cumberland said.

"He just confessed to beating Ronnie Libby nearly to death."

86

Wednesday, October 15, 9:45 a.m

The following morning, Brock made the decision to drop the bad news on Dr. Heiden at the hospital. It was agreed that Brock and Zimmerman would confront him, as Chloe wanted to chase down another loose thread.

As Brock and Zimmerman made their way along the Northern Light Hospital's main corridor, they noticed some type of celebratory commotion near the nurses' station where Brittney LaRoux was showing something to several of the nurses.

"What's going on?" Zimmerman said as they approached.

"Brittney just got engaged," Nurse Nancy Higgins said.

"Congratulations," Brock said.

"Thank you," LaRoux said, beaming as she held up the large sparkling diamond for everyone to see.

"Who's the lucky guy?" Zimmerman said, playing along.

"I am," Dr. Heiden said from right behind them.

Brock turned to face him. "Just the man we're looking for. Mind if we have a word?"

Chloe turned into the LaRoux driveway, where she found an elderly woman outside on the front lawn raking leaves from the flower bed that bordered the front of the split-level home. She parked directly in front of the closed garage door and exited the SUV.

"Good morning," Chloe said. "Are you Ethel LaRoux?"

"Ethel Acheson, actually," the woman said as she leaned the rake against the front steps and brushed debris from her faded denim shirt. "LaRoux was my maiden name."

Chloe was surprised at just how spry the woman was for her age.

"May I help you with something?" Acheson said.

"I hope so," Chloe said as she held up her credentials for the woman to see. "My name is Chloe Wright, and I am investigating the murder of Summer Randall. I was hoping I could ask you a few questions about your granddaughter, Brittney."

"Detective, huh? Well, if you're looking for Brittney, she's at work. On at the hospital until midnight."

"Actually, it's you I came to see, Mrs. Acheson."

"Me?" Acheson said, clearly surprised.

"I wondered if we might sit and have a chat?"

"Certainly, if you think it will help you solve the murder of that poor girl. You know Brittney and Summer were best friends."

"Her death must have been very hard on Brittney," Chloe said.

"It sure was. Why don't you come inside, and I'll get us something cold to drink. Do you like lemonade?"

Brock and Zimmerman sat across the desk from Dr. Heiden in his office at the hospital. Heiden had closed the door of his own volition to allow them some privacy.

"So, what can I do for you gentlemen?" Heiden said.

"We were hoping you might be able to answer a question we had about your previous statement for us," Zimmerman said, taking the lead in a well-rehearsed trap.

The doctor's attention shifted between the two detectives. It was clear to Brock that Heiden was attempting to calculate what misstep he might have made.

"I'll do the best I can."

Zimmerman turned to Brock and beamed a fake smile. "See, I told you he'd help us."

"What's your question?" Heiden said.

"Why did you lie about the nature of your relationship with Summer Randall?" Brock said.

The color drained from the doctor's face.

"I, I'm not sure what you—"

"Sure you are, Doc," Zimmerman said. "You know exactly what we're talking about. You told us that your relationship with Summer was strictly limited to professional friendship. Remember? But that isn't true, is it?"

"I believe you also said the same thing about your relationship with Ms. LaRoux," Brock said. "That big diamond on her hand says otherwise."

Heiden let out a long sigh. It was clear he knew he was beaten. The only question remaining was whether he would come clean or lawyer up.

"How did you find out?"

"The DNA sample you provided," Brock said. "We got a match."

"That's impossible," Heiden protested. "I had nothing to do with Summer's murder."

"Your DNA wasn't found at the murder scene, Doctor," Brock said.

"But you said that was why you needed it. To eliminate me."

"We lied," Zimmerman said.

"Well, if you didn't find my DNA at the crime scene, where did you find it?"

"In Summer's unborn child," Zimmerman said.

The remaining color drained from the doctor's face. He looked like he might be sick.

"Summer was pregnant?"

Brock studied the man's expression. He had met some top-notch liars in his time on the job. People that were beyond convincing. But Brock considered himself fairly astute when it came to reading most people's reactions to unexpected news, and Heiden honestly looked shocked.

"Don't tell us you didn't know," Zimmerman said.

"I didn't. I swear."

"Not sure your word counts for much anymore, Doctor," Brock said. "You have lied to us before."

"Yeah," Zimmerman said. "How do we know you're not lying now?"

87

Wednesday, October 15, 10:15 a.m

While Acheson prepared their drinks in the kitchen, Chloe used the need for a bathroom break as a ruse, affording herself the opportunity to bypass the bathroom and sneak through the door that opened into the garage. As quietly as she could, Chloe closed the door behind her, then flicked on the overhead lights to the garage. The nearest bay was empty. Chloe assumed it was the space where Brittney parked her own vehicle. Occupying the bay farthest from her was a large vehicle covered by a grungy gray canvas tarpaulin. The shape beneath was clearly an SUV. The vehicle Brittney had told her was inoperable and hadn't been driven in over two years. Brittney had even confided in Chloe that she had disconnected the battery so that her grandmother wouldn't try using it in her absence.

Chloe approached the vehicle and pulled back the dusty tarp, revealing the front end, hood, and windshield of the vehicle. It was a Toyota 4Runner. The same make and model that appeared in the game camera video they had recovered from Peter Bragg, right down to the NASA-styled hood Zimmerman had found so stylish. Chloe knew that there was no way to confirm that this was the same Toyota as the one they saw in the video, or even the same year, but she couldn't help but feel the excitement that accompanied another piece clicking into place. She circled around to the front end and knelt down to look at the registration. The plate was partially obscured by mud. Mud that should have been dried out and crusty if Brittney had told the truth about the last time the vehicle had been driven. Chloe ran the pad of her index finger over the mud, and it came off in a brownish clump. The earthy residue was dry on the outside, but moisture was still contained within. In other words, it was fresh. And there was only one explanation. Someone had recently driven the 4Runner.

Chloe rose up and walked to the driver's door, half expecting it to be locked, but it wasn't. She opened the door, then reached inside and pulled the hood release latch. The hood popped up with a loud clunk, causing Chloe to cringe. She only hoped that Ethel hadn't heard the noise through the closed garage door. She gently pushed the driver's door shut until the latch clicked. She returned to the front of the vehicle and raised the hood. As she had expected, the battery was connected to both cables.

"I would have thought the interior dome light would have given it away," a familiar voice said from behind her.

Chloe started slightly at the sound of an unexpected visitor, and her hand quickly moved toward her hip holster.

"I wouldn't do that if I were you," Brittney cautioned. "Get your hands up, and slowly turn toward me."

Chloe did as instructed. Brittney stood at the center of the empty garage bay holding a double-barrel shotgun at the ready.

"Your grandmother said you were on duty until midnight," Chloe said, attempting to keep her voice low and calm.

"I wasn't feeling well. Decided to take a few hours of personal time."

"Sorry to hear that."

"Something about state police detectives paying a visit to my new fiancé that I found disconcerting. And your absence was an even greater concern."

"I figured it might be a good time to double check the alibi your grandmother had provided. As you said, she suffers from the occasional bout of confusion. I wondered whether you might have had a hand in the memory she had of the evening Summer Randall was murdered."

"Oh? And how did that go for you?"

"Very well, actually. She remembered waking up from a nap after you'd brought her some tea. Said she felt funny. Like she does after taking something to help her sleep. She wondered how that could have happened, since she hadn't had anything but the tea you'd given her."

"What are you saying? That I drugged my own grandmother?"

"Actually, you said it. The odd thing was that she forced herself up from the living room chair after you failed to respond when she called out to you. Told me she searched the entire house, but you were nowhere to be found."

Brittney shrugged. "Maybe it was all just a dream. Sometimes she conflates the real world with her dreams. It happens with older people."

"I'm sure you were hoping I'd think that, but there's one problem."

"Oh?"

"I'm not dreaming. And there's fresh mud on the 4Runner. You know, the one you said hasn't been driven for more than two years."

Brittney shrugged again. "Maybe I decided to take it out for a spin after we last spoke. You know how vehicles tend to fall apart if they aren't driven. I didn't want to see that happen to Gran's Toyota."

"And when was this?"

"Um, I forget. You do know you're not talking your way out of this."

"Out of what?"

"Take your gun out of its holster with your left hand and set it on the floor."

"Why don't we—"

"Now!"

Chloe drew a deep breath and reached across her body toward the gun.

"Nice and slow. I wouldn't want to make a mess in Gran's garage."

Chloe slid her gun free of its holster, then bent down and set it on the concrete floor.

"Now kick it over to me."

Chloe complied once again.

"Now what?"

"Now we're going to take a nice leisurely ride in the 4Runner." Brittney tossed her the keys. "I hope you don't mind driving."

88

Wednesday, October 15, 10:15 a.m

Brock and Zimmerman listened intently as Heiden came clean about where he was the night of Summer's murder.

"And that was the reason you lied about being at home?" Brock said. "Because you were with your ex-wife?"

"I didn't want to complicate my personal life any more than it is."

Heiden grabbed a stack of sticky notes and scribbled a name and several numbers on the top sheet before tearing it off and handing it to Brock.

"Her name is Cindy, and those are her home and cell numbers. Feel free to call her. She'll confirm I was with her that night."

"We will," Brock said, handing the note to Zimmerman.

"I'm on it," Zimmerman said as he stood and headed for the door.

After Zimmerman left, Brock changed the subject.

"Why did you keep your relationship with Summer Randall a secret if you had nothing to do with her murder?"

"Because it wasn't a relationship. Just a one-time thing. We'd both been drinking. It was after a party. I know that's not an excuse, but I was seeing Brittney by then. Obviously, I didn't want to screw that up."

"Seems like sleeping with her best friend was a good way to do just that."

Brock thought about adding sleeping with the ex-wife to the list of bad decisions that Dr. Heiden had recently made, but didn't see the need to pile on.

"I can't believe she was pregnant with my child and didn't tell me," Heiden said. "Surely you don't think the pregnancy had anything to do with why she was attacked."

"Would she have said anything to Brittney?" Brock said.

Heiden's eyes widened as he clearly understood the implication.

"You can't possibly think Brittney was involved in this."

That was exactly what Brock was thinking. He checked his cell phone for messages, surprised that Chloe hadn't checked in yet, but there were none.

Zimmerman returned to the office, nodding at Brock. "Cindy just confirmed his account. He was with her the entire night."

"Looks like you're in the clear," Brock said.

"Doc, I know it's none of my business, but you might want to consider what effect this infidelity problem you have is gonna do to your engagement," Zimmerman said.

"Or has already done," Brock said. "We need to speak to Brittney again."

"She isn't here," Zimmerman said. "I just checked. They said she wasn't feeling well and drove home."

Brock stood up and pulled out his cell phone again. He punched up Chloe's number on speed dial and held the phone to his ear.

"What's wrong?" Zimmerman said.

"Chloe went to see Brittney's grandmother to double-check her alibi."

"Shit," Zimmerman said.

"Voicemail," Brock said.

Heiden's eyes darted back and forth between them. "You don't think—?"

Neither Brock nor Zimmerman heard the rest of the doctor's question, as they were already out of the office and racing down the hall.

Following Brittney's instructions, Chloe turned left out of the driveway in the direction of Greenville. The rain had just begun, coating the pavement in a thin oily sheen that held the falling leaves like glue. She felt the barrel of her own weapon pressed against her rib cage. Unhinged or not, Brittney clearly meant business.

"You don't really think you'll get away with this, do you?" Chloe said. "I mean, my cruiser is parked in your driveway. The other detectives know I was going to see your grandmother."

"Shut up and drive," Brittney said as she toyed with the engagement ring. "I need to think."

"What about Ethel?"

"She won't be a problem. I locked her in her room."

"Where are we going?"

"Just drive."

Chloe didn't want to provoke Brittney further, but she needed to keep her talking and engaged. Distracted.

"How long had you really known about Summer's pregnancy?"

"She told me in confidence about a week before she—died."

"Best friends and all," Chloe said. "That's what they do, right? Share secrets?"

Brittney didn't respond.

"Did she tell you who the father was?"

"Not at first. I figured it was Chris Mitchell's. Everyone knows what he's like. And it would have explained Summer suddenly quitting work at the gym."

"When did she tell you the baby was Ivan's?"

"The day before I killed her. I wouldn't have done it, but she forced my hand."

"How so?"

"Summer originally told me that she planned to terminate the pregnancy, but something made her change her mind."

"How would that affect you?"

"She was planning to tell Ivan that the baby was his. And I knew he was about to propose to me. Summer was going to mess up everything I had worked so hard for. She betrayed me."

"Last I checked, it takes two people to have an affair, Brittney."

"Ivan made one silly mistake in sleeping with her, and she was going to make him pay for the rest of his life. Hell, she was going to make me pay. I just couldn't let that happen."

Chloe caught sight of a dark-colored SUV approaching at high speed from the opposite direction. She knew it was Brock and Zim, and she knew she needed to distract Brittney before she noticed it.

"Too bad you didn't know about the game camera."

Brittney turned her head toward Chloe, her eyes narrowing. "What game camera?"

89

Wednesday, October 15, 10:45 a.m

"Right there," Zimmerman shouted. "It's Chloe and Brittney, right there in that Toyota."

"I see it," Brock said.

"That has to be the 4Runner we saw in the video," Zimmerman said. "Quick, turn around."

"Give me a second," Brock shouted back. "I don't want to draw attention to us if I don't have to. Call it in to dispatch."

Zimmerman picked up the mic and radioed the county dispatch center.

"Go ahead," the female dispatcher said.

"10-74. Possible kidnapping of one of ours by a 10-49 suspect. We're following the vehicle now." Zimmerman quickly provided a description of the vehicle sans plate number.

"Your twenty?"

"Um, where the hell are we, Brock?"

"Route 15."

"Route 15 toward Greenville from Monson."

"Ten-four."

"You don't think they saw us?" Zimmerman said.

"I don't think Brittney did. She was facing Chloe when they passed us."

Brock forced himself to wait until the roof of the Toyota disappeared below a dip in the road before reacting. It was a trick he had mastered while working in uniform to keep from alerting a suspect. Never touch the brakes or change your speed until the suspect loses visibility of your vehicle. As soon as he was sure they were out of sight, he got on the brakes hard. He felt the antilock mechanism pulsing against the pedal beneath his foot as he cut the wheel hard left into the oncoming lane. Brock quickly shifted the transmission into reverse, then stomped on the accelerator and cut the steering wheel in the other direction, executing the three-point turn to perfection. The Interceptor's engine responded, rocketing them back in the direction they had come. Zimmerman held onto the dash with one hand and the radio microphone in the other. The only sounds inside the SUV were the racing engine and the voice of the county dispatcher clearing the airwaves and putting out an all-car.

"What camera are you talking about?" Brittney said.

"One of the local poachers caught you tossing Summer's phone shortly after you killed her."

"You're making that up," Brittney said as she pressed the gun barrel harder against Chloe's ribs.

"How do you think I knew to check Ethel's 4Runner?"

Chloe glanced in the rearview mirror again, praying that Brock had seen them. He hadn't seemed to react as they passed by, but she knew he likely hadn't wanted to alert Brittney. At least she hoped.

"Turn here," Brittney said. "Right here."

Chloe intentionally hit the brakes too late, causing the 4Runner to roll past the road.

"Don't fuck with me," Brittney hissed.

"I'm not. You didn't give me enough warning."

"Back up and make the turn. Now."

Chloe did as instructed, her eyes glued to the rearview mirror. She was about to shift the transmission into drive when she saw Brock's Interceptor come over the rise about a hundred yards back. Her heart leapt. They had seen her.

"Drive," Brittney commanded.

"Okay. Okay."

"Eleven oh six, I'm en route to intercept."

"Isn't that—?" Zimmerman began.

"Yeah," Brock said, cutting Zimmerman off mid-sentence and wondering how much worse things had just gotten. "It's Evan Mathers."

"Chloe's life is in danger, brother," Zimmerman said. "We'll take any help we can get."

Brock knew Zimmerman was right, but given his history with Mathers and the very real possibility that he had now likely committed what amounted to a second murder in Brock's eyes, he would have preferred another option.

Brock was doing his best to hang back just far enough to try and avoid drawing unwanted attention from Brittney's prying eyes. The Toyota was maintaining the speed limit, but he had no way of knowing if that was Chloe's doing or if Brittney was hoping not to get pulled over for a traffic infraction.

"Where do you think they're going?" Zimmerman said.

"I wish I knew."

"Piscataquis to SP twelve one three, what is your current twenty?" the dispatcher said.

"Elliotsville Road," Zimmerman said into the mic. "About a mile and a half from Route 15."

"Tell them we're nearing Bodfish," Brock said.

"What the hell is Bodfish?" Zimmerman said.

"Just tell her," Brock snapped.

"We are approaching Bodfish," Zimmerman parroted into the mic.

"Eleven oh six copies," Mathers radioed.

The 4Runner began to pull away from them. Brock punched the accelerator, trying to match its speed.

"What's happening?" Zimmerman said.

"I think Brittney made us," Brock said as he activated the unmarked's emergency lights and siren.

"Suspect made us, County," Zimmerman shouted into the radio in an attempt to be heard above the siren. "In pursuit."

"Ten-four," the dispatcher said. "Eleven oh six, copy?"

"Copy," Mathers said.

"Tell me you've got a plan, Brock," Zimmerman said.

"Working on it," Brock lied as he glanced down at the speedometer.

They were traveling nearly eighty miles an hour now along the twisting, bumpy two-lane road. Even with the Ford's beefed-up suspension, Brock was struggling to keep the SUV on the road and avoid hydroplaning.

"Eleven oh six to SP twelve one three, I'm about three miles ahead of you. Gonna try and deploy."

Zimmerman turned to Brock. "Deploy?"

"Spike strip."

"If you know what's good for you, you'll lose them," Brittney growled as she focused on the right-side mirror.

"Doing my best," Chloe shot back as anger began to eclipse her fear.

"Let me put it another way," Brittney said, her attention returning fully to Chloe. "If your friends catch us, neither one of us will be leaving this vehicle alive."

Chloe was struggling to come up with a way out of this. Without the benefit of a police radio, she had no idea what Brock might be planning. She only hoped that the cavalry was on its way.

"Faster," Brittney said.

Chloe didn't know how much faster she could safely navigate the unfamiliar road without rolling the four-wheel-drive vehicle. Every rise they crested, Chloe felt her stomach flip like she was on a rollercoaster. The drizzle was heavier now, and even on the high-speed setting the wipers were struggling to keep up with the water collecting on the dirty windshield.

Trees raced past in a blur of color to the right while the left side of the road opened into pastureland bordered by a fieldstone wall. Chloe glanced back to make sure Brock and Zim were still there and saw that they had somehow managed to close the distance and were now only about thirty yards behind them.

"Lose them or die," Brittney said as she raised the H&K to Chloe's temple.

As Chloe focused on the road ahead, she caught a glimpse of flashing blue strobes. She could tell by the markings that it was a county vehicle. And she knew by the vehicle's positioning what the deputy was up to. Her eyes flicked toward Brittney to see if she'd noticed, but Brittney had turned in her seat, her attention fully on Brock's SUV now. Chloe accelerated toward the small opening the deputy had provided. She saw a figure appear from behind the cruiser and launch something across the road. She knew exactly what it was, and she fought back a smile.

Brittney's head whipped around just as several of the Toyota's tires burst. Chloe cut the wheel hard left in the direction of the stone wall and braced for impact.

90

Wednesday, October 15, 11:25 a.m

Brock and Zimmerman stared in horror as they watched the 4Runner launch itself over the stone wall and into the air. Broken pieces of the Toyota's front end and undercarriage seemingly exploded from impact, propelled forward by the vehicle's momentum. The SUV landed awkwardly in the field beyond, striking something unseen that sent it end over end down the grassy embankment.

"Holy shit!" Zimmerman said, expressing Brock's own thoughts perfectly.

Brock's attention returned to the rapidly approaching hazard in the road ahead of them. He reacted on instinct alone, standing on the brake pedal in an attempt to avoid running over the spike strip and disabling their own vehicle. The Ford came to a skidding stop inches from the Piscataquis County cruiser and Evan Mathers. Brock and Zimmerman bailed out of the SUV and scrambled over the stone wall on foot.

Every inch of Chloe's body was strained, her muscles screaming in agony. She felt like she'd just spent the last five minutes in a medieval torture device akin to the rack. The 4Runner had mercifully stopped flipping, but Chloe's equilibrium was still off-kilter like she was suffering from vertigo. The smoke hanging inside the passenger compartment was swirling around like a noxious fog, making it difficult to see. It took Chloe a moment to realize that it was coming from the slowly deflating airbags protruding from the dash and steering wheel.

Fighting against the pain, Chloe managed to turn her head to one side and saw Brittney struggling to free herself from the seat belt from which she was still suspended. Chloe followed Brittney's gaze until she saw the object motivating her. It was Chloe's semiautomatic handgun lying in a pile of broken glass gathered on the Toyota's torn headliner.

Despite the pain and increasing nausea, Chloe didn't hesitate as she swung her elbow into the side of Brittney's head as hard as she could. The impact of bone on bone sent a flash of searing pain up Chloe's arm to her injured neck, but the blow had the desired effect, momentarily stunning the nurse. Chloe's attention switched to the handgun as she struggled against her own restraint, stretching her body until her fingers closed around the weapon.

Brittney screamed in defiance as she realized what was happening and clawed at Chloe's eyes with her hands, trying to blind her. Chloe realized that she had just about exhausted whatever adrenaline remained and was in jeopardy of passing out. Rather than risk discharging her firearm inside the closed space and possibly injuring herself further, Chloe held the gun by the slide and swung it like a hammer, striking Brittney squarely across the bridge of her nose. Blood sprayed throughout their inverted world, accompanied by the satisfying crunch of bone and cartilage. Brittney's screams ceased and her body fell limp, suspended in midair like some grotesque acrobat.

Black spots danced across Chloe's field of vision as she released the gun. As the last of her consciousness slipped away, she thought she heard the sound of shouting voices.

91

Thursday, October 16, 10:30 a.m

Chloe found herself lying bundled in a slightly reclined hospital bed, annoyed by the constant beep emitting from nearby monitors, but feeling pleasantly numb, no doubt due to the miracle of modern medicine.

"Well, now," a familiar voice said softly. "Look who's decided to rejoin the living."

"Hey, Brock," Chloe managed to croak in a voice that sounded as if it belonged to someone else. "Where am I?"

"The Northern Light Hospital," Zimmerman said. "Where else? Good to have you back, young lady."

"What happened?" Chloe said as her opioid-muddled memory failed her.

"You caught the bad guy, partner," Brock said.

"Or in this case, the bad gal," Zimmerman chuckled.

"You don't remember anything?" Brock said.

"I remember talking with Brittney's grandmother, Ethel. And Brittney pointing a shotgun at me in the garage. Then I think someone was chasing me."

"That was us," Brock said.

"I had no idea you could drive like that," Zimmerman said. "You were like a stunt driver out there. Chloe Chitwood."

A dark thought made it through Chloe's foggy recall as she remembered fighting for her weapon in the overturned wreck.

"What happened to Brittney?" she managed.

"She's in custody at Eastern Maine Med," Brock said.

"They LifeFlighted her to Bangor after you rearranged her face," Zimmerman chuckled. "She looks like Mrs. Potato Head."

Chloe felt herself cramping up as she fought back laughter, the pain in her ribs worming its way through the morphine to the surface.

"P-please, don't make me laugh, Zim."

"Sorry. I just thought you'd appreciate the image."

"Ah, I see my favorite police detective is back with us," Nurse Nancy Higgins said as she breezed into the room. "And she's being bothered by two people who should be letting her rest."

"Aw, come on, Nurse Nancy," Zimmerman teased.

"How are you feeling, hon?" Higgins said, ignoring him.

"Like a truck ran over me," Chloe said.

"Close enough," Zimmerman said.

"Okay, I need both of you out of here," Higgins said. "Detective Wright will have plenty of time to play cops and robbers later. Now shoo."

Brock stood and placed a gentle hand on Chloe's arm. "We'll be back to check on you later."

"Thanks, partner."

"Hey, what about me?" Zimmerman said.

"Thanks, Zim."

Early the next morning, Brock and Zimmerman sat across from Lt. Cumberland in the empty Greenville Grinds café. Chief Leavitt had once again exerted his not insubstantial influence to gain them early access to the eatery. The aroma of spices and yeasty dough permeated the space.

"What is that incredible smell?" Cumberland asked as she removed the lid from her coffee.

"You'll see," Brock said as he exchanged a knowing grin with Zimmerman.

"So how are you feeling about how everything turned out?" Cumberland said.

"I'm happy we caught Summer's killer," Brock said. "I just wish Chloe hadn't nearly gotten killed in the process."

"She made it out alive," Zimmerman said. "That's the important thing."

Brock knew he was right, but he also knew how many lives had been upended or outright destroyed by Summer Randall's secret. A secret she had only shared with one other person. It was a decision that had cost Summer her life.

"Seems like there are still more questions than answers," Cumberland said.

"Always are," Zimmerman said. "And unless Brittney decides to come clean, we'll probably never know for sure."

"I still don't get why the nurse took the victim's phone," Cumberland said. "I mean, you'd already seen the text thread back and forth between Summer and Brittney, right?"

"I've been discussing that with Clayton Veilleux," Brock said. "The timeline might provide the answer."

"Meaning?" Cumberland said.

"Clayton thinks that Summer's last text to Brittney, the one where she says not to worry, that she'll see her tomorrow, may actually have been written just prior to the attack on Summer."

Cumberland's eyes widened. "By Brittney?"

"Her attempt to close the loop on being a no-show for their training run," Brock said.

"Let me get this right," Zimmerman said. "You're saying that Brittney retrieved Summer's phone and tried to cement her alibi by sending herself a phony text message, stabbed her, then chased her through the woods until she ran into the path of a drunk driver and got hit."

Brock nodded. "I don't think chasing Summer all the way to Lily Bay Road was part of the plan, but she staged the break-in to Summer's car to make it look like a motor vehicle burglary gone bad. We think Summer was on her way back to her car when Brittney attacked her. If she hadn't been caught on camera discarding the cell phone and knife, who knows."

"That's some cold stuff, right there," Cumberland said.

"Hell hath no fury," Zimmerman said.

"Something you would do well to remember, Detective," Cumberland said.

Brock fought back a smile.

"What about Summer's father, Taylor Randall?" Zimmerman said.

"What about him?" Cumberland said.

"Well, now that it looks like Ronnie Libby will recover from his injuries, do you think the prosecutor will go easier on him?"

"Why would they?" Cumberland said.

"Well, he's still the guy whose daughter was murdered."

"And then tried to exact revenge on an innocent man," Cumberland said.

"I'm not sure I would ever describe a guy like Ronnie as innocent," Zimmerman said.

"Be that as it may, Mr. Randall played the vigilante card and lost," Cumberland said. "If there is any hope for leniency, it will come through political channels."

"You mean Congresswoman Randall," Brock said.

"Precisely. After all, didn't they intercede after Ronnie attacked Summer?"

"Indeed they did," Brock said.

"What about Major Malf—Morgan?" Zimmerman said, catching himself before he uttered Morgan's derogatory moniker.

"What about him?" Cumberland said as she eyed him suspiciously.

"Well, he all but came out and told the press that Peter Bragg was responsible for killing Summer Randall. Can't imagine that will help his chances at becoming the next colonel of MSP."

"I don't deal in rumors, Detective Zimmerman," Cumberland said. Her tone implied he should take caution. "And last I checked, Major Morgan doesn't answer to us."

Zimmerman raised his hands, palms out. "Understood, LT."

"Who's hungry?" the café owner said as she appeared at the counter with a full tray of steaming cinnamon buns.

Zimmerman popped up out of his chair so fast he nearly knocked it over.

As Zimmerman busied himself at the counter, Cumberland leaned in close to Brock.

"You and I have another matter to discuss."

"Oh?" Brock said as he cocked his head to one side.

"Unfinished business," she said.

"You mean—?"

"I got a call from Detective Dashofy's boss."

Brock stared at her, unable to mask his surprise.

"We'll talk about it later," Cumberland said. "No reason to drag any more people into that mess."

Brock nodded his understanding.

"Here you go, Lieutenant," Zimmerman said as he delivered Cumberland's cinnamon bun directly to the table.

"Oh my God," Cumberland said. "That has got to be—"

"The biggest cinnamon bun in the entire state of Maine," the owner said, beaming with pride.

EPILOGUE

Brock took one last look around his room, making sure he hadn't left anything behind. The Moose Mountain Inn had been his home away from home for more than a week. Much had changed since the night he and Chloe arrived to find the lifeless body of Summer Randall splayed out across Lily Bay Road. So many secrets revealed. So much pain. He wondered how long it would take the residents of Greenville to begin to heal. Brock knew many of the townspeople never would.

He slid a forty-dollar tip for the cleaning staff under the room card atop the dresser, then picked up the file folders lying on the bed and shoved them inside his cloth briefcase and zipped it closed. He slung his duffel over one shoulder and grabbed his briefcase, then headed toward the door.

The morning sun streamed through the trees as Brock stepped outside into the crisp autumn air. A light breeze stirred the leaves, releasing a cascade of crimson and gold. Brock paused to relish in the moment, watching the leaves drift toward the ground. He closed his eyes and drew a deep breath through his nostrils. The scent of lake water, pine sap, and dying vegetation blended into a pleasing aroma. He opened his eyes and resumed walking across the lot toward his SUV. It was time to bust Chloe out of the hospital and return to Bangor.

He pressed the button on his key fob, unlocking the doors on his unmarked, then tossed his bags onto the rear seat. He opened the driver's door and was preparing to climb inside when he saw a Piscataquis County cruiser turn into the lot and roll toward him. Seated behind the wheel was the smiling face of Evan Mathers.

Mathers parked a short distance away, then exited the vehicle and approached on foot.

"I can't believe you were just gonna leave without saying goodbye, Brock."

"I knew you'd stop by to gloat," Brock said. "Isn't that what guys like you do?"

"What? You're still pissed about not being able to charge me with that whore's murder? I thought you'd be happy to get at least one solved case under your belt. How's your new partner? Figured you two would be checking out together."

"I'm picking her up at the hospital."

"I could give her a ride if you'd rather," Mathers said, in a transparent attempt to goad Brock. "I'm known for having a way with the ladies."

"Thanks anyway, but I think I can handle it."

Mathers shrugged. "Her loss."

"I got to hand it to you," Brock said. "You got away with it again."

"I don't know what you mean," Mathers said.

"Yeah, you do," Brock said.

Mathers looked around the lot, then leaned in close to Brock. "You know, I was surprised that Laura's name never came up during the trial. I mean with you being so forthcoming and all, you'd certainly mention my relationship with Kirke's main squeeze."

"I imagined you already had enough on your plate after killing an unarmed man," Brock said.

"Jury saw it differently, though, didn't they," Mathers said with a wink. "By the way, I must admit I was impressed with the background I found in your hotel room."

"You broke into my room?" Brock said.

"I wouldn't exactly call it a break-in. More like checking up on you. I had a feeling you wouldn't be able to resist poking your nose into Laura's death. Couldn't prove I was involved, though, could you?"

"Nope. But I figure she probably tried to blackmail you after you got away with killing Darrell Kirke."

"You always were the bright one, Brock. And yeah, Laura absolutely tried. Five grand, if you can believe it. Christ, she even expected me to spring for the hotel room."

Brock said nothing.

"You want to know the best part?" Mathers said.

"What's that?"

"The look on her drunk face when she realized I was about to drown her in the tub. It still makes me smile."

Brock waited a long moment to see if Mathers had more to say.

"Well, I can't sit here and shoot the shit with you all day, amigo," Mathers said. "I've got a county to patrol. Serve and protect, right?"

"You don't even know what that means, Evan."

Mathers grinned as he climbed back inside his cruiser. "See you 'round, partner. And hey, don't be a stranger."

Brock watched the arrogant cop make a U-turn before heading toward the exit. As the black SUV reached the main road, multiple police vehicles descended on its location, blocking Mathers in. Brock only wished he could see the shocked expression on Evan's face as he realized he'd been played.

Brock heard footsteps approaching from behind. "You get what you needed?" he said without turning around.

"We sure did," Detective Dashofy said. "Every single word."

Dark Harbor
Detective Justice Book 3

One dead millionaire, one dead intruder, and a detective whose only path forward means exposing the secrets of Bar Harbor's wealthy elite.

Detective Brock Justice never imagined the glittering coastal town of Bar Harbor would be his next battleground. When multimillionaire Granville Warren and an unidentifiable burglar turn up dead in a mansion break-in gone awry, the evidence points straight to Granville's much younger wife, Lily. Her self-defense claim raises more suspicion than sympathy, and Brock must untangle a crime scene awash in contradictions.

Justice's instincts scream there's more beneath the polished surface of Bar Harbor's elite, but the last thing he needs is interference from inside his own ranks. Enter Samantha Osborn, a detective just back from a task force assignment—too polished, too eager, and watching his every move. Brock doesn't believe in coincidences, and Osborn smells like trouble from a mile away.

As Brock and his team pushes deeper into the Warren case, each uncovered clue pulls them further into Bar Harbor's deep-seated corruption. Haunted by past mistakes and facing powerful figures intent on keeping their secrets hidden, Justice must walk a razor's edge to solve this twisted case—or risk losing his career, his reputation, and possibly his life.

Get your copy today at
severnriverbooks.com

30% Off your next paperback.

Thank you for reading. For exclusive offers on your next paperback:

- **Visit SevernRiverBooks.com** and enter code **PRINTBOOKS30** at checkout.
- Or scan the QR code.

Offer valid for future paperback purchases only. The discount applies solely to the book price (excluding shipping, taxes, and fees) and is limited to one use per customer. Offer available to US customers only. Additional terms and conditions apply.

ACKNOWLEDGMENTS

Bitter Fall, my tenth published novel and the second in the Detective Justice Mystery Series, is a milestone I never dreamed possible. If this literary journey has taught me anything, it serves as a reminder of how blessed I am to have the most incredible readers. Thank you all.

As always, I must also give thanks to some amazing folks without whom I might never have gotten this far: Paula Munier and Gina Panettieri at Talcott Notch Literary for continuing to believe in me and my stories; Andrew Watts, Cate Streissguth, Julia Barron, Kate Schomaker, and the rest of the talented team at Severn River Publishing.

My beta readers and fact checkers, Jim Emerson, Eric Berce, Josh Guay, Mark Holmquist, Mike Edes, Peggy Greenwald. Any mistakes were entirely my own.

The countless men and women in the field of criminal justice, true professionals, I was fortunate to have served with, and those who continue to serve (these are their stories).

Lastly, and most importantly, my wife, Karen, for her love, inspiration, and infinite patience. Without you in my life, there would be no story.

ABOUT BRUCE ROBERT COFFIN

Bruce Robert Coffin is the award-winning author of the Detective Byron Mysteries. Former detective sergeant with more than twenty-seven years in law enforcement, he is the winner of Killer Nashville's Silver Falchion Awards for Best Procedural, and Best Investigator, and the Maine Literary Award for Best Crime Fiction Novel. Bruce was also a finalist for the Agatha Award for Best Contemporary Novel. His short fiction appears in a number of anthologies, including Best American Mystery Stories 2016.

Join the reader list at
severnriverbooks.com